THE KEEPSAKE

Sheelagh Kelly was born in York. She left school at fifteen and went to work as a book-keeper. She has written for pleasure since she was a small child, but not until 1980 were the seeds sown for her first novel, *A Long Way from Heaven*, when she developed an interest in genealogy and local history and decided to trace her ancestors' story. She has since completed many bestselling sagas, most of which are set in or around the city of York.

Visit www.AuthorTracker.co.uk for exclusive information on Sheelagh Kelly.

Also by Sheelagh Kelly

SHEELAGH KELLY

The Keepsake

HarperCollins*Publishers*

HarperCollins*Publishers*
77–85 Fulham Palace Road,
Hammersmith, London W6 8JB

www.harpercollins.co.uk

This paperback edition 2006
1

First published in Great Britain by
HarperCollins*Publishers* 2006

A catalogue record for this book
is available from the British Library

ISBN 13 978 0 00 721155 5
ISBN 10 0 00 721155 4

Typeset in Sabon by Palimpsest Book Production Limited,
Polmont, Stirlingshire

Printed and bound in Great Britain by
Clays Ltd, St Ives plc

This novel is entirely a work of fiction.
The names, characters and incidents portrayed in it are
the work of the author's imagination. Any resemblance to
actual persons, living or dead, events or localities is
entirely coincidental.

For my dear daughter, Gayle.

1

Marty Lanegan was skylarking his way along a corridor of the grandest hotel in York, lolloping like an ape for the entertainment of a workmate to have him double up in laughter, when his antics were stalled by a furious argument. Abandoning his audience, he paused to listen and to grin at the choice insults which jarred with this Edwardian elegance, that were hurled like clubs between father and daughter. He knew this to be the relationship for he had witnessed the arrival of the scowling but very handsome young lady and her papa late yesterday afternoon, and had opined to the rest of the staff that she looked a proper handful.

'You mean you'd like a handful,' the page had leered.

Well, that was no lie. She was the most stunning girl Marty had ever seen: hence his unusual keenness for work this morning. He was about to put his eye to the keyhole when the door opened, forcing him to leap back or be bullocked aside by the angry gentleman on the point of exit.

The boot boy sought to explain his proximity. 'I've just come to check if there's any shoes need cleaning, sir!'

This was met by suspicion, the man's cane held at a threatening angle. 'Somewhat late in the day for that, isn't it?' It was well after breakfast.

Marty's reply displayed just the right blend of courtesy

1

and helpfulness, delivered with the faintest lilt of Irish brogue. 'Some guests forget to leave them out, sir, so I make constant trips up here. I like to provide good service.'

'If it was that good you'd be aware that you've already done ours,' growled the man, who, with his bearded face, corpulent build and eyes that bulged with rage, was the spitting image of the King, though his manner was anything but royal. Ramming on his bowler and shoving the cane under his arm, he turned his back on the servant, locked the door and marched to the stairs, but not before both he and Marty heard the sound of a heavy object hitting wood.

Struggling to contain his mirth, the boot boy appeared to go obediently on his way. But a crafty glance over his shoulder told him that the other had descended and, upon hearing noisy sobs, he crept back to employ the keyhole. Maybe he could be the one to comfort her . . .

They were not the feeble kind of tears but loud wails interspersed with frustrated yelps and thuds, as if she were punching some substitute for the one who had angered her. He was still bent over trying to catch a glimpse of anything other than the bedroom wallpaper, when someone nipped his trim, uniformed buttock, shocking him upright.

The culprit stifled a giggle as her victim swivelled in dread. 'What're you up to, Bootsie?'

'Ye daft mare!' He scolded the chambermaid in a forced whisper, and then grabbed her to tussle and tickle her, chuckling good-naturedly. 'I thought 'twas her daddy come back.'

Annoyed to learn that his attention was for another woman, Joanna's laughter dissipated in a blunt Yorkshire response. 'You lecher! Spying on that swanky lass – I might have known!'

'I'm just checking she's all right, that's all!' The tone was innocent, but the cheeky sparkle in Marty's eyes showed otherwise. 'They were going hammer and tongs at each other and then he left in a hurry and locked her in.' Keeping

2

his voice low, and oblivious to Joanna's jealousy, he shoved his cap to the back of his head and bent to the keyhole again. 'Maybe he hit her – she's still bawlin'.'

Smarting over his ignorance of her own feelings, Joanna hissed, 'Why don't you just knock and find out?' And with that she rapped briskly on the door before hastening away with her trolley, leaving him to panic.

He was set to run but the occupant was already at the door, her crying stopped and her voice eager with enquiry. 'Who's there?'

Still unnerved by Joanna's action, Marty gave rapid apology through the barrier. 'Sorry, miss, I didn't mean to distur—'

'Don't go!' Her entreaty was swift but polite, its melodic tone permeating the wood to spellbind him. 'Could you possibly help? My father's gone out and taken the key in error. I'm locked in.'

Marty knew it was no error. He would be in deep trouble if he got involved in this. 'I'm only the boots, Miss er –' He broke off, not privy to her name. But her voice sounded lovely, stroked him persuasively as she begged again.

'Oh please! Couldn't you find a spare key and let me out?'

Wanting to assist, his face contorted with indecision, he glanced along the corridor to where a bad-tempered Joanna was darting in and out of a room changing the bed linen. She would have a key. Still, he dithered for a second, playing with his chin. Why had the girl's father locked her in? It was too impertinent to ask, but he did not like the man who, gentlemanly attire or no, looked an arrogant brute. Thus decided, he straightened his cap and said, 'Hang on, miss, I'll just go see what I can do.'

Hurrying to accost the maid he explained the situation. 'We have to help her, Jo.'

'I don't *have* to do anything!' Edging her way past him to gather dirty linen, Joanna remained cross, white petticoats frothing under the sober dress as she marched to and fro.

Marty tried to cajole sympathy, leaning his attractive head close to her plain one and nudging her arm suggestively. 'I always took you for a kind soul. How would you feel if your da locked you in against your will? Bet you'd want me to come and rescue you.'

For once his rough-diamond charm was lost. Ignoring the smell of buttermilk soap, those kind eyes, the winning smile, Joanna condemned him as a faithless friend. 'It's not my dad, it's hers, and we shouldn't get involved unless we want to lose our jobs!' She stamped off with her bundle of sheets.

Thwarted, Marty grimaced and returned to apologise to the prisoner. 'Sorry, miss, I tried to get a key off the maid but she wouldn't be involved.'

There came a snort of frustration that condemned him as useless and the sound of a body slumping to the carpet. Squinting through the keyhole he caught a wisp of dark hair against the backdrop of pastel wallpaper. 'Maybe your father won't be long.'

Her reply was dull. 'He'll be out all morning.'

Upon learning this, Marty relaxed somewhat to enjoy the romantic notion that he was helping a damsel in distress. He was intrigued to know why she had been locked in, and difference in status had not prevented him from flirting with female guests before, given the encouragement. Some ladies found him attractive, though heaven knew why; personally he saw a gypsy when he looked in the mirror, a face that lacked the finely chiselled features he himself admired, with eyes that were somewhere between grey and green. When he was happy they appeared green, when sad they were grey – that was, if one could see them under those heavy lids. His hair was of a nondescript colour too; one might be kind and call it brown but it was the insipid brown of dried winter undergrowth and its texture similarly wiry, so that whenever he removed his hat it sprang back into place like trampled

4

grass, no amount of oil able to control it. He disliked every-thing about his looks. Still, to his favour he had decent teeth and was taller than average, and he had learned that charm compensated for any other lack of attribute.

Leaning against the door, he voiced a bold and teasing statement. 'Your father took the key on purpose, didn't he?'

There was a pregnant pause, then the glint of an eye as she tried to assess her impudent Samaritan through the aper-ture.

Marty felt no need to apologise, but did offer an expla-nation as to how he had guessed. 'I saw him leave. He seemed quite aggrieved.'

She fixed her glittering dark eye to his green one.

Concerned that he might have overstepped the mark, he added quickly. 'I hung around 'cause I felt worried about you.'

'Did you, really?' She sounded grateful.

Encouraged, Marty prolonged the bizarre method of conversation. 'It's remiss of me to have to ask, miss, but could you tell me whom I have the pleasure of addressing?'

'I'm Henrietta Ibbetson.'

When he did not automatically introduce himself in return, she prompted, 'So, who are you?'

'Oh, like I said, I'm only the boots, miss.' The quality of her voice had him glued to the keyhole. If the hotel manager himself had come round the corner Marty could not have torn himself away.

'You must have a name.'

'I'm flattered you're even interested, miss.' Marty grinned to himself – that's right, lay it on thick.

'Why, naturally I am!'

'Thank you, miss. It's Martin Lanegan.'

'Martin, I'd love to see you, but even with this unyielding timber between us I can tell by your voice that you're a very kind person, very likeable.'

His belly tightened at the artlessly seductive tone.

5

'And that's why I feel confident in throwing myself upon your mercy.'

I'd like to throw myself on you, thought Marty, imagining the gorgeous creature on the other side of the door, but he said, throatily polite, 'I'll do what I can.'

'Might you perhaps find a key at the reception desk?'

The lascivious thoughts vanished. He gasped at the very suggestion. 'That's more than my life's worth, miss! If you're not here when your father comes back –'

'But I will be! I *swear* it. It's not that I wish to run away, but that I don't care to be caged like an animal.'

He endured mental argument, desperate to ingratiate himself but not so keen as to risk dismissal. 'I know it's none of my affair, Miss Ibbetson, but why did he lock you up?'

There was a slight pause whilst Henrietta wondered how much to divulge. He was, after all, just a lowly employee. But it was essential that she lure him to her side. How else was she to keep the arranged rendezvous with her beau at King's Cross?

Keeping this latter part to herself, she injected her sigh with feeling and made a half-confession. 'My father plans to marry me off to an individual of his choosing, a man I find utterly loathsome.' Her tone endorsed this revulsion. 'Two days ago I ran away to my aunt's in London . . .' It had been during her escapade that she had met a more promising match, one who, upon hearing her story, had vowed to help. She should have gone with him there and then but had thought it wiser to go to her aunt's and to meet him in a few days' time. '. . . but she betrayed me and Father came to take me home. We arrived too late in York to continue our journey so he booked us in here. He hasn't let me out of his sight other than to sleep and to breakfast. He's killing two birds with one stone by attending some business whilst in the city. We're to catch the afternoon train home. At which point I shall be condemned.'

But if this dolt would only comply she could be well on her way to her assignation at King's Cross before her father even returned. 'I'd be eternally grateful, Martin, if you could find it in your heart to assist.'

Enthralled that his name had never sounded so wonderful than on these lips, Marty came alive to make a bold decision. 'I'll be quick as I can!'

A gleeful Henrietta gave herself a congratulatory squeeze.

It was no small task Marty had set himself, for the sentinel on the desk was as keen as Cerberus at guarding his post. Much subterfuge and the assistance of another colleague was required to lure him away and for the boot boy to make his daring foray, knowing that if he were caught with the key he would be sacked without reference. The reward, however, was immeasurable.

The brief preview he had had of Miss Ibbetson could not have prepared him for the full magnificence. Upon his excited entrance to the suite he was dealt a vision of pink candy-striped organdie, a tantalising glimpse of bare skin through a diaphanous sleeve, a figure as sumptuously upholstered as the room that was normally forbidden to him . . . Yet it was not any rich accoutrement that so enchanted. The eyes that had been but a glint through a keyhole now totally impaled him, transfixed him to the expensive carpet that his feet were not permitted to sully, as glittering and radiant as lighted coals in a face that brimmed with intelligence – even though at this minute she was gawping at him like some yokel.

Henrietta caught her breath. She had been poised, hat in hand, ready to flee, but upon seeing Martin there came a surge of every corpuscle in her veins, like a spring tide, which swept away all the repressive debris of her previous existence and brought her so overwhelmingly alive that she feared she might choke upon this ecstasy. All reason suspended, utterly immobile with shock, she let the hat fall,

7

unable to perform any task other than to stare at him, totally oblivious that her jaw was hanging open.

A brief awkwardness ensued, arising not from difference in rank but from the palpable desire that exuded from both, each embarrassed at having been caught so unawares.

Normally self-assured, Henrietta fought the constriction in her throat and tried to thank him for liberating her, but found herself stricken dumb. The way he was looking at her, his eyelids droopy as if on the verge of slumber, but the look within them tugging at her abdomen, igniting all manner of extraordinary feelings . . .

Marty noted that she seemed in no hurry to escape now; her eyes still adhered to his face. Something had occurred to change her mind. He could only hope that she felt the same thrilling emotions that bound him captive. What in God's name was happening here?

Eventually breaking free of his trance, suddenly self-conscious under her probing gaze, only now did he think to whip off his cap before enquiring, 'What will you do now, miss?'

Henrietta watched the masculine fingers remove the cap, the springy hair beneath, her eyes fixed to the sensual bow of his mouth though barely hearing the words it uttered, whilst her own murmured vaguely, 'What?' Then, suddenly aware she had been holding her breath, she exhaled on a note of laughter, a happy sound that rippled his belly with its exquisiteness. 'Oh . . . I haven't the slightest idea!' Her plan abandoned, she had forgotten all about the one she had promised to meet, indeed could not even recall what he looked like – certainly not so desirable as this green-eyed young man before her. Oh, he was lovely. *Lovely!* Ignoring the uniform that labelled him minion, her gaze pored over him, constantly lured back to those eyes, which promised kindness yet at the same time danger.

Marty echoed her affectionate laughter and the two stood admiring each other for a while, before she said with a smiling shrug by way of explanation, 'I'm just desperate to escape.'

Until these words, both of them had forgotten her irate father. Misreading her companion's hasty grab for the door-knob and his expression as one of self-concern, she prompted him, though not without a tinge of disappoint-ment. 'Yes, it's unwise to let him find you here! I'm truly grateful for your assistance but I should hate for you to lose your job.'

But instead of running away as she had feared, Marty shut the door from the inside and leaned with his back to it, a triumphant twinkle in his eye. Secure that his feelings were reciprocated, his reply was gallant. 'It'd be worth it. I'm not worried for meself, but for you.'

Her beam was so radiantly affectionate that he wanted to snatch her in his arms, to press the whole length of his body against hers. But that would have been just too brazen. Besides, enough was happening in his trousers already. If that was what she could do to him merely by looking . . .

He mirrored her smile then strolled over to the window, tapping his cap against his leg and appearing to take an interest in the view, though his thoughts were still consumed by the girl behind him. 'It's inhuman to treat anyone in such a fashion – outdated too.' For heaven's sake, they were four years into the twentieth century. 'Most fathers are very particular when it comes to the one who marries their daughter,' briefly, he pictured his own wedded sisters, 'but they usually take account of her feelings on the matter.'

Henrietta wandered over to stand beside the tall figure, her eyes staring out across the beautifully laid-out grounds in full flower, and beyond the river to the Minster that dominated the city, its ancient pinnacles etched against a summer sky. Considering the hotel's juxtaposition with the railway this room was very quiet. She wondered if Martin could hear the rapid thudding of her heart. 'There my father differs, I'm afraid.' Her face was less vibrant now, her tone hollow. 'For he sets his entire store on my brother, John; he places no value on my opinions at all.'

Electrified by her proximity, angry on her behalf, Marty tightened his grip on the cap, whacked it against a piece of furniture. 'Then the man's not only cruel but blind and stupid.' That was audacious indeed.

But Henrietta did not appear to judge it thus, merely dealing him a smile that was both sad and happy at the same time, and saying with feeling, 'It's the worst thing in the world to be bullied, don't you feel? Not that someone of your physical stature would be troubled by that, of course.'

Marty bared his white teeth with a rueful chuckle. 'You don't know my superior.'

Dazzled by his smile, she matched it. Henrietta had never made any distinction between the ranks. Just because someone was forced to do menial work did not lower them in her estimation. 'I suppose we all have someone above us. May one ask how old you are?'

Considering her own mature appearance, Marty added fifteen months to his age. 'I'm twenty-one.'

She looked wistful. 'So in all things that count you are your own man. You could walk out and find employment elsewhere, go wherever you choose. There are four more years before I come of age – not that it would matter, I should still be at that despot's command.'

Shamed by her truthfulness, he admitted, 'Well, as a matter of fact I've a few months to go yet – but it wouldn't make a difference what age I was either, Mr Wilkinson would still dub me a shirker.' He grinned impishly. 'Maybe I am or I wouldn't be up here dallying with you.'

'Well, I'm very glad you are – here, I mean.' Now perched on a dressing stool, her eyes having abandoned the land-scape in favour of her attractive companion, Henrietta marvelled at how easily she could converse with him. 'Tell me more about yourself.'

'I'd hate to delay your escape.'

'We've ages yet. Have you always been a boots?'

'God forbid!' He was delighted by the fact that she had said *we*, as if they were going together. 'I've only been here a year or so. It was a drop in station from my last job, but I'd had that since leaving school at fourteen and was going nowhere, so I decided there was a better chance of promotion in a hotel. It's hard to put your heart into cleaning boots but I intend to work my way up. I was joking about being a shirker by the way.'

'Of course,' affirmed Henrietta. 'But you must have enjoyed your last job if you had it for five, six years?'

He was about to correct her then remembered he had already said he was nearly twenty-one and fobbed her off with a quick, 'Thereabouts – but these are lovelier surroundings. York's a grand place, isn't it? I wasn't born here ye know.'

'I'd never have guessed.' Her eyes teased.

'That obvious, eh?' Marty pretended to be crushed. 'And here's me thinking I'd got rid of the accent.'

'Oh, don't ever lose it!' she begged him. 'It's so pleasant on the ear.'

'Some folk would disagree. There's many can't stand the Irish.' He paused to weigh his words before adding a confession. 'Especially if they're tinkers to boot. Ach, now I've told ye. We only came to live in a house after me grandparents died.'

'How romantic!'

Comforted by her reaction, he chuckled. 'Not what some would say. The insults I've suffered . . .'

Her face oozed sympathy, then she turned slightly sober. 'Well, that's something we share, although I doubt the insults come from your own father.'

Marty was about to make a joke but saw it was not the time. 'I'd like to think you get on better with your mother.'

'Hardly – well, that's a lie, we are really quite at ease when we are permitted to be on our own. Unfortunately

11

that's a rare occurrence. *He* is always there to spoil it.' She looked wistful. 'The trouble is, Mother's a very weak person. That might sound harsh, but it's something I learned very early in life from studying the way she bent to his will, even to the detriment of her children – well, not so much John for he was Father's favourite, but in my case . . .' Henrietta moved her head slowly from side to side, then from her lips poured a torrent of information on her childhood, injustices she had suffered, her feelings on these and on her family, to which Marty listened mesmerised.

'Far from issuing words in my defence,' went on Henrietta, 'Mother saw me as the defiant one, begged me to take what she saw as the easy path instead of fighting his regime. Not once have I seen her stand up to him, not even when he dismissed dear old Nanny, the person who really was more of a mother to me, who raised me from a babe . . .' She scowled in memory of that awful crime. 'It's so long ago but his callousness infuriates me still. He said she wasn't required any more; sent her packing without a care that some of us might love –' Verging on tears, she broke off in mid-sentence to disguise her emotions with a giggle. 'I can't believe I'm confiding all this to a total stranger!'

'*You* can't?' One lithe buttock resting on the dressing table, Marty leaned towards her and laughed even more heartily, relaxing into his normal mode of speech. 'I can't believe I'm eejit enough to ruin me chances with the most beautiful girl I ever met by telling her I'm from a family of tinkers.'

'Oh, but surely they can't be classified as such!' Henrietta reached out quickly to press his arm, the gesture loaded with affection, before it was just as quickly withdrawn.

Wanting to grab her too, despite his enthralment Marty shrewdly divined that his comment on her beauty had gone undisputed, though there was no hint of arrogance in her manner and, as one with no belief in his own attractiveness, he envied her that.

'You did say they live in a house these days,' she reminded him.

'Aye, for seven, eight years or so.' Might he have laid the romantic gypsy thing on a bit too thick? He spoke more truthfully now. 'I suppose we were never strictly part of that community anyway, we tended to travel alone, though I can't deny it was the rover's life. Back and forth twixt Ireland and Yorkshire. As a nipper ye kind o' get sick of it, moving round different schools and the like. I was glad when Da settled for the buffer's life.' Rubbing the edge of the dressing table, he studied the hand that rested temptingly close to his, then exclaimed, 'Eh, don't let on to anyone here, will you? I've never told a soul – man nor woman nor beast.'

'Then I shan't either. But even if they still dwelt in a caravan it wouldn't make any difference about the way I feel towards you.' She herself saw beyond the gypsy, detected some indescribable quality of spirit.

'Wouldn't it?' His green eyes shone and his question was superfluous; had he thought it would affect their miraculous rapport he would never have used the approach. Boldly, he grabbed her hand. 'That's such a relief. I just wanted you to know everything about me so's you're fully aware of what you're getting into.' It was a gross presumption but one that he was confident to make and that Henrietta would accept.

She shook her head in happy amazement, her little pearl earrings trembling. 'It's so strange but I feel as if I already know everything there is to know – as if we've been acquainted for years!'

'I feel like that too,' declared Marty, his eyes running over her dark tresses – the only coarse thing about her – that were swept up at the front and fastened in an elegant twist to frame pale symmetrical features. She reminded him

13

of a ballerina in a painting he had once seen. 'Or is it all my imagination? 'Cause I can't for the life of me believe a girl as lovely as you could bring herself even to talk to me.'

Something flickered over Henrietta's face. The light went out of her eyes as they retreated under dark lashes. 'You seem to set great store by my appearance –'

Not yet realising that her mood had changed, he laughed and butted in. 'Well, if you've been taking the ugly pills I can tell you they're not working.'

But she would not look up at him. '– because that's the second reference you've made to it.'

Taken aback at her sudden coolness, Marty cocked his head and studied her pose for a second, wondering why his intended praise had for some strange reason inflicted huge displeasure. 'Begging your pardon, but what's so wrong with that?' Having sisters, he was not inexperienced in the ways of females, was aware that their moods could turn from honey to vitriol at the drop of a hat, but never had he known one who eschewed compliments.

Eyes still downcast, Henrietta picked at her satin skirt and took a deep breath. 'I've just poured out my heart telling you of the lack of regard my father has for me, yet you –' She broke off, angry and hurt at having her joy ruined so quickly.

Still frowning and totally confused as to how a remark on her beauty could be so misconstrued, Marty was desperate to make things right but did not know how. What did her father have to do with this? Then, as he continued to stare at her forlorn figure, his heart plunging from its former heights to hang like a leaden pendulum in his chest, he was suddenly granted a deeper understanding of this beautiful creature. Confident she might be in her looks, but the years of parental neglect had left Henrietta with the assumption that she was worthless for anything other than to adorn the house of some magnate, to be used as bargaining power for her father's gain. His heart went out to her and he cupped her hand gently in both of his. 'Of *course* I think you're gorgeous, and I can't deny that was the thing which first attracted me – but it's not the only thing – and I don't mean your clothes or your wealth.'

'My father's wealth,' she reminded him.

'That's as may be, but it doesn't count. It wouldn't matter who or what y'are, I'd still like you . . . more than like.' His voice was tenderly coaxing. 'I thought, I *hoped* you felt the same.'

She forced her woebegone eyes up to meet his droopy-lidded gaze, her belly performing a somersault as she admitted in a little voice, 'I do.'

'And what was it attracted you?' he asked gently.

'Well, the way you –' She broke off, her pink lips curling in a half-smile of self-mockery.

'The way I look,' provided Marty, smiling too now as he gave her hand an accusing but playful shake. 'So it's not just me that's guilty, is it?'

'No.' Under his teasing, Henrietta melted, fighting back the tears.

'I mean, it stands to reason that it's a person's physical appearance that first attracts someone, doesn't it? Though what the devil you see in me is anyone's guess,' he added incredulously.

She rose then. Tapered little fingers stroked him, as did her voice. 'I'm sorry, Martin, I didn't mean to sound harsh or arrogant or ungrateful, it's just that –'

'I know,' he told her kindly, going so far as to caress her cheek with his knuckle, wanting to go much further and pull the pins from her hair and the clothes from her body, forgetting that he should not even be there at all. 'It might be the first thing that attracted us but we both know it goes far beyond that, don't we?'

She nodded, blinking away the moisture of emotion. Their eyes held each other adoringly for a while, both still reeling from the impact of their meeting, trying to understand what

15

had happened to them but unable to voice it, until the magnetic charge between them became too strong to resist and they finally pressed their lips together, tentatively at first, but quickly yielding to such fierce passion that it terrified them into breaking away, although not completely.

Marty swallowed, took a deep breath and emitted a delighted laugh. His hands gripping her waist, his eyes unable to tear themselves from hers, he pondered on their glittering depths. 'So what now, Miss Ibbetson? Or should I say Henrietta?'

Equally ecstatic, she said, 'I think you should, especially after *that*. But call me Etta, I much prefer it.' Then she sighed and laid her head against his warm chest, leaving it there even though one of his metal buttons hurt her ear. 'You know, I really do wish you had a caravan, then you could spirit me away.'

He rubbed his chin atop her head, breathing in her scent and smiling. 'Ah, now don't go making rash statements like that or I might.'

'I'm serious.'

'You are?' He pushed her gently away so that he could read her face.

'Completely! Caravan or no, I can't wait here for Father to get back. I'm desperate to leave . . . but not without you. I never want to leave you, Martin, *ever*.' She squeezed him tightly.

Marty let out a happy roar. 'To think when I came to work this morning the only thing I had in mind to tackle was boots! Little did I know I'd be kissing me future wife.'

'And I my future husband!' Etta laughed emotionally, and they hugged again amorously.

Marty was on the verge of announcing that he would run away with her there and then, but how could he do this with no funds? He was lucky if he earned nine bob a week. He wondered if she had any money, but was not

16

about to appear so mercenary for that would indeed ruin his case. Still wondering how to broach the subject, he was forestalled by Etta who urged excitedly, 'Let's leave this minute!'

'Oh, that'd be really bright, us walking through the hotel lobby together. The manager'd be delighted.' He grinned to show he was ribbing. 'Isn't it enough that you're about to sacrifice everything, without me losing my job too?'

'There's nothing for me to sacrifice but wealth, and that means absolutely nothing.'

'It might when you've nothing to eat. If I walk out of here I've lost my income. How would I support you?'

'You could get another job! I'd help.'

'Etta, I'd love nothing more than to run away with you right now, but one of us has to be sensible. I can't promise to keep you in the manner to which you're accustomed but I can at least hang on to the job I have. Now, we must think of a plan. Where are we to go? Where are we to live? I couldn't raise enough for a month's rent so quickly, not to mention what it'd cost even to secure the key.'

'But you won't allow these stumbling blocks to come between us, will you?' she implored him with little kisses.

Marty closed his eyes in ecstasy, fighting carnal urges. 'Do I look as if I'd give up so easily? I'm going to have to enlist help, that's all.'

'From your parents?'

He sobered. 'Ah, no, I certainly couldn't take you home just like that.' Nor could he allow her to think this was some jolly jape. 'It might be that your father's not the only one who doesn't take kindly to this. I don't mean any insult, I'm sure Ma and Da'll be fine once they get used to the idea of me marrying a lady – if the shock doesn't kill them first – but I can't just spring it on them. Besides, what kind of a man would I be if I expected my parents to look after us? No, but I have quite a few friends I can turn to.'

'I knew you'd be popular!' She hugged him.

17

'Thanks, but nobody's that popular when he's asking for cash.' He tried to clear his mind but it was difficult with her pressed so close. His eye caught the carriage clock on the bedside table. 'God in heaven, I've been in here almost an hour!' How the time had flown. 'I'll have to get this key back. Now, sweetheart, nice as it is we've got to stop all this cuddling and be practical. How long before himself returns?'

'I should think at least another hour.'

'Then I'll have to make a start on our relief fund.' He attempted to disentangle himself.

'I have a few coins hidden!' An adoring Etta made a grab for her portmanteau, hurling clothes right, left and centre before pressing the money into his hand. 'Sorry there's so little but I spent the rest on my last escapade.'

Marty accepted the few shillings with grace. 'Never mind, this'll be a big help, though we'll need just a bit more.' He gave her a quick kiss. 'So let me go about getting it, and the moment I do I'll be back to whisk you away.'

Overjoyed, she clung to him all the way to the door. 'Oh, surely I must be dreaming!'

'And I must be crazy!' Loath to drag himself away, Marty kissed her heartily, dealt her one last adoring look, then, peeking into the corridor to check that it was clear, rushed back to his proper quarters.

On the way down, however, he encountered the pageboy, whom he knew received plenty of tips, and, without preamble, demanded excitedly, 'Joe, me old mucker, lend us some cash. I'll pay it back soon as I can.'

The trusting youngster fished a couple of silver three-pences out of his trouser pocket. 'No rush.'

'Thanks, but I meant a bit more than this.' Needing to shout it from the rooftops, Marty grinned and in an excited whisper revealed his intentions. 'You'll never believe this. You know the stunner? She wants me to run away with her!'

Joe gave an impassive nod and made to move on. 'Right
. . . sorry, Bootsie, can't stop, that lady in room one-two-
five's just rang down to ask if I'll go slip her a length. She
can't get enough of –'

'I'm not codding ye!' Marty pressed a delaying hand to
his friend's chest, hissing with bright-eyed enthusiasm,
'We've really clicked. Her dad locked her in and –'

'Oh aye, Joanna's just been ranting on about that!' Joe
rolled his eyes in amused exasperation. 'Proper disgruntled
she was.'

'Will you stop bloody wittering on!' Marty displayed
urgency. 'I have to think of a way to get her out o' here
before he comes back.'

Joe laughed aloud then. 'You soft article! A lady like
her's not really interested in the likes of us. She only spun
you a line to get you to unlock the door. Joanna told u—'

'Ach, I haven't time to sod about!' Marty rushed away,
muttering that he had to get some money together.

Watching the other retreat, the little pageboy shook his
head knowingly, dismissing Marty's outpouring as fantasy.
'She'll be vanished by the time you get back!' he called after
him.

'Don't bet on it!'

But down in the basement Marty was to be shown equal
disrespect. Having been reliably informed by Joanna, everyone
was of the opinion that he had taken leave of his senses.

'I know she's lovely,' said a motherly chambermaid,
'because she asked me to do up her corsets and gave me
sixpence for my troubles –'

'Blimey, I'd've done 'em for nowt,' interjected one of the
boys.

'– but I rather think she's teasing you, dear,' finished the
maid.

'Aye, she's having you for a mug, Bootsie,' sneered a
waiter.

'But will you lend us something, please, *please*?'

19

Clutching his cap to his breast, Marty dropped to his knees, shuffling in this fashion around the workers and making them all laugh.

'Here you are then, I'm happy to bet on a certainty.' Casually, one of the porters dropped a florin into the outstretched cap.

Others gasped at the munificent gesture. 'Bloody hell, I'll have some if you're chucking it about!'

The contributor's face creased in mockery. 'Nah – I'll be getting it back in ten minutes when Bootsie finds out she's done a flit!'

Ignoring the ridicule, Marty lauded his benefactor. And as others good-naturedly followed suit he blessed these too, even knowing it was done out of jest, for they would soon be laughing on the other side of their faces.

'Eh, we'll look daft if he runs off to Timbuktu with her,' joked one of the boys, nudging his neighbour.

'We won't be running that far.' Marty got to his feet, looking smug.

'She might not be but you will! When her dad comes back you'll find yourself travelling to Timbuktu on the end of his foot.'

Marty remained smiling and chinked the coins now in his hand. 'Mock if you will! But Etta and myself will be using this for a deposit on a home.'

Alas, this drew more than raucous guffaws.

'What's this infernal racket? Boots!' Marty jumped and shoved the coins in his pocket as his superior appeared and everyone hurried about their work. 'I might have known you'd be at the centre of it!'

'Sorry, Mr Wilkinson.'

'You will be! The gentleman in room one-twenty has made a complaint that his dirty shoes are still in the corridor.'

Marty retreated quickly with an apologetic bow. 'I must have missed them, sir. I'll go fetch them now.'

'Jump to it, boy – and return those whilst you're at it!' Wilkinson pointed to a lone pair of ladies' shoes, which Marty quickly seized.

'Yes, sir, I'll see to it immediately!' The errand gave him just the excuse he needed to go upstairs again.

On the way his luck increased, for not only was he able to replace the key but he met Joe struggling under the weight of two cases and whispered urgently to him, 'When you've done that will you keep watch for me? I need to know if that Ibbetson gadger comes back – he hasn't been past already, has he?'

Joe said not that he knew of, adding that he would act as lookout so long as he was not needed. 'You'll get me hung, you will!'

'Hanged!' corrected Marty with a grin, and, thanking him, he galloped off to Etta's room.

Yet at the point of entering he stalled – not simply because her father might be there but more because he feared his friends could be right. Had he indeed been fooling himself, caught up in the moment? What could a ravishing, wealthy young lady like her see in him? Moreover, how could he be idiot enough to expect her to give it all up?

But the doubt was transitory. Once inside, everything was all right again. More than all right. In her relief Etta threw herself at him, sparking off a feverish bout of kissing.

Reinvigorated, Marty said cheerfully, 'Right, get your hat on, missus! We're off.'

Giggling and giddy with happiness, she ran to where the hat still lay on the carpet. It was whilst she was picking it up that her father's voice intruded, startling the elopers.

'What the deuce are you doing in here?' It emerged as through a megaphone.

Wheeling to face the imposing presence, Marty blanched – the wretch must have passed Joe on the way. Under threat, he thought quickly, seizing and brandishing the kid slippers that he had thrown aside on entry. 'Just returning the lady's

21

shoes, sir!' He hoped the father did not recognize the lie.

But ownership of the shoes was of no concern to Ibbetson. 'The door was locked – you must have let yourself in!' Stick raised, the man advanced upon the slender youth.

Alarmed that her newfound romance was to be spoiled before it had chance to flourish, Etta butted in whilst trying to appear calm. 'There's nothing untoward, Father, he was passing the room and I commanded him to fetch me something to drink, which involved him also fetching a key. It was stifling in here, I almost passed out.'

Marty chipped in to endorse this. 'I didn't think you'd want me to ignore the lady's discomfort, sir.'

'You are impudent, boy! I shall have you dismissed!'

'For saving me?' Head erect, Etta glided forward, desperate to run but knowing that would ruin everything. As things stood, all was not completely lost. 'I should rather imagine the hotel owner would thank his employee for such quick thinking. He wasn't the one who locked me in.'

With her father's wrath successfully deflected from Martin, immediately she became humble, though it was against her nature. 'I beg your pardon, I didn't mean that to sound in any way defiant. I'm merely trying to explain that the young man was simply doing as he was bidden. Please, Father, you've never been unfair to our own servants.' Etta laid a steadying hand upon his arm, trying not to reveal her true anxiety. How were they to get away now?

Marty was thinking the same thing. Wisely, in the face of Ibbetson's fury he dropped his gaze to the carpet and stood meekly awaiting his fate, though under the surface his mind whirred like clockwork for a solution.

After what seemed like aeons, though his colour remained high, Ibbetson grudgingly decided, 'Very well, I'll give you the benefit of the doubt. You may keep your job – but only because we shall shortly be gone and I shan't have to encounter your detestable face again. Now get out and send a porter to transport our bags immediately to the platform!'

With the man gesticulating for him to leave, Marty gave hasty thanks and obeyed. Henrietta's heart sank into despair as he dealt her not so much as a glance.

By now, though, thoroughly infatuated, Marty had no intention of abandoning his prize. Cursing his laxity at not seeking her precise address, he raced downstairs, and, after bewailing his luck to his colleagues and submitting to their friendly teasing, he threw himself on their mercy yet again. Scribbling on a crumpled bit of paper and electing the chambermaid as his go-between, he begged her, 'Jo, do us a favour! Slip her this message before she lea—'

'He must think I'm barmy!' Open-mouthed, she advertised her scorn to the laughing assembly.

'Ah, go on!' Fraught with desperation, he tried to cup her face. '*Please*! I have to get her address or she's lost to me forever!'

She craned her head out of reach. 'And you expect me to care?' Was he really so insensitive? Could he not tell how much she wanted him herself?

'I thought you were a pal?' he beseeched her, but she just pushed him bad-temperedly out of her way and left.

No one else seemed keen to take the risk, laughing off his frantic attempts as pure whimsy. After an infuriated pause there came a brainwave. Swearing and rummaging through a drawer he finally came up with a piece of chalk. Then, grabbing a tray he scrawled something on the underside and rushed from the side exit. Swearing and dodging his way through a collection of laundry hampers that were being off-loaded, he bounded around to the hotel's main lobby which opened onto the station platform, heading for a spot that Etta would have to pass.

But she was already well on her way, albeit unwillingly, being half dragged by her father after the porter who carried their bags. Hovering anxiously with his tray, Marty silently urged her to turn around, but Etta marched onwards stiff-backed to the waiting train. Panic rose. He couldn't lose her, he couldn't! Almost at the point of risking everything, he was about to yell out for her not to leave, when, miracle of miracles, she turned crossly to take issue with her father for manhandling her into the carriage and at last spotted Marty. In this same instant he tilted the tray to reveal the chalked entreaty underneath: *IF YOU WANT ME TELL ME WHERE YOU LIVE.*

A joyous recognition came to her eyes, igniting a spark of optimism that regrettably was not to last, for at this same time her father spun round too and Marty was compelled to vanish. When he dared to poke his head out again, Etta was in the carriage, out of sight. He wondered miserably, as the train chugged away, if she had deciphered his message or if he would ever see her again.

Ignorant as to the extent of his agony, his colleagues told him mildly, 'Forget about her, Bootsie. The likes of her won't fret about thee – oh, and we'll have our money back if you don't mind.'

'Aw, don't be mean!' Now that the rival had been disposed of, Joanna allowed her compassionate nature to shine through and she gripped his arm. 'Cheer up, Bootsie, me and my friend are off to the theatre tonight, you can come with us if you like.'

Normally Marty would have accepted, but he was just too devastated and did not even acknowledge the invitation, much to his admirer's hurt. He emptied his pockets but, though glum, his tone showed he was not beaten. 'I wonder if her address is in the register.'

'Eh, don't let Wilko hear you!' They grouped round to recover their contributions.

Marty remained pensive. 'She mentioned her dad's a farmer . . .'

There was a cackle from the porter. 'Aye, but not just

24

some clod-hopping smallholder! Haven't you heard of him, you dummy? He owns half the Yorkshire Wolds!'

Unfazed, Marty declared. 'Well, he doesn't own me and I'm going to find her, you see.'

There was no time for the others to enquire how he was going to do this, for their superior came in then to give everyone a dressing down and to make sure the boot boy was kept busy for the rest of his shift.

But that didn't stop his mind being preoccupied, and this mood was to last long after Etta had gone.

It was still with him when he travelled home along Walmgate that evening, a different environment completely to the one he had just left. Abounding with public houses, the thoroughfare reeked of stale beer fumes and the effluvia of tanneries and skin-yards, alleviated only by the more appetising aroma of fish and chips. Ahead of him, a small boy clanked along with a bucket and shovel, stopping occasionally to scrape a pile of dog excreta from the pavement into his bucket. Two hatchet-faced, greasy-haired slatterns called insults at each other from opposite sides of the road, one threatening to, 'Tear the black heart out of yese!' Cringing from such unfeminine behaviour, Marty ducked into a side street and onwards to the tiny terraced house in Hope Street with its soot-engrained bricks, its dull bottle-green door and lopsided shutters, the feeling of discontent plain on his face.

His mother was quick to comment on this as he came through the door. 'Bad day, son?'

He barely glanced at her as he went to wash his hands. 'I met the girl I want to marry, Ma.'

With two children helping her to lay the table and another smaller one using her leg as a support, Agnes Lanegan smiled, arched an eyebrow at her husband and replied facetiously, 'I'd better starch the best linen then, though you don't look too happy about it.'

'That's because her father doesn't want her to marry me,' revealed Marty, hanging up the towel. 'Thinks she's above us.'

'You weren't codding us then?' His mother bridled and pursed her lips.

His normally mild-mannered father showed indignation. 'The poltroon! My son's good enough for anyone . . . lessen 'tis the daughter of the hotel manager of course, now that would be taking expectations a bit too far.' His eyes told that it was meant as a jest. Then he noted his son's expression and his jaw dropped. 'Christ, she's not, is she?'

Marty paused and took a deep breath. 'No . . . but her father does have a bob or two.' Always able to confide in his parents, he was honest with them now, telling them everything that had occurred and rendering them dumb with such astonishment that he had to fill the gap himself. 'I still can't believe it happened so fast! Like an angel she is, an angel.'

His parents looked at each other, betraying dubiety, Agnes breaking the silence first. 'But she's left the hotel, ye say?' She plucked the loose, tanned skin of her throat, anxious that he might be courting trouble.

Marty nodded sadly and tugged down his shirt cuffs.

Somewhat relieved, Mrs Lanegan shared a look of sympathy with her husband, saying kindly to her son, 'There are finer fish in the sea than have ever been caught. Here, come sit down, I've some nice kippers – Uncle Mal, come for your tea now!'

Great Uncle Malachy cast a rheumy eye from his evening newspaper. 'Tea? I only just had breakfast.' But he ambled obediently to sit with the children at the table.

Pulling out a chair, Marty looked wan. 'I don't think I can manage anything.'

'Sure and you will!' Serving him directly after his father, Agnes patted his shoulder lovingly. 'Get that down ye, it'll make you forget about Miss High and Mighty.'

He looked up from his seat, slightly annoyed. 'No it won't.'

'Watch your tone, boy,' warned Redmond Lanegan, his eyes suddenly hard.

'Sorry, Mammy.' Marty was contrite whilst remaining obstinate in his ambition. 'But I couldn't forget about Etta even if I tried. She's the one for me and I'm the one for her.'

'Her father doesn't seem to agree,' Agnes reminded him.

'Then he can lump it.'

The parents glanced at each other in dismay over this all too familiar stance. Marty had always lived life like a terrier fighting the leash: he knew there was something better to be had just over there, if only he was allowed to get at it – and, God, help them, he had spotted something over there again.

'Martin, I'm warning you, put this out of your mind at once!' Grim-faced, Mrs Lanegan turned to her husband for backing, which was granted, though it did not the slightest to change their son's mind. Marty picked at his meal, not offering any further argument, but it was clearly evident in his posture.

Planting herself on the wobbly dining chair, Agnes damned him. 'Ever since you were a bit of a boy you've always wanted what you can't have! I'll never forget that time you set your heart on a great big cooking apple – pestered and pestered till I bought it for you, even after I'd warned that it wouldn't suit your taste. Then you took one bite, made a face and said you didn't want any more – after I'd emptied me purse to get it for you!'

'And you made me sit and eat it if I recall.' Marty cast a dour grin at his younger siblings. 'But this isn't the same at all, Ma.'

Seeing his wife open her mouth for another volley, Redmond commanded tiredly, 'For the love of Mike, leave it, woman!'

And knowing what tiresome repercussions even a tiny argument could bring, she complied, though with bad grace as she repeated primly, 'Always wanted what you can't damn well have!' before getting on with her tea.

Taking his father's raised voice as a signal to desist, Marty offered not another word, quarrel giving way to the brusque scraping of knives and forks.

Old Uncle Mal, searching for something to divert open warfare, ran his tongue around his gums and announced, 'You'll be pleased to hear my diarrhoea's cleared up, Marty.'

'We're overjoyed,' yawned Redmond, as there was a groan of disgust from his wife and sniggers from the youngsters.

But they were an affectionate family and the bad feeling did not last for more than a few hours, Mrs Lanegan clamping her son's shoulder as she served his usual supper of bread and tea, and, without resurrecting the topic, telling him quietly, 'Everything'll turn out for the best, you'll see.'

'Aye, lookit, Marty!' His face wreathed in ambition, Mr Lanegan displayed a picture of a motor car in the book he had been reading. 'How d'ye fancy driving along Walmgate in that? 'Twould get the neighbours talking sure enough. Aye,' he gazed longingly at the picture, 'we shall have one of those some day.'

Marty dealt him a fond but half-hearted smile, knowing it was just his father's way of taking his mind off Etta. As if it would.

Apparently this was to remain a concern to his parents, for as Marty finished his supper and was on his way to bed he overheard his mother trying to reassure her husband, 'Don't go fretting yourself about it, dear. 'Twill be just another of his passing desires. She's gone from the hotel, so there's not much he can do about it. You know what he's like. In a few days he'll have set his sights on something or somebody else and forgotten all about her.'

No I won't, thought her son grimly as he continued up

the stairs. I won't even be able to sleep for thinking about her. And he was right.

The next morning, exhausted and grumpy, Marty was ready to bite the head off the first person who crossed him. As this turned out to be the head porter he held his tongue and was glad he did, because after being upbraided for having his mail directed to the hotel, a letter was shoved into his fist.

Knowing immediately who it was from, he tore it open, receiving a jolt as he read the grand-sounding address of the correspondent: *Swanford Hall*. The note was brief and obviously scribbled in a hurry, but its content was wonderfully explicit. Etta wanted him.

2

Regarding it as too chancy to commit his intentions to paper, besides not being much of a letter-writer, Marty's only option was to roll up at Etta's address on his first afternoon off and hope to encounter her. Sadly, his optimism was outweighed by reality. Not daring to venture as far as the mansion he hung around its imposing gates until nightfall, waiting so long that he missed the last carrier and had to walk the fifteen miles home alone in the pouring rain. Thankfully he had Sunday off too which meant he could sleep in, but this failed to salve the bitter disappointment of not seeing her.

His mother, able to read him like a book, said upon his late-coming to breakfast and the drenched clothes that were steaming over the fire, 'I hope you're not up to divilment, Marty Lanegan, out capering till all hours.'

Knowing she would disapprove he felt unable to confide, mumbling into his dripping sandwich that it was the fault of his chum Joe who had forced ten pints down his neck.

But this did not hoodwink his mother. 'Well, you're drunk with something, that's for sure, but it's certainly not beer, there's not a whiff of it about you.'

Ashamed that she knew he was lying to her, that he had pursued Etta when she had forbidden it, Marty dared not look up from his breakfast. However, this did not deter him from doing exactly the same on his next day off.

To his utter devastation, this attempt was also to end in another drenched failure, and to make it even worse there was a working day to follow. Consumed by thoughts of Etta, teased by the porter and the page alike for his grand ideas, he sought a feminine ear to air his chagrin.

Although wounded that he failed to detect her own heartache while he spoke longingly for another, Joanna was relieved that his expeditions had not borne fruit and she could afford to be magnanimous. 'Ne'er mind, Bootsie,' she comforted gently. 'Sit down there and have a piece of this chocolate cake with a cup of tea. It usually helps to take my mind off any troubles.'

'Ah, you're a good pal.' Martin showed gratitude and accepted the offer. But he was too obsessed with thoughts of the beautiful Etta to be touched for long by this soft-hearted gesture. Sipping his tea, his mind far away, he told Joanna, 'I'm not giving up, though. Next time I'm off right up to the door if I have to.'

Joanna controlled her hurt, murmuring lightly whilst inwardly praying for failure. 'Oh well, third time lucky.'

True to his declaration, Marty did indeed venture much further on his next day off. Using trees and shrubs as cover, he darted from one to another until there was nowhere left to hide, just an expanse of lawn up to the palatial stone residence. Thank heavens that after three weeks of rain the sun had come out. Crouched behind a huge rhododendron, he peeped around it to look up at each mullioned window, trying by sheer willpower to lure Etta to one of them.

Instead, to his horror, three dogs came bounding over from nowhere, hackles raised. He came instantly upright. They sniffed him excitedly, the hound, the Labrador and the flea-bitten terrier, circling him in distrust, but they did not bite, at least not yet. Encouraged, he voiced a cheery greeting, though he could have murdered the canine intruders; at which point they seemed to decide he was no threat and began to snuffle around the bush instead. Keeping a nervous eye on them, he crouched again behind the foliage, whereupon the Labrador proceeded to thrust its smiling, fish-stinking muzzle into his face. Head averted in disgust, he entreated it gently at first, 'Good lad, off you go now.' Then when this did not work, he hissed more forcefully, 'Bugger off!' With a hurt expression the Labrador lolloped away, the terrier pelting after it. Martin cast an eye over his shoulder to locate the hound, found it cocking its leg against his back and lashed out at it. 'Wha – you filthy sod! Take your purple bloody testicles elsewhere. *Go!*' Luckily it did not retaliate to his rash outburst but loped after its companions, leaving him to flick disgustedly at his soiled jacket.

In the house, others were under chastisement too.

'Ow! Blanche, are you trying to assassinate me?' Etta jerked her handsome head out of reach and rubbed the spot where the hairpin had almost lanced her scalp.

'Sorry, miss!' The maid was contrite and paid more attention to her task of getting her mistress ready for her afternoon outing. 'I was just diverted for a second – the dogs seem to have found something interesting in them bushes over there. I just thought it might be a robber.' She glanced anxiously again at the window. 'I'm sure I saw a man.'

Etta was immediately rushing to view the scene, hair only half done. Straining her eyes for a sighting, she fixed them on the bush in question where the dogs did indeed seem to be converging.

Blanche was peering out too now. 'There!' She caught a glimpse of the intruder's face. 'I knew I saw somebody! Shall I inform the master, Miss Ett?'

'No!' An excited Etta grabbed her. 'He's come to see me. I want you to take a message to him.'

Blanche was aghast. Warned to keep watch on her mistress after the recent escapade to London, she was not so treacherous, but was nevertheless alarmed. 'Is that wise?'

'Do you want me to marry that gormless goblin my father has in mind?' demanded Etta.

'Oh heaven forbid, miss!' Loyal to the young woman, Blanche detested the suitor as much as did the bride-to-be.

'You'd rather I was with a man who loves me? Well, that man is there. His name is Mr Lanegan and he's waiting for me to elope with him.'

Blanche gasped, clamped a hand to her mouth and spoke through her fingers. 'It's that one you asked me to post the letter to a few weeks back!'

'Yes!' Eyes bright with zeal the mistress patted the maid's fat arms and went on breathlessly, 'Oh, Blanche, I *knew* he'd come – now, be quick and finish my hair, then I want you to pack as much as you can into a small valise – we don't want my father to be suspicious. Take it to Mr Lanegan and ask him to go to the village and wait by the stone cross.'

Of a similar age to her mistress, Blanche was quickly infected by the romance. 'Ooh, but what will I say if I encounter the master and he asks where I'm off with a bag?'

'Tell him I've sent you on an errand with some old clothes to the almshouses.' Etta rushed back to the dressing mirror. 'Whilst you're doing that I shall set out as if for my afternoon expedition as planned and no one will be any the wiser.' She hoisted her shoulders to express utter delight.

'And what's to become of me, miss?' With a wistful expression, Blanche inserted a swift collection of hairpins. 'I mean, I've been with you all this time and I know how you like things done, and unless this Mr Lanegan's got a lady's maid lined up for you I'd like to be considered . . .'

'And I'm determined you shall, Blanche, you're most valuable to me.' The girls had played together as children and Etta genuinely cared for her. 'But for the moment I don't want to arouse suspicion by us both going out laden with luggage. I promise to send word of my address later, but until then I shall have to manage without your help.'

'Aw, I'm grateful, miss! But I couldn't do it without the master's say so, and he's bound to ask me where you've gone.' Rather more conservative of nature, Blanche envisioned herself being expelled and bringing shame on her parents, who also worked on the estate.

'All the more reason that you don't know what to tell him.'

'I know the gentleman's name.'

'But you won't divulge it.' Etta sounded confident.

'Not if I can help it.' Blanche handed over a pair of earrings, saying anxiously as her mistress's excited fingers fumbled in putting them on, 'I hate to keep putting hurdles in your way, Miss Etta, but what about the coachman?' The latter would be transporting Etta to this afternoon's venue. 'You know, the master's –'

'Got his spies everywhere,' Etta supplied darkly. 'Yes, I'm all too aware of that. I shall just have to risk it. By the time any tittle-tale reaches my father I'll hopefully be far away. Now, shoo!' The command was accompanied by a conspiratorial smile. 'Before anyone should catch my future husband.'

Swept up in the excitement and anticipating someone far more eligible, Blanche was shocked to discover the individual of modest means behind the bush, and her first thought was that Miss Henrietta had mistaken his identity.

'What's your name?' she demanded rudely.

Thinking the game was up, Marty rose and tugged his jacket straight, hoping she wouldn't spot the damp patch where the dog had pissed on his back. 'Lanegan, miss, I –'

'Oh good grief, it is the right one then,' muttered Blanche, and her suspicious frown turned to one of incredulity. Nevertheless, she shoved the bag at him and, to his delight, reported Etta's instructions.

The latter meanwhile was summoning her transport, and,

without a backwards glance, hurrying down the stone staircase and into the coach's leather interior. Only at the gate did her composure slip when she banged on the roof and shouted for the coachman to make a detour from his previously instructed route.

Bag in hand, Marty had barely arrived at the meeting place when the vehicle pulled up and his beloved alighted. It was as if he were seeing her for the first time all over again. He felt he might choke with desire as her face came aglow at the sight of him.

Similarly smitten, Etta wanted to rush to him, but she restrained herself for now, first instructing the coachman firmly to 'Wait here for me, I shan't be long' before approaching Marty at a casual pace.

Her expression told him not to do anything rash, so he followed her lead, initially just standing to admire her accomplished deportment, but especially the sweep of breast and buttock under the pink figure-hugging dress, the froth of white lace at her bosom, privately smiling at the ridiculously large hat, then turning to stroll alongside her as she came past, murmuring to him, 'Just act as if we're discussing the weather.'

Parasol aloft, she sauntered down the tree-lined country road, Marty alongside.

'I thought we'd get the carrier,' he told her, as they inserted some distance between themselves and the coach. 'He goes from the village green so we'd best not walk too far. I know to my cost he's a mean sort and won't pull up except at the proper stop.'

'He will for me,' replied his assured companion. 'I refuse to turn back for anything.' She urged him to keep walking, then linked his arm daringly. 'I thought you'd never come!'

'This is the third time I've been here – third time lucky.' He could smile now at how long it had taken, for during the interim he had accrued a few shillings. Normally his mother would be the one to benefit from his tips, but lately he had become a miser. In addition he had spent the last three weeks trying to earn money in other ways, though it was still barely enough to fund his elopement.

He dared not look over his shoulder at the straight road behind, but felt the coachman's eyes boring into his back and said so. 'Wouldn't it have been wiser to send him away? He's seen you with me now.'

'In retrospect it might have been wiser not to bring him at all but I had to make everything appear normal. If I'd sent him home he'd guess of my intention to abscond and would run directly to my father. By telling him to wait for me I've ensured that he daren't disobey – at least for a reasonable period.'

By the time the carrier came past they were fifty yards or so from the village, but Etta turned out to be right. At the commanding wave of her parasol the driver obligingly halted for the lady and her companion to get onboard, the other passengers shuffling up to make room. Huddled close together on the wooden seat, the horse clip-clopping onwards, she and Marty looked back along the arrow-straight road to where the coachman still waited obediently in the distance.

Marty chuckled sympathetically. 'He won't still be standing there in the dark, will he?'

Overwhelmed by happiness, Etta smiled and gripped his hand. 'Don't waste your pity, he'll have none for us when he speeds off to tell Father the moment this vehicle disappears. But at least we've gained a head start.'

Her suitor felt a pang of concern, wishing he had planned this better. After the previously abortive attempts at elopement he had not visualised success this time and consequently had omitted to arrange anywhere for them to live. However, he didn't tell Etta this, not with a cart full of people eyeing the mismatched couple suspiciously. In fact, under these strained circumstances, they were to say little to each other at all during the two and a half hour journey that followed.

Only when they were finally standing on the antiquated pavement of York and his young bride-to-be looked expectantly at him for direction did Marty confess. 'Sorry, I haven't managed to secure us any lodgings yet.'

Etta was unfazed, deliriously happy just to be with him, clinging to his arm and gazing up into his eyes. 'Didn't you say your work occasionally involves you having to sleep at the hotel? You can sneak me into the room where you stay.'

'I'm sure Ned would be delighted.'

'Who's Ned?'

'The bloke whose turn it is tonight.' Despite the joke, Marty felt inept. 'Besides, it's the first place your father will look for us.'

'I'm afraid I haven't enough money to pay for accommodation,' said Etta. 'I did manage to acquire some since we last met but in my rush to meet you I completely forgot it. I feel terribly foolish.'

'No, you're not.' He patted her. 'There's only one thing for it. It's risky, but if I can find out which rooms are unoccupied I could hide you in one of them for a day or so, until I can organise somewhere else.'

Her eyes sparkled, such intrigue adding spice to the romance. Marty, too, felt not fear but elation as they made their way from the busy Rougier Street, under a carved limestone arch in the Bar Walls, and on to the magnificent edifice that was the Royal Station Hotel. Advising Etta to wait in the sunlit grounds, heavy with the scent of roses, he affected a casual entrance to the hotel via the door marked tradesmen, as if arriving for work, yet his appearance drew amazement from the others. 'Can't stay away, Bootsie?'

He dealt them as carefree a laugh as he could. 'Aye, I love it so much. No, I just nipped in to ask Joe if he wants to go for a drink tonight. Is he about?' Told that the page was upstairs, he made his way there. 'It's Wilko's day off too, isn't it? Nobody to catch me then!'

But upon finding Joe there was no mention of beer. Marty

37

used a different fib. 'I just came to collect something I left behind the other day – busy, are we?'

Joe took the opportunity to slouch against the wall, nibbling a hangnail. 'Nah, there's not that many in.'

'What about that grumbling old sod in eighty-four?'

'Gone, thank God, and not so much as a farthing tip.'

'Got somebody better in there now?'

Joe shook his head, winced and spat out the hangnail. 'Nobody at all, as far as I know.' He studied his bleeding finger then sucked it.

Not wanting to compromise his friend, Marty merely nodded, whilst working out how to get hold of a key. After chatting a few minutes more he said a cheery farewell to Joe and padded downstairs to the lobby. Having scant luck until now he could scarcely believe it when he saw that the area behind the reception desk was deserted. Knowing it would not be so for long, he dashed in, grabbed the key and was outside pressing it into Etta's hand before anyone had noticed its absence.

'You'll have to do this on your own,' he instructed, escorting her as far as he dared towards the east entrance. 'But it shouldn't be too difficult, nobody'll dare to challenge someone like you. Just march through as if you own the place and go to room eighty-four.' He told her where it was.

'And you'll meet me there?' Etta asked eagerly.

'If I can, but I'm not meant to be at work until tomorrow so if I'm accosted and can't manage it don't worry, just lie low till morning.'

For the first time she showed apprehension. 'But how will I survive alone?'

His green eyes turned thoughtful. 'Maybe we could buy some food now before you go in.'

She clicked her tongue and dealt him a gentle shake. 'I meant how will I survive without *you*? I ran away so that we could be together.'

38

'And we will be, always!' His cheery grin encouraged her. 'This is only for a short while until I get us somewhere permanent. I can't stay out all night, my parents will be suspicious. But I promise I'll try my hardest to spend some time with you.'

'And what of my valise?' She pointed to the bag he was holding. 'Am I to carry it myself?'

Agreeing this might attract attention, his worry soon evaporated. 'Why, it'll give me just the excuse I need to come up!' And he urged her on her way, saying he would follow.

Watching her enter, he feasted his gaze on the hips that curved from the nipped-in waist. That she did not come out was a good sign. After a tense wait for the coast to clear – not just of superiors but of workmates too, for he did not know just who to trust – Marty saw an opportunity, grabbed it and pelted to Etta's room, tapping urgently on the door until she unlocked it.

Then they were free to indulge their passion, if not to its ultimate conclusion – although Marty certainly tried. With Etta's breast crushed to his, her lips returning his hungry, grinding kisses, working him into a lustful frenzy, he was positive that she was equally aroused. Hence, whilst one of his hands cupped the small of her back, moulding her groin against his, the fingers of his other hand sought out the buttons at the nape of her neck. To his frustration they were the very devil to undo – and there seemed thousand upon thousand of them. Frustrated but undeterred, he moved his attention to other regions, running his hands around her buttocks, kneading and pulling her into even deeper intimacy. When she did not stop him, but returned his amorous kisses whilst moving her hands as freely over his body, he put one of his feet against hers, and then the other, inching forward, compelling her to walk backwards until she felt the bed pressing against her legs and had no option but to fall back upon it with Marty atop her. After

a brief grunt of impact they resumed kissing, his movements becoming ever bolder, grasping handfuls of silken
pink material and eventually managing to hoist the hem of
her petticoat.

But a farmer's daughter, even a gentleman farmer's
daughter, could not fail to have learned a little about the
facts of life. Though flushed and excited, her eyes glazed
with desire, Etta squirmed violently at the more intimate
intrusion. 'Martin, what are you doing? Put that away!'

'Sorry! I thought you wanted – oh, Etta, I'll be so careful!'

But she was fighting him now, grabbing his shoulders,
straining to lever him from her. 'I've seen the stallion
brought to the mares! It's for one reason only and I've no
wish to be in foal!'

'But they say that can't happen the first time! Please let
me, sweetheart. I can't stop now, you've made me want to
explode!' He fell upon her again, planting fervent coaxing
kisses all over her face and neck, trying to manoeuvre
himself into position.

'Martin, you *can* stop and you will!'

Alarmed that her loud protestation would fetch
witnesses, her ardent suitor issued a gasp of frustration and
allowed himself to be displaced as, with a last growling
heave, Etta hurled him to one side and dragged down her
skirt, her breast rapidly rising and falling.

There was a moment's silence during which he lay beside
her and sulked. Then, with a scissor movement he leapt up
and stalked across the room, his back to her as he adjusted
his clothing. 'I'm sorry I misunderstood – we are to be wed,
after all.'

'And once we are then you shall have the matrimonial
benefits,' came her firm reply. 'But I won't escape from one
bully to saddle myself with another.'

Grossly affronted, Marty wheeled about. 'How can you
compare me with him? I adore you!'

'But you don't respect me,' she retorted.

'I do!' Then his objection gave way to serious contemplation, which terminated in a grin of self-confession. 'Well, sorry . . . I did get a bit carried away.' He rushed to her side again, stroking and petting her in an unthreatening manner. 'It's just that I've never wanted anyone so much as I want you, Etta.' His eyes showed it. 'I thought you wanted me in the same way.'

'Oh, Martin, I *do*.' Hardly able to breathe through passion, she put a hand to his cheek, holding his droopy-lidded gaze earnestly. When the subject of marriage had first been aired she had asked her mother what to expect. Mother had refused to discuss it, saying that it was all rather horrid but a wife must put up with it. None of her friends could enlighten her either. A determined Etta had finally gone back to Blanche, who had previously refused to be drawn but being of a lower class and the dispenser of bawdy jokes must surely be more conversant with such matters than herself. Despite professing to know little more than her mistress, amid great embarrassment, Blanche had finally been coaxed into detail, and had likened the marital act to what happened amongst the animals. 'Or so I'm told! I'm dreading it myself.' Etta had found it repellent too then, but the thought of such a union with Marty was utterly different. 'But I want to be married first. I don't think you understand how shameful it is for a woman to bear a child out of wedlock. You see, I've witnessed one of our maids being sent packing for such a reason.'

'Do you realise how insulting that is?' It was his turn to accuse now. 'You're insinuating that once I've had what I want I'll leave you in the lurch!'

'I didn't mean that, I know I can trust you. It's just . . .'

'It's just you think I'm a lying tinker.'

'No!' Disturbed, Etta struggled to conjure a plausible answer, hating that sullen frown upon Martin's brow, eventually admitting in a little voice, 'It's . . . I'm frightened.'

Overwhelmed with love, he hugged her then. 'Oh, you poor little thing! But I've explained to you, nothing awful will come of it.'

'Is that what you say to all the girls?'

'No!'

'There must have been plenty – you seem very experienced.'

'There hasn't! Well, only one.'

A small voice. 'And did you love her?'

He shook his head, ashamed to tell the truth, that the girl had only been someone liberal with her favours and had meant nothing to him. 'I didn't know what love was until I met you, Etta. The last thing I want is to hurt you.' He cradled her dark skull, kissing the top of it. 'Why won't you believe me?'

'I do.' She suddenly regained her passion, grasping his arms, her face close to his. 'Oh, we can do it if you want!'

Marty was not so noble as to refuse and his question was academic. 'Are you sure?'

At her nod he was instantly eager and upon her again, Etta returning his passion, even removing some of her clothing for him and welcoming the intimacy she had refused before. But at the vital moment he sensed that her invitation still veiled a modicum of doubt and he gave an agonised groan. 'Oh God, Etta, you're not going to stop me again, are ye?'

'No, no, go on!'

Still, as he examined her face he saw fear, and, barely able to contain himself, gasped,

'Oh Christ, look, it's no good if you feel like that. I won't go all the way, just grip it between your thighs like this –'

An anxious query. 'Is that all right?'

'Yes, yes! Now, stay with me!' And hanging on to her tightly he set the bed rocking.

It was over quickly and afterwards he remained on top of her, lungs heaving, breath hot upon her neck.

Etta remained slightly stunned. 'Gosh . . . I didn't expect
. . . that was very pleasurable, wasn't it?'

His body shook in silent laughter and he nodded into
her shoulder. Fancy a lady saying that to him!

She tensed. 'Are you mocking me?'

He lifted his face rapidly to deny this, his eyes warm
with love and sated desire.

Still, somewhat guilty for leading him on, she asked tentatively, 'Did you mind very much that we weren't able to
do it properly?'

'Ah, God love you, my dear, dear sweetheart!' Marty
dealt her a resounding kiss. 'That was as close as dammit.'
He moved to give her breathing space, though not too far,
their bodies remained in contact. 'And very pleasurable for
me too I might add.' He could hardly believe that he felt
so relaxed as to say such a thing, but Etta felt like a part
of himself, always had from the minute they'd met.

'And you don't mind that I'm making you wait?' Her
dusky eyes examined him.

Satisfied now, he was able to give a genuinely kind reply,
his mouth only inches away from hers. 'Of course not.
Much as I want ye I'm sure I can hang on a few days longer.
But I warn you, once we're married I'm going to make up
for lost time.' He pretended to gnaw on her neck, making
animal noises.

Etta giggled and moulded herself to him. 'Could we just
shuffle over a little? It's rather – is it meant to be so wet?'

'Ach, sorry!' He gave an awkward laugh and hauled her
across the rumpled bed where they lay contentedly for a
while, their lips occasionally touching, tasting, reiterating
their love for each other, enjoying the closeness. Then, giving
her a last rapturous kiss, Marty patted her, rolled off the
bed, adjusted his clothing, and in a happy manner went to
retrieve the paper bag he had discarded upon entry, coming
back to hand it to her.

Now discreetly covered, Etta sat up expectantly and,

43

with dark hair all awry, peered into the bag. 'What's in here?'

He threw himself on the bed again to watch lovingly. 'Gingersnaps! While I was waiting down there I managed to cadge them from a pal at the station. Sorry, there's no tray of tea to go with them, I daren't risk that. Nor will there be anything else until tomorrow morning when I can maybe sneak something from the kitchen. I'll fetch you some water, though, before I leave.'

Handing him a biscuit and nibbling on one herself, she smiled contentedly, hardly taking her eyes off him all the time she ate, which precipitated another bout of kissing amidst the crumbs. But this could not continue forever. If Martin should lose his job how would he support them? So, reluctantly, they prepared to bid each other *adieu*.

Coming back to reality, Marty gave a muttered comment on the bed. 'Good grief, look at the mess we've made o' this.' And he dragged off the counterpane. 'Grab the other edge.' Even as he said it he wondered if she might take umbrage at his order, but she seemed not to mind as she helped to turn it over.

A long night ahead of her, Etta showed reluctance to let him go, hanging on to his coat sleeves in concern. 'What if Father should arrive in your absence and drag me back – would you come after me?'

He cupped her face and gazed into it, swearing solemnly, 'Darlin', I'd follow you to the ends of the earth. Well, at least as far as my poor old barking dogs will carry me.' The joke about his sore feet was accompanied by a reassuring hug and a chuckle. 'Ah, don't fret now, with a bit o' luck we'll have you out of here before anyone notices. And now I must be gone too.' After first sneaking off to fetch a jug of water for her, Marty finally took his leave. Clinging to him until the last second, Etta planted frantic kisses upon him, declaring she would go to bed early so as not to feel hungry and locking the door behind her beloved as he went home with a spring in his step.

'I'm glad to see you looking happier,' said his mother when he arrived, though there was more than a hint of suspicion in her eye.

Inwardly laughing at her understatement, Marty dealt her a blithe shrug. 'No point being miserable, Ma.' And, with a happy ruffle of his little brother's hair, he sat to partake of the family meal, his own being consumed in no time.

Still eating, Agnes watched him shrewdly. 'Would you be in a rush to go out by any chance?'

'Ah no, I was just famished,' he replied with an innocent, languorous gaze. 'Tired too. I think it'll be an early night tonight.' He thought of poor Etta, alone and hungry, then turned to his father who was also still eating. 'Da, would you mind very much if I get down and have a little look at the press before bed?'

Granted permission, he went to sit on a more comfortable chair. It was fortunate that the 'houses to let' section was on the first page so that he would not appear to be hunting for something. Having opted for furnished lodgings as he possessed no furniture or artefacts of his own, he sat back to peruse, though it turned out to be an unsatisfying read. Most of the rents were beyond his pocket, for until he was safely wed he still had to pay his dues at home, not just to make things look normal but so as not to deprive his mother. Behind the newspaper, he machinated over how to boost his funds. What if he were to pawn something? In his wardrobe was a decent greatcoat which would be hanging redundant throughout the summer months, along with one or two other items of winter clothing. Maybe combined they would raise enough to secure a property, or at least rooms. His mother did not hold with pawnbrokers, opining that borrowing money was a slippery slope to get

45

on to, not from any high-minded ideal but out of contempt for the interest rates they charged. Whenever his father was out of employment she would work doubly hard herself. Even in the usual course of her day she took on others' laundry or mending, accepting anything rather than having to resort to money-lenders, so there would be no danger she might need the clothes for this purpose. The only difficulty would be in sneaking them out of the house. He cast his eye again over the column of vacancies, taking mental note of suitable addresses.

Earlier than normal, with a nonchalant yawn he bade others goodnight and went to bed alongside his younger siblings, where he lay for another hour planning his next move and imagining himself with Etta, which took him to the brink of tumescence, at which point he forced himself to think of other things and shortly fell asleep.

In the morning he made a bundle of the coat and other items to be pawned and tied it with a belt. As it transpired, it was not so difficult to smuggle it past his mother. After breakfast, during which he folded some bread and butter and slipped it into his pocket, he simply went back to his room, opened the window and dropped the bundle to the pavement, before hurrying outside to retrieve it as he went off to work. On his way, he called at a pawnbroker's, one that was not too close to home; it wouldn't do for Ma to spot his best coat in the window. Having thought of everything, and quite happy with the five shillings raised, he hurried onwards, his keenness not for work but to see his beloved.

It was relatively swift and easy to get to her, for his first act upon arrival was always to go and check the corridors for boots. Today, after collecting a few items in order to feign normality, he tapped on her door using the special knock they had arranged. Within seconds he was inside, the boots were tipped onto the floor and Etta was in his arms.

Relations were even better this morning, for she was wearing a nightdress which revealed every soft curve, her body warm, her black eyes heavy with sleep and looking more seductive than ever. In seconds, without even removing his boots, let alone his uniform, he was in the bed with her, repeating yesterday's excursion. Ecstatic to see him, Etta proved most willing, but eventually pushed him away with a scolding laugh, telling him, 'Enough! I'm absolutely famished. They've been baking bread since the early hours and the scent of it has been driving me insane.'

His senses otherwise engaged, only now did Marty notice the aroma that elevated from the bake house, and apologised for the flattened offering he had provided, but she didn't seem to mind, devouring the bread and butter with gusto and asking between bites, 'Did you manage to find us a home?'

'I did! Or rather I soon will have. I've three addresses lined up, so one of them should come up trumps.' At her look of excitement he added, 'Sorry I won't be able to afford a whole house . . .'

'Rooms will be fine,' she assured him, munching happily. 'Providing I'm with you.' She seemed unable to tear her eyes from him, her roaming gaze making new discoveries. 'Your fingernails are beautifully clean considering what you do for a living.'

Surprised by this sudden tangent, he looked down at his hands. 'Thank you. I always wear gloves when I'm handling boot polish; can't abide filthy nails.'

She nodded approvingly and, still munching, returned to the subject in hand. 'So, when will you have news?'

'I'll try and go in my dinner hour.'

'You know, we should really be arranging our nuptials too.'

'Don't think I've forgotten.' He gave her a kiss. 'But I haven't time to do that *and* look for rooms, and my priority is to get you out of here.'

'My priority too.' She gnawed her way through the crust. 'You can't imagine how bored I've been – so I think I shall go for a walk and at the same time visit the register office.'

'Ye can't go out! What if you're seen? It took me so much trouble getting you in here . . .'

Etta gave a petulant sigh. 'Oh, all right. Perhaps it would be more fitting for the groom to apply.' But her despondency did not last long, as she informed him excitedly, 'Since Father dragged me away from you I've been putting our enforced separation to good use by reading up on the subject of matrimony. Apparently, if time is of the essence, as it is with us, one requires a licence. Once we have that we may marry after one full day elapses. We'll also need written consent from our parents – now, that's something I can be doing whilst you're away, I'm very adept at forgery. Though it might be rather suspicious if I use the hotel writing paper for both letters!'

Marty laughed and said he would compose his own on more suitable paper. 'But how much is all this going to cost?'

Etta had missed this practicality. 'Oh, I'm not sure – but don't worry, I've some jewellery in my bag we can sell.' At his objection she overruled him. 'I insist! Everything is worthless compared to being your wife.' The last mouthful of bread consumed, she leapt from the bed, soon dancing back to him with some earrings and two brooches. 'There are lesser items too if you think you'll be able to get anything for them, a blouse, a skirt . . .'

Reluctant even to accept the jewellery, he told her, 'What sort o' man takes the clothes from his wife's back? I'm not even sure I should be taking these. You realise I could be accused of stealing them?'

'Really?' She projected shock. 'How disgusting. Should I write a note of authenticity?'

'Might be an idea.' After studying the precious items for some seconds, he put them in his pocket. 'But I won't sell

48

them, I'll pawn them; that way I can retrieve them later.'

She replied lightly as she flopped down beside him again, 'I shan't want them, I told you they mean nothing.'

Now that everything had been discussed, she cuddled up to him for more kisses. But soon they had to part again, Etta to pace the room in boredom and to survive on the brief visits that her lover paid her whenever he could.

Noon finally came and Marty approached his superior. 'Mr Wilkinson, please could I go out in my dinner break?'

'What's so important that it can't wait until this evening?' Wilkinson had no reason to forbid it, he just liked to be awkward.

'My aunt's poorly. Mother asked would I call in on her, see if she needs anything. Of course, I could wait till tonight, but if she were to faint and then fall on –'

'Spare me the long list of ridiculous consequences,' replied Wilkinson tiredly, but with a smirk of amusement, for at heart he liked Boots. 'Away with you before I change my mind.'

'Aw thanks, Mr Wilkinson!' Marty decided to chance his luck. 'Er, she lives quite far away, could I tack an extra fifteen minutes on –'

'I'll grant you ten. Any more and you'll make up for it at the end of your shift.'

'Oh, I will, sir – thank ye kindly!' Marty rushed off to inspect the rooms.

His first port of call was to be in what he regarded as a nice area, for if he couldn't keep Etta in the manner to which she was accustomed then he could at least do his best. A stroke of luck occurred when he saw a friend who gave him a lift in his trap, thus saving him precious minutes. Taking this as a good omen, Marty was therefore pole-axed when his enquiry was rudely forestalled. Yes, there was a notice in the window advertising the vacancy, but it was accompanied by a proviso: No Irish.

Dismayed, he wasted no time in proceeding to the next address. Alas, these rooms had been taken at ten o'clock that morning. The third place on his list was closer to home in a street despised even by those of his own class. He had regarded it as a last resort but now dashed there, praying that no one would have beaten him to it. Time was running out. He would have to take these rooms even if they were bug-infested.

He was never to find out, for the rooms had already been taken. By now famished and despondent, he beseeched the woman who had answered his knock, 'Do you know where there might be anywhere else to let – anywhere at all?'

She weighed up his smartly uniformed figure before directing him to a public house along the street. 'I think they've a room going.'

Marty crumpled in despair. The Square and Compass was hardly the sort of place to bring a lady. For a second he considered the gold jewellery in his pocket, yet to be pawned. But no, Etta expected that would pay for the wedding; if he used it to rent somewhere better it might render them unable to marry and then where would he be? With little choice he thanked the woman and went to involve himself in swift negotiation with the landlord.

His return to the hotel was accompanied by mixed emotions. True, the room was not what he wanted for Etta – classed as furnished, it had the barest minimum of items and was somewhat jaded – but at least it was somewhere they could be together as man and wife. It was only two shillings a week, and they could always move later – a definite possibility for he had achieved an excellent price for the jewellery. The moment his workload allowed it, he dashed to tell her this.

Confined for hours like a restless zoo animal, unable to lace her own corset and having to leave it off, forced to occupy herself by brushing her hair a hundred times and inexpertly attempting to fashion it into different styles, an intensely bored Etta was relieved to see him back and even more thrilled to hear him voicing success. 'You've found us rooms?' She flung herself at him.

'Aye!' He swept her up, then tempered his excited response. 'Well, *room*, singular – I'm sorry, everything else had gone, it's all I could manage at the moment – but we won't have to stay there long. Once we're safely wed I'll make a concerted effort to find something better.' He hugged her tightly, releasing her to say, 'You do understand you might have to be there on your own for a couple of nights, just till I can arrange the wedding? I'll take you there when I get off work and make sure you're safe, but I can't sleep there, obviously, before we're man and wife.' Even if Etta had been willing he couldn't let his parents down by living in sin.

She nodded, enthusing, 'Oh, I can't wait to go there!'

He crushed her again. 'Me an' all. How did ye go on with your letter of consent?'

'Oh, that took me all of five minutes!' She prised herself free and skipped away to fetch an envelope, which he put in his pocket.

'That's great.' His arms soon encircled her again. 'Only a few more hours to go.'

Etta pulled a face. 'More hours of biting my fingernails to the quick, imagining my father's going to turn up at any moment. I'll have them down to my elbows before tonight.'

'Ah well, you can chew on mine if ye like – well you did remark on how clean they were, I thought ye might find them tasty!' He laughed as she grappled with him, joyful that she shared his sense of humour.

'I might have to hold you to that! I'm absolutely ravenous.'

Marty admitted, 'So am I, I didn't have time for any dinner. Maybe I can get us something from the kitchen.' Then, he squashed his lips to hers.

It was whilst they were torridly engrossed that someone rattled a key in the lock, forcing self-preservation to override passion. Tearing themselves apart, they turned to stare at the door in horror, having no time to run for the person was entering.

'Oh, I beg your –' Joanna had been about to apologise, but at the sight of Marty in the arms of another she broke off, her jaw dropping and her eyes wide in shock. Then, in the same instant she had spun on her heel.

'Jo, wait!' A panicked Marty raced to waylay the chambermaid, catching her and dragging her back into the room where he forbade any exit by leaning against the door. 'Please don't give us away!'

Joanna demanded to be past. 'I want nothing to do with this!'

'All right, but let me explain!' With Etta an anxious spectator, he grasped the maid's arms.

'I don't wish to know!' Joanna wrenched free. 'I just came to check that the room was fit for the next guest – and I see that it isn't!' She indicated the rumpled bed with the discarded corset upon it, then glared pointedly at Etta and Marty.

'Guest? Oh, bloody hell!' He clutched his head, before gauging her real cause for complaint. 'Eh, it's not what you think, Jo! Etta spent the night on her own –'

'She's been here all night?' screeched Joanna.

'She had nowhere else to go! She's run away.' Throwing a fond glance at Etta he decided to let his friend in on their secret. 'We're going to be married.'

Joanna's homely face looked as if it had been smacked. She became very quiet, staring at him as his excited voice babbled on:

'I've got us a place to live! We'll be going there in a few hours – at least we were, but if someone wants this room . . .' His words trailed away in despair.

'They're not coming until tomorrow,' Joanna heard her

own voice say dully. Why had she revealed this? She could have been shot of her rival in an instant by stating the room was needed now. But that would solve nothing, would only propel Etta further into Bootsie's arms.

'Oh, thank God – saved!' He threw his face heavenwards with a sigh of relief. 'Thanks, Jo. You won't tell anyone she's here, will you?'

Remaining stunned and dull of eye, she shook her mobcapped head slowly. 'I've still got to prepare this room, though.'

'I'm sure Etta won't mind.'

Hurt and furious, Joanna flared then. 'I should think she won't!' Still in awe of her upper class rival, she directed her hissed objection at Marty, 'And I'm not having her sitting on the bed after I've changed it!'

Amused, but feeling pity for the maid who so obviously coveted Martin too, Etta responded quietly, 'I shall endeavour to keep out of your way.'

'And I'd better go before I'm missed,' opined Marty. He dealt Etta a swift but adoring kiss, then indicated the garments that were strewn about the room. 'It might be an idea for you to be packed and ready to leave.'

She sighed. 'I was hoping to have them laundered . . .'

'Perhaps Joanna would oblige,' he said thoughtlessly.

There was a tight reply from the chambermaid. 'Perhaps Joanna's got enough to do. Perhaps on second thoughts she'll come back when the sodding room's empty!'

Watching her stalk out, Marty grimaced at Etta. 'Maungy devil, she's usually a pal.'

Etta beheld him lovingly and stole one of his words to rebuke him. 'She cares for you, you eejit.'

He laughed, then frowned. 'What? No, surely . . .'

His lover experienced a sudden flash of jealousy. 'Was she the one who –'

'No! I've never even regarded her as anything other than a workmate. Oh, bloody hell, Etta, how was I to know?

She never said anything when I poured my heart out about you. What should I say to her?'

Without revealing her deeply possessive streak, Etta prescribed delicacy. 'I think you've said enough. You could provoke her and she might tell.'

He shook his head. 'No, she's not that kind. I'd better go try and make it up to her somehow.' He gave Etta a swift but devoted kiss. 'I'll see you later with some grub, and try not to fret.' Juggling a collection of footwear, he hurried away.

He did catch up with Joanna, but whatever excuse he offered only seemed to worsen the atmosphere between them and, finally heeding Etta's advice, he left her to cool off. Besides, there was work to be done, this keeping him so involved that he never got to discover whether or not she had returned to tidy Etta's room.

Joanna had no intention of going back to that place of sin. In fact, by reliving every sequence of events she had worked herself into a fine lather and was by now so absolutely livid that she even contemplated telling the housekeeper about Bootsie's subterfuge. But that would only get him the sack and it was not him she wished to be rid of. Instead, her anger making her physically ill, she approached the housekeeper with a request that she might be allowed to leave early. Presented with the chambermaid's pallor and bloodshot eyes, Mrs Hardy was sympathetic and agreed. Joanna was on her way out of the hotel when she overheard a loud enquiry that halted her instantly.

'*Ibbetson*,' repeated the elder of the two gentlemen testily. 'Check again.'

Transformed by excitement, she made a detour and crept back to lurk on the perimeter of the resplendently-tiled main entrance. The porter on the reception desk was polite and did as he was bidden, but his answer was the same as before. 'I'm sorry, sir, there is no one of that name staying in the hotel.'

'Then I shall search the place myself!' boomed Mr Ibbetson senior. 'For I have it on good authority that a member of your staff has abducted my daughter!'

With other employees looking fearful that there was about to be a scene, a delighted Joanna rushed forth to solve the mystery, moreover to rectify her own problem. 'Excuse me, sir!' she whispered confidentially, 'but I think you'll find the young lady in room eighty-four.'

No one had time to ask how she knew this, for with Ibbetson rushing off with his son in pursuit, Joanna's superiors had enough to contend with in trying to keep this scandal from other guests. Withdrawing into the background, Joanna's heart pumped with excitement as she awaited the ejection of her rival. With Bootsie safely tucked away in his rightful place there was no one to prevent it.

But the commotion had drawn a gaggle of observers who now smirked and gossiped and craned their necks to witness the fun, amongst them Marty. Joanna ducked out of sight, for he would instantly know it was she who had given the game away, especially now, as an even louder hullabaloo preceded the Ibbetson girl being dragged protesting down the grand central staircase, the thwarted bride-to-be digging in her heels and gaining a grip on the ornate ironwork, refusing to obey, only to receive a vicious rap from her father's cane and her fingers wrenched free.

At the sight of his loved one so mistreated, the levity drained from Marty's face. Immediately he elbowed his way through the watchers, intent on rescue, but Ibbetson had seen him too and roared to his son, 'That's him!' And in seconds they had abandoned Etta and came rushing to tackle him. He saw the upraised cane, feinted to avoid it but only succumbed to a blow from Etta's brother John. Whilst he was reeling from this the heavy silver top of Ibbetson's cane thwacked his cheek, causing him to yell in pain, the crowd to gasp and Etta to scream.

'Stop, stop!' Horrified at the sight of blood upon her

lover's face she tried to get near, to save him, but the windmilling arms prevented it, knocking her off her feet. 'Martin!' Heroically she rose and tried again, but someone pinioned her arms. 'Father, stop!'

But her screaming entreaties did no good, for her father and brother seemed to have lost all reason, ignoring the hotel manager who had finally been roused from his office and tried politely to intervene – lashing, punching and thrashing Matin with no one doing a thing to stop it, knocking him to the ground until his only recourse was to curl up like a hedgehog. Still they showed no mercy, the silver-topped cane berating him again and again.

Appalled to have brought this upon the one she loved, at first Joanna stood frozen to the spot, biting her lip in terror at the violence, but when no one ended it, when it seemed that Bootsie might even be killed, she found the courage to rush forth and protect his cowering body, imploring his attackers to desist, and only now did they do so, standing back to examine their work, panting with grim satisfaction at the vengeance meted out, the victim's blood sprayed upon their clothes.

'Martin!' Etta screamed and struggled to be free, even biting one of the hands that imprisoned her in order to run to him. But she was not allowed to do so, her father and brother grasping a slender arm each and dragging her from the hotel, protesting and shrieking for her lover. 'He's injured! I demand to see him! You cannot keep us apart!'

'I can and I will,' came her father's grim reply, his fingers digging into her flesh as she wriggled.

'I am most exceedingly sorry, sir!' The hotel manager tried to make amends, wringing his hands and hurrying alongside them, but was ignored by all, his voice drowned out by Etta's.

'You can drag me to the altar but you can't force me to utter the vows! I'd cut out my tongue before that! I'll run away again and again! You'll never stop me – Martin, I'll love you forever!'

Through a fog, Marty heard the declaration of undying love, formed a bloody, grimacing smile and attempted to nod, before entering a tunnel of unconsciousness.

Angry at being demeaned by the Ibbetsons, the manager came hurrying back, growling at those who huddled anxiously around Marty to 'Remove him' before shooing the rest of the staff about their business then forming an obsequious explanation for the guests who had been disturbed.

Hefting him between them, Marty's colleagues struggled to convey his dead weight to the servants' quarters, a frightened Joanna hovering alongside, the rest dispersing to chatter about the incident in shocked tones.

'Oh, Bootsie, I'm sorry!' With others laying him on a table, Joanna fetched a cold damp cloth to tend his injuries, wincing and whining as she dabbed at the blood. 'I never meant to get you in trouble.'

'I think he did that for himself,' a porter comforted her, then clicked his tongue at the audacity. 'The scallywag.'

A younger male conveyed admiration. 'Good old Bootsie, I say. What a dark horse – how did you know he'd stashed her up there?'

'I only found out by accident. I thought I was helping him out of trouble by getting rid of her.' Joanna looked shifty, trying to convince herself as much as anyone. 'I didn't know they were going to half-kill – aw, Bootsie, please don't die!' She dabbed at him frantically, nauseated by the sight of blood on the cloth.

To the relief of all, Marty soon came round, and by the time Mr Wilkinson appeared he was sitting up, despite remaining shocked and in terrible discomfort. His superior was relieved too, although he showed no sympathy. Having received a personal grilling from the manager for his lack of supervision, his eyes were hostile and his request was delivered through gritted teeth. 'Would you care to explain yourself?'

At the victim's bruised and bewildered expression, Joanna answered for him. 'I think he's too dazed, sir.'

Wilkinson did not thaw. 'Am I to assume that Lanegan has been consorting with a guest's daughter?'

Unable to defend him, those supporting his battered carcass turned their eyes on Marty, who did not appear to know where he was, let alone what had happened.

'I shall take your silence as an admission, Lanegan,' hissed Wilkinson. 'You will therefore remove yourself from the premises.'

Seeing that the boot boy still failed to understand, his friends exchanged looks. 'You're dismissing him, sir?' ventured one brave soul.

'I most certainly am.'

Feeling guilty, Joanna risked her own position. 'But, begging your pardon, sir, he's the victim of a dreadful crime.'

'The only crime that has been committed here is that Lanegan has brought this hotel into disrepute!'

'But he's too ill to walk, sir!'

'Then fetch a cart and convey him to those who care – and it does not take all of you to do it!' Ordering all but two back to work, the furious Wilkinson strode away.

The page and the chambermaid studied their friend, who had begun to shiver. Marty beheld them too, but did not respond to their questioning for their voices were muffled as if emerging from a drainpipe. 'Oh, look at his eyes,' he heard Joanna say, 'they're right odd.'

Avoiding the nasty lesion, Joe pressed the victim's brow. 'He's really cold an' all. And he looks as if he's going to throw – whoa!' He jumped back as Martin spewed vomit, Joanna taking the full force of it.

Regarding her frontage in disgust, she did not cast blame – it did seem poetic justice after all – but stoically removed her apron and carried it between thumb and forefinger for disposal.

Whilst Joe tended Marty, whose teeth had started to

chatter, she returned with mop and bucket and swiftly cleared the mess. Then the page suggested, 'Away, we'd better get some transport and take him home to bed.'

Averse to consigning him to a handcart as their superior had suggested, they hailed a cab and with the jarvey's assistance bundled him inside, a guilt-ridden Joanna pressing the shilling fare into Marty's hand and closing his fingers around it.

'We can't send him on his own like a parcel,' decided Joe. 'Look at him, he doesn't even know what day it is. One of us should go with him and explain to his ma what's happened.' When Joanna shrank at the thought of her own malicious role in this, he announced, 'Right, I'm off then and bugger me job!'

Marty could not summon the words to thank him. He was hardly aware of anything as he was taken home in disgrace. Dazed, and barely able to hold a handkerchief to his cheek, he stumbled from the cab as, simultaneously, his mother responded to the knock on her door.

'Mother o' mercy!' At the bloodied state of her son, Agnes Lanegan was instinctively protective and, along with Joe, supported him over the threshold to a chair. But then there came fury as the full tale emerged and she raged at him, 'Didn't I warn you about wanting things you can't have? You damned fool, look at the state of ye! What the hell is your father going to say?' But her ire was directed less at Marty's actions, more at the callous treatment that had been meted out to him, and she was swift to see that her ranting was not doing an ounce of good.

Under the wide and watchful eyes of her younger children and her anxious elderly uncle, she and Joe transferred Marty to the sofa then she pounded upstairs to fetch blankets, which were snuggled about him. 'Brandy! That's what we need.' Shoving a cup at Joe and sending him to the Brown Cow, she herself made a pot of tea, and whilst this was brewing she tipped the rest of the contents of the kettle into a stone hot-water bottle, wrapping this in a towel and tucking it at Marty's feet, crooning and fussing. 'Oh, my poor dear boy, what have they done to ye?'

Uncle Mal shook his head gravely. 'Beat near to death, he is.'

Joe returned within minutes, the brandy being dribbled down the patient's throat, followed by hot sweet tea.

'Will I pour you a cup, Joe?' Sounding vague, Aggie stood back to assess the situation. Though swathed to the chin in blankets, her son still shivered and trembled, teeth chattering, his face a swollen mass of lacerations, and he had not uttered a word. It deeply concerned her.

The page backed away. 'No, thank you, Mrs Lanegan, I'd best return to work. I hope he's soon recovered.'

'Dear God, so do I, dear,' muttered Aggie, but, looking at that trembling impostor, she feared her happy-go-lucky son might never return.

3

Wounds knitted, awareness restored, after his ghastly experience Marty felt he had lost a fortnight, but in fact had been lying there only a couple of days. According to Uncle Mal, his mother had barely left his side during those first perilous hours, spooning water through his split lips, performing the most intimate tasks, though he could remember little of them. He still ached in every crevice but now felt able enough for action after his midday mug of oxtail broth.

Forming each move gingerly to lessen the hurt, he rose from the threadbare sofa and waited a while to steady himself whilst his parents, younger siblings and Uncle Mal watched intently. 'Sorry for putting you through all this, Ma.'

'Isn't that what mothers are for.' Aggie's heart bled for him, and she sighed. ''Tis a shame she never even managed to leave you a wee keepsake before they took her.'

Tottering to the mirror above the fireplace Marty grimaced at his pasty reflection, carefully examining the encrusted lesions. 'What need have I of trinkets when I'll soon have a real, flesh and blood keepsake – and now I'm back to normal I can go retrieve her.'

'Normal, says he!' A howl came from his father's chair, making the smaller children jump. 'There's nothing normal about you. What ignoramus would set himself up for another whipping like that? Sure, he must've beat the brains out o' ye.' Redmond was grumpy and tired; he, too, had just been sacked, for taking a nap in work time.

Martin made allowances, his reflection displaying nausea. 'She's in danger, Da, I have to –'

'Did you witness her father whipping her?' demanded Redmond.

'No, he –'

'He reserved his punishment for you, and quite frankly I can understand why!' After trudging eight miles home with no pay for his morning's work, Redmond was abnormally uncharitable. 'What a damn fool to think you could get away with stealing his daughter!'

There was only so many allowances Marty would make. 'She's consented to marry me,' came his obstinate reply.

'Then she's as disobedient a child as you, and if she takes a good hiding she thoroughly deserves it!' Redmond turned to vent his exasperation on his wife. 'He gets this off you! Letting him have his own way in everything . . .'

'I do not!' Aggie was having none of this. 'Did you not hear me warn him about flashing the tackles over that girl? But will he ever listen? He will not!' She in turn chastised Marty. 'Look what your ambition's done, setting us all against each other! What happened to that nice young woman you were stepping out with a few months ago?'

Marty gaped. 'Bridget? Why, you said you didn't want me consorting with a chocolate-basher, said you wanted better for me!'

'There's better and there's downright ridiculous!' Aggie united with her husband to warn their son, 'Now, I forbid you to pursue this crazy notion. I'll not have you putting yourself in danger again – do you hear?'

Looking worn, Marty turned away from the mirror, wincing. 'I hear, Ma, I hear.'

'But do you heed?' His father jabbed a finger. 'Because if you disobey then there'll be nobody to scrape you off the floor next time, and I refuse to have this household upset in such a fashion again. I've never heard such rubbish – you'll be better directing your energy into finding a job and making it up to your mother!'

'Why, of course I will, that was my intention.'

'And you *will* leave that girl alone!'

His son heaved a sigh. 'Have I any choice?'

'Aye, you can do as the mammy and I say or you can sling your bloody hook!' With that his father slumped back in his chair, his energy spent.

Seeing his mother about to set into him again, Marty held up his hands in surrender. But nothing would divert him. He was determined upon this union more than ever.

First, though, he must arrange the marriage licence. Still equipped with the uniform he had worked so hard to pay for, and which was the smartest clothing he possessed, he wooed his mother into sponging and ironing it into shape, saying he was going out to find new employment. Instead, armed with the forged letters, the money from the jewellery and an air of confidence, he presented himself at the register office. Here, much sweating was to take place whilst all the paperwork was gone through, though in fact it all turned out to be very simple and his request was duly granted. Unable to give a specific date for the wedding, he rejoiced to hear that the licence would last for three months. Still, he was wise enough to recognise that the hardest part was yet to come – not just the rescue of Etta but the acquisition of more money, for this arrangement had almost cleaned him out. Hence, the next hours were given to seeking work, though with poor result. Finding it impossible to acquire even the lowliest of jobs with no reference, Marty was pushed into the drastic measure of returning to the place from whence he had been dismissed. Presented with an abject apology, perhaps Mr Wilkinson would take pity and scribble a few lines in order that Marty's family might not starve?

On the other hand he might not. The intrepid suitor found himself once again ejected, and whilst it was not under such violent circumstance as before, it left him under no illusion as to his lack of worth.

His application at the adjacent railway station met with no better luck. Dallying aimlessly by the ticket barrier, to be assailed by clouds of sulphurous smoke, the soot-speckled rush of passengers, the tuneless medley of carriage doors being slammed, the shrill whistle, the chugging and heaving of a departing engine and the cold echoing emptiness that ensued, a benighted Marty racked his brain for a solution. The rescue of Etta would be hard enough, for she could have been locked up or even sent away. However, putting himself in the father's shoes, he doubted if the arrogant Ibbetson would expect him to turn up after such a trouncing, which would at least lend him an element of surprise. So, acting on this theory, he had decided simply to turn up at the mansion and wait for his willing partner to appear. He would wait even if it took forever. But to maintain her safety, he must have a regular income . . . which brought him back to the here and now.

He cast his despondent gaze aloft to the glass roof of this vast structure, and its elaborate cast-iron arched supports that extended along the length of the platform in an elegant curve, like the ribs of some leviathan, and he sighed – Jonah, trapped in the belly of a whale.

Another train came rackety-racking alongside the platform, and more tourists alighted, porters toting their belongings to the lobby of the Royal Station Hotel. He pictured Etta's arrival with her papa that fateful day, wondered what she was doing and if she felt this miserable too. With unfocused eyes he stared as passengers came flooding through the barriers, those unable to afford a cab hailing the services of barrow boys. The scene was re-enacted many a time before the solution hit him. Why, of course! Whoever said that he could not be his own employer? Excited now, his mind began to race, to form a plan, plummeting briefly as he hit a snag: to be a barrow boy one must have a licence – another blessed licence – and whatever the price he was unable to afford it. Still, he remained optimistic enough to accost one such carrier who was standing idle, asking, 'Eh, chum, how much is a licence?'

''Bout half a crown, I think –'

Marty groaned.

The shifty-looking informant then admitted, '– but I haven't got one.'

Marty perked up. 'That's in order, is it?'

'Aye, but it means you only get a job when the permit-holders are all busy. And you have to watch out for Custard Lugs,' he indicated a man with huge, yellow-tinged ears, 'he carries a life-preserver and he'll use it if he thinks you're trying to weasel your way in.'

'Don't worry, I'll keep out of his way!' Grinning his thanks, Marty left the station, feeling more buoyant than when he had arrived and celebrating with a pennyworth of fish and chips. All he had to do now was to acquire a barrow.

Had he not been a popular sort, with very little cash the acquisition might have been impossible, but he knew just where to go. One of his many friends was a collector, preferring that term to a fence of stolen goods, from whose treasure trove was unearthed a rickety barrow.

'Needs a wheel.' Bill's guttural Yorkshire accent emerged from the shadows as he turned to poke around again in the shed. 'But I must have summat here that'll do.'

Marty was delighted. 'Trouble is, Bill, I don't have any cash. Can I pay you when I've put it to work?'

Still searching, Bill said he could, then reached into a cardboard box. 'How about a cheese?'

'To act as a wheel?' asked Marty with a laugh.

'Dozy sod – for your mother. Tell her I've got some nice bacon an' all – oh, there we are!' Bill found a suitable wheel which, affixed to the barrow, was to provide Marty's salvation. He had a barrow, he had a job; now he would have Etta.

Before anything else, he had to conjure an excuse for his parents as to why he might be absent for the next couple of days. It would not work. They would guess at once what he was up to and prevent it. Instead, speaking enthusiastically about the barrow, he explained the difficulty he might have in touting for custom without a licence, and that if he happened to be very late home on his first day they must not worry. They seemed very pleased with his enterprise and he hoped they would not be too concerned when he failed to show. He hated lying but could not hope for them to understand the strength of his feelings for Etta. It was she who commanded his thoughts as he trundled his barrow to the pub in Long Close Lane early the next morning, to be stashed there until his triumphal return.

Everything was in order with the room. How fortunate that he had paid the month's rent in advance. Checking for the umpteenth time that the key was in his pocket, he embarked on his rescue expedition. Admittedly he was terrified of such a powerful man as Ibbetson, but his love for Etta overcame all, and the notion that he was taking the first step towards their reunion filled him with cheer as he set off on his fifteen-mile hike. Occasionally, this lightness of spirit was to evaporate along with the runnels of sweat on his brow as he struggled through the August heat wave that had suddenly flared, plodding along dusty roads and rolling countryside with his jacket slung over his shoulder, hour after hour after hour, his feet on fire, his legs fit to buckle, his throat parched. But, eventually arrived at her gate just after noon, he was imbued with a sense of such overwhelming achievement that instead of lying low and waiting for her to spot him, he summoned every ounce of courage, donned his brass-buttoned jacket and marched proudly up the driveway towards the massive front door. He would show just how serious he was and let Ibbetson admire his pluck.

The door seemingly miles away, his resolve began to fray as he pictured the actions of those inside as they heard the crunch of an impostor's feet along the gravel. He imagined eyes at every window, and steeled himself for the blows that must surely follow.

But lo and behold it was a kiss which greeted him first! Spotting him from her lonely seat by the window as she dressed for luncheon, Etta shoved aside her startled maid, rushed headlong down the staircase and across the hall, and before he even had a chance to ring the bell she had thrown herself into his arms and was pressing her lips to every sweating part of his face in joy and relief.

'I knew it! I knew you'd come!' And she grabbed his arm and hurriedly led him around the back of the house to a more secluded spot near the potting shed, with an anxious Blanche giving chase.

Unrestrained kisses were to follow, the maid averting her eyes, until Etta suddenly commented on the results of his previous beating. 'Oh, your poor face! Have I hurt you?'

'No, no! You make everything better.' A rapturous Marty enfolded her, moulding his body into her soft, hot flesh, breathing in her scent along with the flowers, kissing and caressing erotically.

'You shouldn't have come to the front door!' Her protestations interspersed more breathless kissing.

'Are you saying I'm not good enough?'

Her face scolded him between kisses. 'I meant why did you risk it? Father will be even more furious, I dread to think what he'll do this time!'

'Miss Etta!' Blanche hissed a warning, but was ignored.

'I won't be cowed.' Marty nuzzled the silky white neck. 'I've decided to face him man to man, tell him I've got the licence for our wedding and he'll have to kill me to prevent it!'

'That is a distinct possibility!' interjected another. They whirled to see her enraged father bearing down on them. Informed by a servant, Ibbetson had had no time to grab a weapon but his clenched fists promised retribution. Blanche immediately backed away.

Forewarned, Marty was prepared and squared up to his opponent – at least there was only the one this time – but Etta went to meet her father. 'Please discuss this sensibly!'

However, Ibbetson had never been an articulate man.

'Mother, stop him!'

Along with a gaggle of servants, Mrs Ibbetson had pursued her husband but, afraid of his fury, did no more than hover in the background wringing her hands.

Etta found herself swiped to the ground, much to Marty's disgust, but before he could avenge her honour she was up again and yelling into her father's face. 'Oh, that's right, cast me aside like the dirt you hold me to be!'

Ibbetson wrestled with her, at the same time grappling with Marty. 'You behave like a guttersnipe, and you'll be treated as such!'

Mrs Ibbetson moaned. Blanche burst into tears. The tranquil garden was rent by angry grunts and squeals.

'Call yourself a gentleman!' countered a furious Marty, trying to avoid hitting Etta, who insisted on sandwiching herself between the men. 'You look down on me but I'd never spurn a lady in such a fashion!'

'No, you'd just defile her so no other man'll take her!' yelled Ibbetson, managing to elbow past his daughter and grab hold of the young upstart, tussling with him, trying to aim a good punch, their struggle invading the flowerbeds where geraniums were trampled underfoot.

'I've done nothing to be ashamed of!' Face livid, Marty grasped the bigger man around the waist, hanging on grimly and pulling him in close to prevent Ibbetson landing a blow.

'If you'd granted me the chance I would have asked politely to marry Etta, but you're not a man for reason, are ye?'

Striving with effort, her nostrils tweaked by the anomalous perfume of crushed geranium, Etta heaved on her father's tailcoat, trying to haul him off Marty, whilst her mother merely whimpered and hopped ineffectively from foot to foot. 'Father, *why* in pity's name won't you allow me to marry the man I love?'

'Because you can't be trusted to make an intelligent decision! You'd sooner bring disgrace on this family – a boot boy, for deuce's sake!' Ibbetson staggered as his daughter almost succeeded in pulling him off balance, Marty still clinging on for grim death, both almost ankle-deep in soil.

'Boot boy no more since you kindly had me dismissed!' panted Marty, grimacing with the effort of trying to hang on and reassuring Etta at the same time as informing her father, 'But I didn't stay down for long – I'm to be my own boss!'

Etta might be impressed, but her father sneered. 'If you think that entitles you to marry my daughter then think again! Now will someone remove this parasite from my land!' With the assistance of footmen, a rebellious Marty was manipulated towards the exit.

Jerked back and forth by the violent jig performed by the men, Etta felt his jacket ripped out of her hands and threw them up in a gesture of exasperation, declaring stubbornly, 'You can forbid it all you like, but Martin will be back for me! Lock me in chains, but I'll get out somehow!'

'Like a bitch on heat!' Spittle flew from her father's lips to his beard, showing just how deranged she had made him and causing her mother to reel in shock, the servants too. 'I wager he doesn't know how many more there've been, queuing up for your favours. He wouldn't be so keen then!'

Etta gasped, could hardly speak from outrage. 'And you've turned every one of them away! How *dare* you humiliate me in such a vile manner? What chance have I had to do such things of which you accuse me when I'm forever in thrall to you? I have no value to you other than to be bartered to some rich man, no matter how charmless or ugly, just so long as the union brings you more power!'

This pulled him up slightly, but only to offer derision. 'I don't need some flibbertigibbet to imbue me with power! I've worked damned hard to build all this and I don't intend to lose it to some Tom, Dick or Harry on whom you've conveyed your favours!'

'Pybus, this is intolerable, I beg you, desist!' entreated Mrs Ibbetson, a more genteel person altogether than her husband, braving his wrath to snatch at his arm and condemn him with a whisper. 'It's unforgivable that you address Henrietta like some common ... she's our *daughter*.'

'And how many times I've wished she wasn't!' retorted Ibbetson, but his wife's quiet rebuke had acted as a turning point. Wrenching himself free of Marty, he thrust the hapless youth into the arms of the servants who awaited the order to eject him. But their master signalled them to linger. Brushing and tugging his clothes into some semblance of order, only just able to control his fury, he issued his daughter with an ultimatum. 'One last chance – and I'm being more than generous in the face of such wilful provocation. But first I shall have an honest answer: did this scoundrel at any time take advantage of you?'

Etta toyed with the idea of saying yes – which would, in effect, mean that no other man would want her and she would be of no further use as a bargaining tool – but it would also spell another beating for Marty and she could not bear that. 'You asked me once before. I told you that I intend to guard my honour until I marry. But, let me inform you, Father, I would die before I wed a man of your choosing. This man here, whom you have so cruelly handled, he is the only one I shall marry!' She went to Marty's side and clung to him.

Driven to distraction by this girl who, since babyhood, had never done as she was bidden, Ibbetson ranted, 'You imbecile, he's only after your wealth, can't you see?'

'What wealth?' Etta reflected her father's exasperation, her face pink and her hair tousled from the fray. 'I have none, other than that which you deign to bestow!'

Ibbetson clutched his scalp and gave a delirious moan as if trying to understand how all this had come to pass. How could she depict him as such an ogre, after all he had given her? He got on well with his son John, didn't he? Tremendously in fact, for John had never repaid his generosity and advice with ingratitude or confronted him at every turn of the way, as had this chit here, but gave him all the admiration that was due. Etta seemed only to want to hurl it back in his face, the ultimate display of that ingratitude being here and now in her choice of husband, this damned upstart, this lowest of the low.

A lethal expression on his face, he made as if to grab Marty again, but Etta's mother intervened with a shriek. 'Pybus, must you resort to murder? For nothing short of it will stop them. They are determined to wed.'

It was an unusually brave move for Isabella Ibbetson, who had allowed herself to be passed mutely from an over-bearing father to a domineering husband, and, having learned how spitefully childish Pybus could be if not exalted as the font of all wisdom, preferred to buckle under for the sake of a quiet life. Her prayers that Etta would take this example had been unanswered, but she loved her wilful daughter, empathised with her reluctance to be bartered, and, even if it might be too late, sought to fight her corner now.

Marty saw the mother properly for the first time now, a striking woman with dark looks, and threw her a look of gratitude for her support, though it quickly became evident that she had not an ounce of Etta's staying power.

Receiving a glare for her disobedience, Mrs Ibbetson

sighed and meekly stepped aside for her husband to do his worst. But at least he seemed to have taken her remark to heart. Confining any further violence to his voice, he barked at Etta whilst addressing her via his wife. 'Very well! The unmanageable baggage wants her own way, and she shall have it.'

Thinking there was some trick, Etta did not move, scraping away the hair that was clinging to her glistening brow and exchanging looks with Marty.

But her father said again, directly this time, 'Off you go then! If that's the way you want to repay everything that's been lavished on you, there's no point in dallying. After all, what use are you to me if you won't do as you're bidden?'

Still she was hesitant. 'With your blessing?'

'Blessing be damned! I hope you both rot in eternal damnation!'

Galvanised into action, she replied hotly, 'As you wish, Father! Blanche, go and pack – you shall come with me, of course.'

An admiring Blanche made to accompany her to the house but the master blocked their progress. 'She shall not! The servants are my property, and I didn't buy you those clothes so you could pawn them to subsidise your fancy-man.'

Alternating between relief and anger, Marty rejoined tersely, 'I can support my own wife, Mr Ibbetson, we need none of your help.'

'Splendid! Because you won't get it. You!' He jerked his head at Blanche. 'Back to the house, unless you want to forfeit your livelihood.'

'Don't treat her like a chattel, she's a human being – Blanche, stand your ground!'

But, recognising the futility of siding with Etta, the maid instantly complied with her employer's demand.

'Now let's see how keen you are to take her on, Mr . . . whatever your name is.'

'Lanegan,' provided Marty through gritted teeth.

'Hah! I thought I detected a touch of the bog-trotter. I suppose you're a damned Roman Catholic into the bargain, aren't you?'

'I am.' Marty was defiant, though he rarely went to church and neither did his parents.

'Didn't know that, did you?' Ibbetson took delight in the look of slight surprise on his daughter's face.

'Martin's religion has no bearing on anything.' Etta became haughty.

Ibbetson gave a nasty laugh. 'Let's see what bearing it has when he lands you with a brat every year!' His tone lightened. 'But if you still want him badly enough I'll allow you to walk out of here with the clothes you stand up in, which is more than you deserve. I wouldn't like to guess how long one dress will last, mind.' He saw the flicker of alarm on his daughter's face as she realised what she was about to sacrifice, and drove his point home. 'But then maybe, after what you've just learned, you'd care to reconsider, to admit that you've been an ungrateful fool and put this ridiculous notion out of your head, say goodbye to this bog-Irish fortune hunter, in which case we'll say no more about it.'

Etta tried to appear dignified. 'Presented with such generosity of spirit, Father, you leave us no choice.' She took Marty's arm and headed for the gate.

Her mother panicked – this was not what she had intended at all. 'Henrietta, don't be so rash! Will you not consider your mother? For I must stand by my husband in this, there shall be no return.'

'I'm sorry, Mother.' Etta turned a pitying expression on Mrs Ibbetson, her eyes filling with tears. 'Say goodbye to John for me when next you see him.' Then she turned away to hide her distress.

'Pybus, you cannot allow her to go!' The mother clutched her cheeks in anguish.

Ibbetson was unnerved too at his bluff being called, though he did not let it show. 'You were the one who said she was determined. Well, let's see how determined she is when she has to fend for herself.' And to his daughter: 'Don't come begging to us when you find your boot boy doesn't earn enough to keep you in scent!'

Etta rounded angrily on her father, fighting tears of rage at the blithe manner in which he rejected her. 'If you think that by spoiling Martin's chances of finding work I'll come back to you –'

'You think I'd have you back?' Ibbetson gave an uncaring snort. 'Once you get beyond those gates that's it – and that fellow doesn't need my help in losing a job, he'll do that for himself by his reckless attitude.'

'I know you, you vindictive wretch!' stormed Etta. 'The minute I'm gone –'

There was no chance to say more, for at her father's declaration of 'Enough of this!' she was bundled unceremoniously from the grounds along with her lover and the gates clanged shut in her astonished face. There was nothing else for it but to walk away.

Behind the barricade, watching her go, Etta's father remained furious. Her mother was only sad, her voice caught with emotion. 'We've lost her.'

'Rubbish! She'll try crawling back when he finds he can't manage her either and throws her out.'

In response came a miserable shake of head from one who knew: both husband and daughter were as stubborn as each other.

Ibbetson turned dismissively to march back to the house, the servants scurrying ahead. But his daughter's ingratitude had wounded him deeply. He could never forgive her.

Elated at having won, Marty would have tackled the fifteen-mile return hike with aplomb, but how could he drag Etta all that way in those flimsy little shoes? Especially after such extreme upset as she had endured.

'We'll bide here for the carrier,' he told her kindly, even though he had little cash to spare, as he led her to a bench on the village green. 'Hope it's not too long a wait.'

Etta nodded and sat beside him, constricted, chafed and sweating in the corset that held her upright like a fist of iron but could not prevent her overall subdued bearing.

It hurt to say it but he felt he must. 'There's still time to go back if you're regretting –'

'No!' Her upper lip beaded with sweat, she hastened to reiterate her love for him, trying to appear her bright self. 'I'm not in the least regretful. You're all I've ever wanted and will want, truly.' She laid her head on his shoulder. 'It's just so sad to have to leave Mother . . .'

'Aye . . . but you mentioned she didn't have much to do with bringing you up.' He remembered Etta voicing her sense of loss at the dismissal of her old nanny.

Her head came up. 'That doesn't matter! She's still my mother. Imagine how you'd feel.'

Nodding, he entwined her in comforting arms, coaxed her head back to his shoulder and was thoughtful for a while. 'It's not the same, I know, but I'm sure mine will welcome you as her own once she gets to meet you in person. And my da's a lovely man too.' Perhaps, again, it was the wrong thing to have said, her father being quite the opposite. He rested his chin atop her perspiring scalp, imagining the initial commotion his parents would make. But they were good people, and once they had evidence of Etta's love for their son they would take her to their hearts.

Reassured, Etta cuddled up to him, ignoring the fact that it was far too hot, feeling the heat of his body searing though her bodice, to her heart. Away from the angry voices the atmosphere of the village was one of calm, barely a sound other than that of the hover flies suspended in the sultry air around their heads. Her demeanour gradually relaxed and her mind began to drift.

'I wonder what John will say when he learns of this,' she murmured. 'I know he was beastly to you, but only at father's instigation and because he sought to protect me; he and I used to be close until recent happenings.'

Marty thought he understood. 'I suppose you would be if there was just the two o' yese.'

'I believe there was some sort of crisis when I was born. At any rate, Mother couldn't have any more. But of course that doesn't mean we are Father's only children.' At Marty's frown, she added, 'He has a mistress – in fact more than one.'

'How do you know?' asked her amazed partner.

Her head still upon his shoulder, Etta wrinkled her nose. 'Oh, gossip, you know.'

'It might be just that,' offered Marty.

'No, I followed him one day, witnessed his indiscretion for myself. I feel so sorry for poor Mother, who shows him such devotion – yet I deplore her weakness for allowing it to happen. I tried to tell her, but it was obvious she already knew and was turning a blind eye. I'd never countenance anything of that nature in my marriage.' It was not merely a declaration but a warning.

Marty was quick to squeeze her and voice his own fidelity. She hugged him back, and to pass the time whilst they waited for the carrier asked about his brothers and sisters, whom he had named before but she had forgotten. He listed them: Louisa, Bridget, Mary and Anne, all of whom were older than himself and married, Elizabeth and Maggie still at school, Tom and Jimmy-Joe the youngest – and that was not to mention the dead ones in between.

Etta chuckled. 'My word, do you think we'll have such a clan?'

He wondered how to respond. 'Would you want to?'

76

She toyed thoughtfully with one of his brass buttons. 'Well, maybe not quite so many – and not for years. For now I've no desire to share you with anyone.'

He gave vigorous accord. 'I'd never say anything of the sort to my parents, but too large a family drags you down. All your money goes on feeding and clothing them and there's none left over to spend on things for yourself.'

'And what would you like for yourself?' Etta quizzed with a smile of interest.

Marty grinned, but bit his tongue upon cognising that he had painted himself into a corner: how could he confide his dream of a big house and servants with good-quality furniture and a suit of clothes that didn't have to be kept for best? It wouldn't matter that it was pure fantasy; Etta would think that her father had been right about him only being after her for her money, and that just wasn't true at all. Knowing how touchy she was about her looks, he couldn't even admit that part of his dream had been realised in a beautiful bride-to-be.

But then to his relief he did not have to speak. Alerted by the rumble of a cart, Etta jumped up to hail its driver. 'Are you by any chance going near York?'

The grizzled waggoner tipped his hat. 'All t'way there, lady.'

'See!' Etta turned to Marty, her dark eyes refilled with their usual sparkle. 'Luck is smiling on us already.'

Belying his rough appearance, their saviour showed respect for the young lady's dress and rubbed the seat clean with his hat. The sight of Marty's bruised face caused a moment of doubt, but, a shrewd judge of character, the waggoner quickly weighed the situation and a quiet smile accompanied his invitation for the happy couple to board. It appealed to his anarchic nature that he might be helping them elope, their murmured conversation during the journey confirming his suspicions.

Martin wondered aloud if they would be in York before

the register office closed, thus including the waggoner in their conspiracy.

'I don't want to dash your hopes, but old Snowy doesn't walk much faster than a man these days. However,' he gave a reassuring smile and tickled the horse's geriatric rear with his whip, 'we'll give him a try – gerrup now, Snowy!'

'Aye, gerrup, Snowy!' Marty and Etta shared a loving laugh at their simultaneous command, even though it made no difference at all to the horse's stride.

Against all odds, they did reach their destination just in time to visit the register office, the waggoner bestowing them a wink of good luck as they thanked him and rushed away to make an appointment to marry.

But at the last minute, Etta had a bout of nervous superstition and urged her suitor to enter alone lest all go awry. 'When they see how young I am – oh, I feel so self-conscious, I can't bring myself to go in!'

'You'll have to present yourself some time, they can't marry folk by telegraph – I'm joking!' He gave her arm an encouraging squeeze. 'How can it go wrong? We've already been granted the licence.'

'It's all very well for you, you're almost twenty-one.'

Blushing, Marty was forced to admit then, 'I exaggerated about the couple of months, I won't come of age till next year – but I swear to God I haven't lied to you about anything else!' He crossed his heart.

Forgiving him this trespass, she was finally persuaded that their visit was mere formality, and, with time ticking away, agreed to come in with him for support. Still, she braced herself for an interrogation.

The superintendent registrar was not at all pleased to receive their request so late in the day, and throughout the brief interview there was to be great suspense.

But then, 'We've done it!' Marty broke into relieved

laughter as, wedding arranged, they rushed away before anyone could call them back.

'Almost!' Etta squeezed his arm excitedly. 'Oh goodness, wasn't it such luck he could fit us in so soon? I wish tomorrow afternoon would hurry! What are we to do until then?'

'I don't know about you but I'm famished!' exclaimed Marty, who had not eaten since breakfast.

'Let's visit a restaurant!' At his look of dismay a crafty glint came to Etta's eye. 'I'm not so penniless as I made out to Father. After the last debacle I thought to be better prepared and I've managed to accumulate eight sovereigns.' She laughed at his gasp. 'Don't ask where from! I had Blanche sew them into my petticoat.' Then, taking his arm, she hurried him into the entrance of a dark, ancient passageway that stank of urine. 'Shelter me whilst I retrieve some of it!'

His stomach cramped by intense hunger, Marty was not about to rebuff her extravagant gesture and shielded her with his body whilst keeping a lookout for peeping Toms. He cast furtive glances as she hoisted her skirts and attempted to rip the coins from the petticoat's hem, but they were too firmly stitched. She cursed and applied her teeth to the linen, making him laugh at her antics until frustration drove her to urge him, 'Well, you have a go!'

Wondering what an onlooker might think of him lifting a young lady's petticoats, he nibbled and picked at the hem, which, between the pair of them, was finally rent and the coins retrieved, Marty having to chase some of them down the pavement as they all spilled free at once.

Then, still delirious with laughter and excitement at the thought of their coming nuptials, off they went to find a place in which to gorge.

An hour later, bloated with sausage and mash, strawberries and cream, Marty bestowed an adoring smile upon his bride-to-be across the white table linen, hoping he didn't have gravy round his mouth and admitting he had never been in a place as nice as this. Moreover, there was another bonus. 'I've still got plenty of time to nip home before it gets dark – I mean to Ma and Da's.'

Etta's jaw dropped. 'You can't possibly think to leave me alone! I know you regard it as living in sin, but –'

'Do I look that holy?' He reached for her hand, laughing. 'We'll only be jumping the gun for a single night, that hardly constitutes living in sin. No, I meant just to reassure them. I'll take you to our new home first, get you settled – got to go there to collect my barrow anyway – then I'll call on Ma and Da and tell them I didn't have such a lucrative day as I thought so I'll have to go out again. You know, lay it on thick as to how I feel guilty at not bringing any money home after all the trouble I've caused them.'

'You're used to this, aren't you?' accused Etta with a smile.

He bit his lip. 'No, I hardly ever tell them lies. I hate doing it now really but they've been so blasted obstroculous over this marriage that it serves them right. If they supported their son he wouldn't have to lie, would he? Though what I'll do if Ma wants to feed me . . .' He chuckled and, holding his distended stomach, pretended to retch.

Etta grimaced emphathetically as they paid for the meal and left the restaurant. 'But they'll still expect you to come home some time during the evening,' she reminded him.

'Not if I say I'm going to kip on a bench at the station so's to be bright and early tomorrow.' Marty looked smug.

'Another lie for Judgement Day,' teased Etta.

'Well, only in part. I will be up bright and early, it's not every day a fella gets married.' He linked her arm as they ambled through the city, along narrow streets that boasted elegant Georgian architecture, its symmetry marred by the squat and decrepit medieval buildings that lurked between, their gable-ends plastered with garish advertisements, plus an array of striped awnings, even now at seven o'clock having to shade the goods in the shop windows against an unrelenting sun. 'Mindst, we won't be tying the knot until the afternoon, we might decide we deserve a lie in.' A twinkle in his eye, he nudged her suggestively with his hip.

'Well, I might,' said Etta, 'though I can't see you being very comfortable on the floor.'

At this he looked blank.

'We only have the licence, not the certificate,' she reminded him archly. 'It's rather presumptuous of you.'

Marty's visage flooded with disappointment. 'Aye, well, I suppose it is . . .'

Etta remained aloof for a moment, then could no longer maintain the charade and broke into peals of laughter at his chagrin, clutching his arm as if hanging on to life itself. 'Do you seriously think I'm ever going to let you out of my sight again? Of course you shall share the bed, tonight and always – oh, won't it be wonderful never to be parted!'

He returned her laughing gesture, voicing agreement, but still in the dark as to whether she intended only to let him sleep beside her or to lift the embargo on their physical union before marriage. But at present nothing else mattered other than her vow to be his – as his warning glance told every other man who turned to stare at her, though secretly he enjoyed the kudos of having such a jewel on his arm.

They came out of town via the gnarled stone bridge at Castle Mills, over the scum-laden, oil-dappled broth that was the River Foss, where barges idled in the evening sun, and through the postern gate in the medieval limestone walls. Marty had deliberately brought her this way to avoid any drunken antics along Walmgate, renowned as the roughest thoroughfare in York. Some might have declared it a futile gesture when the room he had rented was over a pub, but he himself was pleased to find the saloon bar comparatively quiet, this being mid-week, albeit reeking of the usual beery fumes and tobacco smoke.

Still, he imagined it must be a shock for Etta.

'It won't be for long!' he assured her again, seeing her face drop at the realisation that this seedy venue was home. 'Had there been anything else –'

'I'm sure it will be fine!' Hiding her disappointment, Etta faked glee. 'It's all rather exciting, come show me the way!'

He led her up a dilapidated staircase and across a landing with nicotine-stained walls, apologising for the room's bare boards and sparse furnishings, drawing the curtains to give them some privacy and repeating that this was purely a temporary lodging.

Etta remained optimistic. 'I didn't come here to admire the furniture.' And, smiling, she opened her arms, into which he gladly stepped.

There followed a passionate succession of kisses. It was such a wrench to leave her, but with a regretful expression he unglued his lips. 'I really should go and pacify the mammy and daddy now.'

'Do they live far?' She stroked him.

'Only a hundred yards or so.' His eyes crinkled in laughter. 'That's why I was so edgy in coming here, lest I was spotted. What will you do while I'm gone?'

Etta planted herself demurely on the edge of the bed, hands in lap. 'I shall just sit here and contemplate my extreme good fortune in finding you.'

'Aw!' Overwhelmed with affection, Marty threw his arms round her again, then, knowing how dusty and sticky he himself felt from their journey, said, 'I should fetch you some water so's you can make yourself more comfy.' There was a bowl and jug on a table. Grabbing the jug, he returned some moments later with a supply of cold water. 'Sorry we've no tap of our own. Everything's a bit primitive.'

She said this was of no matter. 'Do I call someone to take it away when I'm done?'

'No! Mustn't let anyone see you're not wearing a ring, I told them we're already man and wife. I'll shift it later.

Oh, and I'd better light this, don't want to leave you in the dark.' After fumbling over the paraffin lamp, he looked about him, checking for any other addition to her comfort. 'Er . . . there's a whatsit under the bed if you need it.' Then he blew her a last kiss, saying he would try not to be away too long. 'Think of this, after tomorrow none of it will matter.'

He hurried through the dying light to his parents' house, both happy and ashamed that they believed him when he said what a hard day he'd had and did not question when he told them of his plan to return to the railway station. There was no avoiding the meal his mother had kept for him, but luckily it was a platter of cold meat, which he was able to wrap and take with him saying he must get back without delay. It would provide him and Etta with breakfast.

On the way back he relieved his bladder for the night so as not to have to do it in front of his wife-to-be. Expecting that she might have fallen asleep after her gruelling day, he was touched to discover she had forced herself to stay awake for him, although she was in bed, the covers up to her chest and her long, dark tresses spread across the pillow.

She asked how things had gone with his parents, to be told that all was fine, then saw his eyes go to the dress and corset draped over the iron bedstead. 'I had dreadful trouble unlacing without Blanche.'

'Never mind, from now on you'll have me to help you.' He removed his jacket, gave it a shake, draped it over the back of a chair and went to wash his hands and face in the bowl using the sliver of soap that Etta had conjured from somewhere. Then, oddly self-conscious under her drowsy gaze, he snuffed out the lamp before unbuttoning his trousers, carefully laying these aside too and climbing in beside her.

Discovering that Etta, too, had left on her underwear, he refrained from cuddling her for the moment, not just because it was stiflingly hot but because he was unsure what she expected of him. 'I'll bet you're exhausted, aren't you?' he blurted.

The dark outline of her head nodded sleepily. 'But incredibly happy.' She reached for his hand.

A little relieved, he lay back gripping her fingers, closing his eyes and murmuring how much he was looking forward to tomorrow.

4

The next thing he knew it was tomorrow, light streaming through the thin curtains, his body drenched in sweat and his garments plastered to him. Coming round, he stretched uncomfortably, then, feeling the stack of hot coals beside him, rolled his head to view his sleeping partner through a misty veil and smiled when he saw she was not asleep at all but was grinning back at him, her eyes more alert than his.

His first words were unromantic. 'God, isn't it clammy?'

Propped on one elbow, Etta agreed. 'That's what woke me – that and the birds. I've been watching you for ages.' She trailed tender fingers down his sweating face, then dabbed her lips to it.

Smothered by her long hair, he chuckled and fought a gentle way out. Few sounds came from outside. 'It must only be about five.' He kicked off the covers, the erotic musk of her body wafting up to arouse him into kissing her, she meeting him willingly. But the room was like an oven, forcing him to break away abruptly with a grunt of discomfort.

'Sorry, darlin', I'll just have to open the window.' He clambered over the bed and reached through the curtains to open the sash, though this was to provide little relief and he groaned as he slumped back beside her and tried to flap some air inside his shirt.

'I don't mind if you take your clothes off.' Etta dipped her mouth into the socket of his eye then licked the salt from her lips.

His lazy grin exuded sensuality and he ran his hands through his hair to relieve his perspiring scalp. 'I can't vouch for what would happen then.'

'I think it already has happened to some extent.' She rolled a coquettish eye at his groin.

He gasped – 'You're shameless!' – but immediately leapt atop her, eager to find out the extent of her invitation, and was ecstatic upon finding that she did not push his hands away this time, no matter how intimately they pried.

The heat of the day was forgotten as an inner heat took over, overwhelming Etta to such a pitch that in her thrashing she almost rolled off the bed. Between frantic laughing kisses she urged him to stop only so that she might take off her underwear. All self-consciousness gone, both rapidly divested themselves of this last barrier, then hurled their fevered bodies back together, rocking and chuckling and moaning, and, amidst passion, pain and apology, forged their blissful union.

Sweat trickled off Marty's body as, finally, he rolled away from her and lay there panting and victorious, whilst Etta shifted onto her side and continued to kiss him, quiet, loving little kisses on his shoulder, nestling and nuzzling, both of them thoughtful, marvelling at what had occurred. Inevitably, though, much as each loved the other they were forced to move to the outer edges of the mattress, spreading their naked limbs to try and catch what little draught came through the window, yet maintaining contact with each other by the tips of their fingers. The air was pungent with their odour.

'I've no hat.'

Marty chuckled at the inappropriate comment. 'And do you always wear a hat for this kinda thing?'

'For our wedding! I must have one.' On the point of

going to luncheon when he had come to rescue her, she had not been wearing outdoor clothing. It had only just begun to register now what dire straits she would be in when the climate changed. And, 'Oh, look, my dress is on the floor!' She beheld the crumpled garment with dismay.

He threw off his languor and leapt out of bed, giving the dress a shake and hanging it on a peg. 'The creases'll drop out by afternoon. I shall have to sponge me suit an' all, it's carrying half o' your father's garden.'

'You're so capable.' She ran admiring eyes over his naked muscles.

'There's no limit to my talents, but holding my water isn't one of them – could I ask ye to turn your back for a minute?' His bladder swollen to the size of a football, he was finally compelled to employ the chamber pot. 'Stop your giggling! I can't go if I know anyone's listening to me.'

Successfully relieving himself, he enjoyed a lengthy scratch of his torso, raked his hands through his hair that was all stuck up from bed, then went to pour a drink from the jug, sharing the glass with her. Thirst quenched, he lay back beside her nude form, desire already beginning to rekindle.

But before responding to it he felt obliged to murmur amends. 'Sorry.'

She rolled her head to search his eyes. 'Goodness, what on earth for?'

Face thoughtful, his fingers gently strummed her belly. 'Hurting you. I did, didn't I?'

Etta wrinkled her nose and shook her head to reassure him. 'Well, perhaps just a little – but it was glorious too.' She threw herself onto her side to issue fervent kisses.

Encouraged, he grinned and snuggled up to her, to begin the whole sequence all over again. There was still no interruption from the outside world other than the grind of the iron-rimmed wheels of the milk cart.

Perspiring and happy, desire pitted against fragile flesh

and overwhelming all, Etta and Marty were working their way towards another bittersweet union when there came movement from across the landing as the landlord and his wife prepared for the day ahead. Marty put a finger to his lips, but this only made Etta titter even more and he had to stifle her with his palm, whispering, 'You'll get us chucked out!' Making sure she was over her laughter, he withdrew his hand from her mouth and rolled out of bed – but she nipped his bottom causing him to wheel round with a hiss of accusation, albeit amused. 'Behave! Or there'll be no breakfast for you.'

He had intended to save the cold beef for as long as he could, but, ravenous now, he went to fetch the paper bag from his pocket, he and Etta devouring its contents as if at a feast, ignoring the fact that the slices were slightly grey and curling up at the edges.

Afterwards, Etta urged him to perform the same courtesy as she had shown him whilst she used the chamber pot. Whilst doing so she heard muffled amusement. 'What are you laughing at now?'

'Sorry – I just didn't know posh folk passed wind!'

She came at him in a giggling rush to unite yet again.

The hour to their wedding crept nearer. Feeling distinctly grubby, the bride-to-be coaxed the groom into procuring a bath from the landlord. When he replied that this would be deemed a most unusual request, she wheedled, 'Oh, please, I can't go to my most important day in such a state, can I?'

'Well, I suppose I wouldn't mind sharing the water,' he admitted. Concerned that the victualler might have overheard their bawdy antics, Marty nevertheless wanted to do all in his power to please her, and so, after donning his shirt and trousers, he went down to make his request which, as he had feared, was met by a laughing gasp of astonishment.

'What does he think we are?' the landlord demanded of

his wife, then to the petitioner, 'Get yourself down to the slipper baths!'

'Normally I would.' Marty could not give the true reason for wanting to look spruce. 'It's just that I've an important appointment and I don't have that much time.' Fishing into his pocket he took out the change from the sovereign that had paid for last night's meal. 'I'll gladly pay you.'

'Go on then,' said the landlord grudgingly with an outstretched hand, and said he'd send the tweeny up. 'But don't make a habit of this.'

'Thank you, we won't bother you again,' promised Marty. But as he turned to go the landlord's addition made him blush.

'And don't make a habit of all that giggling racket at the crack o' dawn, neither!'

Ducking in embarrassment, but stifling laughter too, Marty rushed back upstairs to inform Etta that, hereon, they must bridle their unrestrained lovemaking. Far from this affecting them, though, it only inspired another bout of gleeful kissing whilst they waited for the bath to arrive, and only when the maid and the landlord's wife brought it in did they hastily separate, Etta whipping her left hand behind her back to hide the lack of a ring.

That plain and simple water could provide such ecstasy – Etta had never realised it before today. She sank into the lukewarm tub, luxuriating for so long that a sweating Marty had to beg for his turn. Whilst he watched from the bath, she took her time in dressing, eschewing the corset as too cumbersome.

'And unnecessary,' Marty added, observing her perfect form.

Unselfconscious in her nakedness, she bent to examine her legs and frowned at the red blotches that had sprung up overnight. 'There must be a midge in here, I'm bitten to death.'

Marty chose not to correct her, merely nodded and

scratched at his own flea bites, then finally emerged from the water and began to dry himself.

Stepping into the crumpled underwear she had worn in bed, Etta said she would have to purchase more. There were also other indispensable items she was missing, such as a hairbrush. 'It's fortunate I was wearing this yesterday.' She held up the gold locket and chain that lay on the table. 'I should be able to acquire several items in exchange for it.'

'Oh, I couldn't have you sell that!' Anxious not to detract from his bride's aristocratic appearance, Marty tied the towel around himself and went to fasten the chain around her neck.

Etta acquiesced with a smile and continued her toilet whilst he went to dress. Still unable to take his eyes off her, he studied the way she was sitting now in her rumpled bodice and drawers, hair about shoulders, a golden locket around her neck, one leg spread, the other raised on the edge of the bed whilst she picked at a jagged toenail, more like a scene from a bordello – not that he had ever been in one – and he thought how marvellous she was to remain genteel whilst being so sexually alluring and down to earth at the same time.

She turned to her hair, for now using his comb, but seeing how badly this coped with her severely tangled locks and pitying her, Marty said he would go to the shop to get those items necessary to her wellbeing.

'Apart from the drawers,' he said cheekily as he breathed on the brass buttons of his uniform and gave them a rub with his cuff. 'I wouldn't know what size and I'm not asking for those even for you.' He donned the coat. 'There, am I good enough for a wedding?'

'Good enough to eat!' Etta provided the money but showed reluctance to let him go, dragging him back to kiss him more than once, both of them groaning at the separation.

In his absence, Etta was to rack her brain as to how she could acquire a hat without actually paying for it. Only able to afford the common or garden variety, she rebelled against sullying her head with one of those. By the time Marty returned she had her plan. Under her direction, whilst she held the curls in place, he helped to insert her pins so that with such splendidly combined effort her hairstyle was not so unrecognisable from the one normally completed by her maid. Finally, checking both their appearances, she took Marty's arm, voicing her intention to purchase the hat on their way to the register office and announcing gaily, 'Let us be wed!'

A clock in town informed them that they had emerged far too prematurely, but with Etta intent on dragging him to every milliner in York this was just as well. Trying to be diplomatic, Etta said that he would be much too bored watching her try on hats and should wait outside if he preferred, in truth knowing that his bruised and lowly appearance would hinder her deception. Glad that she did not want him to accompany her inside, Marty sought out a patch of shade provided by a church spire. This was to be re-enacted at various other shops, waiting and wilting, his heart sinking every time she emerged empty-handed, worrying that a member of his family might spot him, until Etta eventually tried on a hat she approved.

'Hallelujah!' he declared, half laughing, half exasperated.

'You could say you like it.' She was rather hurt and cross, having taken so much trouble.

'It's grand,' he was quick to say of the veiled and flow-ered creation. It worried him that she saw fit to squander what little they had on such frippery, but he would not have hurt her for the world. 'Looks expensive.'

'Only the best for my wedding day.' She tilted the brim coquettishly to display silk roses and violets. 'Doesn't it go well with this dress? Thank goodness I was wearing one of my better ones when you rescued me.' She laughed at his obvious dismay. 'Don't panic, I didn't pay a sou. Aren't I clever?'

His jaw dropped – surely she had not stolen it?

Etta spoke conspiratorially, her glittering eyes lauding her own acumen. 'I explained my predicament to the milliner, told her how a wretched bird had defiled my own hat whilst I was on my way to a most important engagement – my maid found it simply impossible to remove that dreadful stain! I equipped them with my identity and told them to send the bill to Swanford Hall –'

'Etta!'

'– and to send a number of other hats on approval as they were all so delightful that I could not decide which to choose!' She laughed softly. 'Oh, I know it was mean of me but the woman was such a snob – besides, you never know, Mother might like them and coax Father into footing the bill. Serve him right, the miserable swine.' Her face laughed but her eyes betrayed the pain he had caused her.

'I always knew you'd be a handful,' Marty chastised her, but warmly.

It then occurred to him that he had yet to acquire a much more necessary item than the hat and, hence, they went to visit the nearest jeweller.

By the time they had lunched, the occasion for which they yearned was almost arrived. Soliciting two strangers along the way to bear witness, Marty led his beloved to the register office.

In the slippery heat of the afternoon, reclining close beside him in their rumpled bed, after their finest, most passionate, most spiritual coupling to date, Etta leaned on her elbow, gazed into her beloved husband's green eyes and said, tenderly profuse, 'I've never in my entire life felt such happiness.'

Marty wholeheartedly agreed. He was a happy sort of person anyway, but for him too this elation was something special. Cupping the back of her hot skull he caught her lower lip between his, drawing it in and caressing it with his tongue.

Breaking free to recoup her breath, Etta threw herself back, stretching and purring. 'Oh, how wonderful to be free of that tyrant! To do as I please, to know he can never dominate me again.' Then she hurled herself back at Marty.

In the knowledge that he would have to go out and earn a living tomorrow, they lay entwined in love for the rest of that afternoon, undisturbed until a dray wagon came to deliver, whereupon the loud rumble of barrels being transferred from pavement to cellar caused them to rise and dress and Etta to tidy her hair. Pulling two wooden chairs to the window, they sat side by side to watch for a while, then, after the drayman had gone, just to lift their eyes beyond the roofs of the slum dwellings to the glorious sunlit day, and to smile contentedly at each other.

Had the position of the sun not informed him that it was almost time for tea, Marty's grumbling stomach would have done. Still, he sat for a while longer, smiling at his bride and waiting.

Eventually she rubbed the knees beneath her silken gown. 'Well . . . shall we dine?'

He brightened. 'I was beginning to think my new wife lived on air!'

She laughed lightly, but made no move to rise.

After another short period of waiting, Marty prompted her. 'So, are you going to get it then?'

'I?' Etta looked astonished.

'Well it won't appear on its own, will it?' he said, amused.

She looked nonplussed – yes, it usually did.

He watched the incomprehension spread across her face, indeed, shared it.

After some indecision, she lamented, 'I wish I could have brought Blanche, she'd know what to do.' Then, before he could broach the distinct possibility that Etta might have

93

to look after herself, she announced brightly, 'No matter! We'll eat at a restaurant until we can hire someone.'

Marty had no time to comment on the ridiculousness of this statement, nor opine that the sovereigns she had brought would not last long if she were intent on lavishing them on restaurants. She looked so excited and lovely that he could not bear to spoil things. He must let her down gently. 'Perhaps we shouldn't fritter the money we have. Let's go round to Ma and Da's. They'll feed us.'

'But won't they be furious?' Etta knew how he had been dreading the event.

'Highly likely, but I'll have to make the confession some time. Best get it over with – and I doubt they'll make a scene with you there.' He raised a grin. 'Then tonight we'll make a list of things we need and you can go and buy them while I'm at work tomorrow.'

Looking bemused at this last statement, Etta nevertheless expressed a desire to meet her in-laws. 'I do hope they like me.'

'How could they not?' He curled an arm round her and squeezed as they went to the stairs.

His parents' home was only in the next street, but, avoiding the more insalubrious shortcuts that he himself would have taken if alone, Marty led Etta in a roundabout fashion down and then up grimy rows of terraced buildings. However, there was no evading the fact that several occupants of this impoverished area were acquainted with Etta's husband, for they called out to him along the way.

And, self-consciously, he answered, 'Hello, Mr Bechetti. Good evening, Mrs Cahill.'

Breaking away from his peers, a small Yorkshire lad came to trot alongside his hero. 'I like your new sweetheart, Marty. Better than t'old one.'

'Such cheek! I'll tell your mother, Albert Gledhill.' Marty

tried to sound scolding but the youngster only laughed and ran away, chanting, 'Sweetheart, sweetheart!'

Feeling Etta's inquisitive gaze he laughed off the impudent remark, but there was no way round what was to follow: the thing he had dreaded most.

Etta exclaimed, 'Oh my goodness, there's a drunkard fallen in the gutter!' The man had been staggering some way ahead of them when suddenly he capsized.

Marty's spirits sank. Bidding Etta to stay where she was, he rushed to attend the collapsed figure. However, after brief hesitation she disobeyed and wandered up to find the man unconscious and her husband anxiously patting his cheek.

But others were here to assist, one of them providing a wheelbarrow and treating this in somewhat cavalier fashion, she thought, as he announced with a bow, 'Your carriage awaits, Mr Lanegan.'

Suffering deep embarrassment, Marty steadied the barrow whilst others loaded the body aboard. Then, with grim face, he thanked his helpers and wheeled the perpetrator away.

Much bemused that her husband assumed such responsibility, Etta padded alongside, querying apprehensively, 'Where will you take him?'

'Home.' He struggled to keep the three-wheeled barrow level under the dead weight of its load.

'You know where he lives then?'

'I should do – he's my father.'

Whilst a shocked Etta halted in her tracks, Marty carried on, though went only a little further before yelling through an open front door, 'Ma! Can you give us a hand?'

Etta watched as Mrs Lanegan sauntered out and, with resignation as if this were a frequent occurrence, helped to transport the recumbent occupant of the barrow into the house.

She wandered in quietly after them and stood unnoticed

as mother and son tended the drunkard, her eyes flitting briefly over the other residents who eyed her back curiously, before travelling to a row of empty beer bottles in the scullery.

His father deposited in the armchair, Marty clicked his tongue as Redmond slowly emerged from his trance. '*Now* he comes round!' He turned an exasperated face on his mother, but at that point followed his wife's gaze to the beer bottles and hastily sought to explain. 'Sorry, Etta, it's not the way it looks.'

Aggie turned a quizzical expression which quickly changed to one of astonishment at the vision in lilac silk and cream lace. There was no need to ask who this was. Her eyes hardened and flew to Marty as if demanding to know how he could have brought the Ibbetson girl here. She was unprepared for an even bigger shock.

'Mother, I'd like you to meet my wife, Etta.'

Too deafened by the thudding of her own angry pulse, Aggie did not hear the collective intake of breath from her children and Uncle Mal, and also her husband, who was fully conscious though still a little dazed.

'Did I hear right? Did he say *wife?*' Redmond gawped blankly from one family member to the other, then promptly swooned again.

'We were married today.' Etta stared at the father in perplexed concern, yet, noting that none of the others seemed remotely worried and were more intent on her, she formed a tentative smile and extended her hand to her mother-in-law, for a second thinking that it might be refused. The other Mrs Lanegan was prematurely grey, and with her high cheekbones must once have been attractive but was now quite wizened. Clad in a faded dress, her chest was exceedingly narrow, giving the impression of frailness, but this was misleading for her lips were sanguine and her eyes lively and strong with that special blueness only encountered in a glacier as they fixed themselves on this intruder. Here was a woman who liked folk to keep their place, and heaven help Etta, who had come and upset all that.

But the handshake was accepted with a formal nod. Though devastated that her son had defied her to marry in secret and to one of such different class, Aggie was unable to express her wrath in front of so illustrious a stranger, and, summoning politeness, invited Etta to take a seat at the table that was set for tea, brushing deferentially at the chair to make sure it was clean. 'Won't you join us, Mi – I mean, Etta?'

Etta glanced apprehensively at Mr Lanegan who was once again conscious. 'If my presence would not be too much of an imposition?' Told that it wouldn't, she thanked her hostess and sat down, aware that her every movement was under studious examination from several pairs of eyes.

'Is she a fairy?' whispered little Tom, entranced.

'Sure, and she'd give the little people a run for their money, Tom.'

Etta turned her beguiling smile on the white-haired speaker, Uncle Mal, who had the weathered air of one who had lived all his life in the open and was poorly attired with a neckerchief in place of a collar, and trousers that were bagged at the knees, but otherwise had a pleasant manner and at this moment was directing the full force of it at her.

'Put those eggs on!' Aggie growled at one of her daughters, indicating the pan of water on the range, whilst she herself disappeared into the scullery with another child following, the youngest two staying behind to stare at Etta, in whom they seemed rapt.

Despite the childish scrutiny Etta felt a little easier with her mother-in-law gone, for of the pair Mrs Lanegan seemed the formidable one. Studying Marty's father now she saw a delicate countenance framed in bushy brown hair, calm if watery eyes with a kind look about them, which Marty had obviously inherited. There was not a whiff of alcohol. Believing Marty when he had said things were not how they seemed, she could see that this man was no drunkard, yet was puzzled as to what might have caused the initial collapse plus the subsequent fleeting departures into unconsciousness she had witnessed in the few moments she had been there, deducing that his frail physique must be responsible. Whilst his wife only appeared to be fragile there was stronger evidence of it here in the pronounced slope of Mr Lanegan's shoulders, his posture deplorable as he shambled out to the backyard, excusing himself to Etta as he went. That she smiled at him seemed to pacify Martin, who had been agitated since they entered. But she was not to be provided with an explanation just yet.

Murmuring reassurance to his bride and hoping Uncle Mal would not yield to his uninhibited penchant for describing bowel movements, the groom slipped away to the scullery where he disturbed Aggie in the act of trying to calm herself.

'Mammy, I'm –'

'Don't you dare say you're sorry!' Nearly choking herself in trying to dispose of the sherry, which had come by dishonest means, she slammed the empty glass down and stabbed a finger at him, hissing the words through clenched teeth. 'You treacherous spalpeen, you're not sorry at all!'

'I'm not sorry for marrying Etta, but I'm sorry you made me have to lie in doing it!'

'Oh, so it's my fault! God damn you – here, give me that bloody glass before your father gets back – that's if he hasn't collapsed again out there from the outrage!' And she tipped another tot of the illicit sherry down her throat before hiding the bottle behind bags of flour and dried peas and reaching for the bread knife, which was first levelled threateningly at Marty before being used to more legitimate purpose.

Reappearing from the privy, Redmond found his wife carving a loaf, his son standing by shamefaced.

Shaking his head in disgust, he told the latter tersely, 'We'll have this out later. Back to the table with you, you're neglecting your wife.'

In between discussing the hot weather with Uncle Mal, Etta had been examining her surroundings, a small but tidy room displaying religious pictures, many china ornaments of surprisingly high quality, gleaming brass oil-lamps with elaborate cowls, and lace antimacassars all pristine, but as her husband re-entered she turned to feast her attention on him as if he had been gone years. Marty sat beside her.

Competing for her attention, Uncle Mal leaned towards her mouthing boastfully, 'I'm seventy-eight, ye know.'

Etta tore her eyes from Marty. 'That's a remarkable age.'

Then, a plate of bread and butter was delivered to the table and tea began. The pampered Etta might have no idea as to how meals were produced, but she could not fail to notice that there were insufficient boiled eggs to go round. Presented with one herself, she thanked her mother-in-law but said, 'I do hope by our impromptu appearance we haven't deprived anyone?'

'No one in this family is deprived,' replied Aggie firmly.

'Of course, I didn't mean to imply . . .' Etta's hands remained in her lap as she watched her mother-in-law deftly slice the top off one diner's egg and give it to another, performing this thrice more until everyone had a share.

'Nobody will go hungry. Please be at liberty to begin.' Obviously unhappy, but, out of courtesy, not going so far as to voice this, Aggie passed around the bread and butter.

Etta removed the top of her egg and began to eat, her every mouthful under surveillance from those children who had already scooped up their meagre ration and were now reliant on bread.

Beside her, despite being one of the lucky few with a

whole egg, Marty festered. Was his mother deliberately trying to make him feel guilty?

Both he and Etta were glad when the meal was over, yet it would be impolite for them to rush off after being fed and they were obliged to sit a while longer. Voicing more thanks, Etta moved aside to allow Martin's sisters to clear her plate and others. They were several years younger than herself, their skinny, shapeless trunks belonging more to monkeys than women, yet Elizabeth and Maggie emitted an air of competence as they moved around the table, stacking the crockery and taking it away. Her eyes moved back to the ornaments on the sideboard upon which she commented to no one in particular.

'I must say, you have some very handsome china.'

Before thanks could be issued, Uncle Mal raised white eyebrows and emitted cheerfully, 'Those? Pff! They're just Aggie's gimcracks.' He inflated his chest and hoiked up the waistband of his trousers. 'You want fine china, ye should've seen the collection I used to have, shouldn't she, Red? 'Twould have graced a palace –'

'Probably did before you got your hands on it, Unc,' joked Marty from the side of his mouth, then shrank at the glare from his mother.

Mal was oblivious. '– but that was before my dear Bridget passed away and her sisters grabbed the lot and I was forced to come and live here. Never left me so much as a spoon to stir my tea, so they didn't . . .'

'You've talent enough for stirring without spoons,' accused Red, but Mal just heaved an emotional sigh and pulled out a handkerchief to mop at his glistening eyes. 'God love her, she had real style, my Biddy. I'm not saying Aggie doesn't try her best of course . . .'

Grossly insulted and too furious to sit still, with face a-thunder Aggie marched off to the scullery where, against habit, she aided her girls with the washing up.

Meantime, a child was ousted so that Etta could get to

100

one of the more comfortable seats, the youngest planting himself at her feet.

'Jimmy-Joe seems to have a fascination with your shoes, Etta,' observed Redmond in his soft brogue, between taking puffs of a pipe.

Responding to his kind attempts to make conversation, she agreed and smiled down at the toddler, who played with the tassel on one of her kid shoes – but fondness swiftly turned to dismay when, with one crafty sleight of hand, the tassel was ripped from its moorings and was spirited away as Jimmy-Joe made his gleeful escape on all fours.

'Catch that wee divil!' Redmond signalled to Maggie, who grabbed the toddler before he managed to scramble between her stick-thin legs, upturning him and retrieving the tassel, which was apologetically handed back to its owner.

Marty saw Etta's crestfallen face at the disfigurement of her only pair of shoes, and said hastily, 'Don't worry, I'll stick it on when we get home. Have you any glue I can borrow, Da?'

Redmond gritted his teeth to smile contritely at Etta. 'Why, to be sure.'

'Will I fetch it?' offered Uncle Mal, rising. 'I want to go for a –'

'Thanks, Uncle.' Marty pre-empted any rude utterance.

'– drink of water, anyway,' finished the old man before tottering off.

The washing-up done, Aggie was forced to return and to undergo dialogue with Etta, perching herself uncomfortably on a dining chair. Informed of the vandalism and seeing an unrepentant Jimmy-Joe bound for Etta's other shoe, she snatched his dress and hauled him back, advising the rest of her youngsters, 'Take him out to play for a while afore bed.'

Excited by their brother's choice of bride, the children were loath to miss any crumb of information and had to be forced outside, twelve-year-old Elizabeth tutting sulkily, 'Just call your slave in when you want any more washing-up done!' Then quick as a sprite she ducked outside to escape retribution. However, nothing of much import was to follow, the topics ranging from the hot weather to Etta's outfit, which Aggie deigned to compliment. Her daughter-in-law was indeed a very pretty girl, she could see how Marty would have fallen for her, and she went so far as to say this, Etta's response being equally gracious.

Uncle Mal re-entered then, carrying the glue-pot, which he placed on the table for Marty to collect when he left.

Whilst the old man lowered himself into his chair, Aggie resumed the chit-chat, but the polite conversation was halted by an agonised yelp.

'Sat on me nuts,' explained a pain-faced Uncle Mal.

Redmond cleared his throat noisily, signalling for his wife to say something. Marty wanted to die and dared not lift his eyes from his shoes. Etta fought laughter and pretended she had not heard, saying, 'It's remarkably light still, isn't it? The children must appreciate these summer nights.'

'Indeed, indeed,' nodded Redmond, puffing embarrassedly at his pipe and brushing at his trouser leg to remove imaginary specks.

'Right, enough of this codology,' said Aggie from her seat at the table, her tone quiet but determined, her eyes on the newly married couple. 'I want to know where we stand.' She dismissed her husband's look of quiet recrimination. 'We've a right to know if the girl's father's going to come around and knock us flat.'

'He won't come here,' said Etta, beating Marty to this disclosure. 'He's washed his hands of me.'

Holding her daughter-in-law's eyes, Aggie saw the flicker of pain in them and allowed slight compassion into her voice. 'Well, I'm sorry about that, but I can't say I'm not

102

relieved that my son isn't to get another beating on your account.'

Etta felt immediately challenged, a sense of rivalry forcing her to declare, 'And so am I. It wasn't my intention that he should receive the first.' She looked at Marty's father to include him in her answer, but to her dismay he seemed so uninterested as to be nodding his way towards sleep, and so she addressed herself solely to the matriarch. 'Your son is very dear to me, Mrs Lanegan.' It sounded idiotic saying that when she was Mrs Lanegan too, but at that moment she could never contemplate addressing this woman as Mother; nor, she felt, would the other countenance it.

'Dearer than your parents, obviously.' Aggie remained cool.

Marty showed slight annoyance at the hurt inflicted on his loved one. 'Ah well, what's done is done.'

'Doesn't mean it can't be undone,' retorted Aggie. 'You're both under age.'

He looked aghast. 'You're not saying – Ma, surely you wouldn't have the marriage revoked?'

Aggie rapped the table, jolting her husband awake, and projected her full ire at them.

'God almighty, is that all you're bothered about? Don't you know you could be sent to prison for this, the both of yese?'

The newlyweds were flabbergasted.

'For making false declaration! You've both presumably told the registrar that you had your parents' consent when that's a patent lie.' Aggie watched the horror spread over their young faces, letting them stew for a while.

Etta was on the verge of tears at the thought of being parted from her beloved. 'Oh, I beg you not to be so cruel!'

'Cruel?' Aggie's temper was rising. 'You turn a son against his parents, make him lie like a serpent to them, and you tell me I'm the cruel one!'

Marty fought to save the situation. 'Etta didn't mean it

like that, Ma! Aw, you wouldn't really ruin our happiness? Not after all Etta's been through. I've told her how great you and Dad are, how you'd understand why we had to do this, that you'd take her to your hearts!'

'Aggie, stop torturing them, they've learned their lesson.' Redmond's quiet intervention put a stop to this, leaving Etta surprised that he had been listening after all, and also grateful when he told the pair, 'We won't give you away, there'd be little point, the damage is done. Oh, but you've hurt us, Marty, by doing it this way.' He shook his head, his voice bitterly accusing. 'You surely have.'

Marty dropped his eyes to the multi-hued clipping rug at his feet. Etta too showed repentance, but both were utterly relieved.

Studying her daughter-in-law's face, Aggie tried to read if her motive was genuine or whether this was all just a big adventure. Only time would tell. After an awkward period, she enquired with a sigh, 'So, are you thinking we'll put the pair of you up?'

Again it was Etta who delivered hasty reassurance. 'Oh no, Mrs Lanegan, we have a place of our own.'

'Thought of everything, haven't ye?' Aggie looked piercingly at her son.

Marty was beginning to tire of the interrogation, saying to Etta, 'Maybe we'd better go now – thanks for the tea, Ma.'

'Our pleasure.' The reply was ironic, Aggie rising with the couple, as did Redmond and Mal. 'Are we permitted to know where you live?'

'Long Close Lane,' Marty told them. 'The Square and Compass.'

Withholding their opinions, his parents merely nodded, but it was obvious what they were thinking.

Etta and Marty took their leave of Uncle Mal, the old man wishing them, 'Good luck now to the pair o' ye. Aye, good luck.'

Accompanying them to the door, Aggie cast her eyes at the neighbours who had dragged chairs onto the pavement to enjoy the evening sunlight, gauging their inquisitive reaction to her elegant guest. What would they say when they found out Marty had married Etta?

'Come to dinner on Sunday,' Redmond suddenly invited.

Marty glanced at his mother, who nodded her permission. But when she had closed the door on them Aggie crowed at her husband, 'Sure and what did you tell 'em that for?'

'Ach, they're a pair of blasted eejits but I feel sorry for them,' admitted Redmond, going back to his chair and his pipe. 'The poor girl, it must have been a terrible shock to find out where Marty was taking her.' He stalled Aggie's objection. 'I don't mean here, you goose! I mean the room above that filthy pub. What a comedown for her.' He cocked his head with a thoughtful air. 'I like the lass, she seems genuine – a real looker, too.'

'A lively and good-looking animal indeed,' agreed Uncle Mal and chuckled wryly. 'My, who would've thought the likes of us'd be marrying into quality.'

'Aye, though how long it'll last now that she's heard your uninhibited talk – sat on your nuts indeed! What a thing to say in front of a lady.'

'She can take us as she finds us,' scoffed Mal. 'She'll hear worse.'

'That's for sure.' Redmond noticed his wife was quiet. 'And what did you make of her, Ag?'

Mrs Lanegan remained grim. 'She strides too proud for my liking.'

'Heavens, what a relief to be out of there!' exclaimed Marty, gripping his wife's hand as they made their way home.

Etta agreed, but smilingly. 'Still, the ordeal is over now.'

'That wasn't a true indication of my mother's nature,' he hastened to say.

'I fear she didn't like me very much.'

'It was just the shock. Once you get to know each other . . .'

'It didn't help that I was unsure how to address her.'

Understanding why Etta might not feel much warmth towards his mother after that display, Marty just shrugged.

But Etta was more interested in his other parent. 'Your father –'

'Ah, yes,' his expression changed. 'You must want to know . . .'

Etta thought she already did in part. 'He appears to have suffered ill-health for a long time. His bearing is very stooped, as if –'

'That just stems from years of being hunched over driving a caravan back and forth across the Pennines.' Marty went on to divulge his father's true affliction. 'He has this illness that makes him fall asleep all the time. He can be anywhere, at home, talking to you quite normal like, or even walking down the street, when he'll just drop off.'

'Goodness! How debilitating.' Etta's face was grave.

'The worst thing is, people think he's a drunkard.' Marty saw her cheeks flush upon recalling that this was the term she herself had used for his father. He smiled and patted her hand. 'Ach, it's a reasonable assumption. In fact, he's abstemious – those beer bottles ye saw were Uncle Mal's. No, Da has very few vices at all, and you'll rarely hear him say a bad word about anybody else – apart from me.' He grinned.

Along the way he provided her with more information. Redmond was unable to keep a post for long once an employer discovered his habit of falling asleep on the job, so relied on casual labour, agricultural or otherwise. He also indulged in a spot of hawking. 'So don't think because you find him home in the middle of the day he's a slacker –'

'Oh, I wouldn't!'

'– when the work's available he drives himself like an ox, and he's a grand man even if he is my father.'

'I thought so too,' smiled Etta.

'Just a bit of a dreamer whose dreams come to nothing – unlike those of his son, whose all come true.' He grinned again and squeezed her acquisitively.

But even having equipped her with this knowledge, Marty was aware how disconcerting it could be when Father slipped into a narcoleptic state. 'You'll still find it strange when he nods off during a conversation with you, but try not to worry, it's not because he isn't interested. Ye'll get used to it, as we all have.' His face altered as he envisaged the depleted sherry bottle. 'Well, Ma sometimes gets worked up about it, says she's sure he could prevent it if he had a mind – 'cause often days'll go by when it doesn't affect him at all. If she seems bad-tempered towards ye it's only 'cause he's been keeping her awake all night with his funny goings-on, nightmares and things. Must've been terrible for her all these years. Anyhow . . .' his voice faded into the night.

Etta was left to utter the last word on the topic as they reached the pub overlooked by the medieval city wall. 'Well, it was very kind of them both to invite us to dinner on Sunday. I shall look forward to it.'

Marty was unconvinced, but nodded and led her up the creaky staircase to their room. 'Ah dear, work tomorrow – how I'm going to miss ye.'

'Better make the most of it then.' Etta shoved him playfully then pelted upstairs. With him hot on her tracks, they slammed the door on the world and went early to bed.

5

What torment it was to leave her the next morning. Mother had always been the first to rise at home, having breakfast ready for when he came down and making sandwiches for his pack-up, but Etta was as yet unused to the household programme so, out of love, Marty rose at five and, besides looking after himself, took a slice of dry bread and a cup of water over to her bed. But at least being his own boss gave him the privilege of deciding what time to start work and he could sneak back into bed and devote half an hour or so to the more vital husbandly duties before finally dragging himself away from her to earn a living.

However, his assumption that possessed of a barrow he would automatically have money in his pocket was to be quickly disproved, as hour after hour the licence-holders took precedence. In fact, by midday he was beginning to feel rather grim, having watched an endless procession of locomotives arrive without him earning so much as a farthing. Previously able to filch dinner from the hotel kitchen, now he had only a paltry wedge of bread to see him through the afternoon. Time and again hope soared as another train disgorged those passengers who were unable to afford a cab and hailed the barrow boys instead, at which point a mad rush for custom would ensue with Marty hovering on the periphery, only to feel like the runt of the litter as the permit-holders grabbed the spoils.

By four o'clock in the afternoon he had collected just a measly sixpence and a spattering of lime from one of the dirty pigeons that perched on the overhead iron supports. Only the thought of Etta kept him going. Hardly a minute had gone by without him thinking about her; not merely lusting – though it was difficult to concentrate on anything else – but also wondering if she was coping with her unfamiliar role as badly as he was. Last night they had drawn up a list of household commodities, which his wife intended to purchase today. He wondered if she had done so yet, and pondered whereabouts she was now . . .

Etta was in fact in the city centre, enjoying afternoon tea at a café and feeling rather smug. With no coachman to drive her she had come here by omnibus: yet another new experience. She was certain her mother had never shopped for food supplies, only for garments of fashion, but with no one to instruct her she had been forced to cope and had done so remarkably well. Aside from the necessary victuals, which she had bought this morning and had stacked away in the cupboard, she had made other purchases: new sheets and pillows for their bed, the ones included in the furnished room being rather fusty and bearing the smell and imprint of previous lodgers' heads; a dress for everyday wear, a pair of summer gloves, two aprons and some underwear. These were being delivered later, along with several yards of material to make new curtains, which was very daring as she had not made anything like this before. Achieving all of these at a bargain price enabled her to buy an artist's pad and a small box of watercolours without feeling extravagant – oh, and a bottle of rosewater – and she was feeling very proud of herself as she perched here sipping tea. Further purchases of some canvas and skeins of embroidery silk were enclosed in the brown paper parcel on the chair beside her. What luck that, being a skilled needlewoman, she could soon make their home much more congenial – and still have money left! With a surge of happiness she consumed the last crumb of cake, the final sip of tea, and made for home, imagining how equally proud her husband would be at her thrift.

Ashamed of how little he had earned, Marty now leapt at any opportunity of enterprise – tuppence for giving directions to a lady, sixpence for looking after a gentleman's horse – but was still left wondering what to say to his wife as he finally trundled his barrow home that evening.

As it transpired he was to be rendered totally speechless, first by Etta's mouth as she ran to greet him with a devouring kiss, then by the pristine linen that graced the bed, its whiteness leaping out from the drab background – then by the new dress she wore. Oh Lord, how much had she spent?

But she was so excited that he did not have the heart to scold her for such extravagance, nor for the fact that no meal awaited him as it had always done at home. Besides, Etta rattled off an explanation for this.

'I've arranged for the landlady, Mrs Dalton, to cook that meat you instructed me to buy – did you realise it would have to be cooked? I got it home, then thought, How on earth shall I roast it with no fire?' Displaying all the innocence of a newly hatched chick, she indicated the empty grate with its pile of grey ashes.

'There is a kitchen downstairs for our use,' Marty told her, smiling.

'I'm aware of that now! There's also a sitting room, but it's far too smoky for my liking – besides, we prefer our own company. Anyway, Mrs Dalton was very nice, asked if we wanted anything to go with it, so I told her some potatoes and beans would be very acceptable. I hadn't bought any of those so she said we could have some of hers – naturally I expected to pay for it.'

'Naturally.' Marty smiled at her childlike air and embraced her. In fact they spent a good while after this hugging and kissing, until Mrs Dalton finally disturbed them with the prepared meal.

Shocked but delighted by the size of the joint of beef – the butcher had certainly seen this ingénue coming – Marty wondered whether he would find anything in the drawer with which to carve it, making do with a small but sharp knife he unearthed from the odd assortment of cutlery. He had not realised just how many items one took for granted.

The meal was delicious. Moreover, the joint being so large, it would see them right through to Saturday night. Etta looked delighted when he mopped the last of the juices from his plate, patted his stomach and told her how clever she had been.

'And just how clever you have yet to hear!' She sprang up, cut the string on a brown paper parcel and ripped the latter open to display the fabric therein. 'I intend to make curtains and tablecloths – you won't know this room by next week!'

Marty congratulated her, but tendered uneasily, 'Better not get too many things for this place though, we'll be moving as soon as I have the means.' He rose and wandered over to cast an eye into the cupboard to see what else she had bought. After spending over a guinea on the wedding ring he needed to keep a check. Thankfully there seemed only items of necessity here, bread, butter, cheese and a few other things. 'How much did you have to part with?' He tried to sound casual.

'I can't recall how much the groceries were – but I managed to acquire everything here for less than five pounds.' Unaware of how shocked Marty was, she quickly totted up the coins in her purse. 'Two pounds, two shillings and threepence left!' Her satisfied smile turned to guilt. 'Oh, here's me forgetting to ask! Did you have as successful a day?'

It was Marty's turn to feel guilty then. 'Well, not really – but I'll set off earlier tomorrow so as to beat the competition.'

111

My God, he would have to do much better than today if that was the way she was accustomed to spending. He was diverted by something else, frowning as he looked about. 'You know, there's a queer pong around here.'

'I know!' Etta wrinkled her nose too. Not even the smell of roast beef could mask it. 'I shut the window to keep it out but it became so terribly hot and the wretched smell seeped through regardless . . .'

'I think it's something in here.' Following his nostrils that were flared with distaste, Marty discovered the source of the offending stench. 'Oh . . . the potty hasn't been emptied.' Stooping by the bed, he levelled a finger at the chamber pot, almost full to the brim.

'Ah!' Etta gave a nod of disgust. 'Who should we send for?'

He was about to laugh, but felt that she might take offence, and, as kindly as he could, attempted to inform her of her housewifely duties. 'Well, 'twas always a woman's job at home.'

Etta had never given the slightest thought as to who was responsible for this task in her previous household, but now, as she contemplated the revolting vessel, the fact that she had no servant was reinforced, and from the way that Martin was looking at her it slowly dawned that he was implying the job fell to her.

Seeing the look of revulsion spread over his wife's patrician features, Marty took pity on her. 'Oh, I'll do it this time, it's a bit heavy for you.' Trying not to disturb its layer of scum and so create a worse reek, he dragged the pot from under the bed and, treading gingerly to avoid slopping its contents over the rim, bore it downstairs and out the back to the water closet.

'We'll try to use it as little as possible,' he told her upon his return with a clean receptable. 'Then there won't be so much to empty.'

'I shan't use it at all,' vowed Etta, shuddering.

'Well, you women can hold your bladders better than we fellas can,' grinned Marty, shoving the pot under the bed. 'But a little bit of tiddle during the night shouldn't be too much of an imposition.'

That being the summit of their conversation about such mundane subjects, they were soon falling into bed to initiate the new sheets.

As reluctant to leave her the next day as he had been the one before, somehow he managed to tear himself away and off to work, only the thought of being with her again helping to drag him through each hour as he strove to earn a decent day's wage. But by evening, with just another shilling in his pocket, it seemed as if this was going to require drastic action.

He arrived home to find the table once again divest of food, his wife intent on her embroidery, though this didn't matter for the cold meat would quickly be served and Etta jumped up to greet him in her usual passionate manner and to declare how much she had missed him.

'I wasn't so clever as I thought yesterday,' she laughed as, after filling his stomach, her husband asked what she had been doing. 'I omitted to buy a needle, so I had to go down and ask to borrow one from Mrs Dalton. It took her so long to find it that I felt I must offer her sixpence for her trouble.'

Marty bit his tongue, and instead of saying that Etta could have bought a whole packet of needles for that, he observed her handiwork and said how pretty it looked. 'I'd no idea you were so talented.'

'Oh, there are lots of things you don't know about me,' she laughed teasingly.

That was certainly true, conceded Marty. Just because he knew her in spirit did not remove the fact that there was much to learn about her good and bad points, but then the same must be going through Etta's mind. 'Still,' he

113

offered a little judicious advice, 'maybe we shouldn't keep bothering Mrs Dalton. Ma should be able to provide anything you need. She's only round the corner.'

'So she is,' replied Etta brightly. 'I shall make a list and present it to her on Sunday.'

Marty wondered what his mother's reaction would be when shown the list.

But he was glad when the Sabbath came, in more ways than one. Saturday night at the pub turned out to be rather boisterous and the drunken goings-on were to keep him and Etta awake into the early hours. Just as well that the day afterwards he could legitimately take a day off work and linger in bed with his ravishing wife, and upon becoming too hungry to laze there any longer, could rise and, as his father had always done, shave at his leisure and put on his best clothes, not because he was going anywhere special but simply because it was Sunday.

Getting spruced up and having a gorgeous companion on one's arm was pleasure enough, but more importantly there was a decent meal to look forward to, for since Mrs Dalton had cooked for them he and Etta had not enjoyed anything more substantial than bread and cold meat and the latter was now gone. Hence, the young couple were to arrive early at the family abode, finding Mrs Lanegan sweating over a hot range. There were no assistants today; all the children were at church.

Etta was concerned that she might be responsible for keeping her husband from similar devotion, but Marty just grinned and exposed the holiness as a sham. 'Ma only sends them so's they won't cop a beating at school on Monday for not going to Mass.'

Invited by her mother-in-law to remove her hat and to sit down, Etta took this at face value, oblivious to the toil around her, and, along with her husband, set to chatting with the quiet, unassuming Mr Lanegan and Uncle Mal, both of whom she found just as affable as on her previous

114

visit. Though annoyed that the other failed to volunteer, Aggie said nothing, just got on with what needed to be done.

Even later when dinner was served and Etta allowed herself to be waited on hand and foot, the mother-in-law remained polite, though she inwardly damned the girl for her airs and graces.

Ignorant as to how she was perceived, at the end of the meal Etta thanked her hostess for such generous provision. As if to some servant, griped Aggie to herself, but inclined her head graciously as she and her daughters cleared the table and said, 'Maybe everyone would care to sit in the front parlour now.'

Etta went to sit amongst the males, feeling somewhat conspicuous in the same lilac dress she had worn upon first meeting the Lanegan family, but the one she had bought during the week was far too plain for Sunday wear so she had sprinkled the lilac one with rosewater and made do. Everyone else had on their Sunday best, and though she could not help noticing that Redmond's waistcoat bore a few holes and scorch marks, he had made an effort to dress up. As had Uncle Mal, with a gleaming white collar instead of the neckerchief and his white hair neatly slicked with oil. This, however, was where the observance to dress code ended. Etta was accustomed to changing several times a day, especially for dinner, which in her own household had taken place in the evening, afternoon tea having been between four and five, but she had found that this did not occur in Marty's circle, who would have their tea as soon as the breadwinner came in from work and then little else until breakfast. On the one hand she preferred this less restrictive atmosphere, yet on the other it was nice to looks one's best and she wondered how long it would be before she could acquire more decent apparel. But, compared to a smile from her beloved, this was as nothing. Catching Marty's gleaming eye, she smiled back at him, each bestowing quiet adoration.

'Are you a fairy?' enquired four-year-old Tom, who had been dying for confirmation since the young woman's last visit.

Etta chuckled delightedly and said, 'A mere mortal, I'm afraid.'

Tom gave a disappointed nod. 'I thought you were too big to fit in the clock.'

Seeing his daughter-in-law perplexed, Redmond explained as he reached for a pipe. 'We have the little people living in our clock, don't we, Uncle Mal?'

'We surely do, Red,' grunted old Malachy, sharing a pouch of tobacco with him.

Etta caught the barely perceptible wink. 'How wonderful! And what are their names?' she asked Tom.

The little boy listed them. 'I've never seen them, but Daddy has, haven't you, Daddy?'

Redmond nodded and, glowing pipe in mouth, dragged Tom onto his bony knee. 'And very good-looking they are – that's why the lad thought you must be related.'

Etta thanked him, both fascinated and envious at the ease with which father and child related. Never had she sat upon her father's knee, not even as an infant.

Aggie came back in then.

'We were just telling Etta about our little people,' divulged Redmond.

'Were you indeed?' Aggie wondered how he could find conversation so easy with the girl. She herself was struggling.

'Sometimes they leave me money when one of my teeth falls out,' said Tom, then gave a theatrical sigh of disappointment and surveyed Etta from beneath long eyelashes.

Interpreting the hint, and remembering how she herself had received monetary gifts from visiting aunts and uncles, a smiling Etta delved in her pocket. 'Well, it's a curious thing but last night a fairy came to visit me,' she saw the little boy's face light up as she proffered a coin, 'and she asked that, should I happen to see a boy named Tom, I pass this on to him.'

Delighted, Tom slipped off his father's knee to accept the penny.

Albeit enchanted at the way his wife played the game, Marty wished she was not so free with their funds.

Aggie, too, deemed it most extravagant, though she told Tom to thank his benefactor before leading him from the room. 'Better come and put it in your moneybox, so it'll be safe.'

And, under his mother's careful instruction, Tom went to the understairs cupboard and inserted his penny in the gas meter.

Redmond maintained the conversation with his daughter-in-law, an engaging smile on his frail countenance as he puffed on his pipe. 'So, and how are you managing with your new life, Etta? I expect you find us a strange lot.'

'Not at all, Mr Lanegan,' Etta assured him, noting that Jimmy-Joe had sidled up to kneel at her feet, and she quickly moved her tasselled shoes out of temptation. 'I'm managing very well. It's very good of you to ask, and so kind of you to invite us to luncheon – Martin, we must return the favour.'

Re-entering with Tom, Aggie pursed her lips at the way this was delivered, as if Etta were dealing with some mere social contact. 'It wasn't done out of politeness. This is Marty's family, and yours too now.'

It held the slightest barb but Etta caught it. Mrs Lanegan had not yet forgiven her. Very well, if she wanted to be so petty, Etta would turn that last statement to her advantage.

'You're so kind. In that case, might I perhaps borrow one or two items until Martin and I have found our feet?' She produced a scrap of paper and began to recite from it.

Recognising that she had brought this on herself, Aggie was magnanimous. 'I expect I can provide them before you go.'

'Thank you,' smiled Etta. 'And you really must come to tea with us one afternoon – perhaps next Sunday?'

'Us too?' came ten-year-old Maggie's eager query.

Marty leapt in. 'Maybe just the grown-ups for now, Mags, we haven't room for everyone.'

Etta sought to appease the crestfallen girl. 'But you and Elizabeth are welcome to call through the week whenever you like. I should be glad of the company whilst your brother is at work.'

'We've got school through the week,' provided a sulky Elizabeth.

'Afterwards then.' Etta looked envious. 'Oh, I should love to have had an education but my parents didn't see the need.'

'You can go in my place,' came the suggestion.

'Enough of that,' scolded Red. 'An education is important if you're to get anywhere in life.'

'Some of us still end up doing the washing-up,' muttered Elizabeth.

But Maggie had taken to her sister-in-law and also to her clothes. 'I love that dress, Etta.'

Red assured her, 'You shall have one like it yourself some day.'

'So may we expect you on Sunday?' Etta asked her mother-in-law.

Aggie nodded. 'Thank you, we'll arrange what to –' She broke off as a familiar couple passed the window and a tap at the door quickly ensued. 'Oh, there's only one reason *she*'s here!'

Nobody rushed to respond for now, Marty explaining in a whisper to Etta, 'Aunty Joan and Uncle John. We don't see them very much, Aunt Joan's a bit . . .'

'More than a bit,' came Aggie's sour interjection. 'Sure, I wondered how long the news would take to reach her.' She grimaced at Redmond who seemed none too keen on the visitors either, but, as the front door was already ajar because of the heat and signified that the family was at home, he had no option but to shout, 'Come in, we're open for public viewing!' Though the look on his face belied his cheery invitation.

Mr Lanegan's brother seemed inoffensive enough, if anything a little reserved. His wife too appeared quite timid, everything about her being mouse-like, from the colour of her hair and her tiny pointed chin to her dainty feet, but it quickly became evident why she was unpopular. Etta sensed embarrassment from everyone as, ignoring them, Martin's aunt came directly to her with an ingratiating display that almost bordered on genuflection.

'We're so privileged to meet you!' beamed the mousy woman with a hushed, reverential tone, her Yorkshire accent polished around the consonants though not the vowels. 'We've heard so much about you – how fortunate our nephew is!'

Etta replied politely, 'I assure you I am the fortunate one, Mrs Lanega –'

'Lane!' corrected the other quickly, whilst maintaining her fawning stance.

'I'm sorry, Mrs Lane.' Etta looked to her husband for explanation.

Marty used his eyes to warn her not to say more. He would have to tell her later: whilst Redmond Lanegan celebrated his Irishness, the bigotry of others had scarred his brother John, who preferred to Anglicise his surname and temper his accent, which was how he had acquired his snob of a wife.

'But you must call me Aunt, now that we're related,' Joan told Etta, her perky rodent face beaming.

'How are you, Aunty Joan?' Marty conjured a smile but was granted the briefest of acknowledgements, her sights fixed solely on Etta, guzzling every detail of the lilac and cream silk dress, every tuck, ribbon, pleat and sprig of lace.

119

'What an exquisite gown!' she breathed. 'Such a shame you've nowhere more decent to wear it.'

Stunned by such rudeness, Etta sought to defend her hostess. 'Martin's mother cooked a wonderful luncheon.'

Joan beheld her pityingly. 'You must come to us next time.' Then her eye was briefly drawn to the hostess's outfit, which she eyed with an enquiring smile. 'Is that a new dress, Agnes?'

Aggie seemed mildly surprised that Joan had noticed. She looked down at herself. 'Aye, I got the stuff in Hardings' sale – two and eleven.'

Joan reached over to rub the material between her fingers as if admiring it, then said quietly, 'Yes, it is a bit cottony, isn't it – nice though.'

Aggie looked at her son with an expression that asked why had she fallen for it? The only reason she suffered Joan was because of her marriage to Redmond's brother.

But Etta saw the hurt face and, feeling sorry for her mother-in-law, enquired admiringly of Aggie, 'Did you make it yourself? How clever. I could never hope to achieve your expertise, nor match your cookery skills. I don't know how I shall compete next Sunday, or any other come to that.'

Aggie was grudging. 'Ah, well, I'm always here if you get stuck.'

Somehow – possibly on purpose – Etta mistook this offer of assistance as a regular invitation to Sunday dinner. Aggie could not say in front of Joan that this was not what she had meant at all. Feeling trapped and more agitated than ever, she excused herself, ostensibly to put the kettle on; in reality to take a calming glass of sherry.

Joan hardly missed a beat. 'So, erm, tell me, Etta, when shall we meet your family?' She perched genteelly beside her, desperate for an invitation to what must be a grand house.

'Regretfully, never, Mrs Lane,' replied Etta sadly. 'My elopement with Martin put paid to further contact.'

120

Her hopes dashed upon learning that Etta had come here with nothing, Joan clutched the pearl brooch at her throat. 'So, you weren't able to bring any servants? Oh dear, but I must lend you mine!' Never in her dreams had Joan hoped to make such a statement to so illustrious a person.

Redmond glanced at Marty, both inwardly cringing for the husband, though mild-mannered John barely flinched.

Aggie came back just in time to catch Joan's offer. It was obvious to Marty that his mother had been at the sherry, for her cheeks had that telltale flush and her voice was bolder. 'And how long have you had a servant?' she demanded of her sister-in-law.

The latter smiled condescendingly. 'You know very well Edith's been with us for ages!'

'Oh, you mean the lodger.' Aggie sniffed and handed a cup to Marty, who caught the glint of malice in her eye and tried to hide a smile.

Joan was huffy. 'Well, of course she lodges with us, servants do lodge with their employer.'

Aggie merely nodded, though the action was loaded with disbelief. It seemed not to dampen Joan's enthusiasm, for she continued to fawn over Etta throughout the afternoon, and as the hours progressed it became obvious that both parties were intent on stopping for tea. It would have been bad enough having to cope with her sister-in-law at the best of times, but with Red succumbing to one of his bouts of narcolepsy in mid-sentence and Etta here to witness everything and think them all crazy, the pressure began to build. There was a limit to how many times one could keep disappearing to the kitchen for alcoholic support, but her disapproving husband was unconscious, and besides, there was justifiable reason to bring out the liquor.

'I've just realised we haven't toasted the bride and groom,' announced Aggie, going to a cabinet that held glasses, Marty's new wife being the first to be asked, 'Would you care for a sherry?'

Etta showed misgivings over the size of the tumbler in her mother-in-law's hand, but, not wanting to offend, replied, 'Thank you, perhaps a smaller glass.'

Aggie stiffened at the implication that she did not understand etiquette. 'Well, I wasn't thinking to offer you it in this! We might be poor but we do have the correct receptacle. This is for those who prefer beer.'

Feeling that she could do nothing right, Etta apologized. Unobtrusively, Marty gripped her fingers in a gesture of support as his mother took a selection of glasses to the scullery.

'Can I carry anything, Ma?' he called in afterthought.

'No, stay there!' her voice came back. Measuring out a glass, she threw it down her own throat – her fifth today – before pouring some for Etta and Joan, overfilling the glasses and transporting these gingerly to the front parlour.

Marty beheld his mother, saw that a film of inebriation coated her eyes, and rose to take one of the glasses for Etta. Aggie made to hand the other to Joan, but as she went so carefully forward she lurched, and, by accident or design, half the contents of the glass were spattered down her sister-in-law's blouse.

Joan squeaked and demanded her husband's handkerchief with which to mop frenziedly at the brown stain.

'Oh dear.' Aggie swayed tipsily. Her glazed eyes looked at the glass in her hand and saw that it was not quite empty – and she knocked back the remaining dregs before asking Joan, 'Would you care for another?'

'I think I've had sufficient,' mumbled the victim, still dabbing. Totally humiliated before the guest, she and her husband were immediately to depart.

The others managed to stifle their merriment until they were out of earshot, Uncle Mal wheezing and mopping his eyes, the children giggling into their chests, Etta looking first unsure, then joining in.

'– so, all in all I think I prefer the subtle approach.' Redmond woke as abruptly as he had dropped off, finishing the remainder of his sentence as was common to these episodes.

Marty laughed outright, braying to Etta, 'I think Aunty Joan would have preferred it too!'

Retrieving his pipe from his chest, where it had singed yet another hole in his waistcoat whilst he slept, a bemused Redmond looked round. 'They've gone then? Thank Christ. God knows what my brother sees in that woman. But then love knows no bounds, as they say.' He grinned at Etta and puffed happily to reignite the pipe, before noting with a frown of disapproval that there was alcohol about. 'Where did that spring from?'

Her attention drawn to the glass of sherry in her hand, Aggie manufactured surprise. 'This? Oh, 'tis that bottle I've had since Christmas.' In fact it was the third this year, provided by a relative who worked for an unsuspecting wine merchant.

Marty covered for his mother. 'Ma was very kindly just about to toast me and Etta, Da.'

Redmond eyed his wife's florid countenance, but made no recrimination. 'Well, as you know, I'm not a drinking man, but I will wish you both good health and a thousand blessings – not all of them children I hasten to add.' He smiled at his daughter-in-law.

Glasses were raised. Unable to avoid it, Aggie said to her son, 'I suppose you'll be stopping for tea?'

In view of the meagre pickings at home, Marty hastily accepted. 'That'll be grand.'

'But you really must allow us to entertain you next Sunday afternoon,' Etta reminded her in-laws.

'Oh, that we will!' Sick of being taken for granted, Aggie spoke assuredly. 'Won't we, Red?'

Her husband seemed dubious, shaking his head as he weighed the matter. 'Well now, that rather depends –'

Etta held her breath, awaiting some stern condition as her father-in-law directed his question solely at her.

123

'– on whether your relatives are as bad as ours, and whether they'll be dropping in unannounced.'

Spotting the mischievous gleam, she chuckled with relief. 'Whether they are or not is debatable, Mr Lanegan, but I rather doubt that any of them will be dropping in unexpectedly, next Sunday or otherwise.'

'Thank heaven for that,' said Red with a humorous wink at Uncle Mal. 'Then we'll look forward to it.'

Aggie heard Etta chuckle too, but unlike the others and despite her alcoholic intake she saw past the amusement, gauging the hurt in the girl's response. How dreadful to be ostracised by one's family. Aggie felt mean now at begrudging the lass a sporting chance, for wasn't it natural that it would take Etta a while to get to grips with her new life – and there was no doubting that she held Marty in great esteem when she had given up so much to be with him. How could one deny her a bit of leeway? Aggie stumbled off to make tea, not minding so much now that Etta did not offer to help, even saying as the young couple finally departed, 'Now remember what I said, I'm always here if you need anything.'

Marty tendered a cautious plea. 'Er, in that case might we nab a few lumps of coal, Ma, so's we can boil a kettle?' Quickly taking advantage of the generous response, he went out to the yard and filled two buckets.

'A few lumps, says he!' observed Red to Uncle Mal when it was time for his son to leave. 'And his arms swung low as a monkey's under the weight of it.'

'It's only slack in the other!' Marty showed them.

'Slack's the word,' muttered Red.

Etta promised swiftly, 'We'll return it as soon as we're able.'

'Sure he's codding yese.' Aggie swiped at her husband, who smiled to show this was true.

Etta gave warm thanks as she left clutching the bag of items that her mother-in-law had supplied in response to her list, feeling so much more confident than upon her first meeting with Aggie.

'You were right about your mother.' She clutched Marty's arm fondly. 'I think we shall be great friends.'

6

On Monday morning, Marty was first up again to light a fire for Etta, because despite the heat wave being unabated she would need it for all that must be done today. By the time his wife rose he had made a pot of tea and buttered some bread and had also made extra to take with him for lunch. Knowing how completely ignorant she was of housework, once the fire took hold he banked it up with slack, advising her to make sure it did not go out by adding a lump from time to time whilst he was at work.

Once Marty had gone, having swept up the crumbs from breakfast, stamped on any beetles and silverfish that happened to scurry her way, smoothed the bedclothes and filled the water jug from the tap downstairs, Etta forced herself to empty the chamber pot – a disgusting chore even though the contents were shallow. Downstairs, in the passageway to the yard she was forced to step over the landlord's daughter who was on her hands and knees scrubbing the floor. The publican himself was in the taproom cleaning out the spittoon and looked up as she passed the doorway. It was hard to maintain one's dignity when carrying a chamber pot, but Etta managed a smile and a good morning to both as if merely out on a stroll and not to the lavatory. The latter could only be accessed by passing through a urinal. Praying there would be no one in it, she rushed through, completed the deed, then hurried back upstairs to stow the pot under the bed.

Then, in happier vein, she dabbed her complexion with rosewater, put on her hat and white gloves and went to restock provisions. During her leisurely stroll to the shops she happened to notice youths on bicycles with large wicker baskets calling at certain households, and ascertained that they were making deliveries from various trades persons. Ah, so that was what one did! She made a mental note to give regular instruction to the butcher, the baker and the grocer – though of course their commodities would still have to be turned into meals and she had yet to acquire this trick. So, heeding her mother-in-law's previous generosity, on her way back she sought Aggie's guidance.

Aggie was out in the yard, one sinewy arm winding the mangle, the other steering countless items between its rollers. The sun was almost to its zenith now and the yard was like a furnace, but this was one day when she would have no complaint, for the bedding that had been hanging out since just after breakfast was already dry. Shaking off the flecks of soot that had floated down from the chimneys, she removed the sheets and pillowcases from the line and replaced them with another selection of wet articles. Having pegged out the final garment she could now go in and snatch a bite to eat before an afternoon's work. Thank heaven the girls had returned from school and could serve up dinner.

She had just mopped the sweat from her brow and seated herself with Uncle Mal and the children when a polite tap came at the open front door. Tutting, she craned her neck to see Etta there with an expectant smile.

'You did say I could call on you should I need advice . . . ?'

'So I did, come in.' Aggie rose as her daughter-in-law entered. 'Will you take a bit of dinner with us while you're here?'

'I should be delighted.' Etta dealt her a pleased smile and took a chair at the table, engaging in small talk with the others whilst Aggie fetched an extra setting. 'Will Martin's father not be joining us?'

'He's found work over at Poppleton,' supplied Uncle Mal, leaning nearer for his white-stubbled jaw to murmur a winking addition, 'That's why herself is in such a grand mood, she likes the spondulicks.'

Etta smiled as her mother-in-law came back and laid a plate before her.

Her hostess returned the amiability. 'Washing done already?'

Glancing through the window and noting the clothes hanging on the line, Etta misinterpreted this as a statement and merely nodded in acknowledgement.

Aggie looked impressed. 'You'll be spending the afternoon like me, then.' She was forced to add a word of explanation to the somewhat puzzled listener. 'Ironing! Normally I wouldn't do it until Tuesday – it would be more sensible, I suppose, to wait until it's cooler, but this sun's got them dry in no time so I might as well make a start.'

'Quite . . .' Etta remained nonplussed.

'Not till after dinner but.' Aggie laughed and doled out a ladle of hash. 'Here, tuck in. 'Tis only the beef left over from Sunday, but there's plenty of spuds. Hope it's to your liking.'

'Thank you, I'm sure it will be,' said Etta, even though it was obvious that the best of the meat had been consumed yesterday, the contents of her plate having a rich vein of fat.

However, the gravy was extremely tasty and after a great deal of trimming she enjoyed her dinner, during its consumption telling Aggie and Uncle Mal and the children what she had learned that morning about the tradesmen making deliveries, announcing proudly, 'So, this afternoon I shall set about organising my own supplies of groceries and bread, etcetera.'

Aggie's own enjoyment of the meal was fast becoming spoiled by her daughter-in-law's finicky eating habits and the mound of perfectly edible meat that was building up on the side of Etta's plate. Consequently the tone of her reply was distinctly unimpressed. 'Most folk around here make their own bread.'

'Oh . . .' Taken off-guard, Etta looked crestfallen, but soon rallied. 'Would you perhaps teach me then?'

'On a Monday with all this washing? If you've a mind to be here at five tomorrow morning, maybe.' Then, feeling churlish, Aggie reminded herself of yesterday's resolution and added more kindly, 'Still, you'll have Marty to see to then. I'll write the instructions down for you after we've eaten, 'tis easy enough.'

Etta thanked her, daintily speared the last few pieces of potato and duly laid down her cutlery.

'Have you had sufficient?' Aggie eyed the other's leavings.

The reply was polite. 'Yes, thank you, that was excellent.'

Uncle Mal's clouded blue eyes were in fact as keen as a hawk's. 'Can I be having that if she doesn't want it?'

Aggie responded with a terse nod, at which a bemused Etta watched the old man snatch the plate from under her nose and devour the bits of fat in no time.

Annoyed at them both – Mal for showing her up with his lack of manners, Etta for her prissy habits – Aggie finished her meal in silence, then laid down her own knife and fork and rose with a gruff command to her daughters. 'Come on now, you've school to get back to.'

There was a hasty scraping of plates, which the girls then took to the scullery where Elizabeth wrinkled her nose and whispered to her sister, 'For somebody posh she stinks awful bad.' Both tittered as they set about washing up before going off to class.

Whilst Aggie checked her washing, Etta sat and chatted

happily to Uncle Mal and the little boys, all of whom seemed to hang on her every word, much to Aggie's disgust.

'Now, you'll be wanting that bread receipt so's you can get on with other things!' Coming back into the room, she searched for a scrap of paper and a pencil.

'Oh, there's no need for you to hurry,' said Etta brightly.

'Best I do it now so I don't forget. I'll just put these on to warm while I write it out for ye.' Firm of hand, Aggie set a couple of irons near the fire and spread an old blanket over the table ready to tackle her linen, hoping Etta would take the hint.

But no, even after receiving instruction on the baking of bread, her daughter-in-law was to sit there well into the afternoon, chattering contentedly about all sorts of nonsense as Aggie herself laboured non-stop.

Halfway through the first stack of ironing, her brow dripping, Aggie paused to brew tea. Only at this point did it occur to Etta that perhaps she had been there long enough, though she did not actually leave until having partaken of a cup; after all there was nothing other to do at home once she had spoken to the tradesmen but to wait for her husband to return. 'Thank you for the bread receipt,' she smiled at Aggie upon exiting. 'I shall certainly try it out tomorrow.'

Aggie made sure her daughter-in-law had gone before spluttering her objection to Uncle Mal. 'Wouldn't you think she'd at least take it upon herself to mash a pot of tea! Letting me wait on her hand and bloody foot, and me with all this ironing, the dilatory biddy. I don't know what she expected marriage to be. Did she imagine she'd sit on her arse all day playing madrigals?'

The old man's watery blue eyes turned to slits, his laughter rattling up from deep within his chest. 'Looks like it'll be lean pickings for poor Marty.'

'Puh!' Aggie seized a fresh iron, aiming a contemptuous spurt of saliva that evaporated with a hiss. 'He's too besotted to notice she isn't feeding him – but he

130

needn't think he can come round here every Sunday for a decent meal.' She dashed the hot iron at another pile of linen, working it into pleats and tucks. 'I'll put up with it for so long whilst she sorts herself out, but I won't run around after them forever. He's made his bed, he can lie on it.'

At that moment Marty was wishing fervently that he was in that very bed, cuddled up beside his heavenly wife instead of in a bleak railway station being aggravated by the inane cooing of soot-covered pigeons. The morning had been another complete disaster; not a penny had he made. One small mercy: still in possession of her own money, it had not occurred to Etta to ask him yet how much he had earned, but that time would surely come. How could he admit that his retort to Pybus Ibbetson about being able to look after her had been an empty boast? The pittance he had acquired would not even keep himself, let alone a wife. What kind of man would she think he was? It was the thought of Etta's disappointment that inspired him to take a drastic step. There was no alternative but to risk the other barrow boys' wrath and muscle his way in.

Alas, lack of muscle was part of the problem. He had tried to push to the front before and all it had earned him was a blow to the kidneys from the man nicknamed Custard Lugs. Knowing that in addition to his fists the latter also used a life preserver, and having seen the damage it had inflicted on others, did not bolster Marty's confidence either. But he was not without guile, and during his hours of boredom he had noticed a nice little hidey-hole from where one might make a sudden dash – so long as the station master who enforced the rules was otherwise engaged. Being an affable sort, Marty had previously tried to curry favour with the head man, confiding his newlywed status and his lack of funds, but, though gaining sympathy, it had not done him much good in the short term for the other had

131

said there was no way he could help unless Marty had a licence.

In desperation, he decided that the time had come for ambush. Keeping alert to the position of his rivals and to the whereabouts of the bowler-hatted station master, he hid himself away to await the next train.

Upon an echoing announcement from the loud-speaker, Marty tensed himself for action and, with the subsequent rumble of an approaching engine, made ready to bolt. The train ground to a halt, doors were thrown open, the porter stepped forth to assist the alighting passengers and raised his hand for a barrow boy. This was the signal for which Marty had been waiting and he shot from his hiding place as if from a canon, hurling his barrow before him, its wheels rattling fit to fly off as he pelted forth, his face a picture of joyful expectancy.

But another had set his sights on this customer too, and with neither being willing to give way it became horribly apparent that there was to be a collision of barrows. Marty flinched as he saw it was Custard Lugs, but there was no backing down now. Urged on by thoughts of Etta, face displaying his determination to his opponent, he injected every ounce of energy into his limbs, but at the last minute, when his barrow seemed set to collide with the other, he performed the most daring of moves, halting stock-still as if to allow Custard Lugs past, but instead, with a deft flick of his barrow, sweeping the man's feet from under him and sending him tumbling with a violent clatter, at which point he propelled himself forth again, slewing around the obstacle and continuing his sprint, to arrive triumphantly before the customer, who placed a shiny reward into his hand.

With his most violent rival nursing an injured kneecap it was to be the first of many rewards that afternoon as Marty hurtled his barrow frantically to and fro. So hard won, this chance was not to be wasted. Initially he had proposed to throw the money on the table in a theatrical gesture of largesse, smiling to himself as he pictured Etta's happiness and admiration in his enterprise. But then, sense prevailed. Once this cash was spent there was no guarantee of more, for Custard Lugs would soon be on his feet again and seeking retribution; whereas if he bought a licence – and there was enough in his pocket now to do so – this would ensure future earnings without him having to fight for it. Pleased with himself for such a mature decision, he set about acquiring the means to a brighter future.

All this was relayed to Etta at the end of a very eventful day, but he confessed between chuckles and kisses that, 'Custard Lugs has marked my card, though, you can expect me to come home with an egg on my skull when he's fit enough to catch me.'

She frowned. 'He throws eggs?'

'No, you clot!' He kissed her, laughing. 'I mean a bump from his cosh.'

'Oh, goodness!'

'Don't worry! He's not up to your father's standards of violence – sorry, I shouldn't have said that,' he added hurriedly upon seeing her hurt expression and kissing it better. 'It was thoughtless of me, I'm sorry.'

'It doesn't matter – but he won't really hurt you, will he?' She was greatly concerned.

'Nah! I'll keep out of his way. He can't do much to stop me earning money now I've got a licence, so things are looking up, me darlin'.' His happy smile convinced her. After a few more kisses, he said, 'Will we eat?' And he let go of her, rubbing his palms together and looking around the room to see if anything was different, his eyes settling on the weak glow of embers in the grate. 'I expect you'll have had a busy day yourself.'

'A busy afternoon, certainly.' Briefly, she showed him how far her embroidery had progressed, then put it aside to attend to the tea. 'The fire made me so hot during the morning that I was forced to leave the house. Once the sun moved around it wasn't so bad but even with the window open I was stifled. I did heed your advice about adding the occasional lump of coal, yet I was also conscious of the need to conserve our little bucket of fuel. That's why the fire's so low, if you're wondering.' There had never been a fire in summer in her parents' drawing room, but now she recognised that perhaps the servants must have had to suffer one in order to boil a kettle. Using a poker to swing her own kettle off the embers and a rag to hold its handle, she proceeded to brew a pot of tea, which Marty had shown her how to do.

'Ah! Well, concern yourself no more, I ordered ten stone of coal on my way home and it'll be here tomorrow. Mr Dalton's promised to section off a corner of his shed.'

Etta gave a nod of pleasure. 'Splendid. Should I pay the man?'

'Yes, one and fivepence. So, you'll have all the fuel you want for boiling kettles and the odd pot of stew – well, let's be having that tea!'

'Very well, my lord!' Tripping happily to the table, she whisked aside a tea-cloth to reveal a dainty arrangement. 'Cucumber sandwiches – and I bought some little buns too.'

Gazing upon the offering, her young husband's smile barely faltered. 'Great, I'm famished.' And he sat down to eat.

Next evening there were sandwiches again, this time made with bread from Etta's own sweet hand. But pride soon turned to disappointment.

'Sorry, it's a little crisp,' she sought to warn him as he was about to bite into it.

'That's all right, I don't like it soggy.' This was just as well, for he almost broke his teeth in an effort to tear off a chunk.

'I don't know what went wrong,' said Etta rather indignantly. 'I followed your mother's receipt to the letter. Perhaps she omitted an ingredient. I shall have a word with her tomorrow.'

Unable to speak whilst gagging over a mouthful of what felt like stiff cardboard, Marty just nodded until he was capable of swallowing, at which point he told Etta, ''Tis fine enough for me.'

That was just as well for this menu was to be repeated the next evening. 'It's far too hot for anything else, isn't it really?' opined Etta.

Unaware that she herself had enjoyed dinner at his mother's house for the past couple of days, Marty readily agreed, even though he did not see the logic for there had always been a cooked meal on the table at home whatever the weather.

However, after coming home to this same fare on Thursday evening, having eaten it for breakfast and pack-up too, he was to voice a hint: 'Let's pray for cooler weather soon. I love a good stew.'

'I'm trying my best,' said Etta, somewhat crossly, sawing at the flat round loaf, which might have been better employed as a discus on the sports field.

'Aw, I know that!' Immediately he reached out to pat her.

'I just can't seem to get the hang of it.'

'It could be something wrong with Mrs Dalton's oven,' he said kindly.

'Everyone else seems to cope. No, I'm forced to admit, the fault is all mine.' She sighed, though she did not sound too unhappy, as she added, 'Oh well, I shall have to buy it from the shop tomorrow. Your mother will no doubt frown upon that, but some of us are just not cut out for baking.'

Dispensing with the need for food, Marty hauled her to him, his expression one of cheerful lust. 'I know something you are cut out for, though – ooh, but put that bread knife down first!' He carefully removed it from her hand before transporting her to the bed and slaking his hunger in a much different fashion.

Perhaps he should have been grateful upon receiving edible bread the following night, but as it arrived yet again in the form of sandwiches, Marty determined to ask his mother if she would teach Etta how to cook.

There was another matter he had been wanting to broach too. 'Etta, love, I don't like to mention it, but, well, my shirts are getting a bit mucky. Might you be able to wash one tomorrow? And maybe some pants and socks?'

Her face showed that it had not even occurred to her, but she had been wondering over the grubbiness of her own attire and responded willingly. 'Certainly! Just show me what to do and I'll oblige.' She turned rather bashful. 'I'm afraid I haven't the slightest idea how to go about it.'

'Neither have I,' he admitted. 'But I think you're supposed to do it on a Monday, that's why I lit the fire for you, to heat the water . . .'

Etta remembered the lines of laundry in Aggie's yard and uttered a murmur of recognition.

'Never mind, me mother'll tell you what to do, I'm sure.'

She bit her lip. 'How embarrassing to have to make such an admittance, though.'

'No! She understands that you come from a different world.'

'I confess there must be a thousand things I took for granted – but I'll learn, truly I will. I so want to be a good wife.'

'I know! Mother will teach you, she's very patient.'

To Etta that sounded as if she was just being tolerated and this caused slight offence. There were plenty of things she could teach Martin's mother, though she chose not to say this to him. A moment of contemplation occurred; then a solution. 'I know! Just for this week I shall pay Mrs

Dalton's maid for the task.' She quickly soothed his worried expression. 'It's not being wasteful, I shall use the opportunity to spy on her so that I can learn how things are done, and next week I'll be able to do it for myself!'

Marty projected admiration, but privately hoped Etta would not make a habit of this and he began to see that he had to get her away from the pub, or in one way or another she might eventually end up handing all his hard-earned cash to Mrs Dalton. Not understanding Etta's reluctance to enlist his family's help, he asked, 'Why pay when Mother will show you for free?'

'Because she'll think me a fool,' said Etta firmly.

Marty assured her this was not so, but with his wife insistent on her plan, as usual he acquiesced. However, this would not prevent him from seeking his mother's guidance on the other important matter, and he decided to call there on his way to work the next day.

Aggie showed no surprise at his request that she teach Etta to cook. 'Well, I suppose I'd better before you fade away to a shadow,' she told her son, looking him up and down as if for signs of malnutrition and smiling wryly at Uncle Mal.

Marty felt he ought to stick up for his wife. 'Oh, I've never gone hungry! But you see it's difficult for Etta without her own oven.'

'Ah, so that's why she's turned up here every dinnertime this week.'

At his mother's words, Marty looked nonplussed.

Aggie's face turned crafty. 'She didn't mention it, then?'

Marty shook his head. No wonder Etta had been satisfied with sandwiches for tea. Though slightly miffed, he was quick to provide another reason for her regular visits. 'Maybe she's lonely on her own all day.'

Aggie pooh-poohed the lame excuse. 'She wouldn't have time to be lonely if she were doing her job. Look at the cut of ye!' She poked him in the ribs. 'Sit down and have breakfast.'

'I've had it.'

'A *proper* breakfast!' She reached for the frying pan and, along with a lump of dripping, slapped three rashers of bacon into it.

Uncle Mal objected. 'How come his "proper breakfast" is bacon and I had to make do with bread and scrape?'

Aggie beheld him witheringly. 'He's not taking your breakfast . . . this was for your tea.' She winked at her son.

Marty laughed but said, 'I don't want to go taking anybody's tea.'

'Don't worry, you're not,' said Aggie. 'I'm expecting another delivery of bacon this morning. In fact,' she glanced at the clock, 'it should be falling off the back of the cart right now.'

Marty dealt a grin of surrender. 'Well, seeing as how you've put it on I won't waste it.'

'Oh, 'twon't go to waste.' Old Mal began to reach out. 'Sure, I can always manage –'

'Leave off you old bugger!'

There was no offence over the irreverent reply, only chesty laughter.

Almost drooling at the aroma, Marty hovered whilst the bacon sputtered and spat. 'Once I get us a house with a proper range I'm sure things'll look up.'

Aggie dropped a slice of bread into the sizzling fat. 'I'm sure they will, but until then I'll teach the lass what she needs to know. 'Tis more than likely she'll be round at dinnertime, I'll get her involved then.'

'Thanks, Ma.' Marty watched the bread turn golden brown, ready to snatch this and the bacon the minute it was done and wasting no time in devouring it. 'It'll only be for a week or so. I want to be out of the pub by the end of the month.'

'Ah well, till then you must have your dinner here on

Sundays. At least it'll give you one decent meal a week.'

True to expectations, Etta did turn up at midday, and, whilst surprised to be included in the preparation of dinner, made no objection but happily joined in, telling Marty when he arrived home from work, 'Your mother seemed grateful for the help.'

This was contrary to what Aggie had told him when he had called in on his way home. Indeed, to listen to his mother it sounded as if Etta's contribution had been particularly inept, but of course he would never reveal this to his wife and he felt Ma's comment was unjust, for Etta really was trying. This was exemplified by the neat stack of clean clothes that awaited him, all sweetly laundered and ironed as he had requested. No matter that she had not done them herself, she had succeeded in organising it and he was proud of her. Etta meant far more to him than any drudge, and to illustrate this, he took her in his arms and spent most of the evening making love to her.

Happily, under Agnes's tuition, Etta's culinary skills immediately improved. Marty supposed anything was an improvement on sandwiches after a hard day's graft, even if it was not yet up to his mother's standards. He had professed a love of stew and now he got it, but served alongside was an apology that it had stuck to the bottom of the pan and was therefore a little tainted.

'Your mother advised to keep stirring it.' Etta looked slightly disparaging. 'But how could one stand there all afternoon with more pressing things to be done . . . Do you like my egg cosies, by the way?' She reached for the creations, each comprising a little satin and lace skirt topped by the china torso of a miniature lady. Inserting her forefingers under the skirts she waggled them about as if making the ladies dance.

Marty imbibed another mouthful of burnt stew, smiling gamely and praising her creativity and her cooking. But privately he continued to look forward to Sunday dinner from his mother's hand.

Aggie Lanegan was a godsend in other ways too. Knowing her son had little time in which to look for another dwelling himself, she had been keeping her ears open, and that Saturday waylaid him in the street to say she had found one vacant in a nearby courtyard.

'It's not furnished,' he relayed the information to an excited Etta when he got home, 'we'll have everything to buy, but Ma's promised to dig some things out for us and she's already got the promise of a sofa from one of my aunties and a bed from a neighbour.'

'Our own home!' Ignorant as to the amount of work that lay ahead, Etta was thrilled and asked, 'When may we move in?'

'Well, we've paid the rent on this place until the end o' next week, so maybe Friday.' His wife never bothered to enquire how much things cost, but money was all important to Marty, who told her, 'It's half a crown a week, only sixpence more than here so I should easily be able to manage that. Hopefully Mr Dalton'll be all right about us not staying longer. I did warn him.'

Etta clasped her hands to her bosom. 'That being so, do you think your parents would mind if we postpone our invitation to tea on Sunday? It would be wonderful if we could welcome them into our new house!'

He felt irresponsible for whipping her into this over-enthusiastic mood. 'Don't expect too much, you know, it's only round the corner.'

'But it's ours – without someone else being across the hallway! It won't matter how much noise we make!' And she hugged him, rubbing her soft body against him erotically.

Easily seduced, he responded by picking her up and carrying her, giggling, to the bed.

*

140

On Sunday, Etta first thanked her mother-in-law for finding them the accommodation, then apologised for having to postpone their arrangement for afternoon tea. 'I'm so sorry for the short notice. I just want it to be perfect. You'll be our very first guests! Will you mind awfully – because you can still come this afternoon if you prefer?'

Aggie said it was no imposition at all.

'In that case you must at least allow me to prepare tea here!' Etta seemed oblivious to the amused smiles, and that she was in effect inviting herself to tea.

Aggie shook her head, as much in despair as amusement. God help poor Marty if he thought his wife would improve with a change of house. But true to her promise she went through her cupboards, unearthing anything that was duplicated or no longer of use, and, these being trundled on Marty's barrow, towards the end of another week the young couple moved into their own home.

It was hardly an auspicious occasion, the dwelling being situated down a narrow cobbled alley and bereft of sunlight due to the tenements that overshadowed the courtyard, but Etta was determined to make it one and announced that she would soon have the place habitable by the use of bright materials. Marty admired her optimism, for he himself saw only the dank little hovel it was, one room up and one down and a single point of entry. Unlike his parents' home which had a separate scullery, this had just a tap in the living room, which was leaking and had been for some time judging by the green slime and the cracked bricks beneath. Closer examination showed that it was not something he could fix himself either. But for his wife's sake he cheered up – after all, if anyone was downhearted it should be Etta, who was accustomed to so much more – and he told her that a friend of his would mend it for nothing.

'I'll light a fire right away so's to get the bricks warmed through. Once it's dried out we can put a bit of lino over it and nobody will be any the wiser!' For the time being

141

he stuck a bucket under the drip then began to rake out the hearth. Her clothes protected by strategically placed bits of sacking, Etta looked on, planning what she herself was going to do with the room.

Having got the fire going, Marty found himself enveloped in smoke, and, his eyes streaming and lungs choking, immediately set to rectifying this. Unfortunately his activity dislodged a nest, which came tumbling down the chimney like a fireball, along with a cloud of soot, that saw the pair of them rushing to escape outside in a fit of screaming laughter – though the cleaning-up operation that followed was far from hilarious and it was well into evening by the time they were done.

But once the water was heated and transported jug by jug between them, there was fun to be had in the tin bath, and, tucked up in bed, a beautiful naked wife at his side, Marty could afford to be magnanimous. 'I suppose we'd have had to clean it anyway. I can't abide other people's muck.' Exhausted but happy, he kissed and stroked her and spoke of his plans for the morrow. 'I'm taking a day off and we'll go buy a table and chairs, maybe a chest of drawers –'

'And a carpet?' Etta made a sudden clutch at his bare ribs making him jump and squirm laughingly.

'Agh, don't tickle! Well, maybe a small little rug. I know a fella who runs a second-hand shop, we'll get heaps for our money there.'

Etta squeezed him again lovingly, projecting her joy. 'Oh, we're going to be so happy here. I know it.'

Throughout Saturday there was to be further hard work. Whilst Marty went about household repairs, Etta slipped into town to visit the market. Returning laden at midday, head in the clouds at the joy of having Marty to herself all day and consumed by exciting plans, she failed to hear a greeting from one of her neighbours and went straight indoors without reply.

142

'The snotty bloody cow!' The one who had been rebuffed marched back inside to address her husband. 'Did you see that? She cut me dead!' And within seconds this was to be relayed to every other household in the courtyard. 'I knew she'd be like that. Why's she living round here in the first place, that's what I want to know? Dressed up like a dog's dinner and talking with a plum in her gob, thinking she's better than us . . .'

Etta was oblivious to this slander, too involved in showing Marty her latest discovery. 'Look what I've found!' She held up a tin of meat. 'Isn't this a boon? I didn't know such a thing existed.'

He smiled. 'Grand – did ye get the ducks? I tell ye, I'm ready for me dinner.'

She beheld him dubiously. 'Marty, I don't know who informed you that one could buy a duck for a penny but I've been all around the livestock market and –'

He burst out laughing. 'Sure, I didn't mean *real* ducks! I meant those square, faggoty things ye get for a penny.'

'Oh!' She hooted with embarrassment. 'I'm such a juggins . . .'

'No, you're not!' He soothed her with a smile.

'Well,' she announced, still laughing as she put aside the tin, 'we might not have ducks but we shall have our own eggs – in time.' And, from a box, with gentle hands she scooped two fluffy yellow chicks that peeped anxiously as she set one on each of her feet, where they were to remain like pom-poms as she paraded them for Marty's amusement.

As if adopting Etta as their mother, the chicks were even to travel on her slippers as she went to the privy and back, which again attracted much ridicule from her neighbours.

Wrapped up in her own little world, Etta was to spare nary a thought for this gossip, and though Marty thought he detected a less than friendly response to his own greeting to a neighbour when he went out to fetch a celebratory jug of ale at the end of the day, he was too tired and happy with Etta to care.

Alas, by Sunday morn the chicks had been devoured by a predator, leaving only a few telltale downy feathers in the yard. But there was no point in dwelling on this, with other matters taking precedence. With the windows cleaned, curtains affixed, the fireplace black-leaded, lino and a rug on the floor and food in the cupboard under the stairs, Etta now felt able to make that invitation to her parents-in-law. From his friend at the second-hand shop Marty had purchased a whole box of crockery for a few pence, much of it matching so that it appeared to be a set, although it wasn't. Some of the saucers were chipped but the cups would be perfectly all right once the thick veneer of tannin was removed. Anxious to impress her mother-in-law, Etta wondered aloud how to get it off. Marty didn't know and so she relied upon a box of crystals that had successfully removed other engrained filth and employed them to great success. By the time her guests arrived the table was set with a white cloth and crockery that was just as spotless. Now that she had an oven she had also managed to bake a cake, though it had taken much practice and the one that took pride of place was not her first effort. Wisely she had steered clear of making bread for the sandwiches, for which the basic ingredients had been purchased from the shop.

Nevertheless, Aggie was to pass compliment as she handed over some buns in a paper bag. 'I brought you these though I can see you don't need them. My, this all looks very inviting, that cake especially.'

'Thank you, but you're responsible, it's from your own receipt.' Etta's reply was modest, though she felt immensely proud of herself as she poured tea for everyone and smiled at Marty, who winked back at her.

There was compliment over the cups too. 'Lovely china, isn't it, Red?' murmured Aggie, and took a sip, at which her face changed slightly.

144

Thinking she might be mistaken, she did not immediately remark on the contents and tasted the tea again to make sure. Her husband and uncle looked at each other suspiciously.

But Marty gagged and pulled a face, blurting, 'Jesus, Ett, what the hell did you use to clean them?'

Stricken, Etta took a sip from her own cup, casting an agonised look at him before admitting, 'Borax.'

'I think you forgot to rinse them out, dear.' Mouth pursed in distaste, Aggie grabbed the cup from her husband who had been trying to remain polite and, needlessly warning the others not to swallow another drop, she put herself in charge, collected the rest and tipped the contents outside down the drain.

Guilty over his rash outburst, Marty tried to make a joke of it, but, annoyed at being made to feel stupid, Etta retorted stiffly, 'I did rinse them. Anybody would think I was trying to poison you.'

'Ach, we didn't think that, deary, these things happen.' Red murmured words of comfort and along with the others tried to rid himself of the vile taste by tucking into the sandwiches and saying how good they were, but for Etta the afternoon had been ruined. She could not wait for the guests to leave and was to voice her upset the moment they did, berating Marty in harsh manner:

'Did you have to make such a fuss about it?'

'Sorry, sorry!' He hauled her into an embrace, plastering her with conciliatory kisses until she began to lose her scowl. ''Twas unforgivable, I'm just a blasted eejit who says the first thing that comes into me head, please forgive me, aw, please, *please* . . .' He wriggled his groin suggestively against hers.

'I *might.*'

Despite the jutting lower lip and the forceful response, a softer expression underlay them, luring Marty to form a roguish grin. 'You only wanted them out o' the house so's

145

ye could get your wicked way with me, didn't ye?'

Etta scoffed, but there was glee in her eye. When he seduced her with that droopy-lidded gaze she could deny him nothing.

'Ye know, if ye'd wanted rid of them so badly there are easier ways without poisoning your husband too – aagh!' He ran laughing to the stairs with Etta in pursuit.

'Poor old Marty's copping it now.' Misinterpreting the squeals, Uncle Mal threw a sympathetic grimace at Red as they made their exit along the cobble-stoned alley.

Aggie was more concerned with the awful taste in her mouth. 'Dilatory, she is!' she spat her favourite denouncement of Etta. 'I thought her sort were meant to be more intelligent than us? All those privileges and she hasn't the sense she was born with. Wasn't trying to poison us, says she – well, trying or not she almost succeeded! I'm still crunching on that blessed grit.'

Mal threw a wheezy laugh at Red. 'At least we'll have nice white gnashers.'

But Aggie did not share their amusement, especially when having to keep catching her husband, whose laughter caused him to buckle into a faint every few seconds. 'I swear, I've never known anyone so bloody dilatory! Well, this week, come hell or high water I'm going to take that girl in hand.'

And to some extent she succeeded, managing to convey all manner of valuable information to Etta during the week that followed. But for all her intensive training, her hopes that this might encourage her daughter-in-law to provide her own dinner the following Sunday were shattered when Red heard the front door open and informed his wife drolly:

'Looks like Pyramus 'n' Thisby will be dining with us again.'

Oblivious to the sigh of exasperation from the kitchen, Marty entered chirpily and explained away his wife's short-comings. 'I think the chimney's still got a nest up it. It's blocked with something anyway, 'cause I couldn't get a decent fire going for Etta to cook dinner. Is it all right if we . . . ?'

Aggie bit her tongue and sighed, 'Sit down. Lizzie, fetch two more plates.'

'Maybe you should have the chimney swept,' Redmond advised his son, his face a mass of abrasions from a recent fall. 'Best to have it done every quarter.'

Marty shrugged carelessly. 'Ah well, we won't be there long if I have my way.' He rubbed his palms together merrily at the sight and smell of the roast mutton. 'By, 'tis a good job you're just round the corner, Ma, we'd have had no dinner, would we, Ett?'

Mellowed by a morning's lovemaking, Etta did not infer from this that she was useless, and nodded benignly.

Aggie returned an affable nod, but later, after the uninvited guests had gone, she complained to her husband, 'God Almighty, you think you're getting rid of them when they wed! I see more of Marty than ever since he married that useless girl.'

'Ah well now, you shouldn't have been so good to him,' joked Red. 'He'll still be turning up when he's a bloody pensioner.'

'Bedad, he won't! One pensioner's enough for me.'

'Sure, is that any way to treat an old soldier?' gasped Mal, offended. 'If you'd sooner I take my annuity elsewhere –'

'Oh, whist you silly old donkey, who else would have yese, money or no.' Aggie continued as if there had been no interruption. 'Anyway, 'tis not entirely Marty's fault, you can't blame him for wanting a decent dinner. It's that dilatory cuckoo he married, there's always some excuse as to why she can't provide for him. Too used to servants, that's her trouble.'

Young Lizzie was quick to whisper to her sister, 'Just like Ma!'

Aggie did not hear. 'Well, she needn't think I'll put up with her treating me like one. I'll fettle that one, see if I don't.'

To this end, the following Sunday when the young couple inevitably turned up, she awaited the opportunity to deliver the bad news, although now having had a week in which to cool down she found it more difficult. It would have been easier to blurt it outright had Etta been an unpleasant sort, but she wasn't and Aggie felt obliged to opt for a gentler, diplomatic approach, especially as the girl had been unusually helpful that afternoon, undertaking all the washing-up herself.

This task done, Etta spread the damp tea towel on a line above the fireplace and smiled in response to her mother-in-law's thanks. 'Well, it's only right that I should take my turn. You've made me feel part of your family. I'm so grateful.'

Aggie gave an inward groan, for Etta's warmth made her own task harder. Yet it did give her an opening. 'Speaking of family,' she said casually as her son wandered outside to the lavatory. 'Are you thinking of letting your own know where you're at?'

Smote as if by lightning, Etta cooled. 'Had they wanted to find me they would have done so already.'

'As I understand it, your argument is with your father. Speaking as a mother, I'd want to know where my daughter was – especially if I only had the one.'

Etta felt tears prick her eyes and was angry at herself for being so affected. 'My mother isn't like you. She's too influenced by my father even to contemplate tracing me.'

'That's sad.' Aggie hesitated, but then persisted. 'If you want me to act as go-between –'

'No!' Curbing her outburst, Etta was to moderate the rest of her reply. 'Thank you, it's very decent but I've no wish to be reunited with any of them.' She couldn't bring herself to say that she had already tried the written approach

148

but through fear of being rebuffed had torn the letter up. 'Martin and I need only each other.' Immediately realising she had insulted her mother-in-law, she tried to apologise, but it was too late, the response was stiff.

'Aye, well, maybe you'll realise just how much you need others when you start a family of your own.' Her ire rekindled over being taken for granted, Aggie added, 'By the by, we won't be eating at home next Sunday, we've been invited to Louisa's.' This was her eldest married daughter.

Etta misinterpreted and, thankful to have the subject changed, said more brightly, 'Oh, I shall look forward to meeting her!'

Aggie was not about to let her get away with this. 'When I said *we*, I meant Red and Uncle Mal and myself and the children. You and Marty'll have to fend for yourself I'm afraid.'

Seeing Etta's face droop, Red felt a rush of pity. 'Well, maybe –'

'Aye.' Uncle Mal leaned forth to croon in sympathetic tone.

'It's not our place to go inviting other folk,' pronounced Aggie firmly.

Her husband remained equable. 'Strangers, maybe, but Marty is Lou's brother and I'm sure she would be as pleased to meet Etta.'

'And she will meet her some other time, but next Sunday I'm afraid Etta and Marty will have to rely on their own devices – sure, it'll be no hardship for those who prefer their own company.' Aggie looked Etta in the eye so that they were both clear as to where they stood.

When Marty came back into the room he sensed an atmosphere but assumed it was because his father had instantaneously dropped off to sleep. However, on the way home not long afterwards, he enquired of his wife who was unusually quiet, 'Did something happen while I was in the lavvy?'

'I've upset her again,' Etta revealed dully.

'What did you say?'

She related the brief exchange. 'Consequently, we're to provide our own Sunday luncheon in future.'

'Don't fret, Ett. You haven't poisoned me yet.'

She punched him playfully.

He overreacted with a melodramatic performance that brought the sparkle of laughter to her eyes as he had hoped, and soon she was back to her animated self.

'Oh well!' she exclaimed, hugging his arm, 'It was a bit much to expect your mother to put up with us every week. After all, we are an old married couple now.'

'Aye, almost a month!' He pulled her into his side, their hips jostling as they made their way down the street. 'We must think of a way to celebrate our anniversary. Though I'm sure I can't imagine how.' Then he gave her a sly sideways glance that set her giggling and had them speeding home to bed.

7

Etta quickly recovered from the altercation with Aggie, and the latter, gracious in winning the battle of Sunday lunch, proceeded to teach her daughter-in-law how to manage a household. But tuition was only part of the equation: it had taken years of experience to perfect Mrs Lanegan's pastry, she could only pass on the method not the skill, and judging by the younger Mrs Lanegan's efforts, hers would have been better employed in making bricks. Still in the blissful newlywed stage of marriage, Marty was laughing to himself about this as he came through the courtyard, wondering what Etta had in store for him this evening. She was a dreadful cook, but oh, how he loved coming home to her.

It had been hell at work. Still limping, Custard Lugs had not yet been able to wreak vengeance, but the promise of it was simmering in his eyes every time Marty looked at him. It was only a matter of time, and the dread of this had concerned him for most of the day. His was a tiring enough job without the extra stress of having to dodge that ruffian.

But for now he felt safe. Grinning in preparation of seeing his loved one, he grasped the door knob and entered – but before he had a chance to lay eyes on his wife someone leapt from behind the door, threw a blanket over his head and to all intents rendered him blind and almost suffocated as it was swathed tightly about him, pinning his arms to his sides and imprisoning him. More alarmed for Etta than himself – please God don't let her be harmed – he twirled violently to dislodge his assailant, who gave a squeak and thudded to the floor, whereupon Marty fought his way out of the blanket, his face red with fury as he made to deliver retribution.

Etta cringed and yelled as she looked up at him with tears in her eyes, half of laughter, half of pain from the bloody nose he had inflicted. 'Stop, it's only me!'

Aghast, Marty clutched his head and shrieked, 'You stupid bloody woman!' Then he bent to help her.

Furious at the insult, she immediately dispensed with the laughter and lashed out with her foot. 'It was a joke, for heaven's sake!'

He leapt back. 'Some joke! I thought I was being attacked – and even worse, I thought they'd hurt you!'

'Huh, well *someone* has!' Having been fantasising about him all day, Etta had worked herself into a frenzy of lust, and her practical joke had been meant as a precursor to sexual frolics. Acutely disappointed and furious that her plan had backfired, she refused his help and got up, testing her throbbing, bloody nose gingerly. 'I think you might have broken it.'

He heaved a sigh of exasperation and made to dab at the trickle of blood with his handkerchief, but she shrugged him off pettishly.

It took both of them a long time to calm down, Etta turning her back on him and going to fetch their meal. Marty was first to tender his regret. 'I'm sorry,' he muttered as she laid the plates none too gently on the table. 'I was terrified 'twas your father come to beat me inside out again and snatch you away.'

'You don't know him like I do.' Etta remained morose as she set out the knives and forks. 'Never concern yourself that he'll want me back.'

The underlying poignancy to this remark caused him to

reach out to her. 'Then he's a downright fool and it's his great loss – but others have it in for me too, Ett, I wasn't to know. I'm *really* sorry for hurting ye, I wouldn't do it for the world, you know that.'

She pretended to sulk but allowed herself to be pulled into his arms. 'I intended to grab you and whisk you off to bed.'

'Well, you still could.' He grinned suggestively.

'With this conk?' She pouted.

'True, it is a bit off-putting – like making love to a walrus!' He laughed and jerked his head away as she squealed and tried to hit him. 'Calm, calm! Now ye know what it's like to be on the receiving end of a joke. But, sure, have you ever known anything to put me off?'

Responding to his lazy grin, she was grudging in her forgiveness. 'Too late now. You'll have to make do with kippers.' But from the way she pushed her lower body at him, her head cocked slyly and her eyes bright over the crimson nose, he knew there was to be an erotic dessert.

'I wonder if we'll still be like this when we're old and grey,' sighed Etta as she lay beneath him later, glued together by sweat.

Totally forgiven, Marty was almost asleep and snuggled into her neck. 'Mm, of course . . . though I hope we won't still be stuck in this dump.'

After all her hard work to prettify the house, it rather hurt that he damned it so. But she stroked his back lovingly and told him, 'It wouldn't matter a jot to me.' To her, the pursuit of happiness had been all-consuming. Before meeting him, her lonely existence had caused her often to question what purpose life had. Only in marriage to this adorable, loving man had she realised her destiny. 'I'd face any hardship so long as I can be with you.'

It dawned on Marty then that his wife had never once complained about the poor conditions into which he had plunged her. She seemed perfectly content to make the best of things so long as she had something pleasant to do like her embroidery or reading a novel or one of her other hobbies. Oh, his adoration was equal to hers if not greater, but for him that was only a part of it. He hadn't unearthed this gem simply to bury her in squalor. Kissing her, he peeled himself gingerly away, rolled into a more comfortable position and declared, 'There's got to be something more for us than this.'

'What more can there be but to care for the person you love?' came Etta's gentle query.

'There is, and I'll get it,' swore Marty. Touching her cheek in the dark, he allowed his hand to fall back to the mattress and was soon asleep.

Etta lay there listening to the sound of his breathing for a while, then soon she too drifted off.

Ironically, the day after Etta's practical joke, that which he had been dreading finally came about: one second Marty was poised to make a dash for a customer, the next he felt a painful blow to the back of his neck, then inky darkness washed over him.

Apparently he was unconscious for no more than a few minutes, but the nauseating headache induced by Custard Lug's cosh was to disqualify him from work for the rest of the day and was still there next morning. 'Ooh, look!' he winced at Etta. 'Come and feel this hard swelling.'

'I've been caught like that before,' accused his wife, trying to make light of a situation that had alarmed them both.

He pointed a scolding finger at her. 'I'll remember that when you're looking for sympathy!'

She chuckled and petted him. 'Only teasing – oh, my poor love, I trust that brute will be punished.'

But with no proof that the man with yellow ears was the culprit, Marty was unable to lodge a complaint. Back at work, he was also forced to endure malicious smirking

154

from his antagonist for the rest of the week. Had that been the end of the matter he would have called it quits – after all, it had been he who inflicted the first injury – but it was made very clear to him that his enemy considered this to be a lifelong blood feud. Hence, he would forever require eyes in the back of his head.

At least, joked Etta, her husband had some sort of contact with people other than his family, even if it might be unwelcome. She herself found it nigh on impossible to commune with anyone other than him. Oh, she had tried, but though some of the neighbours had greeted her in passing, they were unwilling to prolong the experience, seemingly awkward in her well-spoken presence – apart from the men, who might openly admire her but were no company, being too restricted by their wives. 'Not that I care,' she told Marty, echoing the declaration she had made to his mother. 'As long as I have you, no one else matters.'

But it mattered to Marty that his wife might be ostracised, and the next day on his way home from work he took a detour from his usual route in order to call on his eldest sister, whose home was on the northern side of town in the shadow of the Minster. By coincidence, two of his other married sisters, Bridget and Anne, who lived outside the city, were here on a visit too, all three chorusing their surprise at his entry to the small courtyard dwelling and jumping up to encircle him.

'Well, I never, if it isn't the married man!' Louisa was a female version of her father with a bush of light brown hair and a kind face that broke into smiles upon sight of the brother who had not visited in many a week. 'Get yourself in here, we've a bone to pick with you, sneaking off and not telling any one of us!' Her voice was bossy and she pinched his cheek as if he were still a little child, but her blue eyes were warm, as were those of her sisters as they poked and prodded him accusingly.

Whilst Marty gave laughing apology and fought off their

tickling fingers, Louisa's stick-thin husband Dan rose from his seat to reach out and shake his brother-in-law's hand, saying in a deep Yorkshire accent, 'By, you little rascal, I bet you copped it when you told Ma!'

'You're not joking,' said Marty with a rueful grin, then to Bridget and Anne, 'And what are you two doing here? Have your fellas got sick of you and chucked you out? Sure, I'm not surprised.' He cowered away, laughing as, playfully, they attacked him again.

'They're at the market, cheeky!' Bridget told him. 'Came in to buy some stock. So we thought we'd come with them, didn't we, Annie, and take the opportunity to come and visit our sister.'

'And your husbands have taken the opportunity to sneak off to the pub,' teased their brother. 'Still at market at this time of evening? They'd tell you anything!'

'Come on then, you lasses,' ordered Dan, 'leave the newlywed alone and let him sit down. He needs to conserve his energy.'

'Oh, Marty, I can't offer you anything substantial.' Louisa looked pained as her brother perched on the edge of a sofa that was full of children. 'We've already had our tea. Our visitors have eaten me out of house and home.'

'You cheeky article!' Bridget threatened her jokingly, as did Anne.

'But we can offer the man a drink,' cut in Dan. 'Fred, grab a jug and nip to the pub!'

'No, not for me!' Marty prevented his six-year-old nephew from his errand, grabbing him and undergoing a brief wrestling match in which two other little boys joined, the other occupant of the sofa, a wide-eyed baby girl, being scooped away from the danger by her mother Bridget.

'Tea then?' jumped in Louisa.

'No, no, I can't stop!' Marty broke off to calm the boys down. 'Thanks all the same, but *my wife*'s waiting for me.' Everyone laughed at the proud emphasis he laid on this.

156

'Ooh, she's got him under the thumb already.' Dan nudged his wife.

'You wouldn't say that if ye saw her,' riposted Marty.

'So when *are* we going to see her?' demanded Bridget with a gleam in her eye, bouncing the baby in her arms. 'We've been thinking she must be right ugly, you don't seem so keen to show her off.'

Marty pretended to deal her a backhander. 'Get away with yese, I know full well Ma must have given you a detailed account!'

Louisa flushed and tried not to look at the others, recalling her mother's opinion that Etta had some 'filthy, dirty habits', which in fact she herself had just been relaying to her sisters when Marty had arrived. Feeling her husband's sly gaze she chattered hastily, 'Well, we've been told she's a stunner but we'd like to see for ourselves, wouldn't we?'

This statement was echoed by her sisters, as was her following invitation. 'You must bring her round.'

'I'm glad you said that,' smiled Marty. ''Cause Etta's a bit lonely when I'm out all day at work and the neighbours aren't very forthcoming, so I hoped she might be able to pop round here if she needs a friendly face – she's got Ma of course, but just somebody nearer her own age.'

Louisa seemed hesitant at first. 'Well, I was meaning the pair of you should come round for your tea this Sunday – but yes, of course Etta will be more than welcome to call if she can find the time.'

'Great!' Marty slapped his knees and leapt up. 'I'll get home right away and tell her. Give my regards to Mick and Joe!' With a kiss to each cheek, he departed.

'My God, what have I agreed to?' Louisa clasped her cheeks with a fearsome look at the others. 'And her so posh. I won't know what to say to her nor nothing. What if she should want to use the lavatory?'

Dan beheld her with pity. 'Don't you know anything? Posh folk don't go to the lav. They have a different biology to the rest of us.' He grinned at his sisters-in-law, who tittered along with the children.

Oblivious to his teasing, she pondered on the difficulties. 'Maybe I should buy some proper toilet tissue . . .'

'You're frightened she'll get newsprint on her bum?' Dan roared with laughter. 'My God! You'll be painting the seat gold next.'

''Tis all right for you!' Louisa slapped him, then turned on her sisters who found this almost hysterically amusing. 'And the pair of you can stop wetting yourselves, I'll be sending her round to your houses next!'

And for the rest of the week she was to fret, rushing to the window every five minutes in case Etta should turn up, practising what she might say to her, forgetting all that Aggie had said about Marty's wife being lax with the housework, remembering only that Etta was posh, and posh people were different, weren't they?

But she need not have worried, for when Etta did turn up it was on Marty's arm on Sunday afternoon, and she was not the imperious creature Louisa had feared but was very warm, charming and friendly, not hoity-toity at all. Even if her confident manner was a little intimidating, Louisa could see why Marty had fallen for her, and so for his sake she agreed that if Etta ever needed the company she should feel free to visit. 'Though not on Wednesdays 'cause that's when I clean for the doctor's wife – and Thursday is a bit awkward as I usually go to market – but any other day . . .'

Etta voiced her gratitude, but sensed that her presence made Louisa feel awkward and that the offer was made out of politeness rather than true kinship, and though she promised to call occasionally she had no real desire to, for Marty was the only member of this clan that she would ever really need.

For all this, there were some closer to home with whom she really should try to make a connection. And the next

morning, Monday, she was granted the opportunity to culti-
vate friendship with all of her neighbours at once, at least
the female ones, for they were congregated in the yard, busy
at their laundry. Marty had bought her an iron-hooped tub
which stood outside the back door, and now seemed a good
time to put it to use. Trying to recall what came first, Etta
carved some slivers from a large bar of soap then wandered
out to tip these into the tub, nodding tentatively to the
other women before going back in. Then came the trans-
portation of water from the copper in jugs, a seemingly
endless task. Finally she gathered the articles to be washed,
and, hoping her ignorance would not be too obvious, went
out to join the women.

Though many of them had Irish surnames, over the sixty
years since their ancestors had come here to escape the
potato famine, the accent had become Yorkshire. They were
laughing raucously over some shared joke, but when Etta
came amongst them they controlled their amusement. This
somewhat exasperated her, for even though Marty's parents
told her she was part of the family they often reacted in a
similar vein, clamming up in case she overheard their earthy
joke, as if she wouldn't understand. In fact she did enjoy
such humour and felt excluded and sad that they felt so
constrained by her presence. She told the women, 'Don't
mind me,' and introduced herself for the benefit of those
she had not met, but though they smiled and gave their
names and did not actually state that she was intruding,
this was the way she felt.

Many of them were laundering sheets. Etta briefly entertained the idea of doing her own, but then, preferring to
finish the embroidery she had been working on, decided
against it for today and concentrated on underwear and
stockings, a shirt and a few muslin aprons. As an afterthought, whilst these were soaking in the tub, she went
back inside to fetch her lilac dress. Even kept for Sunday
best, its cream lace was looking slightly worse for wear, its

ribbons grey around the edges. Too daunted to immerse the entire garment, she opted to dip just these parts in the wash tub, but after barely any rubbing on the washboard they became distorted, the ribbons fraying and requiring a trim, and Etta despaired that her lovely gown would never be wearable again.

Possessing no mangle, she asked politely if she might have the use of her neighbour's, which was granted. Whilst working, she tried to chat to the woman, but this only extended to comments about the weather, and however much she tried to keep it going it soon petered out, so she was glad not to have many items to do and was soon finished.

Her washing dangling from the communal line, Etta left everyone else still pummelling and wringing amongst the suds and went to make herself a cup of tea. First, though, after a look at her red hands, she reached for a little cardboard pot of salve.

Hearing the clink of crockery, the one whose mangle she had borrowed looked round expectantly, but when no cup of tea was forthcoming she sniffed to her companions, 'Too posh to offer us one. Let her buy her own bloody mangle then.'

Another tittered. 'She hardly needs one for the few things she's washed. Two pairs o' drawers and a sock.'

'And have you seen the colour of her doorstep?' asked another, at which all turned to behold the scuffed and dirty tread. 'I've never seen her stone it yet, nor wipe her sills.' To those who cleaned theirs every day of the week except Sunday, this was a capital offence. Hearing their amusement and suspecting that she was the butt of it, Etta could not imagine why they were all so uncharitable. Telling herself to ignore them, she sat down with her cup of tea and read a few chapters of a romantic novel, before turning to her embroidery.

Apart from a break for a cold luncheon, this was to

involve her for most of the day. Whilst the women were still scrubbing at their washboards, boiling and rinsing, bluing and mangling, brows dripping sweat, engaging in banter, she poured all her energy into French knots and long stitch. Let them make fun of her, see if she cared.

Only much later in the afternoon was there someone to talk to. No longer plagued by Etta every lunchtime now, her mother-in-law decided to call around half past three to see how the younger Mrs Lanegan was coping. Aggie was a scrupulously clean person – one had to be round here in the shadow of iron foundries and factory chimneys, the moment one cleaned one's sill the flecks of soot were already beginning to settle again – but, raised with servants, Etta had yet to grasp the concept of hard work that went into the upkeep of even a modest abode and gave more relevance to which colour thread she was to employ on her embroidery. The blissful ignorance that so endeared her to Marty only served to infuriate Aggie, who did not hold back in her criticism, though only after she had returned home.

'Here's me taking them a bit of pie for their tea, thinking she'd be rushed off her feet, what with it being washing day an' all, and what do I find her doing? Sitting embroidering on her backside –'

'Embroidering her backside?' Uncle Mal gave a laugh of interest. 'Sure, is it not pretty enough?'

But his niece remained grim, '– and not a soap bubble in evidence!'

Aggie was not the only one to think this odd, though it took Marty a while longer to voice it. Monday had always been a nightmare for the men he knew, not even a downpour able to delay the ritual wash, and the clothes being dried in front of the fire so that no one could get near it. Not so under Etta's management. Sun or rain it seemed not to matter to his beautiful wife.

Smitten as he was with her, he could put up with

unwashed sheets for several weeks before this became a problem, but even one so besotted could not fail to notice that there was now a brownish, body-shaped imprint on either side of the bed.

On the third Monday running, after he had lighted the copper for her and still there appeared little hint of activity to come, he stroked his chin as he wondered how to phrase this to Etta, finally suggesting that he put the bed linen on to soak before he left for work. 'To make your job easier.'

Dabbing her face with rosewater, Etta apologised, though did not seem too upset over the fact that he had had to remind her of her duties. 'Yes, I suppose I had better do them. It just never entered my head. I've had so much else to do.'

'So will I put them on before –'

'No, leave them to me.' She sprang up to kiss him goodbye. 'Off to work with you now, and leave wifey to her business!'

How she was to regret this blithe response. The laundering of the sheets turned out to be horrendous from start to finish. Inflicting a scald on her hand as she tried to hook the steaming linen from the boiler with just a stick, drenching herself as she struggled to transfer them to the wash tub, arms aching like they had never ached before after pummelling and scrubbing against the washboard all morning, she felt utterly exhausted – and still her sheets did not bare comparison with others on the line, which she graciously voiced to the women before going inside to put more ointment on her smarting hand.

The reason was given to her in an overheard comment from one neighbour to another: 'She might see a difference in her piebald sheets if she bothered to do them every week like normal folk.'

Etta was flabbergasted. Suffer that every week? How would she find time to wash her clothes as well? They might be happy to waste their energies, but she had far better things to do. After greasing her sore hand and protecting it with a glove, she ate lunch. Then, suddenly remembering she had not topped up the boiler after using it, she hurried to the cold tap with a jug. Having replenished it, she set about finishing her embroidery. If uninterrupted she should be able to complete her project this afternoon and have the cloth on the table for when Martin came home for tea.

There was slight irritation when her mother-in-law turned up at three, causing work on the tablecloth to stop. As Aggie had brought a letter from Aunt Joan and also half a pie, Etta kept her tone civil and chatted for a moment, but did not offer her guest refreshment, for she itched to get back to her embroidery. This did not pass unnoticed, nor had the inadequately laundered sheets that hung in the yard, but Aggie said merely, 'Well, I'll leave you to it then . . .'

Etta grinned eagerly and retrieved her needle. 'I'm hoping to finish this before Martin gets home.'

'I trust he'll appreciate it,' sniffed Aggie, and left with another disparaging glance at the stained sheets, muttering to herself. 'And they call us dirty tinkers.'

'Thank you for the pie!' called Etta in afterthought, before quickly reverting to her task.

Her fingertips burning from having spent most of the day pushing a needle in and out of thick linen, not to mention the painful scald on her hand, Etta was further hurt that evening when Martin failed to comment on how she had improved the house for his homecoming, finally having to demand of him, 'Haven't you noticed my table-cloth?'

Food being one of his main priorities these days alongside sexual intercourse, after partaking of his wife's lips with gusto, Marty's eyes had homed in on the mouth-watering pie on the table – obviously one of his mother's – and not the cloth beneath. He had wolfed half of it down before Etta's injured enquiry pricked his conscience. 'Sorry! I was just enjoying your apple pie so much.'

'I didn't bake it, your mother brought it round.'

'Oh, I thought it was yours, it's hard to tell the difference these days.' Covering his flattery with a more genuine compliment, he made great play of studying the embroidered cloth, proclaiming it, 'The most wondrous piece of handiwork I've ever clapped eyes on!'

She looked suitably appeased, but told him, 'I didn't think I was going to be able to finish it in time, I scalded my hand trying to lift the heavy sheets out of the copper – look.' Her lips pouting, she peeled off the glove.

'Aw!' Marty cupped the hand gently, frowning over it. 'Maybe I should have stayed behind to help you.' He kissed the skin around the injury. 'That looks nasty. Ma'll have something for it in her medicine chest.'

Etta remembered then. 'Oh, your mother brought a letter from Aunt Joan. She's invited us to tea on Saturday week.'

'Great,' said Marty without much enthusiasm, before the memory of Joan's baking won him round.

'I suppose we'll have to return their hospitality,' said Etta.

'You can't invite them here!'

She frowned. 'Are you ashamed of our home?'

'No! I just can't abide the old witch, that's why.' He chuckled and examined her hand again. 'Did you show Ma when she came round?'

'No, she seemed in a rush.' Etta winced. 'Gosh, it's really throbbing now.'

'I'll pop round and ask if she'll take a look at it; you'll never sleep for the pain otherwise. Take it easy while I'm gone.'

Exhausted after her own washing day, and irritated with Redmond for falling asleep halfway through their conversation, the last thing Aggie needed was a request for her to trail round to her son's abode and her response was grumpy. 'Etta never said anything while I was there.'

'Well, you know Etta, she wouldn't like to make a fuss. She struggled with those steaming sheets all on her own.'

'We all do, son.'

He conceded this, then wrinkled his nose. 'Aye, but she's not born to it, is she, Ma? And it's a right nasty scald, I'm worried it might turn poisonous, told her you'd know what to do . . .'

His mother rolled her eyes. 'I can see I'll get no peace if I don't come now.'

Marty dealt her a thankful grin.

Taking with her a pot of home-made ointment, she threw a parting line at Uncle Mal. 'If His Majesty wants to know where I am when he deigns to wake up, tell him I'm gone to perform a resurrection.'

However, after viewing the scald she was less than sympathetic. 'Martin Lanegan, is this what you dragged me out for? Why, from your tone I thought to find her stitched into her shroud – and that scald no bigger than a cat's bottom!'

Marty reflected his wife's look of indignance. 'Aye, but that doesn't stop it hurting! Often the tinier things are more painful than the big ones.'

'Are they indeed?' muttered Aggie, in no mood to suffer such foibles tonight. 'Well, I'll leave you the pot of ointment and let you apply it yourself.' Handing it over she turned to go.

Grimacing at Etta, Marty hurried after his mother, telling her in the yard, 'Sorry to drag you out, Ma, I wasn't sure what to do. I've told Ett to take it easy for a while.'

Sick of this besotted pampering, Aggie could withhold the caustic retort no longer. 'She'll have no trouble doing that, to be sure!'

Marty was irked. 'That's not fair!'

'No, I suppose it isn't, just like it wasn't fair of your wife not to offer me so much as a glass of water when I'd gone to the trouble of fetching Joan's letter and a pie for your tea – just like I do every week because I know if I don't my son won't get anything decent in his belly! After she's enjoyed my hospitality for the past two months!' Too annoyed to stop now, Aggie let her objections flow. 'You know what that one's trouble is? She's never had to put herself out for anyone, thinks we're all there to run about after her.' Seeing that Etta had overheard and come out to join them, she did not halt her complaints but addressed them to the culprit herself. 'Just wait till you have children, milady, then you'll know!'

Taken aback by the sudden vehemence of all this, Etta was swift to retort, 'Then I shan't have any!'

'Then I'll congratulate you on being a lot cleverer than the rest of us!' Aggie wagged her finger. 'But it'll be your loss, because you won't be any good till you have had any!'

Conserving any loyalty for his wife, Marty scolded, 'I think you've said enough, Ma.'

Aggie had meant to leave at that point but now turned her anger on him. 'Son, if you want to stand like a dummy and have her walk all over you then that's your affair, but I don't and I'll say my piece. Ever since you brought her here I've held my tongue, made allowances because of the different background, but there's a limit to my patien—'

'I *beg* you,' Etta cut in imperiously, 'not to stretch your patience on my behalf. I was unaware that I was such a burden to you, but now that it has been made abundantly clear I'll endeavour to amend the situation. We shan't trouble you again. Goodnight.' Eyes burning, she turned and went indoors, indicating that she expected Marty to follow, but, by no means certain of this, she was to suffer agonies when he remained outside.

Shocked by the exchange, trapped between one and the other, Marty gave an anguished look at his mother.

Even before he dealt her that helpless shrug, Aggie knew what lay ahead. 'Right, if that's the thanks I get for all

166

I've –' Too furious to say more, tears of rage in her eyes, she spun on her heel. 'Ah, to hell with ye!'

'Ma-a!' Marty called after her, but, suddenly realising this was providing a show for his neighbours, he uttered a feeble gasp and hurried inside to his wife.

How on earth had this happened, Marty asked himself a week later? One minute they had been sailing along fine, the next, a few ill-chosen words and a moment's irritation had escalated into a family feud.

Remaining furious over his mother's denigration of her, Etta refused to have anything to do with Aggie. Well, that was understandable, Marty supposed. He was angry with his mother too and had not felt like speaking to her either for a couple of days after the altercation. But his hope that this would eventually blow over was to be dashed when Etta discovered that he intended to go round to his parents on his way home from work that night.

'As if nothing has happened?' she demanded of him, looking hurt. 'I thought you were on my side?'

'I am! But you want to get this fixed, don't you?'

'No! I told you I don't wish to speak to your mother again and I meant it – you said you agreed with me.'

He gave an awkward laugh. 'But now things have cooled down . . .'

'I meant it!'

'Etta, she's done a lot for us.'

'And I've thanked her, but what she said to me was unforgivable.' Around the jet-like pupils, the whites of Etta's eyes were tinted an angry red.

He frowned. 'Are you asking me not to go and see my own mother?'

'And are you saying that what she said to me was just and fair?' volleyed his wife.

'No, but surely –'

'Of course, it's up to you to decide whom to support.'

Etta folded her arms and shrugged, but left him in no doubt as to what she expected.

He scratched his neck, for the moment saying nothing, his troubled eyes on a woodlouse making its laborious way across the brick floor. 'What if Ma and Da should turn up here, would you expect me to ignore them?'

Again she shrugged uncaringly.

Marty ballooned his cheeks. She was making this terribly difficult for him. He made no decision one way or the other, just took her in his arms and promised that everything would turn out all right.

But it didn't. The incident had disturbed Etta more than she chose to admit – made her physically ill, in fact – although she did not have to confess it because Marty could see that for himself. Each evening when he came home he now found her lying on the bed, not with that mischievous promise in her eye but instead wearing a look of nausea. Mercifully this was to wear off after an hour in his company; he made sure that it did by cosseting her with little treats, pandering to her unusual craving for porridge at the oddest hours. But still the nausea returned on a regular basis to cause them both unrest.

'Maybe we should have you to the doctor,' he said as he cuddled her through yet another bout.

'No need,' sighed Etta, nestling against him on the sofa. 'We both know what's upset me.'

Aware of how sensitive she was, he nodded, but then added, 'As long as that's all it is.'

'*All?*' Her indignant face jerked round to confront him.

'Oh, I didn't mean to sound dismissive!' He lured her back with a pacifying hug. 'I know how deeply she insulted you. What I meant was, what if this is actually a serious illness?' His cousin had suffered from regular bouts of sickness that had terminated in a fatal haemorrhage. Loath to mention this to Etta, he cuddled her and thought for a while. 'Is there any other symptom apart from feeling sick?'

168

Etta pondered, then shook her head. 'No.'

Marty looked relieved – then at her tiny exclamation he turned to see her expression change and demanded, 'Love, you must tell me!'

Etta had turned pink, her eyes suddenly alert. There *was* something else, though it had always been classed as too indelicate to mention between ladies of her former acquaintance and certainly not to menfolk. But then she was not such a shrinking violet as some. 'It's nothing really. Just that I haven't been ... *unwell*, for, oh, I can't recall how long.' At her husband's frown, she attempted to clarify. 'The curse that visits women every month.'

Stunned by her candidness, Marty made a little noise of embarrassment and averted his gaze.

There was a hiatus, during which each of them ruminated on the cause, minds beginning to tick. Marty recalled how, prior to his younger sisters and brothers being born his mother had always been incommoded by sickness. He remembered this so well because of the inconvenience it had caused him. But that had been a morning occurrence; Etta suffered hers on a night. Even so ... Glancing at his wife, he wondered if the same suspicion had crossed her mind.

Until this moment, Etta's thoughts had only been ones of gratitude that the monthly visitation had not chosen to ruin her idyll. Faced with the combined evidence, even now other young ladies might not have put two and two together. But an earthy interest in the sexual whys and wherefores of life had always led this one to seek answers, and the thought that suddenly exploded in her brain was horrific. Looking back at Marty she wondered how to voice it, but as he had watched the expression in her eyes quickly turn from incomprehension to terror, she did not have to.

He put his hand over his mouth, his shocked voice emerging through his fingers. 'You're having a nipper!'

Etta was too stunned to speak. What an innocent, what

a dolt to think she could prevent pregnancy simply by wishing it!

'God . . . well, I suppose it was bound to happen, but . . . Holy Mother . . .' Marty performed a deep breath, then an exhalation of laughter. Now that the truth had registered, he was overcome with happiness over the idea of becoming a father. 'Oh Jazers, oh bloody hell, I'm lost for words!' He seized her in a hug.

Even snuggled within his embrace, Etta could not feel the same elation – she knew only fear. Something, some*one*, had invaded her body; it would live there like a parasite for months, swelling her to the size of a house before bursting its way out – and then what? There was no one to tell her, no one to show her, no one on whom to lean. Never had she needed a mother more than now. Even Blanche would have done, dear Blanche, more like a friend than a servant. But she had no one. In her hour of travail she would be alone.

Bursting with his good news, Marty jumped up and declared that he must go round and convey this to his parents.

'Don't leave me!'

'You can come too!' Smiling, he held out an encouraging hand.

Etta grimaced up at him in disbelief. 'Didn't you hear anything I said before?'

He sank again to the sofa, grabbing her hand to exhort her. 'Oh, but Ett, think about this! We don't know anything about bab—'

'I'll learn! Martin, I don't want to tell anyone else about this at present, it's too much of a shock.' Shock was too mild a word. She fought to contain the nausea that had come rushing back with a vengeance

'But they'll be so pleased! Ma will bend over backwards to hel—'

'I don't want her help!' shrieked Etta. 'Martin, please, I

know she's your mother but she isn't mine and I'd rather you didn't tell her for now.'

After an anguished snort, he abandoned the pressure. It was childish and petty of his wife, but he adored Etta, thought her lovelier than ever with their child growing within her, and though it cut him deeply he acquiesced to her demand.

Folding her in his arms again he vouched it would be their secret for now. But privately he did not know how long he could stop himself from leaking this wonderful news.

In fact, it took less than twenty-four hours. Bumping into his mother and father in the street the next evening on his way home, first he apologised for not seeing them for a while. 'It's been a bit awkward, Etta hasn't felt too well.'

Though tired and grimy from his day's toil in the fields, Redmond was as kind as ever. 'Ah, sure, we're sorry to hear that.'

Aggie merely nodded and, without referring to Etta, asked, 'How are you, son?'

Itching to shout out his news, he replied that he was, 'In the pink.'

'Good, good . . .' She nodded again.

It was evident to Marty that he was in her bad books. Well, what did she expect him to say? Was he meant to tell her it was all right that she had said those awful things to his wife? That she was forgiven? Well, he wasn't going to, for her words had stung him too. Nevertheless, bursting with joy, he wanted to share his news. 'As a matter of fact . . . oh, look, I'm not supposed to tell yese but I'm going to be a daddy!'

Redmond's delicate face creased into a smile. 'Why, isn't that great!' Then immediately his jaw went slack, as due to his condition it was wont to do in times of emotion, and he sat down on the kerb in anticipation that his knees might follow suit.

171

Ignoring her husband, Aggie trained her ice-blue eyes on Marty, her tone guarded. 'What do you mean, aren't supposed to tell us?'

Marty's flush of excitement was further coloured by guilt. 'I didn't mean just you! I meant anybod—'

'No, I think you did mean just us,' said Aggie, grossly offended, 'and we all know who gave the instruction.'

'Ag . . .' From his crouched position, Red tried to mediate.

But Marty interrupted. 'Etta just wanted to keep it between us for a while, Ma. We're not even sure yet whether she is in a certain condition.'

'But whatever way, we'll be the last to hear of it,' snapped Aggie with assurance.

'Ma, don't be like this,' wailed Marty. 'You did upset her.'

'And what of the way she spoke to me?' demanded his mother.

'Aye, now, be fair, son.' Redmond tried to sound firm, though being down in the gutter lent him no gravitas. 'Your mother was awful hurt by Etta's –'

'"I shan't be having any!"' Aggie mimicked her daughter-in-law's retort. 'Not so clever now, is she? I should've thought she'd be glad of any help – even mine.'

Had Marty been dithering over which side to choose, the sheer mean-spiritedness of this comment helped him make up his mind. 'Well, I'm sorry, Ma, but Etta hasn't forgiven you. I've tried to talk her round, persuade her that you didn't mean what you sai—'

'Oh I meant it all right!'

'And you really hurt her! So, yes, if ye must know she's asked that you don't come round.'

'Does the man of the house have no say?' A glacial eye looked him up and down.

'Well, judging by your attitude now,' rejoined Marty, 'I tend to agree with her that it's best if the two of yese stay apart.'

'I can see the sense in that.' Tired of being ignored, concentrating hard to try and maintain consciousness, Redmond grabbed a handful of his wife's skirt and hauled himself to his feet. 'But you'll keep in contact, won't you, son?'

'It's difficult, Da. I'd love to come round sometimes but I have to support my wife . . .' Marty's voice trailed away.

'I suppose you do,' said Aggie, deeply injured. 'In that case, son, we'll wish ye good luck and maybe see you again when you've come to your senses.' Taking a firm grip of her husband's arm, she led him home.

Anxious not to be denied access to his grandchild, Redmond craned his neck and called over his frail shoulder, 'You'll let us know when the baby's born?' But Marty was already on his way.

'He will, of course he will.' Redmond spoke as if to reassure his wife.

Her jaw clamped, Aggie remained mute.

Uncle Mal could not believe it when they informed him, echoing Redmond's sentiments that the birth of the child would change Marty's view.

Close to tears, Aggie disagreed. 'If you were in his place would you choose your mother over your wife?' She shook her head. 'And wasn't he always a law unto himself.' In despair she began folding things that did not need folding. 'Ah well, I suppose I'm partly to blame. I made him what he is.'

Redmond tried to comfort her. 'How can that be? People are what they are.'

She corrected herself. 'Not what he *is* but rather what he does, what he's allowed to get away with. All this business about him always wanting what he can't have and to go where he wasn't allowed; perhaps if I'd not been so accommodating . . .'

'Ah well, maybe once he's thought about it a while he'll

make Etta listen to reason,' said her husband softly, mopping his watery eyes and fighting to stay awake.

Old Malachy nodded. 'She's going to need ye.'

'I won't go where I'm not wanted,' rejoined Aggie. 'Sure, I'm willing to help, but it's got to come from her. If she wants me she knows where I am. They both do.'

'Aye, they're only a couple of streets away,' nodded her elderly uncle comfortingly.

Streets away, thought Aggie, but from the coldness that emanated from her erstwhile loving son, it could have been miles.

8

The feud was to intensify. People took sides, boundaries were set. Once so popular, now judged on his ruthless behaviour towards the matriarch, Marty found himself barred from places he had always been welcome before, including the home of his sister Lou, who had informed him in a rancorous letter what she thought of him, though Dan still said hello if they passed each other in town. Obviously, the embargo was not upheld by Aunt Joan who, upon hearing of the row, could not restrain her glee at playing Lady Bountiful to Aggie's wicked witch, though her zeal was to be sapped by the eventual dawning that Etta had nought in her favour save a beautiful façade, and could never be, as hoped, Joan's visa to a higher social position. Henceforth, the invitations were performed in the manner of a benefactress to those unfortunate souls at the work-house gates, any attempt from them to return the favour being turned down with the kind words that it would be much nicer for Martin's wife to dine in these pleasanter surroundings, 'As a replacement for all that Etta sacrificed for you.'

After such an insult Marty swore that even if Aunt Joan was the only one speaking to him, he would never visit her and Uncle John again. In fact, with Joan obviously writing Etta off as a dead loss they were not to hear from these particular relatives in months, which gave him no discomfort at all, his sadness being reserved for closer kin. Such alienation was to cause much despair, not simply because he was a loving son and missed his family, but for practical reasons too. Having a wide circle of male friends was all very well when one needed a plumber, but a different matter entirely when another human life was involved. In a few months his child would enter the world, and neither he nor his wife had the slightest idea how to care for it.

An avid reader, Etta set aside her romantic novels in search of more vital content, managing to lay her hands on a volume concerning childbirth. What she read terrified her even more. She tried to convince herself that others got over it, that it could not be so bad if they went on to do it time and time again – could it?

Marty reassured her that it couldn't and truly believed this, for his mother had borne a dozen without difficulty. However, he was also aware that one needed the aid of a midwife; and neither he nor Etta knew of any. Still, there were months to go yet. He would ask around and when her time grew closer he would have one. He urged her not to worry.

In the beginning, Etta did worry about the coming ordeal. Using lack of funds as an excuse not to visit a doctor, in reality it was that she dreaded his confirmation. Until then she could put it to the back of her mind and pretend all was well. However, the time arrived when medical verification was no longer required, for it came in the slightest, strangest fluttering within, and Etta knew with a jolt that her life would never be the same again. Never had she known such abject terror. But gradually as the new life swelled inside her it seemed to bring with it courage, and one morning she awoke to find the horror fading into acceptance, and thenceforth turned her energy to the more positive act of creating a layette.

Clothes were required for the mother-to-be too as her girth expanded. It was Marty's turn to worry then over the amount of money she was spending, for Etta's idea of making do consisted only of buying cheaper material, not less of it, and the funds she had brought to the marriage were expired. Still, he hadn't the heart to condemn her. She looked so exquisite in her floaty creation of ribbons and lace, and, after all, one could not go without clothes, especially now that the mornings held a definite chill. The moment it became unpleasant to get out of bed he encouraged his wife to buy a thick shawl, though he himself continued to hold out. Rarely idle for a second, he could soon get warm.

For a while Etta managed to cope with all that needed to be done about the house, but the grind of having all these chores day after day, week after week, eventually began to annoy. Under the excuse of her delicate condition, she elected to do only the absolute necessities, leaving the rest in favour of her sewing. It helped that Martin did not seem to mind, in fact he was of great assistance.

Others thought differently. 'That poor young man, I feel real sorry for him,' murmured one of the neighbours, Mrs Kelly, spying on Marty through the open door as he swept around Etta's feet whilst his wife sat embroidering. 'Sure and he deserves more decent respect than she shows him. What man wants to do for himself after a hard day's labour? She'll lose him if she's not careful.'

'I'd swap him for mine in a flash,' said her companion, eyeing Marty's attractive proportions as he came out to beat a rug.

The other agreed, both blind to the small gestures of love that passed between man and wife, attuned only to what they saw as exploitation.

Marty did not see it as such. Still in the throes of adoration he was quite happy to take the load off Etta until her confinement was over, and, even with her shape distorted, he was proud to be seen with such a gorgeous companion. He preened under the looks of admiration from other men, in the knowledge that she was his and his alone.

The weather grew steadily colder, the air racked with bronchitic coughs. That the house and courtyard had always been in shadow had not mattered much before, when one knew there was sunshine on the far side of the wall. Now, though, as winter set in, Marty and his wife were beset by other defects. A heavy rainfall revealed that the privy roof let in water. Etta returned from her visit squeaking with indignation and thoroughly drenched.

'It's an outrage when one needs an umbrella *inside!*'

Immediately the downpour ceased, Marty went off to the gasworks and fetched a bucket of tar with which to fix the roof, clambering up and risking injury to daub the tiles so that his loved one might not receive another dousing whilst he was out at work.

His neighbours voiced appreciation, for the leak had been an annoyance to them too.

'Why didn't any of them get their husband to mend it then?' retorted Etta, upon overhearing the women's thanks. 'Instead of leaving it to mine.'

But Marty was more generous, especially when one of the women showed her indebtedness by handing over some freshly baked scones, telling her, 'It's no trouble. I couldn't have my wife getting wet, now, could I? But I'm glad you benefited too.'

'Well, even if he did do it for Lady Muck,' the giver told another neighbour, 'I thought he deserved a reward – I've smelt the burnt offerings milady serves him.'

Savouring the treat, Marty was to perform other tasks around the yard in the hope of procuring more home baking, but alas this was not to be forthcoming – certainly not from Etta. It was not that his wife did not care, he told himself, for she showed her love in many other ways.

For example, noticing him shivering and unable to get warm after another day on the cold stone platform of the railway station, she commanded her husband to, 'Buy an overcoat! It's December, for heaven's sake.'

Hunched over the fire, examining his boots that were in need of mending yet again from all the miles they had travelled, he confessed, 'I've already got one, in a manner of speaking. I pawned it in order to get us a place to stay.'

'Why didn't you say?' Etta was concerned for his well-being. 'You must retrieve it!'

He tried to remain nonchalant between bouts of shivering. 'I've been holding out till the weather gets bad.'

'How much worse does it have to get!' She tightened her shawl about her swollen abdomen and, with some difficulty, knelt to wrap newspaper around the pair of house bricks that had been warming in the oven.

Still he resisted as he took over her task and went to insert the bricks under the bedcover. The amount of patrons needing his service had been drastically reduced lately. He would have to seek other work to make up his income. 'We haven't that much to spare, Ett, we'll need it when the baby's bor—'

'And the baby needs a father! You'll perish before he even draws breath. I order you to get that coat.' His wife took a half-sovereign from the mantelpiece and thrust it at him.

'Yes, ma'am!' Marty jokingly adopted a servile pose, tugging his forelock and cringing before her. 'Anyt'ing ye say, ma'am.'

But when the teasing and laughter was done he mulled her words over as they prepared for bed. The retrieval period was almost up. If he didn't get it back now it would be sold and he would have to pay more for a new one.

So, equipped with the pawn ticket, the next day he went to recover his coat and was thankful for the warmth it provided. It came in handy during the night too, as an extra cover for the bed.

If only the chill were skin deep. Christmas was an especially bad time to be estranged from one's kin. His little brothers and sisters, uninformed of the dispute, called out

179

to him and Etta gaily upon seeing them in the street – 'Marty, we haven't see you for ages! Will you be round for Christmas dinner?'

What could he tell them? Etta seemed content enough with only her man for company, with his help cooking them a reasonable dinner, enjoying silly games afterwards and singing carols in front of a roaring fire – indeed she was to make much of the fact that they were similarly placed now in that both had been abandoned by their families, and was not that a reason to feel even closer to each other? Whilst taking delight in her too, for she could teach him many things and was a great conversationalist and much fun as a companion, a small part of him longed to go round to his parents, who would have a full house. But he had sworn his loyalty to Etta and would not leave her for any reason . . . though he could not resist a wistful fantasy over what the other Lanegans would be having to eat.

The feelings of abandonment were to increase. In summertime, with sunrise at half past four, it had not been such hardship to be first out of bed, to light the fire and attend to other chores that should rightly have been done by his wife. Now, in the pitch-black, teeth-chattering chill of those long winter months as he stumbled off to work through fog and rain, snow and ice, returning to a stack of things that Etta had left undone, he could not avoid feeling slightly vexed at times. It was not that he resented helping his wife – he still adored her – but the marked lack of contribution from Etta proved very wearing.

From her words and behaviour he was confident she loved him equally, but, oh, if only she would pay as much attention to the food as to the furnishings, would try to ensure that, under their fancy little cosies, the boiled eggs were not as hard as rocks, would bake him a competent pie from time to time, it would make everything so much easier to bear. Marty had always loved pies – apple pies, mince pies, but particularly rabbit. In times of strife a well-made pie could be such a comfort. His mother had always provided them regularly. Now there was only the memory.

Perhaps it was his imagination but this winter seemed to be an exceptionally long one, January, February and March crawling by, the pall of smoke from iron foundries and thousands of household chimneys obliterating what little sunlight there was.

But at last the bleakness gradually began to lift, and it seemed as if Marty's situation might improve too with the bursting of spring when a friend was to share the benefits of a poaching excursion. Alas, his hints to Etta that she might like to make a pie with the rabbit did not go down as hoped, in fact she balked just watching him skin and gut it. When she refused even to touch the wretched thing he was compelled to have a bash at a rabbit stew himself, but this only extended to dropping the puny carcass into a pan with some water and vegetables, and the result what not exactly what he had hoped for.

Whilst his spirits slowly deflated, his wife swelled riper by the day, signalling that the time was nigh to find a midwife.

'You said you'd do it,' an anxious Etta reminded him.

Marooned in foreign territory, Marty suggested tentatively, 'Couldn't you ask one of the neighbours?'

'They'll have nothing to do with me,' stated his wife, who, even after several months of living there, had not formed any kind of intimacy with the other women and only greeted them in passing. She shrugged. 'I've tried to be friendly, but . . .'

Marty nodded, acknowledging that this was more their fault than Etta's, for they mistakenly surmised that because of her well-bred mannerisms she was a snob too – and if only they bothered to get to know her they would see that this was not so, she was quite a commoner at heart. But, as ever, it was left to him to remedy matters. 'Don't worry,'

181

he reassured her. 'I'll find someone to help you.' Though he was still unsure how.

Confiding his woes to a chum that same day, he was finally provided with the name of one who might help, and, thus equipped, went to visit the elderly woman on his way home from work. She seemed nice enough, if a little untidy, her robust proportions emanating self-assurance which lent Marty confidence in her aptitude too, though her request for five shillings met with dismay. It seemed an awful lot of money.

Catching the look of doubt upon his face, Nancy Dowd said quickly, 'I'm not asking that you give it me now, my dear. I never charge till the babby's born, and from what you say you'll have a week or so to save it up.'

Searching her softly wrinkled features for signs of duplicity, Marty saw none, but even if he had there would have been no choice for one so desperate, and he agreed to hire her services. At least that was one thing out of the way.

If only his desperation was restricted to fiscal concerns. With Etta so large it had been impossible to make love to her for weeks and, this being the very foundation of their rapport, Marty had lately begun to feel that the withdrawal of it would drive him mad. Any excitement over the imminent arrival of his son or daughter was tempered by a greater apprehension. Would things ever be the same again?

Thoughts of pleasures lost were to consume him as he made his way home from work along a back lane that Monday noon. It was unusual for him to be home at this time of day – even though everyone else might be enjoying an Easter holiday it was a busy time for those at the railway station – but as the birth loomed he had taken to checking on the mother-to-be at dinnertime. Not that there would be anything much on offer for him, he thought miserably. Passing an open gateway he glanced in and was about to walk on, but what he saw there drew him back immediately to look and to lust after. Every scruple demolished, he gazed longingly inside, almost drooling as the voluptuous woman went about her business. Making himself less obtrusive he peeped around the gatepost and watched her for a moment. It was as if she had known he would be passing at that very minute and extended open invitation. His heart thudded as she made for the privy, that wonderful, beneficent angel ... In his mind he went through the moves that would take place behind that door, imagined her occupied in lifting her skirt, drawers round ankles ... Now was his chance ... in those few seconds he tried to resist, truly he did, but the desire was just too overwhelming. He *must* have it.

Bracing himself, he dashed on tiptoe into the yard, at the same time pulling his cuffs down over his hands as a means of protection, and in an instant had reached through the open window and had snatched the steaming pie from where she had displayed it, and was in the lane running before the woman could even cry out. Fleeing to a derelict shed, he kicked the door shut behind him and, heart soaring in triumph, lifted the hot plate to his nostrils in an effort to distinguish the contents of the pie. Steak, he thought ... or some sort of meat anyway. A fresh stream of saliva gushed into his mouth. It didn't matter what variety it was, the surprise of biting into it would be equally thrilling. Wasting no more time he used his penknife to forge a way in and awkwardly scooped a portion into his mouth – immediately cursing and wafting as scalding gravy dribbled down his chin. Oh, but it was glorious!

Again and again he attacked it in the manner of a dog, drawing in quick gulps of air to cool his mouth between bites, gorging and licking and slurping, eating every bit of it himself, and, finally replate, delivering a long ecstatic belch.

Then he took a deep breath and looked down at the empty plate – and all at once felt sick. Sick with pie, sick with guilt. Whilst seeing no wrong in pilfering from the masters who could afford it, he had never stooped so low as to rob his neighbours. What kind of charlatan stole another's dinner? And he hadn't even saved any for Etta.

If the guilt was bad then it was to be exacerbated upon reaching home, for whilst he had been stuffing his face with pie his wife was in the throes of labour.

Pacing the floor, clutching her back, Etta wheeled at his entry, her expression a mixture of relief and annoyance. 'Where have you been? You said you'd be here at –' Her criticism was displaced by a long drawn-out groan and she held on to a chair to steady herself.

Immediately he came to her, hovering ineffectually, trying to support her huge belly. 'Ett, how long have you been like this?'

'*Hours!*' She had been plagued by a nagging backache since last night, but had not recognised it for what it was until, just after her husband had left for work, an unstoppable waterfall had occurred.

He stared helplessly into her contorted face. 'What shall I do?'

The contraction was beginning to recede. Etta released her breath and told him, 'Fetch the midwife.'

'But will you be all right on your own?'

'I'll have to be, shan't I? Now hurry!' Irritated and terrified, Etta gave him a shove, desperate to have someone here who knew what they were doing, to have this ordeal over.

Marty rushed back outside, along the alley and into the street, dithering there for a second over which direction to take, for the midwife's address had completely evaporated in panic. Thankfully, after a moment's swearing it came to him and, running full pelt for almost a mile, he was to find the woman at home. Mrs Dowd being halfway through lunch, the return journey was to be delayed. Hovering whilst his elderly companion finished off her bread and dripping, anxious to assuage his wife's concern, he told the midwife, 'I'll run on ahead if you like!'

She did not share his haste, chewing leisurely. 'Carry my bag for me, would you, dear? I'll follow on when I'm done.'

He belched, apologised, grabbed the satchel and fled back along Walmgate, leaving the old woman to sup her tea.

When he got back, Etta's pacing had become even more agitated. Marty remained by her side, feeling helpless at being unable to alleviate her pain. Mrs Dowd took an age. On finally arriving she seemed no less casual as she waddled in, took a brief, authoritative look at Etta, packed her off to bed, then said to Marty, 'Shall we have the kettle on and have a cup of tea? In all the haste I never got to finish mine.'

His jaw dropped. 'Aren't you going up with her?'

She tried to calm him with a laugh. 'She'll be ages yet. Might as well sort out my fee whilst we're at it.'

'You want it now?' He was amazed that she could be so mercenary whilst Etta's groans could still be heard downstairs.

'Are you telling me you haven't got it?' Mrs Dowd looked suspicious.

'No! Of course I have.' Fortunately he had kept five shillings in a pot on the mantel and delved into it now, for there seemed in her attitude a threat to leave if he didn't cough up.

Pocketing the coins, she instructed him again to make the tea, which he did. Far too restless to join her in a cup, and becoming aware that she smelt like overripe cheese, he headed for the stairs.

'Where do you think you're off to?' she boomed.

'To see my wife.' Under her eagle eye he was made to feel an intruder in his own house, and his gaze dropped to the greasy stain on the bosom of her serge dress. 'If that's all right,' came his mumbled addition.

'And what use will you be?' asked the big woman airily.

Marty bristled yet felt powerless. If he argued with her

she might leave, and then where would he be?

But then she seemed to undergo a change of heart and flicked her hand at him. 'Oh, go if you must – but I don't want you under my feet when I do come.'

Granted permission, he bounded upstairs and held his wife's hand, though he was forced to acknowledge that the midwife was right, Etta didn't even seem to want him there.

After an unhurried cup of tea, Mrs Dowd finally made an appearance, huffing slowly up the staircase with her greasy old satchel and proceeding to lay its contents out on the bare floorboards.

Gripping Etta's hand, Marty's worried eyes examined the midwife's accoutrements: a ball of string, a pot of what looked like lard, and other unrecognisable objects.

'Off you pop now, young fella-me-lad,' ordered Mrs Dowd.

Thankful to be released, Marty bent to murmur in Etta's ear as she writhed in agony. 'You'll be all right now, love, Mrs Dowd'll take care of you.' And with an anxious backwards glance he left the women to their business.

But instead of the midwife making the situation better, it grew steadily noisier. Downstairs, trying and failing to occupy himself by repairing his boots, he was alarmed at the crescendo – his mother hadn't made such a din when giving birth to his younger siblings. The volume became so bloodcurdling that he slapped his hands over his ears in an effort to block it out, though this was futile. Etta's yells would have pierced armour. Unable to bear it, he strode into the yard but the screams were to follow. Whilst he walked back and forth, a neighbour came out to the privy, glanced at him sympathetically, but was too wary to offer help. Embarrassed and upset at the thought of Etta in such torment, Marty quickly went back indoors – sweet Jesus, how much longer could this go on?

'Is everything all right up there?' he called aloft.

Receiving no answer, he took a few steps up the staircase, not daring to go further, watching Mrs Dowd's black-stockinged ankles below the old serge dress, the huge tattered slippers galumphing around the bed.

'Let's slap some grease on, dear, and make its passage easier!'

Her mind and body overtaken by another fearsome contraction, Etta was barely conscious of the jolly voice, the dirty old fingernails dipping into lard that was coated in dust, her only response to squeal long and loud.

Creeping higher, Marty blanched at the horrible indignities perpetrated upon his wife and promptly ducked away, though out of fear he demanded again, 'Is everything all right?'

This time Mrs Dowd answered cheerily, 'Fine enough, lovey!'

'Are you sure? She sounds in terrible pain.'

The midwife shuffled over to look down at him, the revolting cheesy smell wafting from her and her manner infuriatingly calm and somewhat belittling. 'Everything's normal. Eh, you young chaps – you're nobbut a bairn yourself – stop worriting.'

Annoyance flared at her derogatory tone but he tried not to let it show. 'I can't help it! My mother didn't scream so loud.'

In a moment of respite, Etta overheard and misinterpreted his words, and before her body was seized by another contraction she vented her fury: 'Oh, I suppose *she* laughed! I suppose *she* gave birth between washing the sheets and mangling and stirring the bloody stew at the same time – aagh!' Her face was riven with venom and agony and a long drawn-out groan overtook the oaths.

Afraid to see those pale and intelligent features so contorted, Marty shrank inside himself, not recognising his wife at all.

The agony went on all afternoon.

Outside, the rest of the world carried on as normal, many

of the inhabitants of Walmgate gone to the local stray to perform an Easter custom. Children who had spent hours diligently painting patterns onto hard-boiled eggs now hurled them down the grassy incline and raced excitedly after them, the idea being that the shells should smash at the bottom and so complete this ancient fertility rite; but the slopes of Low Moor were too gentle, the eggs' journey constantly interrupted by hummocks of grass or, even worse, a cowpat, and in the end the shells had to be broken by hand. After a rare visit to church for the parents, the Lanegan children had also taken part in this festivity, then had seated themselves beneath a budding chestnut tree where they picked off the shells bit by bit, and, despite the whites being stained with red and green paint, had enjoyed their eggs as a picnic tea before continuing their stroll to the nearby village of Heslington, from where they were now making their way home.

It was incredibly warm for the time of year; the sun still as bright now as it had been all day, the sky as blindingly blue, the fields a-skitter with lambs. Amidst such enjoyable milieu, Aggie was in benevolent mood and, spurred on by watching the frolicking little creatures, murmured to her husband who shambled alongside, 'She'll be about due by now I should think.'

Not needing to ask who *she* was, Redmond tilted his delicate face and breathed a sigh of regret over the rift. 'Aye . . .'

'It'll be difficult for her, giving birth without her mother there.' Over the months, Aggie had seen her daughter-in-law occasionally, noted the progressive increase of her girth as they passed without speaking in the street, and at such points had asked herself: wasn't it easy for her to condemn the Ibbetsons, but was she not behaving in exactly the same manner by cutting off her son? But the answer was always no, because this feud was not of her doing, it was Marty who was avoiding her, not the other way round. Had she seen him face to face she would have broken her silence, despite the hurt he had inflicted on her in his stubborn defence of his wife, just as she might have smiled at Etta had the latter deigned to look at her, but the other's eyes were always averted as she crossed the road to avoid any unpleasantness. Still, she could voice pity for a girl approaching labour. ''Tis a lonely time at best.'

Redmond sensed that his wife might be weakening and, detesting this current state of affairs, sought to take advantage by confirming, 'It'll certainly be a fierce struggle for them both. I wonder how himself has been.'

'Probably disappeared down the cracks in the pavement, the way she neglects him,' said Aggie, intransigent again. 'But that's of his own making. God help that poor child of his. I mean, it will be our grandchild after all. I don't like to think of it born into hardship, nor of Marty struggling . . .'

'Should we call in on our way back, then, do you think?' posed Redmond hopefully. He had tried to bring about a reconciliation at Christmas but Ag had had none of it.

This time, though, she paid him more heed. 'I suppose it wouldn't harm to see how the land lies . . . just you and me. Himself could take the nippers home.' She referred now to Uncle Mal, who shuffled ahead with the children, occasionally stooping to wrench handfuls of spring flowers from beneath the hedgerows. Deliberating for a few seconds longer, she finally uttered, 'Aye, maybe we should – but any of her lip and that's it!'

Some twenty minutes later, upon reaching the deserted pens of the Cattle Market, they instructed Uncle Mal to continue home with the children, they themselves making a detour into the alleyway that led to their son's abode.

Even before they were half a dozen paces along it they could hear Etta's bellows and curses.

Red winced and stroked his bushy hair, his eyes wary. 'Maybe it's better I don't . . .' His comment tailed away as

189

his knees suddenly buckled and he fell to the ground, momentarily paralysed.

His wife sighed in quiet exasperation and bent to tend him, waiting for the couple of minutes it took him to recover, then propping him against a wall whilst she went into the yard, tapped at Marty's door and waited.

Marty had never been so glad to see her. 'Oh, thank God, Ma! I don't know what's happening up there but it can't be right.'

Immediately past slights were forgiven. 'Do you want me to –?'

'Oh please, yes, yes!' He dragged her in and almost bundled her up the stairs.

Rarely had Aggie heard so many oaths strung together as emerged from Etta's mouth – where had a young lady learned such things? She was glad that it was the midwife who was subjected to it and not herself. What a fuss! But that was Etta through and through. She herself had bitten the sheets, twisted them into knots, anything in order to avoid upsetting others, but Etta had no such reserve. Closing her eyes against yet another obscenity, her step was tentative as she approached the bedroom. But once in there she saw what lay behind the commotion.

'Push, woman, push! There where you feel my fingers!'

Aggie cringed – then was immediately furious. There was no delicacy in childbirth but the way that old sow was jabbing at Etta was downright inhuman.

'What in God's name are you doing to that poor girl?' She surged forth now, taking the other by surprise.

'I'm trying to deliver her if she'd heed!' Mrs Dowd wheeled to complain.

'Look at your nails, they're filthy!' Aggie was horrified. 'Away with ye now, you unsanitary old creature!'

Pricked, the old midwife refused to budge. 'I was hired fair and square!'

'Well, your services are no longer required!' Slender of

body, Aggie employed strength of character to drive the bigger woman away from the bed, watching her like a hawk whilst she packed her satchel, to much muttering and grumbling.

'You needn't think I'm giving the money back!'

'Is that right?' countered Aggie. 'Well, I suppose you'll be needing every penny of it, considering you're facing a five pound fine!'

'What?' shrieked Mrs Dowd.

'That's what the penalty is for an unregistered – I *was* going to say midwife but I'm damned if I'll flatter you with the title!' Gladdened by the look of fear she had inflicted, Aggie added in a more reasonable tone, 'Then again, if you hand back the cash you undoubtedly cheated out of this trusting young couple, I might just see my way to not involving the law!'

'Oh, take your blasted money!' In a fit of temper, Mrs Dowd hurled the coins on the floor, and huffed her way downstairs, throwing an insult at Marty on her way out.

His frantic face appeared in the bedroom. 'Ma, what's going on?'

'Have you lost your mind?' Aggie demanded of her son. 'Allowing that great moose of a midwife near your wife!'

He made a gesture of helplessness. 'I wasn't to know!'

'You would have done if you hadn't cut me out of your life,' scolded Aggie.

'I'm sorry, I –!'

'That's good enough! Get round to Mrs Cahill in our street and tell her to come at once – everything's going to be all right now, Etta!' She hurried over to reassure the groaning mother-to-be. 'I'll take care of you.'

Gripped by the most excruciating waves of agony, feeling as if her body were being turned inside out, Etta's only response was to bawl long and loud.

'Won't be two shakes!' Shoving her son before her, Aggie hurried downstairs.

191

Racked by conscience, Marty sped from the house, issuing a swift greeting as he rushed past his father who still sat in the alleyway. A dazed Red barely had the chance to answer before his wife accosted him.

'Do you think you can manage an errand?'

'I'll try.' With her help he hauled his slight frame up.

'Nip to Falconer's and get me some antiseptic.' Aggie gave him some money then dashed back inside, took a bowl of warm water upstairs and proceeded to sluice Etta down where the dirty old fingers had invaded her, crooning, 'Soon be over with, pet, soon be over.'

Time and again this phrase was to be uttered, repeated by the more competent midwife who arrived to take over from Aggie and had been met with much ungrateful abuse from the one in turmoil, until finally the prophesy was realised in an abrupt flesh-splitting scream of release, and a hot, wet slither of new life.

Downstairs, every muscle knotted from having to share his wife's prolonged agony, Marty was jolted by the sudden momentous hush. His eyes flew to those of his father in an instant of shared panic – then came a newborn's cry, and an astonished smile began to spread across his face as his relieved father reached out to grip his hand.

'Will I go up?' After a few vigorous shakes he broke away and made straight for the stairs, but was gently restrained by Redmond, who said kindly:

'Best not just yet. There'll be things for the women to see to.'

And indeed there were. Yearning to see his wife and child, Marty was compelled to wait another full hour until the doctor had been fetched to insert stitches in torn flesh – which drew forth even more piercing screams, much to his horror for he had thought it all over – then for the women to clear up after their grisly business and for Etta to be washed and made comfortable before finally it was his turn.

Excitement in his heart but caution in his step, he felt almost like a thief as he crept up the stairs, especially upon infiltrating the serene oasis. Etta's eyes had only ever been for him, yet now they seemed totally unaware of his presence, her face, radiant but exhausted, concentrated intensely on the bundle that lay alongside her. For a second he endured a terrible sense of exclusion, all the fears of those winter months cascading back to rob him of any joy. Then her eyes lifted and, seeing him, flooded with all the affection that he had come to claim as rightfully his, and though her limbs might be weak her smile was strong as she beckoned him, eager for the kiss he rushed to bestow, responding as if she had not seen him for years.

Then, 'Look what we've done, Marty,' she murmured adoringly, her eyes and voice brimming with emotion.

Greatly moved, unprepared for the tears that sprang to his eyes as they took a first glimpse of his baby daughter, and flooded with an all-encompassing urge to protect her from the world, Marty blurted an emotional laugh and explored the tiny pink face with a wondrous finger. Unable to speak, he could only stare and sigh in awe.

9

Overwhelmed by the birth and the responsibility of having this tiny human being to care for, it was not until a whole day had gone by that Etta experienced a twinge of remorse over other participants. After being so snubbed, Martin's mother could have abandoned her daughter-in-law to her fate, yet here was Aggie, despite all her own commitments, running around after the new mother, treating her only with kindness and showing her how to look after the baby, whilst taking care of the house and Martin too. Unable to find sufficient words to express her gratitude other than a simple thank you, Etta could only convey it in her demeanour, hoping this was enough to make up for her part in the rift.

And indeed it seemed to be, for, even after a fortnight when Etta was up and about, Aggie continued to arrive every day to see if there was anything she could do for the mother and child whilst Marty was at work, all bad feeling completely behind them. As endorsement of this, younger family members also felt able to come and visit the newest Lanegan. Louisa, Bridget, Mary and Ann all arrived in turn with their gifts, to coo over the sweet little thing and to instruct Etta, quite genuinely, to call on them if ever she needed help; and, understanding their previous aversion, she welcomed each and every one, determined not to rebuff their friendship a second time, glad that the feud was over.

Other visitors were not quite so welcome. 'I'm so sorry

194

I haven't been earlier but *nobody* bothered to come and let us know!' Scurrying in on her dainty feet, Aunt Joan delivered a belated gift for the new baby into Etta's hands whilst eyeing her sister-in-law reproachfully. 'If I hadn't bumped into Agnes in town I don't suppose I'd have ever learned of your addition.'

Saying nothing, Aggie turned to put the kettle on whilst her accuser bent over the apple crate that had been padded with blankets to serve as a crib, uttering genuine compliments over the black-haired babe.

Then, coming back to earth, Joan properly took in the newcomer's living conditions, and tried but failed to hide how appalling she found them. Somehow, though, she managed to overcome her aversion to the greasy old sofa and perched on the very edge of it beside Etta, mouthing tentaively under her breath, 'I heard relations have been restored . . .'

'Yes, everything's fine now,' Etta murmured with a smile, nothing and no one able to ruin that glow of maternity.

Joan gave a pleased nod, whispering, 'She can be very difficult can Aggie.'

Seeing her mother-in-law's lips tighten and not wanting to jeopardise their new rapport, Etta said brightly, 'Would you care to see the lovely things Grandmamma has made for Celia?' One by one she displayed a selection of stitched and knitted garments on her lap.

Joan raised a mousy eyebrow. 'How lovely! If you hadn't told me Agnes had made them I'd never have guessed.' She fingered the tiny items with a patronising smile whilst Aggie scowled witheringly behind her back. Adopting a confidential, sisterly air, Joan then leaned towards Etta and divulged, 'She never did believe in quality over quantity.'

How could Aggie fail to overhear in a small room such as this? With the slandered one remaining quiet, Etta felt she must again spring to her defence. 'I think they're splendid and was very grateful for them indeed.'

'Why, naturally, dear! And I suppose you can use those

cottony ones for everyday wear and keep the things I've brought for Sunday best. Aren't they beautiful?' Joan sighed over her own bestowal, a lace dress and bonnet. 'I'd dearly love to be buying them for my own grandchildren, but then we were never blessed.'

At the poignant air, Etta felt rather sorry for Martin's aunt now. 'Well, you'll be most welcome to come and visit your great-niece whenever you wish.'

Still presenting a wistful smile, Joan accepted a cup of tea and examined her surroundings again. 'Thank you, dear, but best you continue to come to us. I wouldn't like to deprive you of a pleasant venue once in a while.'

It was a measure of their new relationship that Etta and Agnes could laugh about this once Joan was gone, Etta marvelling at the other's restraint. 'How do you manage to keep your hands off her?'

Folding napkins, Aggie gave a careless shrug. 'She's married to Red's brother, and him such a nice, inoffensive fellow. How can I upset him by sniping at the woman he loves? And sure, she's a decent enough person at heart. We might not like every member of our family but we must overlook their faults.'

Etta felt chastened over the way she had cut Martin off from his kin.

'Doesn't stop you moaning once they've gone, though,' said Aggie with a wicked grin.

Relieved, Etta's eyes glowed with the warmth of a peat fire as she grinned back, then looked down with fondness upon the little occupant of the apple crate who had been responsible for mending the split.

The observer tendered a grudging compliment. 'I'll say this for you, Etta, you never feel sorry for yourself.'

Her daughter-in-law looked up in amazement. 'What earthly reason do I have? I've never been happier. You can't imagine how wonderful it is to have the freedom to live my own life.'

196

Aggie conceded this, but took the opportunity to offer a suggestion. 'Ah well, so long as you appreciate that freedom brings its own responsibilities.'

Etta gave an apprehensive sigh. 'This little mite for a start.'

Aggie had not merely intended to implicate Celia, but said now, 'Sure, I'm here if you need help on that score. But I was also thinking of Marty, ye mustn't forget him in all this.'

Alas, Etta did not recognise this as a hint to adopt a more housewifely approach, merely smiled lovingly and asked, 'How could anyone forget Marty?'

'Indeed,' said Aggie, and smiled with her.

Relations might well be repaired, but once Etta had overcome the initial awkwardness of caring for this tiny scrap, she quickly reverted to her natural bent and became even more blasé in matters domestic – and so continued to infuriate Aggie with her ineptitude. Still, the two women decided they must tolerate each other for Marty's sake; Aggie biting her tongue upon finding Etta blithely embroidering whilst the windows needed cleaning; Etta overlooking Aggie's interference in Celia's baptism, and even going so far as to sanction a Roman Catholic ceremony in an effort to keep her mother-in-law happy.

'And all of it thanks to you!' Marty whispered into his baby's ear whilst doting upon her, as he did every evening on coming home from work.

Etta pretended jealousy, demanding, 'Put that woman down and attend to your wife!'

With a dutiful laugh he obeyed, though the kisses he bestowed upon her were certainly not from duty, but out of gladness and relief that his wife's indisposition to physical love seemed to be on the wane at last. For the way she was looking at him now held a promise that the time was nigh to resume their intimacy.

And, when that time eventually came, their passion for each other was as robust as ever – better even, with the added joy of sharing this exquisite creation.

Besides reuniting mother and son, little Celia also helped to forge a link with the neighbours, who now stopped to pass the time of day with Etta and admire the new arrival, some even bestowing gifts. Which was all very welcome after such a frosty start, Marty agreed with his wife, but would not be much use as they would be starting all over again in a matter of weeks. When Etta asked what he meant he revealed his surprise.

'I've found us a better house!'

She squealed. 'Where?'

He braced himself to stave off any objection. 'Hope Street – but at the opposite end to Ma's so we're not really that much closer than we are here.' Miraculously, Etta did not appear to mind, or rather he did not give her the chance as he rushed on to inform her that, 'It's got two bedrooms, so Celie can have her own and we can do what we like without fear of waking her!' He picked her up and swirled her round the kitchen.

Recognising the nervousness that lay beneath the gaiety and feeling sorry that she had caused it by her attitude towards his mother, Etta withheld any misgivings on the dwelling's proximity. Besides, Hope Street had a curve to it, which meant that the folk at the top end were not under constant observance from the folk at the bottom end and vice versa. She declared her eagerness to investigate. In fact, she could hardly contain herself until the previous occupants had moved out, at which point she was to discover that the house had even more benefits.

'Ooh, we have a sink!' She clapped her hands in child-like glee. 'No more having to trail into the yard in all weathers.'

Charmed that one so previously accustomed to luxury could express such joy over simple things, Marty put down the chair he was carrying, sat on it and dragged her onto his lap, where they kissed and cuddled for some minutes, making the most of their baby being cared for by her grand-mother, until Etta tore herself away, saying they had better start to unload the furniture.

He gasped in mock outrage that she could regard this as paramount to her husband, then nevertheless went outside with her to transfer their belongings from the cart to the house. Afterwards he lighted a fire, for despite being early summer it was very cool. Once it was going, Etta put the kettle on and rubbed her hands whilst she waited for it to boil. 'Eh by gum, it's fair nitherin' in 'ere, in't it?'

Marty burst out laughing.

'Well, one has to make an effort to fit in with the neighbours,' she smiled primly.

'Don't you ever dare talk like that for real!' he warned her, still chuckling.

'Why, wouldn't you love me any more?' She sashayed over to plant herself on his lap again.

He kissed her, scolding softly, 'You know better than to ask that. I just prefer you the way you are, that's all. Should we test the bed, d'you think, just to check if I've erected it right?'

Etta writhed against him in delight, murmuring a vulgar response but with a reluctant addendum: 'I should really go and fetch Celia, she'll need feeding soon.'

Marty groaned in frustration. 'I love her dearly but I'll be glad when she's not so reliant on you.' He rubbed his face against his wife's swollen breasts.

Etta crooned her sympathy, this leading to more kisses which were inevitably to lead to bed.

Sighing with happiness afterwards, watching her husband hop about on one foot as he hurried to dress, she uttered sincerely, 'Thank you for finding us this nice house, Marty dear.'

'God love you.' He threw her an adoring smile. 'I wish

it could have been more – it will be one day.'

'I don't need more, I didn't marry you for your money. I know we're going to be so happy here, I can feel it.'

Sitting on the edge of the bed, Marty tied his boot laces. 'I feel it too, and I know you're not after me for my money, heaven help you if you were, but I want to give my fine wife a place that befits her.' He fell back on top of her to deliver a last kiss, then levered himself away towards the door. 'Now get your fat arse up and cook my dinner while I go fetch our daughter.' He laughed at her roar of protest and ran off before she could throw a pillow at him.

Once he was gone, Etta's glower melted into a smile and she stretched her arms wide to enjoy a moment of reverie, reliving the act of love in Marty's arms, before jumping out of bed to start on the enhancement of their new home.

With Celia an undemanding baby who hardly ever cried except to announce hunger, Etta was able to spend many hours on improving her home, making curtains, embroidering cushions and painting pictures for the walls – all of which to welcome her dear husband home from his labours, though often at the price of more mundane chores. A nicer house had certainly brought with it extra work – a range to black-lead, copper pipes and brass taps to polish, and numerous other things – but what was the point in wasting all that elbow grease on things that would soon get dirty again? Others frowned on her for such a view, Etta realised, though it did not worry her in the slightest, for, judging by general comments, her neighbours always had something to grumble about.

Hope Street was certainly well-named, many of its residents living in the hope that something better might come along, and even her own husband amongst these. Determined to keep his promise of obtaining the kind of house his wife deserved, Marty strove to enhance his earnings. When business at the station became slack he would

200

turn his hand to house-painting, or portering at a furniture warehouse, indeed anything that brought in cash, rarely idle for one moment. He could never aspire to buy his dreamed-of residence but he could earn enough to rent one – but this, sadly, meant an increase in the hours he and his wife spent apart. Missing him, Etta repeatedly voiced her own contentment, told him time and again that she was not here for material gain, that all she and Celia desired was him, yet no matter how fervent, her pleas seemed not to register.

'I know you don't expect it but I *want* to give you it,' Marty would reply, his voice just as ardent as hers.

Hence, no words to the contrary able to dissuade him, she was forced to make the most of what little time they had together, snatching every opportunity to foist the baby on others now that Celia was fed from a bottle, and to concentrate her loving attentions on the father . . . a consequence of which, alas, was another pregnancy.

Initially furious at being caught out before Celia was even half a year old, Etta was soon pragmatic. 'Oh well, I suppose we do have several months before the onslaught.'

Equally peeved at having his coming-of-age celebration ruined by this announcement, Marty appeared to resign himself too. 'And this one might be a son.' Though in truth he remained rather deflated at the news. Just when he felt he was getting somewhere, a new drain on his finances had to come along, and, apart from fiscal hardship, he dreaded a repetition of the last pregnancy when Etta had isolated herself from him for months. The rejection he had felt had been almost unbearable. Moreover, in addition to his own paid work he had had to do the domestic chores with which his wife had grown too large to cope. But then, as she stated, there were several months before that happened – and she might just feel differently this time.

'And at least with your mother and I not at loggerheads we'll have her help a little earlier,' added Etta.

Marty nodded, but inwardly he balked at the thought of what his mother might say at being expected to look after his family as well as her own. 'I'm sure we'll manage,' he concluded.

To a certain extent they did manage, this confinement being attended from the start by a registered midwife. But other than this, to Marty's chagrin, events gradually began to take a similar course to the last affair, Etta abandoning more and more of her household tasks to concentrate on trivia.

But she was so joyful to see him at the end of a working day, coming directly to embrace and kiss him as if he had been away for months, that he didn't have the heart to scold her if she had done nothing in the house or his tea wasn't ready. And despite being exhausted from his own labours, he even took on her neglected chores too, so that Etta would not come under scrutiny from his mother. Things had been good between them since Celia's birth and he had no desire for Aggie to abandon him again.

Alas, in a roundabout way, this was what was to occur, though through no fault of his mother nor of his wife. Just as Etta gave birth in the spring and her mother-in-law was required to take charge of Celia, Aggie suffered an early miscarriage, discreetly termed a bilious complaint. However, in her usual competent fashion, even from her sickbed Aggie managed to delegate one of her friends as a stand-in until Etta was back on her feet.

What with one thing and another, it was over a fort-night before the two women saw each other again. Having briefly popped in on his way to work to enquire after his mother's health and also to herald the birth of his son, Marty had allowed sufficient time to pass before inviting his parents round to visit, not least because the house was in such disarray now that the neighbour who had assisted had gone and he and Etta were fending for themselves.

'But come after tea,' he told them hastily.

'Ever the philanthropist,' jested his father, impaling a slice of bread on a toasting fork and holding it to the fire.

'I wasn't meaning to be stingy.' Marty looked awkward. 'I just meant I won't be home till sevenish . . .'

Aggie knew what he meant – he needed time to clear up Etta's mess before receiving visitors – but she made allowances. 'Don't you worry yourself, son, this mob needs feeding at five. Your father and me'll nip round after Tom and Jimmy-Joe are in bed.'

Her son was relieved, adding as he left for work, 'Will you be coming an' all, Uncle Mal?'

'He will.' Red answered for him. 'Sure, the ould sod needs an airing.'

The house could have done with an airing too, thought Marty with dismay when he arrived home that evening to be greeted by the combined stink of nappies and burnt food.

'Oh, I'm sorry,' lamented Etta, one baby at her breast, the older one toddling to meet her father who had rushed to salvage the meal. 'I just couldn't smell it.'

'I'm not surprised!' With the pan off the hob, Marty picked up Celia and held her at arms' length with a laugh of disgust. 'God in heaven!'

Etta looked flustered over which task to handle first, but the moment she removed the baby from her breast in order to clean up Celia, he let out a screech, forcing Marty to object.

'Christ, I can't bear it,' he begged above the din. 'Stick him back on and I'll see to her!'

Etta looked apologetic. 'Oh, but your tea . . .'

'I couldn't eat with that in me nostrils – away with ye, clarty drawers, let's get you cleaned up before anything else.'

During the past couple of weeks, the young father had been forced to learn how to change a napkin – oh, Etta had been perfectly competent when there had been just the one babe, but she was struggling to answer the demands of two, which Marty found perfectly under-standable, and which was why he had undertaken the task. However, he was far from adept and Celia always seemed to treat the matter as a huge joke. Tonight was to be no exception. There followed a laughing struggle to lay her down and to try and keep her still whilst he fumbled over the removal of the safety pin and gingerly peeled aside the offending garment – and then, to his dismay, freed of the restriction, Celia made a sudden break for freedom, deriving great joy from kicking her heels violently in the air and also into the contents of the napkin, which were broadcast to every corner of the room. Laughing and swearing, he reared away to avoid being soiled, and quickly grabbed the napkin and bundled it out of the toddler's reach, before pinning on a clean one, his attempts to do so causing her to gurgle and laugh like a drain and squirm even more enthusiastically.

Afterwards, he examined himself distastefully and asked Etta, 'Have I any on me?'

Laughing fondly, she said she didn't think so.

'I must be the only thing that hasn't.' He studied the suckling babe for a moment, his eyes doting but his voice stern. 'Has that man not finished yet? How come he always wants his tea the same time I have mine?'

Etta apologised again.

'Ah, don't fret, darlin'.' His tone forgiving, he swiped at various suspicious stains on the wall, spent a moment looking here and there for more, then went to wash his hands. 'Now, let's see if I can salvage any o' this stew before Ma gets here.'

There was nothing unusual in having burnt stew, and this was duly consumed, which was just as well for the visi-tors arrived soon afterwards – although Marty was still slightly embarrassed to be caught washing up. But any unto-ward observations were quickly displaced by compliments over the baby boy in his new wicker cradle, whom Marty proudly displayed whilst Etta went to make a pot of tea for the guests.

No longer in awe of her, the in-laws felt comfortable enough these days to speak openly. Cup and saucer in hand, waiting for the insipid brew to cool, Red cast an eye upwards and, after a pensive moment, asked in a calmly reasonable tone, 'Would that be shite on your ceiling, Marty?'

Groaning, the young father hurriedly pulled up a chair, used it to clamber onto the table and removed the offensive blemish with a cloth.

'I've a suspicion there's a bit here too.' Uncle Mal nodded at the arm of his chair whilst sipping unperturbed from his cup.

Marty jumped down to rub at this also. 'Ach, sorry, Unc! I thought I'd got it all.'

Red chuckled deep in his chest and, in mock fear, eyed the ceiling again. 'Christ, how much more of it is up there? Have ye got cows on the roof, son?'

Whilst Marty was a little put-out, Etta was not offended in the least and laughingly explained, 'I'm afraid Celia's responsible for that.'

'She's an awful good shot,' observed Red.

'Martin was forced to change her napkin whilst I was busy with Edward,' added Etta, using a foot to rock her son's cradle. 'She was very naughty for him.' Her words scolded the toddler on its grandmother's knee but her tone was kind.

Fearing disapproval, Marty darted an apologetic eye at his mother, but Aggie chose to swallow any condemnation and laughed kindly too. God love him, her poor son had enough to contend with.

Only an hour later when they had gone did he feel able to relax with a sigh. 'Phew, the mammy must have mellowed!'

'I think it's rather that she prefers not to waste her breath on me any more,' Etta grinned, and, after taking Celia up to bed, she fed the baby and laid him down, enabling her and Martin to share precious time alone for what remained of the evening.

'How soon before we can go all the way again?' he enquired eagerly between kissing and nuzzling and caressing her curves. At her murmured response that it would be several weeks yet he groaned in frustration. 'God, it seems like an age!'

Etta laughed softly and was less fervent than he in delivering kisses, though equally affectionate. 'And from now on we really shall have to be more careful – though how I just don't know.'

'I hate rules and regulations!' he grumbled with feeling.

'As do I,' she administered a humouring pat, 'but we don't want another child so quickly, do we?'

Marty reluctantly agreed and tore himself away to enjoy vicarious pursuit. 'Better get the playing cards out then, hadn't we?'

And this was the most he could enjoy for several weeks to come.

But, finally, to great applause, the time came round when Etta and Marty could indulge themselves in what they really did best, when any pre-arranged rules went out of the window and passion was allowed free rein. And in such a spirit of abandon was child number three conceived.

10

Born in the late summer of 1907, Alexandra Lanegan was as pretty a child as her siblings and equally undemanding. For now she posed no financial burden, but in a few years she would. Was Marty the only one to recognise this? Annoyed at his own laxity in begetting her, he declared that only by working longer hours could he provide for the additional family member. This might also help to take his mind off the sexual famine that had arisen.

'But you're away from us for twelve hours a day already,' objected Etta.

'And now I'll be away fifteen.' He tried his best to sound flippant. 'It's a man's job to provide, Ett.'

'But Alex doesn't cost us any extra –'

'I've just forked out twenty-five bob!' he interrupted with a laugh.

Etta acknowledged the second-hand perambulator he had bought for her. 'Yes, but you'd saved up for that reason. There won't be anything else to buy, she takes sustenance from me and wears hand-me-downs from the others.'

Marty gave mirthless dissent. 'For how long? Anyway, it's not just food and clothing that matters. We don't want three of them crammed into the one bed. I want better for my kids than I had myself – no disrespect to my da. No, I intend to keep my promise, they'll have a room each before they're much older.'

Etta began to suspect that his ambitions were not founded on the reasons he had given, but rather from a need to show off to others. But this was too hurtful and she put it aside to enquire, 'And what about your wife?'

'Don't tell me you want a room to yourself too!' He looked aghast, then chuckled at his own quip.

'I might as well have, the way things are going.' Etta did not find this so amusing.

His face crumpled and he hugged her. 'Ah, now, honey, I know, I *know* it's murder.' He rubbed his hands over her longingly. 'But we can't afford to risk having another nipper.'

Subdued, she nodded. 'I thoroughly agree, but we could at least find the time to chat as we used to.' Marty was so tired when he came home that often she found herself performing a one-sided conversation, her partner fast asleep in the chair. Now she knew why Aggie was so irritable with Red.

'And we will on Sunday, I promise,' he told her. 'Here now, cheer up! I forgot to tell ye me da's got me a couple of inside jobs lined up for the bad weather – house-painting and the like.'

'More work, how wonderful,' murmured Etta facetiously. 'Wouldn't he rather take them himself?'

'You're joking! Me father an' ladders are a dangerous mix.' He smiled, then dealt her arms a last scolding pat before releasing her. 'Ye should be grateful I've plenty o' work for the winter.'

Nodding again, she allowed him to make ready for his labours.

'Just concentrate on the nice house this is going to get yese,' advised Marty as he slung the haversack containing his lunch over his shoulder, then left.

'I'd rather have a husband,' Etta murmured worriedly to herself, before turning to make the children's breakfast.

True to his promise, by that winter, through extremely hard labour and enterprise Marty had managed to improve his finances to such an extent that he could afford to move his family to a house with four bedrooms. Whilst not that far from his parents' home, less than a mile away in Lawrence Street and near enough for Etta to pop round to her in-laws if she needed anything, the living conditions were poles apart.

'A bay window!' breathed Aggie, examining the interior with awe, fingering a white lace curtain though wondering how long it would remain so pristine under her daughter-in-law's misrule. 'Sure, the lad's done you proud, Etta.'

Red, taking slight umbrage that Marty was deemed the better husband, merely nodded his approval and opined to the children, 'Then we'd better have ourselves a place like this too, some day.' But knowing their father so well the girls rolled their eyes at Marty and proceeded to compliment him. And at last he began to feel he was getting somewhere in his quest to provide his wife with the accommodation she deserved.

He must have done well, for, whilst it composed barely a twentieth of the Ibbetsons' grand mansion, Aunt Joan, who had regarded their previous abode unworthy of a visit, now deigned to call on a regular basis, fetching little gifts to further beautify their home – crocheted antimacassars and the like – not that this was particularly appreciated by Marty. But other than this, with a neat little garden at the front, a freshly painted entrance, and white lace curtains at the windows, now he felt able to invite just about anyone over his threshold, to display his wife and children in their best attire, even if this meant he was compelled to scoot round tidying up in order not to be embarrassed by Etta's mess on catching sight of an uninvited guest coming up the path.

Watching him do so again today at the arrival of his aunt and uncle, Etta was at first amused, then irritated.

Martin was becoming something of a busybody. Why did he care so much what people thought, especially someone so shallow as Joan, when he cared not one jot for his wife's opinion? Why did he not attend when she begged him to stay in bed for an hour, not to enjoy some raging passion, just a little intimate cuddle like the ones they had shared before the need to work took over? But all Marty could think about was where this might lead. Ironically, just at that very moment, as she watched her husband welcome the dreary Aunt Joan and Uncle John in with their Christmas gifts, it led Etta to think what she had given up to be here, and there came a fleeting glimpse of a dazzling ballroom bedecked with festive greenery and laughing revellers. Why, even the cottages of the tenant workers whom she used to visit with her mother to bestow charity had boasted more warmth and cheer than did her present domicile, which would be even less festive with the husband absent, as Marty would soon surely be in his haste to get back to earning a living.

But then the thought was just as quickly cast aside. Clinging to the belief that he was doing it for her, Etta forced a smile and went to assist in the management of Aunt Joan, laughing affectionately with her husband – once the relatives had gone and the children were in bed – over how bad his aunt had been, and making the most of her time with him before he must return to work.

Work, or rather the division of it, was finally to become a bone of contention in the coming year. Up before dawn, home after dark, Marty's job was not simply a matter of transporting a couple of suitcases across the platform; amongst his clientele were commercial travellers whose wide variety of goods required a good deal of stamina to heft them a mile to the city shops and often beyond. He was far too exhausted to do anything other than sleep when he got into bed, leaving a saddened and frustrated Etta to channel her energy into other things. Having often professed a desire to be educated, she was now at liberty to make a start on this, her borrowings from the library including mathematical tomes as well as the normal literature. Many hours were spent poring over these when the children were in bed, to no particular end other than a need to feed her brain – though of course the edification of their mother would benefit the children too.

She adored heaping attention upon the trio. After such a loveless childhood as she had suffered, Etta was adamant that her own babies would always know how much they were loved. But delightful though it was to take them for rides on a bus or walks in the countryside, to read them stories, to show them how to blow bubbles or to daub paint upon paper, there were times when she preferred to indulge her own artistic skills – apparently at the expense of others, Martin noted to his disconcertment when, on occasions, he came home to find no meal, his youngsters frolicking unattended whilst his wife sat reading or attempting to create some masterpiece. What had originally seemed a novelty – a reminder of his wife's fine breeding – now began to pall.

The paints were in evidence again at his homecoming this April evening, and the baby still up, though thankfully the two older children were in bed.

'Oh, hello, dear, is it that time already?' said Etta, rather too gaily for Marty's liking. 'I haven't even peeled a potato yet!'

Once he had overlooked her failings because he loved her. Lately, though, he had found himself doing things simply to prevent an argument. But, with every muscle of his body aching, he felt one brewing now. 'I'll feed myself then, shall I? Good job I'm used to it.'

Taken aback by the terse response, Etta immediately abandoned her portrait of Alexandra and rushed to hug and cajole him. 'Now, now, that's most unfair! You know how I've improved!' Having paid great application to her

211

culinary shortcomings, she had for some time been able to provide an edible meal, notwithstanding her tight budget. 'It's just that I never know at what time to expect you and I don't want to risk it burning. Wash your hands and I'll have it done in no time!' She pinched his cheek good-humouredly, but this time her affection was poorly received.

'You'd better clear those up or there'll be no room for the plates.' Sick with tiredness and hunger, he did not look her in the eye but made a bad-tempered gesture at the cluttered table before rolling up his sleeves and grabbing a knife and two large potatoes.

The skin was whittled away in thick strips as the one wielding the knife tried to keep his anger at bay. Marty had always been a home bird who wanted nothing more than to have a house of his own, albeit a better one than his father, and a family with whom to enjoy it. Now, when he had achieved all of this, home had become the last place he wanted to be. Why should he be the one doing this? Why? He grafted all day long, the last thing he needed was another stack of work in what was meant to be a refuge – and it was not simply the lack of food which caused distress. Look at the place! One after the other he hacked through the potatoes and dropped them into a pan, which was noisily deposited on the stove. Did she not notice the tarnished brass, the greyness of the lace curtains? Did she imagine that they would maintain their newness without attention from someone? Did she not mind that some might perceive her a slattern. Well, he minded! He was embarrassed to invite anyone here now. What was the use of him working his backside off for Etta to reduce this lovely house to a hovel? The kitchen stank of ammonia from the yellowed napkins that were draped on the rail over the fire, whilst his eight-month-old daughter rolled happily back and forth across the rug, baring her bottom for all to see. Coming in and seeing her sitting there merrily painting amongst the chaos, it had been just one time too many.

He swiped at the offending articles. 'What are all these nappies doing here?'

The portrait of Alexandra, done on the back of some old cardboard, was now propped on the sideboard, Etta hastening over the clearing away of her artist's materials, a cheap tin of watercolours and some jam jars of water. 'I'm just drying them over the fire.'

'Aren't you meant to wash them first?' His tone had a sting.

'I rinsed them,' she objected evenly. 'It was only a little bit of moisture. Hardly worth the bother.'

Glowering with aggravation, Marty set upon some onions with his knife. 'Aye, but a little bit every day all adds up to a big stink. You've probably grown immune 'cause you're with it all day long.'

'Don't exaggerate!' Etta tried to maintain her lightness. 'She's only a babe, how can her napkins stink as bad as you make out?'

'Believe me they can! And it's not just that.' With a distasteful curl to his lip he tweaked the squares, which felt as rough as hessian. 'It must be like wearing sandpaper for the poor little sod.'

Confused by the suddenness of his attack, for he had always been so tolerant before, Etta was too shocked to object, and, feeling guilty at being exposed as neglectful, she hurried to the drawer and withdrew a tablecloth, mumbling defensively, 'I was only trying to keep the amount of washing to a minimum; I find it so exceedingly dreary.'

'Then you should've married someone who could afford servants!'

He had gone too far. She wheeled on him. 'And you should have married a washerwoman!'

Marty's anger intensified. 'Is it too much for a man to expect a meal when he comes in? I mean, I am the one paying the bills after all.'

'Really, Martin, I've never known anyone with such a

213

capacity to slander!' Efficient now, she spread the cloth and laid the cutlery. 'I usually have something prepared.'

'I should hope so, you've had all bloody day to provide it!' In his heart he knew that in this one respect he was being unfair on her; but this wasn't just about the food.

'You speak as if it's a regular occurrence!' rallied Etta. 'If I had some idea of when to expect you ... I've got to have something to do whilst I'm waiting.'

'Waiting for what? For the work to do itself? I've never objected to you having your hobbies but there is a limit!'

Alarmed by the raised voices, her blue eyes widening, baby Alexandra started to cry.

'And what's she doing up at this hour?' demanded Marty.

'I was about to give her her bedtime bottle when you surprised me!' Red-faced, Etta set down a cruet then picked up her daughter. 'I just wanted to put the finishing touches to my painting fir—'

'Well, I'm sorry for coming home and spoiling your evening – better feed her now then, while I sort the bloody supper out!'

Eventually slammed onto the table, after the wailing child had been pacified and put to bed, the meal was eaten in silence, merely picked at before being scraped into a bowl and shoved away in the larder.

Later though, after washing up and having come to accept blame, Etta sidled up to join her husband on the sofa, apologised, attempted to coax him with kisses, and to some extent this worked, for he did lay a hand over hers as if putting the argument to rest. Yet not quite, for when she suggested they go to bed his agreement did not stem from the usual reason.

'Yes, I'm worn out.' Grim-featured, he made to rise from the sofa.

'I didn't mean for sleep.' She gripped his arm and cuddled up to him like a kitten.

'Anything else would be a bit risky, wouldn't it?' His

voice was slightly less cool than it had been before, yet lacked enthusiasm. 'That's if I could find the energy.'

'I'm sorry about my painting,' she told him yet again, softly. 'It's no excuse I'm sure but I was just so absorbed with catching Alexandra's likeness. Of course, I'm aware it wouldn't bear comparison with that of a true artist . . .'

'No, you were right to be proud, it is a grand likeness. It'll look great on the wall.' For a moment he allowed his tired eyes to sweep the room, admiring the others she had done. He supposed he was partly to blame for not instructing her as to what was expected of a housewife early in their marriage. 'It's not that I'm asking you to stop doing your hobbies, just that, well, we all have our quota of work, Ett.'

Etta found this slightly ignorant. Her husband might voice an appreciation for beautiful things but he had no concept of the amount of hard work that went into their creation. And the children were always beautifully turned out, weren't they? That in itself required effort, what with all the starching and ironing it involved for three of them. How could he suggest she was a stranger to work? Still, she was not totally blind to his meaning, nor was it the time to argue, so, despite her loathing of the mundane aspects of housekeeping, she forced herself to say evenly, with a hint of amusement, 'Then if, by default, I haven't fulfilled my own quota, I swear here and now to be more diligent, you have my solemn oath, signed in blood if you so desire.' And with this she nuzzled him seductively. 'Now, will you come to bed, or am I to polish the fender before you'll succumb to my wifely charms?'

But there was little amusement in response. 'The only thing I'll succumb to is sleep, if I can drag meself from this sofa. Three children in less than four years of marriage, Ett . . .' He shook his head despairingly. 'We always said we didn't want lots. And here we are . . .' Impatient fingers drummed his thigh. 'Anyway, I really am jiggered.'

Removing himself from her grasp, he went around extinguishing the gaslights, then waited with his hand upon the last one in order for his devastated wife to climb the stairs, before turning it out.

Fighting tears, nausea churning the pit of her stomach, Etta lay awake in the darkness, wondering how to prevent her marriage from descending further into worthlessness. In the beginning they had made love at every opportunity, but now Martin seemed reluctant even to be near her! There had to be something she could do, just *had* to be, for, envisioning the four or even five decades of married life stretched out ahead, she could not bear the thought of spending them in such ghastly opposition. Tentatively, she stretched her arm across the chasm in the mattress, administered a tender stroke to his thigh. He did not respond, though she knew by his breathing he was not asleep. Further wounded, she withdrew her touch.

Did she know he was pretending to sleep? Marty didn't care. Lying there, despite his desperate need to rest still as taut as a primed crossbow from the earlier angry exchanges, he began to question his attraction for her, asked himself had he been smitten only because of her beauty and status, flattered that she could want him? When – *how* – had everything changed?

Aching from rejection, Etta was asking herself the same questions. She had always been an idealist, refusing to marry for anything other than passion: had it merely appealed to her deeply romantic streak to run away with a gypsy? She began to think of all she had given up, the beautiful house and clothes, the afternoons out riding in the countryside, the lavish Christmas parties she once attended . . . Her children could have had those same things had she married someone of her own class. But she hadn't wanted someone else, she had wanted Martin . . . still wanted him, wanted things to be like they were . . .

*

Only through exhaustion had Marty fallen asleep that night, and on many miserable nights to come. Etta was to feel quite exhausted and miserable too, in her attempts to meet her husband's approval, for no matter how she exerted herself it did not achieve the intimacy she craved, and, gaining no reward from all that endless polishing and cleaning, her good intentions were soon to relapse.

There was no one upon whom to unburden her heart, for one could not complain to a man's mother. Besides, Aggie had never been sympathetic; and pleasant as Etta's sisters-in-law were on a superficial level, she sensed that their allegiance, too, would be with their brother. As for her neighbours, she was barely on nodding terms, let alone such intimate ones. It hadn't mattered so much before when she and Marty had had each other; now, though, Etta became acutely sensitive to her isolation. She yearned to reach out to someone, anyone, but who? Her own mother? No, if Isabella had wanted to get in touch she would have done so long ago. Besides, the longer Etta was exiled from her family the harder it had become for her to renew contact. Despite her adoration of the children, there were days when she felt completely marooned.

The problem could only worsen, both husband and wife growing more discontented by the day. Even an unusually warm spring did nothing to alleviate matters between them, for Marty had no time for Sunday afternoon strolls in the sunshine as he used to enjoy with Etta, and on the rare occasions that he was not catching up on sleep his attention must also be shared with the children – and others, came Etta's grim thought, as the former resentment of her mother-in-law began to resurface.

Summer came, and with it a rash of marriage announcements in the press, reminding Etta that her own wedding anniversary was imminent. She wondered miserably, as she broke off reading the morning newspaper to tend the baby, what this might bring. Did Marty even consider it still to be a cause for celebration? Not if one was to judge by his eagerness to leave their bed on a morning. How could such a turnabout occur in four short years? Pensive all the while, she fed, washed and dressed Alexandra, tied the bow on her frilly bonnet and, with a kiss, sat her in the pram outside in the front garden where, through the iron bars of the gate, the other two were eagerly watching a herd of cattle being driven along the main highway from the outlying fields to market. The air was thick with the scent of cow dung, the shouts of the rough-looking drovers and the panting and yapping of their dogs.

'See, cows!' shouted an excited Edward, pointing at the jostling multitude of black, brown and piebald creatures with their muck-caked hides and wary eyes and drooling wet muzzles, lowing and clattering to meet their fate; and Etta stayed to watch for a while, hoping the childlike enjoyment might rub off on her.

But before long, re-absorbed by her tribulations, she went back indoors to a half-hearted tidying of the breakfast pots, a deft concealment of crumbs under the rug, then a return to her wistful perusal of the engagement and marriage announcements.

After a while, though, she chided herself – this was no way to forget one's troubles – and was about to put the newspaper aside when her eyes rested on a familiar name. A Mr Gerald Fenton and his bride, formerly Miss Victoria Netherwood, had just returned from their month-long honeymoon in Venice. Why, it was an old friend, one she had known since childhood. Too wrapped up in Marty she had never bothered to communicate with Victoria since her elopement, had consigned her to the past along with all the other acquaintances of her previously wealthy existence. But now . . . now in desperate need of a familiar face, Etta decided there and then to reach out, to write via the family address and congratulate this old friend on her marriage, eagerly awaiting the reply.

With the postman rarely visiting this abode, it was such a grand occasion some days later to receive Victoria's letter and, with Marty at work and therefore sparing her any interrogation or interruption, Etta was able to savour the thickness of the envelope for some while before ripping it open. Whilst the infants played around her feet, she read it at leisure, a lovely long epistle informing Etta how delighted Victoria had been to hear from her after all these years. She devoured every word, the most exciting of them saved for the last paragraph. Victoria would be coming to York next week, they must take tea together! Perversely Etta's heart sank then. How could she possibly entertain Victoria here without a maid? But in the next line her friend suggested a time and a meeting place at one of the best cafés in town, stating it as her treat.

The wave of exhilaration carried her to its crest, only to be followed by another trough of despair. How could Etta go on such an important outing accompanied by three children? Desperate to go, she thought about it all morning, pondered telling Marty, who would always have understood, at least in the old days . . . But that was the whole point, these were not the idyllic days of old, and he was in such a bad mood when he got in that she thought better of mentioning it.

A week later with the rendezvous looming she had still not divulged it, nor even told Marty of the letter. Why? She could not say. Perhaps it was born of fear that he would not understand, would feel threatened in the assumption that she had tired of him and was aching to get back to her own kind. This was untrue, of course. Had Etta possessed a friend nearby she would have had no need for such subterfuge, but she did not. So, equipped with the suitable excuse of not wanting to be encumbered by the children whilst she went to find a treat for Martin to mark their anniversary, she took them round to her mother-in-law's house, informing Aggie that the baby had just been fed and was asleep in her pram outside and she herself would be back in an hour or so.

'If that would not be too much of an imposition?' Her enquiring glance took in Uncle Mal too.

Aggie was obliging as ever. 'Sure, they're no trouble at all – hello me little darlins.' She wiped her hands on her apron and bent to welcome Celia and Edward.

'How do you do, Grandmamma?' Clad in a white lace bonnet with an ostentation of frills, the three-year-old peered up as if through a froth of bubbles and extended her hand as she had been taught by her mother.

'Such wonderful manners!' Even having witnessed this a dozen times, Aggie's face creased in fond laughter as she shook the little hand. 'And the conversations she can hold for one so young! Take as long as ye like, Ett, we'd gladly be entertained by these three all day long, wouldn't we, Uncle Mal?'

The old man nodded and patted his knee as encouragement.

Thanking them, Etta rushed home to prepare for her outing, unwinding her hair from its usual chignon and paying a great deal of care in its re-arrangement, dabbing rosewater on her face and inducing some colour to her cheeks with a brisk rub of her palms. The outfit was a harder problem to solve. Even reserved for special occasions the lilac dress was past its heyday, the cream lace grubby and frayed, but it would have to do. Excitement and apprehension churning her stomach, she donned her gold locket, hat and gloves and set out to meet her old friend.

They arrived simultaneously, one on foot, the other alighting from a highly polished carriage with liveried footman to assist. But if Victoria was horrified by the obvious deterioration in Etta's circumstances then she did not mention it, only the merest hesitation giving it away before she hurried forth to meet her friend.

220

'My dear, how wonderful to see you after all these years!'
She gripped Etta's hands and beamed into her face. 'Still
as lovely as ever!' The recipient gave a self-deprecating laugh
and thanked her as Victoria went on, 'I attempted to send
you an invitation to my coming-of-age ball last year but
no one appeared to know where we might find you. I gather
your family have cut you off.'

Etta gave a soulful nod, and, being given the reminder
that her own twenty-first birthday was nigh, knew better
than to expect similar celebration and felt worse than ever.

Victoria sympathised, then added, 'Mother asked me to
say how much she misses you.'

'Do apologise to her for not letting any of you kno—'

'Oh, my dear, there's no need, it was so romantic!' Her
friend adopted a highly envious expression. 'You caused
such a scandal – it was doing the rounds for months! Come,
let's acquire a table and you can tell me all about him.' She
hooked her arm through Etta's and steered her into the
café. 'Then I shall bore you with accounts of *my* beloved!'

Infected by the other's happy enthusiasm, Etta felt her
own spirits raised as she sat down to enjoy an assortment
of delicacies. The only trouble was that the afternoon was
passing much too swiftly, an hour being wasted on eating
and small talk when what she really wanted to tell Victoria
was how miserable was the reality of her existence.

However, Victoria was an intuitive sort, and during a
lull she detected an air of wistfulness in her friend. 'So . . .'
she posed a leading question '. . . has life with Martin been
as you imagined?'

Sensing an invitation to come clean, Etta looked her in
the eye. 'In general, yes . . . though I didn't imagine we'd
be joined by children quite so early on.'

Victoria arched her eyebrows and took a sip of tea.
'Children?' There had been no mention of them until now.
'How many do you have?'

'Three.'

Victoria was stunned. 'Goodness! But you've barely been married that amount of years.'

Etta nodded ruefully, blinking away a tear of embarrassment and despair.

Realising her faux pas, Victoria said kindly, 'I should love to meet them. Where are they – with their nurse, I expect?'

All of a sudden Etta felt like slapping her friend. 'Victoria, how do you suppose I could afford a nurse?'

Startled, the other blushed. 'I'm sorry, I –'

'No, I'm sorry,' Etta did not sound too repentant. 'I didn't mean to snap, especially after you've so generously treated me to tea, but really, have you so little understanding of anything I've told you? Martin is a labouring man, can you not imagine how tiny a budget we have on which to live?'

Victoria winced and apologised again. 'How dreadful . . . I saw only the romantic side.'

'And that's the awful part of it,' mourned Etta. 'I'm as passionate about Martin as ever. I adore him, but he no longer –' She broke off as a waitress passed the table, then continued, 'he won't come near me. I hope it's only out of fear of starting another child. I don't know what I'd do if he –'

'Oh, I'm sure it is, dear,' Victoria patted her friend's hand comfortingly, then after a sidelong glance, murmured, 'I can at least empathise there. I know what it is to be so in love one cannot keep one's hands off one another. Gerald is quite a bit older than I and was divorced. Father didn't regard him as suitable and took an age before permitting us to marr—'

'But what can one *do*?' Focused on her own problem, Etta interrupted with a helpless sigh.

Victoria took another sip of tea and glanced around again before leaning over to whisper a confidence. 'How do you suppose I'm not yet enceinte?' This was not a subject

222

normally aired between ladies, but her friend's desperation called for radical measures, and besides, it pleased Victoria to be so avante-garde. 'There are items one can buy to prevent it, you know.'

Etta did not delay matters by asking how her friend had found this out but showed immediate interest. When Victoria divulged further information, Etta blushed, not through delicacy but because of her shameful financial position. 'I couldn't afford such luxuries even if I knew where to purchase them.'

Victoria was a kind person and did not hesitate before asking, 'Then would you permit me to send you a couple of dozen?' Seeing Etta about to shake her head she raised a firm palm. 'Before you refuse you must put aside any notion of charity or pity or anything else. I'm doing this as one friend to another – even though it might seem an odd sort of gift.' She gave an impish smile.

Etta was too desperate to risk another refusal. 'But your husband –'

'Would never notice, we go through so many!' Victoria butted in eagerly, then snorted behind a hand. 'Oh goodness, that sounds depraved – but what I mean to say is that it will be perhaps less of a problem for us to obtain them than it would be for you.' Her voice lowered again to a whisper. 'Gerald buys them in bulk, he's somewhat the optimist.' She tittered; so did Etta.

Victoria was in full flow now, the content of her information most unsuitable for such a genteel venue but causing hilarity between the two friends, even more so when this drew disapproving looks from others. 'You can use each of them four or five times – depending on how rough you are,' divulged Victoria, blue eyes a-twinkle.

Exhausted by trying to restrain her laughter, as their meeting gradually drew to a close Etta mopped her eyes and gushed sincerely, 'Oh, I can't tell you how much I've enjoyed seeing you again, Vicky! It must have been fate that led me to see your name in the press, for I truly believe you've helped to save my own marriage. I'm so sorry for not writing earlier to say where I was, it must have seemed as if I'd abandoned you.'

'Oh stuff and nonsense.' Putting on her gloves, Victoria gripped her friend's arm warmly. 'I fully understand what it is to be so in love that one can think of no one else. I hardly see any of the people with whom I used to socialise either. I'd love to meet you again –'

'Oh, so would I!' Etta leapt in.

'– but unfortunately Gerald and I will be moving to London shortly.' Victoria's face mirrored Etta's, which was now swathed in disappointment. 'I *know*.' A look of empathy creased her powdered complexion. 'It seems so unjust after fate has brought us together again. But perhaps we can meet once in a while when I come to visit my people.' Etta nodded half-heartedly, noting that Victoria had not sought to invite her and Martin to visit.

Victoria paid the bill, gathered her belongings and dealt her friend a final peck on the cheek. 'Goodbye, my dear, it's been so lovely to see you again – and I promise I shan't forget the what-d'you-call-its!'

Reliving every minute of that wonderful afternoon again and again, Etta went home in a spirit of hope.

Noting her bright eyes, Aggie remarked as she handed over the children, 'You look as if you've enjoyed yourself. Managed to get himself something nice, did you?'

Only then did Etta remember that the object of her outing had been to buy a gift for Marty. But her intended groan quickly became a smile. 'Yes, I'm having it delivered later,' she informed her mother-in-law.

'Oh, too large to carry, was it?' Aggie looked impressed.

'Mm, not large, no,' said Etta with a sparkle, 'but I think it's something he'll appreciate.'

'Ah, I know that look.' Aggie winked. 'Something you can enjoy as well, is it? Something nice for tea?'

Etta laughed at Aggie's unwitting response. 'You know me so well, don't you?' Gathering her children, gaily she took them home.

'Yes, I know you,' murmured Aggie to herself whilst smiling and waving at her grandchildren. 'Whatever it is, you can be sure she'll have it burnt to a cinder by the time Marty comes home.'

Ironically, the what-d'you-call-its were to arrive bang on their wedding anniversary – at least Etta surmised that this was what was in the package which Marty had just unwrapped, judging by his puzzled expression. Being Sunday, he was not at work and was therefore free to answer the postman's knock. She had tried to intercept the parcel which, despite it bearing her name, he had begun to open, but she was too late, his eager fingers had wrenched off the string and torn the brown paper.

Wondering what on earth his wife had spent their money on now, Marty unravelled one of the unfamiliar items and held it up for a second before the shape of it caused suspicion and, finally guessing what it was, he gasped and rewrapped it quickly. 'Etta, are you out of your mind sending for these?'

'I didn't buy them!' She was anxious to assure him.

'The children might have seen them!'

A scornful laugh. 'They won't know what they are.'

'Maybe, but what if somebody else had been here? You could have warned me!' Was this what had made her behave so strangely during the past few days?

'Sorry I didn't realise they'd be here quite so soon. A friend of mine suggested they might be useful.'

He gasped again, this time with condemnation. 'You've been discussing our private life?'

'No! No, not really.' Her bosom heaved as she confessed, 'I bumped into an old friend, Victoria, and when she learned that we have three children after only four years of marriage she was horrified and said she could help!'

'What is she, some kind of prostitute?'

Anxiety turned to outrage. 'No! How *dare* you malign my good friends – and now who's being irresponsible in front of the children!'

Still aghast, Marty looked down at the package and shook his head, whilst little Celia looked anxiously from one to another.

Etta went on in clipped tones, 'Victoria is a respectable married woman who wishes to delay starting a family of her own, and envisaging me in another ten years with another ten children she thought to provide a serv—'

'Does she think I'm so stupid and low that I can't take care of my own affairs?' demanded Marty.

'She was merely trying to be kind!' Etta's fury amplified. 'Wanted her friend to have a similar kind of happiness that she has with her husband, but I'm beginning to wonder why I married you at all!'

He retaliated. 'You said you wanted to be part of my life!'

'But I didn't know there'd be so many others in it!' She went on hotly, 'There's always somebody else here, your mother, your father, your Aunt Fanny – I never get to be with you alone. What's the matter, don't you want things to be like they were? Are you deliberately trying to drive me away?'

He looked stunned. 'Well, yes – no! I mean, of course I want things to be like they were, Etta, of *course* I do. But this is . . . sinful.'

'Who says?' she grilled him.

'The Church.'

'You hypocrite, you never go to church!'

A loud wail interrupted the argument.

'See what you've done now!' Etta grabbed her little son and tried to comfort him, which was difficult as the other two had also become infected by the upset. 'There, there, Father didn't mean to frighten you, have this.' In a few deft movements she had set Edward down, scooped a spoon into the jam pot and inserted it into each little mouth. Succeeding in pacifying them, she stood glaring at her husband.

Having put aside his anger and embarrassment in order to help soothe the infants, Marty became contemplative. Delving into the package again, he held up one of the sheaths – though used his body to shield it from tender eyes. Perhaps this was not such a depravity after all if it meant he could still have access to the one he so desired.

For a moment he beheld his wife's angry stance, then, regretting that he had upset her needlessly, he dealt her a bashful smirk. 'Hell, Ett, what have you told her about me? This'd fit a bloody stallion.'

Her angry mask immediately collapsed and she came to him slyly. 'Well, that's what you are.'

He laughed aloud and curled his free arm around her to kiss her, this also serving to remove the children's apprehension.

'I thought they might be a suitable anniversary gift. Would you care to put one to the test?'

'God, you're shameless! Oh, go on then.' He feigned a look of duty but beat her to the staircase.

'Celie, make sure Edward doesn't touch the fireguard,' Etta instructed her daughter, whom she trusted to be sensible. 'Mother and Father need to do something. We'll be down shortly.' Happiness restored, she pelted after Marty.

Whilst not wholly satisfactory, the first of the what-d'you-call-its did succeed in bringing the couple back to intimacy, and more importantly resurrected their shared sense of humour. There was some small inconvenience for Etta in that it required washing after use, but this in itself was to provide amusement from an unanticipated source.

That same afternoon Marty's parents called in on their

way home from a country walk with the children and Uncle Mal. With no time to hide the sheath that had been put to dry on the hoist above the fireplace, Marty tried to keep his gaze from straying there, babbling like an idiot whilst at the same time exchanging a look of panic with his wife.

Not to offer her guests tea would have seemed rude, and so, with no way of avoiding it, this is what Etta did – though she was acutely conscious that by picking up the kettle she was also drawing attention to the fireplace, and that which hung above it. Seeing Aggie quizzically eyeing the object that dangled from the rail, she bit her lip and cast a sideways look at Marty but dared not move it for fear of inviting a question and, instead, removed herself.

'I hope we're not depriving Marty of his anniversary gift?' said Aggie.

Etta, now carving slices from a piece of boiled bacon, almost choked. 'I beg your pardo— oh, I see what you mean! No, this isn't the gift I bought him. I'm afraid we ate that as soon as it arrived, didn't we, Martin?'

'We did, aye!' Flummoxed, Marty sought to follow his wife's lead.

'Well, and you both seem in very good spirits the pair of you,' offered Redmond in his gentle brogue, noting their shining eyes and lips that twitched with suppressed laughter.

'Oh, we are that, Da!' Marty nodded vigorously, wishing Etta would put away that mischievous look that made him want to erupt. 'And what have you been doing with your-selves, boys? My, that's a big bag you've got!' He nodded encouragingly as his brothers displayed the items they had collected from the hedgerows, showing much more interest than was due, hoping to hold everyone's attention.

''Tis my opinion you've been feeding the lad too many oats,' Aggie announced smilingly to Etta. 'Sure and he's never shut up since we got here.'

At the mention of oats, Marty dared not meet Etta's eye.

'Oh well, that's a nice how-do-ye-do, sorry for boring you, Ma!'

Aggie chuckled and was about to say more, but then Etta came forward with plates and a pot of tea and the conversation turned to other things.

It appeared that Etta and Marty might well have escaped embarrassment, for the object that dangled from the rail seemed to have been forgotten by the time Aggie and the others made to leave.

Relieved to have got away with it, the couple allowed themselves to relax a little – but right at the point of exit Aggie turned and frowned. 'You know, I've been racking my brain trying to make out what that there thing is, but I can't for the life of me –'

'It's a piping bag,' said Etta, quick as a flash. 'I've been learning how to ice a cake.'

Marty could not help a snort and quickly bent down, pretending to tie his shoe as he felt his ears turn red, barely able to contain his laughter.

'Oh . . .' Aggie looked as if to show interest.

Pre-empting a request to see the said cake, Etta added quickly, 'I'm afraid my first effort wasn't good enough so I scraped it off. No one shall see it until I've perfected the art.'

Aggie looked most impressed, calling over her shoulder as she left, 'We'll know where to come when one o' the girls needs a wedding cake then.'

'Icing cakes indeed!' blurted Marty when it was safe to do so, he and Etta falling into each other's arms laughing uproariously that she had unintentionally created a euphemism for intercourse. 'She really believed you! You'll get your comeuppance when you're called upon to produce the evidence.'

Etta laughed so hysterically that she could not speak for some moments, the children looking up in bewilderment. 'Oh stop, don't set me off any more, it hurts! Oh, dear!'

She wiped her eyes and took a deep breath.

'When you've finished laughing I've got one question for you,' said Marty, straight-faced now.

'What?'

'Do you fancy icing another cake?'

11

There were to be many cakes iced during the following weeks, Etta and Marty greedily retrieving the joy of union after famine. However, both were quick to see that the source would not last indefinitely and, sense overruling passion, chose to eke out the remainder of Victoria's gift so as to enjoy it as long as possible before fate would inevitably step in. In consequence, though Marty still laboured from dawn to dark, somehow he managed to reserve sufficient energy for loving liaisons with his wife, and the rest of the year was happy, as were the first few months of the next.

But, regrettably, as the last of the French letters disintegrated, so too did the laughter, and when Aggie sought to enquire in all innocence, 'How's the cake-icing progressing?' Etta took no amusement in her answer that she had given it up as useless.

To her shame she had considered writing to her friend Victoria, even though it was obvious from the lack of correspondence from the other that there was no longer any common ground between them. But, pitted against carnal desire, her self-respect had finally won and she tore up the humiliating petition and instead looked to Marty for action.

'I got them the last time,' she told him firmly, 'now it's your turn.'

Contemplating the embarrassing act of having to walk

into a shop and ask for prophylactics, Marty reached the conclusion that such a moment's awfulness would be worth it, and asked her, 'Did your friend say how much they cost?'

'I think those were quite expensive,' Etta pondered, her face hopeful, 'but I recall Victoria saying there are cheaper varieties. They begin at two shillings per dozen . . .'

'Oh, well, that's it then!' he snapped in bitter disappointment.

'Don't dismiss it yet!' she urged. 'We could do without something else.'

'Like what?'

'Well, I don't know!' Even by dint of cutting down on small luxuries such as her rosewater their income was stretched to the limit. 'You think of something, you're the man!'

'Well thank you for reminding me of that!' He was furious.

'I didn't mea—'

'I know what you meant!' replied Marty before striding off to work.

What else could he do? Who could he ask? The men of his acquaintance were as unequipped to deal with their fertility as he. Nothing. He could do absolutely nothing.

Forced apart once more through fear of pregnancy, the only spark of passion now displayed itself in arguments as frustration lured petty niggles to the fore. Marty supposed he should be grateful that the mother of his children had learned to ensure they were clean and well-dressed and well-cared for; instead he displayed resentment over his own feelings of neglect; began to complain more forcefully about the lax manner in which she ran the household; took great pains to point out that what Etta eschewed as trivia were in fact essential chores. 'You'll see what consequence it is when your children fall ill!'

Still, she refused to be worried by it, saying calmly in that maddening manner of hers, 'I fail to see how my reluctance to waste time in cleaning the windows or scrubbing the step every day could result in a case of measles.'

Robbed of answer, Marty could only fume as she added: 'I'd much rather expend my energy on the children.'

And there lay half the problem. But what kind of man was jealous of his own children? Ashamed of himself, he could only respond with anger. 'Sometimes you drive me bloody mad, woman!'

And then it was his wife's turn to take umbrage, and Etta in a tantrum was not a pretty creature, throwing at him whatever it was she held in her hand, along with a stream of oaths.

Unwitting of the fact that this was the only way she knew how to respond at having her emotions so ravaged, that she saw these painful criticisms as a retraction of his love, there were times when he genuinely wanted to walk away from her.

Nobody else would have known, at least not his work-mates, from the way he managed to maintain his comical banter outside the house.

'By, I hate to say it but you really make it a pleasure to come to work, lad!' old Arthur wheezed with hilarity and mopped his eyes, as did the rest of the group of barrow boys whom Marty kept entertained with impressions of the station hierarchy whilst they waited for another train to come in. 'It's like being at the bloomin' music hall!'

Inspired by their laughter, Marty had not finished yet. 'Eh, look!' Pouncing on a pair of yellow gloves which someone had left behind on a bench, he held one to either side of his head and waggled them at his audience. 'Custard Lugs!'

The barrow boys burst into renewed noisy laughter that ricocheted off the station walls, drawing disapproving eyes, including those of the impersonated one.

'Jesus, I didn't mean to cause a seizure.' Grinning, Marty put a supportive arm round Arthur's shoulders as, on the point of hysteria, the old man fought for breath, the others almost paralysed with amusement too.

'Ooh-hoo!' Arthur struggled to compose himself, puffing and wheezing, tears streaking his leathery cheeks. 'You could even make my missus laugh and that's saying something – eh, Marty, you don't fancy coming home with me and keeping her happy while I sneak out for a pint?'

'Now you all witnessed that!' declared the entertainer to his audience. 'There's an invitation if ever I heard one!'

'Nay, you wouldn't say that if you saw her,' chuckled Arthur, shoving away his handkerchief and making ready with his barrow as a train pulled in and the group broke apart. 'Miserable bugger, only thing she's good for is deterring burglars.'

Marty issued a final laugh as the train came to a hissing standstill. 'It's cheaper than buying a dog licence.'

Arthur agreed, then mellowed a little. 'Oh, I'm being a bit mean, she looks after me well.'

'That's something to be grateful for.' Rudely reminded of Etta's shortcomings, Marty relapsed into a grim mood, wondering what would be in store for him when he went home tonight, but was soon to don his cheery mask again, for a grumpy mug did not attract the customers. If only he could have put up a similarly convincing show of happiness at home.

Both he and Etta hoped to conceal this state of affairs from the rest of the family, putting on a brave smile whenever they were invited round. But unlike Marty's workmates his parents knew him well enough to guess something was wrong.

'Take the lad aside and talk to him,' Aggie urged her husband as he passed her in the scullery during one of Marty's visits. 'There's been some kind of argumentation. See if you can find out what's amiss – as if I didn't already know who's to blame. You try to tell them but they won't listen – this is what comes of marrying out of your kind.'

Though anxious to help, Red pulled awkwardly at his

earlobe. 'Well now, talking's more in your league.'

'Not when it concerns her ladyship and it surely will. I always put my foot in it. You have a go.' And she gave him a push.

Though unnerved, Red fought his inclination to fall asleep by concentrating hard on the matter in hand as he re-entered the parlour to ask, 'Will you be for looking at my new rabbits, Marty?'

The latter, who had been immersed in brooding melancholy, now looked up sharply.

'May we see them, Grandad?' Edward leapt to his feet.

'Sure, and you've seen them already,' Red dissuaded the little boy in the sailor suit with a kind pat. 'I'd just like your father's opinion on them, then you can come out.'

Faced with this odd request, Marty had the feeling that the rabbits were only an excuse to get him out there for private discussion. Casting a glance at Etta, who had been equally subdued, he reluctantly trailed after his father.

But outside, though Red was desperate to raise his son's spirits he did not know how to begin. Hence, the talk hedged around the real subject and moved in desultory fashion from the price of rabbit feed to other such mundane things, before Red inevitably succumbed to his narcolepsy and, upon waking, forgot what he had come out there to do.

Consequently, when the pair came back indoors Aggie was to be no wiser.

Annoyed at her husband's failure, she ran a hand over her mouth and decided, ''Tis left to me as usual to take the divil by the horns, dammit!' And she shoved a bemused-looking Red back towards the parlour before steering Marty outside again.

This time he knew he was for it.

'What's ailing ye, son?' she wheedled. 'Don't bother with the codology, your father and me can tell you're unhappy.'

How could a man voice such things to his mother? He sighed. 'Oh, it's nothing . . .'

'Sure, it must be something, there's never a word passed between the pair o' yese in the last hour and her with a face dripping icicles.'

Marty heaved another sigh. 'It's just . . . me and Ett are having a few disagreements at the moment, that's all, Ma. It's best we don't speak.'

'You won't leave her, will ye?'

Though shocked by this forthright question, only a fool would not grab the opportunity to share his troubles. 'I feel like it,' he replied bluntly, shaking his head at the thought of Etta's recent intransigence. 'By God I do.'

'But you wouldn't?' There was a note of panic in her voice. 'This isn't the same as pestering for a cooking apple then not eating it, this is a marriage.'

'Well, I know that, Ma!' He looked scathing.

'Of course you do, of course,' she soothed. 'I'm just worried about you. Ah, God love ye, I know Etta can be difficult, but tell me ye won't leave her, son?' She had been dreading this all along, knew he would eventually tire of the wretched girl.

Is that what you really think of me, an offended Marty wanted to ask as he stared at her.

But at last, to his mother's relief, he shook his head. 'Of course I won't.' Then he sighed yet again, and struggled to explain how he felt, but could only grasp at metaphor and she would not understand. It was like when, as a child, he had left a glass of lemonade on the outside windowsill in January and come out next day to find the glass cracked open and the lemonade frozen into a block. At first it was such a novelty, such an obsessive treat to cup it in his hands, to lick and gnaw and suck the fruitiness imprisoned within the ice. But then he had found his mouth totally stuck to it, burning and hurting, and he'd tried to pull away but he could not free himself without tearing the skin from his lips. Well, that was how he felt about Etta.

His lack of words was misinterpreted, Aggie shaking her

236

head disapprovingly. 'You'd think she'd be grateful to have a man who slaves as hard as you do.'

'But that's half the problem, Ma! She complains that I work too much, that I don't spend enough time with her.' He felt disloyal just saying it but he wanted someone to confirm he was right in feeling aggrieved.

'But she can't expect to live in a house like that without someone having to work for it, and it sure as hell won't be her. Stuck with her head in a book half the time . . .'

Marty scratched his head. His mother wasn't getting this at all. When he said Etta wanted him to spend more time with her he meant intimate time. He ached for this too – oh God, how he longed for the old days, to let his passion run its course without hindrance – but that could spell only one thing. 'I don't know what to do, Ma. We can't cope with any more children . . .'

'Ah . . .' Now the issue became much more delicate. 'I'd offer to have a word with Etta but there's nothing much I can do to help ye there, son.' Only her decrepitude had prevented any more babies after Jimmy-Joe. She played with her lower lip, pinching it with slight embarrassment.

Marty was embarrassed too. 'No, no, that's all right, I don't expect you to. I was just getting things off me chest. Don't say anything, will you?' Etta would be furious to hear he had been discussing their marriage with his mother. 'We'll be fine.'

'Sure ye will.' His mother touched him. 'These rough patches happen to us all.'

But does it ever come right again, he wanted to ask? For if life were to continue like this for much longer, he would rather be dead.

For twelve more miserable months, through lengthy, aching periods of abstention, he and Etta managed to stave off pregnancy. But a marriage born of physical attraction could never hope to stand the strain. If there were no happy

237

medium to be had, both decided that they would rather take the risk than watch love die. Hence, as a new decade brought the sad announcement that the King had expired, Etta found yet another new life begat within.

Poor William, the Christmas child, totally innocent to the strain his arrival put on his parents' marriage. Would that this were true of Marty and Etta's other issue, but for Celia, Edward and Alex, their parents' encounters, however brief, had become synonymous with angry disruption.

'You've forgotten to empty the pisspot again,' accused Marty, sniffing the air the moment he came in on this wet and freezing night.

Etta had been standing by to welcome him with a warm broth, but now felt her spirits descend. 'What kind of a greeting is that?'

'My sentiments exactly.' Looking jaundiced, he shrugged his drenched coat into her hands and squelched towards the fire. 'Not exactly the aroma a man fancies coming home to.'

She stood up to him, giving the coat an angry shake. 'Why should you expect me to empty it? You're the one who uses it!'

'Ma never complained, nor my sisters.' He went to wash his hands.

Hanging up the coat, Etta grabbed a ladle. 'I'm not your mother – why should you automatically think it's my job? You use it, you empty it!' She served the broth.

Livid, he retaliated. 'If that's the way it was meant to be, everyone cleaning up their own mess, then you'd be a damned sight busier than you are, milady! Christ, you don't know you're born. I'd like to hear what Da had to say if me mother sat on her arse all –'

'Oh, and don't we all know what a paragon of domesticity your mother is!' chafed Etta. 'You're always ranting about how marvellous she is, or your sisters, or anyone else you care to mention except your wife!'

'Maybe that's because me wife never does a bloody thing for me!'

'And what do you call this?' Etta gestured at the steaming bowl on the table. Hours it had taken her, cutting up vegetables, slicing her fingers into the process when she would much rather have been sewing, but it had all been worthwhile for it tasted delicious – as good as anything Aggie had ever produced, and Etta had been dying for Marty to come in and praise her wonderful achievement.

'Oh, well! Sorry, I'll get down on my knees then, shall I? Oh yes, so bloody wonderful – it's a bowl o' frigging soup, for Christ's sake! You've had all day to make it, ye hardly needed to call in Jason and the Argonauts – why, *why* in God's name is it always me who's doing the giving? What have you ever given, tell me that?'

Etta was devastated, so devastated that for the moment she could hurl no response. How could he ask what she had given? She had given herself.

About to take advantage of her stricken silence, Marty opened his mouth to press home his assault when the sound of a crying child interrupted the exchange. Instead he gave a snort and made towards the stairs. 'Oh *shite!*'

'Sit down,' Etta found her voice. 'I'll go.'

'No, *I'll* go.' He could be very anarchic when told what to do. 'Christ, I hardly ever see them.'

'And whose fault is that?' Etta returned to form. 'It isn't I who insists you work all hours God sends.'

'Hah!' He paused. 'No, but you like the money, don't ye? How d'you think you'd be able to afford all these doodahs if I didn't work me nuts off?' He jabbed a finger at examples of her paintings and needlework that dotted the room.

'There's no call to be vulgar!' Her eyes bulged red with the threat of tears. 'I only indulge in such pastimes because I'm on my own! I'd much rather my husband were here on an evening.'

'Well, he's not because he has to work to earn a living – and d'you know why else he works so late? Because his wife makes it so damned unpleasant to be at home!' At this, Marty went upstairs to calm his distressed child.

Too furious and upset to eat, Etta hurled her own broth into the sink along with the bowl, which smashed and sent the contents spattering up the wall. Then she flopped into a chair, listening to the sounds from upstairs, the murmurs of the father, the child's sobs gradually fading.

Even after Celia went back to sleep, Marty remained upstairs for a considerable time, seated on the edge of her bed, just watching her angelic features. This was wrong. He and Etta could not go on upsetting their children like this. He supposed a lot of it was his fault for rubbing her up the wrong way – and what was the point, for it was impossible to change the idle baggage. Every night upon coming home he told himself to stay calm, not to bother if there was a mess or whatever, but he just could not help it. He had worked so hard for this and yet she treated it with such disdain. Even thinking about it made him angry. Something must alter, for he was fast approaching breaking point.

When he finally went downstairs, Etta had reheated his broth and now fetched the bowl back to the table. For the sake of his children he tried to be civil and thanked her, but instead of eating with him, she resorted to her usual tactic, encased herself in frost and turned to concentrate on some mending.

'This is grand,' he said truthfully of the broth.

But his attempts to appease her met with monosyllabic response. Knowing how he hated to be ignored, Etta took revenge for his deeply wounding comments by paying more heed to her stitches.

'You'll hurt your eyes doing that,' he told her between spoonfuls.

240

'I'm used to being hurt,' she deigned to respond, though without looking at him.

He had been meaning to patch things up but now exasperation flared again. What the hell did she expect? Yet, bearing the children's sensibilities in mind, he managed to curb his temper enough to say, 'Look, I'm sorry, I didn't mean it to happen . . . we're hardly ever together but even in the small time that we are all we seem to do is argue, so maybe it's best if we try to stay out of each other's way altogether. In future, just feel free to leave my supper on the stove and go to bed.'

Etta slammed her mending onto her lap and looked at him directly. 'Oh yes, and have you abuse me for neglecting you again!'

'I'm trying to think of a fu—!' Marty fought the inclination to swear at her but it took all his resolve as he laid down his spoon and continued with great deliberation, 'I'm trying to think of a solution, if only for the kids' sake. Jesus, they must get awful sick of listening to us tearing the heart out of each other. I know I'm sick to death of it. I love you, Ett. God, I do, but . . .' He shook his head and made a sound of such utter despair that she ran to him, her face oozing repentance as she knelt by his chair.

She wrapped her arms around him, pressing her lips to his arm, his hand, his fingers, reciprocating his endearments. Equally strenuous in his embrace of her, he sighed and rubbed his cheek against her dark head, his heart feeling as if every ounce of energy had been wrung from it, Etta feeling just as wretched.

After each had confirmed their regret several times over, her face resting on his chest, she tendered carefully, 'You didn't mean it, did you, about not wanting me to be here when you come in?'

He moved his head in an act of negation. 'But we have to try and stay civil to each other somehow . . .'

'It's all this work,' she scolded gently, stroking him. 'It's making you ill.'

'If I don't work we don't eat, simple as that.'

'But you don't need to work so hard! Rather than seeing even less of each other, as you suggest, might it not be better for you to be home more often? To try and regain what we had? I ran away so that we might be together, yet I've ended up lonelier than before.'

But rather than be encouraged that she wanted to be with him, Marty saw it as yet another demand for attention. 'I don't like it any better than you, but if I worked less hours we'd have to give up all this.'

'Would that be so bad?' pleaded Etta. 'I'd rather live in a smaller house and see more of my husband.'

'I don't want to live in a smaller house!' His voice began to rise again.

'No, and there's the crux of it!' She sprang away from him and went to perch stiffly in the chair on the far side of the room. 'You don't care for what I might want, it's always been about what you want. You're afraid of moving to a smaller home because you'll no longer be able to brag! You're just like my father! See me as nothing more than some ornament –'

'I bloody do not!' But Marty looked decidedly abashed for she had hit a nerve. 'Look, see what I mean? We're at it again!' He rose and headed for the back yard. 'Now, I'm off to the lav, and it would be a good idea if you were gone to bed when I get back.'

Etta threw up her hands. 'As my lord and master pleases! I shall make certain I keep out of your way from now on.' But as she dashed for the stairs she knew that this would solve nothing, and her heart was fit to break.

Of course, it was impossible for two people living in the same house not to see each other at some point, and with the quarrels continuing to flare, even during the odd occa-

242

sions they did come together, Marty was forced to concede that it had been a ridiculous suggestion; at least to himself. To Etta he would admit nothing and continued to stick to his guns, even as the daffodils unfurled into trumpets of gold, then shrivelled to make way for summer blooms.

But just because he saw less of her, that was not to say she was never on his mind. He thought of her constantly, veering between a desire to kill her and then, remembering how magnificent their passion had once been, wanting to rage out loud at the terrible injustice of it all, but instead wreaking his malevolence on strangers.

Today it was a little barrow boy, who was blocking his passage along a narrow, congested thoroughfare.

'Get on the proper side of the road!' He hollered ahead. 'How many brains does it take to steer a barrow, for God's sake?' And a muttered addition to himself. 'Fucking halfwit.'

The youth blushingly apologised. Remaining grumpy, Marty barged his way onwards through streets that were ripe with odour, the dung and sweat of horses as they heaved their loads, his own perspiration trickling down his brow as he tried to steer his cumbersome barrow into Spurriergate, giving frustrated growls at being constantly impeded, stopping and starting, stopping and starting, until he finally came to rest outside Leak and Thorp's department store. Here he was commanded loftily to wait, whilst the commercial traveller who had hired him went inside.

Marty slammed the heavily laden barrow down in protest, angered by the way he was treated by people of no higher rank than himself – go here, go there, carry this trunk – jumped-up peasants, the lot of them! His hands relieved of the weight, he rubbed the numbness from them, picking at the calluses and glancing idly about him, his envious eye taking in the odd toff, the ladies in their large feathered hats and going-to-town costumes.

The narrow street was crammed with two-way traffic,

amongst the carriages and horses the occasional motor car and a multitude of bicycles. With a care as to his safety from one of the latter, Marty heeded the furious tinkling of the bell and took a quick sideways step into the gutter, complaining forcefully as the cyclist passed. How much longer would he have to stand here? After an upwards glance at the landmark figure of the Little Admiral and the clock on which this stood, he gave an irritated sigh at how long the traveller had been inside, before resuming his disgruntled observation.

Then his expression froze. An open-topped motor car was attempting to emerge from New Street, driven by a man in a top hat. But it wasn't the hat which caught his attention. Alongside the driver sat Etta. His heart came up into his mouth. Oh Christ, that was it, she was finally sick of him and going back to her own kind!

His heart started to thump in panic. Would the car turn to right or left? If the former it would pass the spot where he was standing. No, it was turning left, carrying her away from him. But he could not move to stop it, could only watch her lovely mouth – a mouth that had not graced him with a tender word in months – laugh prettily, seductively, at her stylishly dressed companion as the vehicle slowly edged its way across the double stream of traffic. Oh God, what should he do? Any husband worth his salt would accost the pair and challenge them, demand to know what was going on, drag the bastard from his car. There was still time, for it was moving at snail's pace – but, too stunned, his whole body a-tremble, Marty could not budge an inch.

'Move along now!'

For a moment he ignored the command, barely heard it above the fevered thumping of his heart as he watched her go. Where was William, the only one to be left at home since Alex had started Baby Class? Obviously she had dumped him on her mother-in-law so that she might keep her tryst. My God, how would he break this to the others when they came in from school?

'I said, move along,' ordered the constable sternly, endorsed by honks and tinkling bells and shouts from the rear. 'You're causing an obstruction.'

But Marty's eyes were glued to his wife, who, from the way her head moved, was still flirting outrageously with her wealthy male companion as the vehicle moved away. 'I've been told to stay here,' he murmured distractedly, never taking his eyes off the adulterous pair. How long had this been going on? Oh, Christ, he was going to vomit.

'Well, *I'm* telling you, if you don't move you'll be arrested!'

Marty suddenly became alert, though not to the constable. The car was picking up speed now – if he didn't act now she would be lost to him forever. With a frantic gleam in his eye he made to run after her.

But the constable, near to losing his patience, grabbed his arm. 'Take your barrow with you!'

Marty struggled to free himself. 'No, my wife! I have to go –'

'The only place you're going is the bridewell,' responded the policeman, and promptly arrested him.

Upon release, he did not return to work but went straight home, fearful of what he might find. It was such a huge relief to see Etta there – and actually smiling as she hurriedly placed his meal before him – that he could have wept with joy.

But this mood was short-lived. What if she were only being nice to him out of pity, lulling him into a false sense of security, her real intention being to sneak away when he was least expecting it?

Etta had been at first pleasantly surprised by his early homecoming, but now, noting that he was picking at the meal – after she had gone to the trouble of cooking his favourite – she felt impatience begin to rise. 'Is there something wrong with it?'

Marty glanced up at the crisp enquiry. 'No, no, I'm just . . .' Then he lowered his eyes again and stared at the table. 'I'd better warn you, I got arrested today.'

'What?' The word was loaded with accusation.

'I was in Coney Street, about two o'clock, and a copper told me to move on.' He looked at her closely as he spoke, watching for her eyes to betray that she had been there too. He thought he saw a flicker, then it was gone. But she had always been a good liar – she was lying on the day he had first met her – he had thought it reserved for others but now he was not so sure.

'Then why didn't you?' demanded Etta.

Mind a-whirl, he frowned. 'Why didn't I what?'

'Do as you were told and move on!'

'Oh, and you like me to do as I'm told, don't you!' He slammed down his cutlery.

'Be quiet,' she hissed, 'you'll wake the children.' She made to take away his plate.

But he grabbed its rim with both hands. 'I haven't finished yet!'

'Let me heat it up then, it must be cold the time you've taken.' Etta felt cold too. Her marriage was falling apart.

'Just leave it,' ordered Marty through clenched teeth, and finally she let go. 'Now, have you anything else to say?'

Confused and unhappy, she shook her head. She had been going to ask him to fix the baby's pram – a nut that secured the chassis had sheared off whilst she had been crossing the road this afternoon. It had been extremely hazardous, the battered old pram had almost collapsed – but with the mood he was in she chose not to mention this.

'Then I'll get on with it!' And he set about the rest of the meal in ferocious manner, clearing the plate in some five minutes and giving himself indigestion.

'May I remove it now?' His wife, who had been patiently standing by, reached out.

But before she could take hold of the plate, Marty gripped her wrist and looked up at her. 'Don't leave me, Ett.'

Stunned, she saw the greyness of desperation in his eyes. Immediately, she repented her condemnation of him, her icy protective casing melted and she looked upon him with compassion. 'As if I would!' She tried to make light of the arrest. 'Don't concern yourself, I'm sure some of these policemen are rather too zealous.'

I *saw* you, he wanted to say, but it hurt too much. Oh, how it hurt to remember the way she had looked at that fellow . . .

Gently, she removed her wrist from its shackle, using her liberated hand to stroke his face. But to Marty it was the kind of stroke she might use on one of their children. And so was her tone of voice. 'Now, let me get rid of that plate and then you can take yourself up to bed. Why, you looked quite worn out.'

'Will you join me?' he asked softly.

She smiled and nodded, but, 'I shall have to give William his bottle first.'

This pulled Marty up sharp as he was about to take the stairs. There was a thing: would a mother run off and leave her babies behind? His mother wouldn't; but he was not so sure about Etta.

Perhaps if he had come right out with it, admitted he had seen her with that man, it could soon have been resolved. But he didn't. For he was afraid that bringing matters to a head might have the opposite effect to that which he desired, might send her away more quickly than she had planned. Instead, he became more and more worked up, so paranoid that the slightest adverse comment from Etta made him think this was the end.

Things were getting Etta down too. It seemed that everything she said to Marty lately was misconstrued and so she had been forced to ask Red to mend the pram. Even so, her husband remained tense. Following his arrest for obstruction, he had just returned from his morning court appearance to announce he had been fined five shillings.

'*Five* shillings?' The moment she opened her mouth she knew he had misunderstood again.

'Oh, don't worry!' he fobbed her off nastily. 'I'll make it up by working on Sunday.'

'I didn't mean that!' Etta looked fraught. He seemed to think she was blaming him for the loss of precious income. 'I was commenting on such harsh . . . penalty,' she finished sadly as the door slammed behind him.

Marty strode directly to the railway station. He had gone home with the intention of having lunch with his family, but Etta had made him so angry that he could eat nothing. He made no diversion from his route. How could he tell his mother what was going on? She had warned him about marrying out of his class all along.

He barged his way through streets festooned with Union Jacks and coloured bunting to mark the King's Coronation. Throughout the week there would be parties galore, but he himself would have no time to attend festivities, oh no, he would be rushed off his feet trying to make up his earnings. And for what? He had four children but hardly ever saw them except on Sunday – and now he had just promised to work on Sunday to prevent his wife carping about money. Damn her! Damn her, bloody damn her!

Reaching the station, he took up his position by the other barrow boys, his agitation still in evidence.

'What did you get, Mart?' asked old Arthur, knowing he had earlier been to court.

'Five bloody bob!' spat Marty.

Arthur winced, unsettled not just by the fine but by his

248

pal's uncharacteristically aggressive mood. 'Ooh dear, have a fag.' He extended a packet.

Though he rarely smoked, Marty snatched one, gave cursory thanks, then dealt an additional few words of venom for Custard Lugs, who seemed to be taking an interest. 'What are you looking at, arse-face?'

'Not sure. It could be a monkey, it could be a pile of turds,' the man with yellow ears replied disdainfully, then made ready for the train that was just chugging in.

'Eh, steady on, lad,' warned Arthur uneasily, like so many others afraid of the man with the cosh.

'Ah, let him go bugger himself,' replied Marty, drawing violently on his cigarette, exhaling the smoke just as force-fully. There had now been rivalry between the pair for years, insults being exchanged, and occasionally an incident would occur, arising from nothing more than that they could not stand the sight of each other. Custard Lugs did not partic-ularly like anyone, but he seemed to detest Marty more than most and the feeling was mutual. In fact, at that moment, Marty felt like punching him in the face, and with his mind in turmoil it was all he could do to stop himself.

A few hours later he was to wish that he had taken the opportunity.

With his licence up for renewal, he was not unduly surprised to be called in front of the relevant authority. However, he was soon to be disabused as to the reason for this summons.

'I have to inform you that we intend to rescind your licence, Lanegan,' said the official.

'Wha— but why?' A look of sheer disbelief joined the beads of perspiration on Marty's face.

'Your recent conviction.'

Utterly devastated, he threw back his head and groaned. It was obvious who was responsible for leaking news of his downfall, for the incident had not yet appeared in the newspaper. 'Sir, please, it was only a paltry offence . . .'

'Irrelevant, I'm afraid, the rules state that –'

Marty didn't wait to hear any more, but swivelled on his heel. He was going to get that bastard. By God he was. But his fury was so clearly evident that Custard Lugs saw the danger long before it occurred, and when Marty unleashed his wrath, all that it earned him was a swift cuff and he was flat on his back. Immediately, he struggled up to try again, cursing and spitting as he launched himself, and indeed he did manage to land a few blows of his own before being hauled off by a much heavier-set platform inspector. But it failed to satisfy, and, furthermore, he was ordered to go home or he would find himself arrested yet again.

Happy, happy, happy! Everybody was fucking happy apart from him. Marty raged at the smiling faces that loomed at every turn of the way, all in party mood, buying new frocks and hats to celebrate the Coronation. He lashed out at a balloon that floated away from the bunch and loomed into his face.

'Watch it, chum!' warned the balloon-seller, as irritated as he by this stifling heat.

'Or what?' snapped Marty, marching straight on.

Only when he was almost home did he ask himself why on earth he was heading back here. There was bound to be another argument when he told her . . .

His children were delighted to see him, though, and he to see them, and even whilst anger and frustration simmered inside he managed to contain it sufficiently to show interest in the decorations they were making, and forced a pleasant laugh as they paraded before him in their paper crowns.

But he could gladly have strangled Etta, who as usual had become carried away with her own interests, allowing the living room to be strewn with paper and scissors and glue and coloured tissue, whilst the pots went unwashed and the bucket used for soaking Will's dirty napkins was full to the brim with yellow stinking water.

'You're early,' she said.

'My, you're observant.' He tried not to shout and frighten the children, but his tone and his eye were severe. 'Maybe that's 'cause I've lost me bloody licence.'

Etta sagged in dismay.

'So!' He dug in his pocket and carefully but deliberately set a handful of coins on the table. 'You'd better make the most of these – they might be the last you see.' He warmed to his theme. 'In fact, make the most of this house, for we'll probably have to move to a shack.'

Trying to hang on to her own temper, Etta demanded, 'What happened?'

'I'll tell ye what happened!' Marty's voice began to rise, his intention to say *I was watching you and your fancy-fella canoodling when I got arrested*. But he did not get the chance, for Etta cut in.

'Oh, damnation, it's Aunt Joan!' Through a gap in the grubby lace curtains she had seen the trim little figure mincing up the path.

'Christ!' Marty raged at the heavens. Then, 'Quick, kids, tidy all your things away!' And he too began to help clear the mess, clattering the pots into the sink in an attempt to hide them. 'At least if we move to a smaller house we won't have the dubious pleasure of her visits!' He noted Etta's worried mien. 'Well, I can't see why you'd be concerned, you've treated this one like a dustbin.'

Too deeply wounded to give any constructive response, Etta flung at him before stalking off to admit Joan, 'Do you think we might have a little courtesy whilst the guest is here?'

Marty rushed to move the stinking bucket of dirty napkins outside, but was caught in the act.

'I hope I haven't come at an inconvenient time?' The visitor wore a smile that became edged with distaste upon sight of the bucket.

Marty had not the inclination to force politeness today.

251

'Couldn't be better, Aunt Joan. You can help wash these nappies if you've a mind. Make yourself useful for once,' came the added mutter.

Joan delivered a light laugh but her nostrils flared and a mouse-like hand twitched at the lace on her bosom. 'Someone had a little accident?' Her eyes viewed the rest of the disarray, smiling unsurely at the children.

'No, it's one big bloody accident,' seethed Marty.

'You must take no notice of my husband's mood, Aunt Joan!' Etta stepped in with a calm apology, at the same time ushering the guest to a chair and throwing a look of recrimination at Marty. 'There is no excuse for his rudeness but there is a reason: Martin has lost his licence.'

'Oh, dear.' Seated now, Joan donned a look of understanding for her nephew. 'I hope that doesn't mean you can't work?'

Marty suffered no guilt at having vented his spleen on her, but now sought to moderate his reply. 'Fortunately no, I can still earn a bob – will you have tea, Aunt?' When Joan said she would, he assisted Etta in getting out the cups and saucers, not because he had any wish to help but to keep himself occupied.

'We might have to move to a smaller house,' five-year-old Edward told the guest.

Both parents looked daggers at him for this indiscretion.

'Oh, Martin, do you really?' The mousy face portrayed the enormity of such a move. 'It would be such a come-down for poor Etta.'

'Not in the least.' Etta saw her husband's dangerous expression and sought to avoid further upset by conveying nonchalance. 'I'm sure we'll be happy wherever we live – children, why don't you finish off your Coronation hats?'

'They are finished,' pointed out Celia.

'Then do something else. Write a story.' Fighting her misery, Etta piloted the small bodies to a corner, providing

252

them with writing and drawing materials. 'Sit quietly now and let the grown-ups speak.'

'Still, it will be a great shame to lose this place,' opined Joan, clinging to the theme.

Deciphering censure in her tone, Marty bubbled with unspoken insults, becoming angrier and angrier as half an hour was to tick by and still the conversation revolved around the same subject. Why was everyone blaming him? The one responsible for all this was sitting right there. He glared under his lashes at Etta, who chose to ignore him.

'Father, may I ask something, please?'

Marty turned at Celia's polite interruption and, over-coming his anger, responded to her query over how to spell photograph. 'Pee, haitch –'

'Aitch,' cut in Etta impatiently. This particular failing had always irritated her. The entire Lanegan family said haitch. She had always bitten her tongue until now, but Martin's obnoxious comments had injured her deeply; two could play at that game.

Marty bristled at being corrected in front of his relative. Why was she treating him so abominably? Did she not realise how much he had sacrificed to put her here? Had she no appreciation of the countless excuses he had made for her, no inkling how much he loved and adored her? *Had* loved . . . but she seemed intent on killing that with her petty attempts to belittle him. '*Haitch*,' he repeated deliberately, before spelling out the rest.

Etta felt his eyes boring into her, feeling just as angry as he, but trying to maintain some semblance of dignity in the face of such provocation. Why, why was he treating her like this? Did he not realise how much she had sacrificed to be here? Had he no appreciation of the way she had defended him in the face of her parents' disapproval? She had not uttered one word of complaint when he had taken her to live in penury, because she had loved and adored him. Why was he now so intent on killing that love?

Made awkward by the atmosphere, Joan formed an excuse to leave. 'Oh dear, I do believe I might have left the gas on – I shall have to go!'

'Every cloud has a silver lining then,' sallied Marty.

The insult went undetected as Joan rushed away, wishing them luck in keeping the house. Marty could barely wait for her to exit before exploding, 'Did you have to make such heavy weather of correcting me?' The children looked up collectively, a flicker of alarm in their eyes.

'It wasn't I who made heavy weather of it. I simply wanted the children to receive the correct example.' Clad in her armour of ice, Etta began to remove the teacups and plates from the table, clattering them along to the scullery and then coming back for the teapot.

'Making out that their father is an ignoramus!'

'You did that for yourself, taking it out on Joan because you lost your licence!'

'Oh yes, and didn't you just make the most of that! Couldn't wait to tell her we'd have to mo—'

'I said no such thing!' Not wanting to blame Edward, Etta clenched her fist around the teapot handle and snapped at him, 'You're deranged.'

'If I am 'tis you who made me so! And that's a good one about teaching our children by example, a really good example *you* set for them! Well, go on, then, bugger off with your fancy-fella, see if I care.'

The children started to cry in unison. Etta spared them only a harassed glance before demanding, 'What the devil are you talking abou—'

'I *saw* you!' bawled Marty above the din of his crying children. 'The day I got arrested in Coney Street 'twas because o' you! I saw you with that man in the car!'

Etta looked puzzled at first, then she let out an incredulous laugh.

Marty was outraged. *How could she laugh in the face of his agony?* He seized at anything now, however ridiculous it might sound, so long as it injured her as much as she had injured him. 'Now I see why your father let me have you. He was probably glad to get bloody rid!'

With nary a signal of warning, Etta lifted the teapot and smashed it down on his head.

Marty staggered, his feet crunching the shards of white pottery and his eyes glazing over as he struggled to right himself by means of a dining chair, then underwent a moment of stunned disbelief, blood and tea leaves running together down his face.

Beholding this tragi-comic sight, teetering on the verge of madness, and dangerous and as unpredictable as a wounded lioness, Etta wanted to laugh and to cry, to fling back at him that the man whom he accused of being her lover was in fact just a stranger who had kindly offered to transport her and William home when the pram had collapsed.

But there was no time, for Marty roared at her, 'It's like living with a fucking animal!'

And, completely blind to his children's distress, he stumbled from the house. 'That's it, I'm gone for good!'

Without enough arms to go round, Etta left the baby to screech in his cot and rushed to cuddle the three sobbing children. 'Don't worry, don't worry! Father didn't mean it, he'll be back.'

'You hurt him!' stammered Celia, her body racked with tears.

Etta groaned. 'I didn't mean to, he just . . . oh, come here!' Fighting her own upset she set to cuddling them again, shushing and soothing and kissing, dabbing at tears. 'I swear it was all a silly mistake, he'll be back before bedtime.'

'Promise?' Edward's lower lip juddered, his puffy red eyes showing a desperate need to believe.

'I promise,' soothed Etta, granting each a final pet and saying evenly despite her own senses being much assailed and her heart pounding like a drum, 'Now buck up whilst I go quieten Willie, then we shall all have some milk and buns.'

Marty strode away without knowing where he was going, trying to pace out his anger until he could walk no more, whereupon he threw his upper body over an iron rail that overlooked the River Ouse and stood there, chest heaving. It was late in the afternoon but still quite hot, the sun reflected in the brown ripples where barges and rowing boats jostled for position. Underneath a bridge on a patch of mud, children frolicked. He leaned there for a time, grimly watching the scene but not really taking in any of it except for the sour tang of the river, his throbbing head awhirl with all manner of thoughts.

'By, you look like I feel.'

Accompanied by the droll Yorkshire comment, he sensed a shabby male presence drape itself next to his and, without interest, turned to see a boyhood friend. 'Oh . . . now then, Ged. How are you?'

A cryptic grin from Ged Burns. 'Not much better for seeing you, that's for sure – you certainly know how to make a chap feel wanted.'

'Ach, don't mind me.' Marty dredged up the energy to pat his companion, but then leaned back on the rail and sighed. 'Wife trouble.'

Ged winced at the congealed blood on his friend's temple. 'She did that, did she?' At Marty's nod he looked sympathetic and offered a thinly rolled cigarette, then, when it was refused, inserted it between his own lips. 'At least you've got a wife. No bugger'll have me.'

'Count yourself lucky then.' His expression glazed, Marty picked at the hard skin that surrounded his thumbnail.

'Struth, you have got it bad. What's happened?'

Marty shrugged and took a while to answer, his eyes

following the group of barefooted youngsters who squelched laughingly amongst the mud, faces alight with glee. Was he ever so carefree? 'Ah, one thing on top of another. One minute there you are, booling along fine, and the next . . .' His voice trailed away into a distant gaze of unhappiness.

'You're in the shit,' finished Ged, his eye holding a glimmer of empathy. 'Got any kids?'

'Four,' sighed Marty.

An untidy eyebrow was arched in envy. 'Can't be that bad between you and the wife then. How old are they?'

'Six, five, Alex's nearly four and Willie's just a bairn.' His heart ached at the thought of them. He shouldn't have ranted and upset them like that.

Ged unleashed a stream of smoke through the gap in his brownish teeth. 'Not bad going. Look at me, twenty-seven, same as yourself, no kids, no wife, no house even, I doss where I can – and you think you're hard done by?' He dealt Marty a laughing, persuasive nudge. 'Fancy coming to drown your sorrows? I don't mean in there,' he nodded at the river and laughed again. 'I mean in a tastier liquor.'

Marty would rarely contemplate imbibing during the day, but this afternoon the thought was tempting. However, remembering he had tipped all his earnings on the table he was forced to tell his companion, 'I haven't a meg.'

'Wife grabbed it all, did she?' Before Marty could reply, Ged patted his own pocket and added, 'Ah well, at least that's one thing I'm not short of.' He displayed a handful of coins and jerked his whiskery chin as a sign of invitation.

After only the slightest pause, Marty murmured, 'What the hell.' And he went with his friend to a quayside hostelry.

Here, in the dank interior, his companion, obviously eager for company, was to keep the drinks flowing for the rest of the afternoon, indeed well into the evening, and Marty was content to let him. Unaccustomed to alcohol, he became quickly inebriated and eventually his troubles began to seem not so bad. Through the murk of insobriety, he vaguely recalled someone else joining them, a blur of laughter and a feeling of freedom he had not enjoyed for many a month, daylight fading and the lamps being turned on. But after that . . .

Returning to some form of consciousness, Marty gradually became aware of a painful jarring motion and his head banging rhythmically against a darkened window, and realised with a start that he was on a train. His befuddled slits of eyes took in the man who sat opposite, the only other person in the carriage, and he recognised him as the friend he had not seen since boyhood. Finally coming to, he managed vaguely to recall their reunion – but that had been in daylight. Now it was pitch black outside and a train was carrying him to heaven knew where. The compartment smelt like a brewery.

Dishevelled and still dazed, Marty threw his companion a look of alarm. 'What're we doing on this train? Where's it go?'

'Lichfield,' said the other on a yawn.

Even more perplexed, Marty rocked with the motion of the carriage. 'Christ, where the fuck's that when it's at home? I don't even remember buying a ticket.'

'You didn't,' slurred Ged.

'Oh, don't tell me I owe you money,' Marty groaned.

The reply was affable. 'No, that sergeant gave us both a travel warrant.' Ged produced his and waved it.

Swaying in his seat, brow furrowed, Marty fumbled automatically in his pockets and came up with a similar document, his confused, bloodshot eyes examining it. 'Sergeant?'

'The one what recruited us.' Arms folded, Ged closed his eyes and wriggled back in his seat as if to sleep.

Panic flared in Marty's breast. God almighty – he had joined the army! Kicking his friend awake, he demanded frantically, 'How long did I sign up for?'

'Ow! Watch it, you bastard.' Ged clasped his shin, then prefixed his reply with a lazy belch that filled the compartment with yet more beery fumes. 'Same as me, six years.'

Marty gasped, moaned and clutched his injured head.

He could have wept. But what would have been the use in it? Tears would not wash his signature from that form. There could be no going back now. And upon serious reflection did he even want to? What was left for him in York? Apart from his children, his dear, dear children – but a fatherly instinct to protect them told him that his being at home was doing more harm than good. Even if Etta did deign to have him back, he could not tell how long he could tolerate being taken for granted. He was sick and tired of looking after everybody. Why couldn't someone look after him for a while?

In a mood of dark resignation, he settled back, folded his arms and closed his eyes again. Yes, this might be just what he needed. Let the army look after him until he could decide what to do next. It didn't seem too big a risk. With England enjoying *entente cordiale* with her old enemy France, and the Boers no longer a problem, it was doubtful there would be another war during his stint, for such hostility blew up rarely. True, he could be ordered to put down foreign natives, but with a gun against their spears that didn't seem too hazardous, and the further away from his wife this train carried him the better the idea seemed to be. At this moment, it was his greatest desire to put as many miles as possible between him and that idle, selfish shrew.

12

She had not waited up for him that night, but, bubbling with anger whilst at the same time listening out for his tread on the stair, she found it impossible to sleep. Yet she must have dozed eventually for it was now daybreak. The other side of the mattress remained cool. Though sick with foreboding, Etta managed to adhere to normality for much of that day, fobbing the children off with the lie that their father had come home very late and was now at work, and answering any dubious query as to whether he would be home that night with the breezy response, 'I'm sure he will!'

But he wasn't. And neither had he appeared by the next morning. Etta was extremely worried by now. What if she had really injured him? What if he had collapsed and was lying unconscious somewhere? No, someone would have found him and taken him to hospital. Should she go there? Yes, she should, and upon taking the children to school she did so immediately.

But there was no record of any such admittance. Nor was there anything in the local newspaper, for she had pored over every word of it.

Whilst this brought vast relief, conversely it resurrected her anger, for there could be only one explanation: he was staying away purposefully to make her suffer.

Where the devil was he? If he did not come back soon it would not be just her marriage that was at stake: she could pay the rent this Friday, but after that . . .

It was no use sitting here wondering, she must go and search for him, the first place being his parents' abode. But Aggie, Red and Uncle Mal looked at her askance when she asked if they had seen Marty in the last couple of days.

She lowered her voice, though the child in her arms was far too young to understand and the rest were at school. 'I didn't want to worry you but he hasn't been home.'

Aggie slapped her palms to her high cheekbones. 'Begor, he could be lying kilt!'

'No, no, I don't think so . . .' Etta turned sheepish. 'We had a row – it was all a silly misunderstanding. When the pram broke that time in town, a man gave me and William a lift in his car. I'd forgotten all about it, but apparently Martin saw us and assumed the worst.' She omitted to mention that she had hit him over the head with a teapot.

Aggie clicked her tongue and shared a despairing glance with her husband. Both had feared it would come to this.

'He charged out saying he was gone for good. I thought he was just saying it to frighten me . . . but I'm beginning to think he meant it.' Etta appeared sick and afraid. 'I don't know what to do, I've hardly any money once this week's rent's paid.'

Red felt responsible for his son's behaviour and, rapidly alternating between sleep and wakefulness, was to react with logic. 'Aggie, give the lass some cash out o' the tin.'

'Is that all the pair of you are worried about?' demanded Aggie. 'Paying the rent? The lad could be kilt, I tell yese!'

Red swooned again.

'I'm sure not,' Etta was quick to say, jiggling William, who was showing apprehension over the raised voices. 'Otherwise I'd have contacted the police.'

'The hospital!' barked Aggie.

'I've already checked there,' her daughter-in-law assured her.

'Ach, your man'll be fine enough!' retorted old Mal

dismissively. ''Tis plain as the nose on your face what he's at – a law unto himself as usual.'

Awake again, Red tended to agree. 'Aye, now come on, deary, how much is this rent?'

'Six and six.'

'*Six and six!*' shrieked all in unison, provoking the baby to tears and worsening Red's narcoleptic fit.

Etta reared defensively, jouncing William even harder. 'Well it wasn't my idea to move to such a large house! Martin was the one who insisted upon it – and now he runs off and deserts me!'

Despite the baby's noise, Red fell in and out of sleep, his wife throwing up her hands in despair. 'Well, for sure, we can't find that amount,' sighed Aggie, joining Etta in trying to calm William. 'I could maybe spare a florin . . .'

Etta was quick to refuse. 'Thank you, but I can survive for now. By staving off the rent collector this Friday I can hang on to my funds another week. By that time Martin should be back.' And, fighting her anxiety, she smiled and kissed the baby's wet cheek in an attempt to show she believed it.

For two Fridays after Martin walked out, Etta did manage to avoid the rent collector, but on the third week running she was finally spotted crawling on all fours beneath the window.

'Have you found it yet?' The man's voice yelled through a gap twixt sill and lace curtain, obliging her to freeze. 'Yes, you on your hands and knees! I presume you're down there looking for the money you've dropped. That's if one takes the charitable view, of course. Anybody with a suspicious mind might think you're trying to get out of paying.' When Etta still did not move, he concluded, 'I'll be back next Friday. If I don't get what's owed you'll be evicted!'

Relating this to her mother-in-law later, after first making

262

sure the coast was clear, Etta declared it, 'The most embarrassing moment of my life – oh, I could kill your son for what he's put us through. Well, I shall just have to pawn this to raise the money.' She tugged at the gold locket and chain around her throat. 'But if he doesn't come back soon I've no idea how we're going to cope.'

Aggie voiced the obvious. 'You'll just have to find a job.'

'How, with four children?' demanded Etta.

Unimpressed by her son's abrupt departure, even though she was worried about him, Aggie felt a sense of responsibility. 'You can leave them with me.'

Whilst not overly thrilled by this offer, Etta mulled it over and eventually saw it was the only solution. 'I suppose I must until your son decides to turn up. But what kind of employment should I seek?'

There's a thing, thought Aggie, for the girl was pathologically workshy.

Uncle Mal sought to help and, with a palsied hand, reached out to tap one of the boys. 'Here now, Jimmy-Joe, get that press off your father, he can't read it while he's asleep.' The nine-year-old prised the newspaper from his sleeping father's grip and took it to the old man, who instructed him to hand it to Etta. 'There's a list of jobs on the front page.'

Etta thanked him unenthusiastically, then, whilst her children skipped and toddled in the evening sun, she perused the situations vacant. House maid? No, she just could not face that. Ah, this was more like it, a high-class store required a seamstress for its ladies costume department. Naturally inclined towards needlework, it seemed perfectly reasonable to take this direction. She pointed it out to Aggie. 'Should I apply, do you think?'

Her mother-in-law shrugged her narrow shoulders. 'It's that or starve.'

Etta felt her hackles rise at such lack of sympathy, overlooking the fact that Aggie was being more than generous by offering to mind her children. She stood abruptly. 'I'd better not waste any more time then.'

Gathering her brood, she went home to pen a formal application and was gratified to receive a reply on Monday asking her to come for interview that afternoon. Donning her best attire, she took the children round to their grandmother's then made her way into town.

Upon following directions from an assistant in the ladies department to an almost bare vestibule with wooden seating, she found three other applicants outside the interviewer's office. Etta observed them from the corner of her eye, wondering if they needed the post as desperately as she. Waiting in line to be interviewed, she watched each of them go in and come out, searching their faces for signs of triumph or disaster. Then it was her turn. Summoning a smile, she entered to face her inquisitor, who sat behind a desk.

'Good afternoon, Miss Lanegan, please be seated.' The prim-looking woman in the gabardine costume smiled up at her, bolstering Etta's confidence.

'Thank you,' she sat on the wooden chair. 'But as a matter of fact it's Mrs'

'Ah . . .' There was a swift change of mood, the middle-aged spinster frowning and briefly perusing the letter of application. 'My secretary must have made some mistake, we don't normally have occasion to employ married women . . .' She glanced up again, saw the pretty young woman's anxious expression and underwent a rethink. 'Still, as you are here I feel obliged to examine your references.'

'I'm afraid I don't have any,' confided Etta.

The other blurted a little laugh of disbelief. 'But I cannot employ you without!'

Etta explained hurriedly, 'I've never required payment for my efforts before.'

A supercilious, rather disbelieving smile twitched the interviewer's lips. 'Then how am I to know you are suitable?'

Somewhat taken aback by this tone, Etta delved into her bag and fetched out an embroidered handkerchief, offering humbly, 'This is a sample of my work.'

'Very pretty.' The woman allowed it a cursory glance before handing it back. 'But I should require much higher qualification than that little scrap – do you even have the proof that you stitched it yourself?'

At first shocked by the implication that she was a liar, Etta was then suffused with fury and embarrassment, but managed to bite her tongue and said tightly, 'I was unaware when I came for interview that my character would be called into question. Perhaps you'd care to contact Mrs Isabella Ibbetson of Swanford Hall? I am sure she will verify my fitness to work in your establishment.'

A knowing smile from the interrogator. 'A pity you didn't see fit to acquire the lady's commendation in writing before you came here.' But then, moved by the glint of moisture in Etta's eyes, she chose to relent. 'If you wish to return with such a letter I should be happy to set you on as a trainee.'

'And what remuneration could I expect?' Etta inwardly chastised herself for appearing so desperate.

The interviewer was incredulous. 'You expect to be paid in addition to receiving the benefit of our experience? Oh no, my dear, it would require a good deal of training before you could hope to earn anything.'

Etta's heart sank and she said abruptly, 'That's no good to me, I have children to feed.'

The other's face lost any trace of nicety, resorting to its former primness. 'Then, my dear, I suggest you alter your forthright views before you next apply for work. Please ask the next applicant to come in as you leave.'

Etta remained in her seat for a moment, feeling helpless and absolutely seething. Then she rose as majestically as she could and turned about with a caustic, 'Goodbye.'

Relating the entire debacle to her in-laws, she embellished

it with sweeping gestures and finished with the declaration, 'I don't know who on earth she thought she was, treating people with such contempt!'

'Sure, you're in good company,' quoth Mal. 'Red knows all about that, don't ye, son?'

'I surely do,' sighed Red, whose agricultural work had become increasingly irregular due to the use of new technology. 'There's no greater disrespect than being replaced by a machine.'

'Though machines are not all bad,' mused the old man. 'If ye'd money to burn 'twould be novel to have one that did everything for ye.'

'Sure you've got one already – 'tis called Aggie.' The speaker sipped her tea then steered the conversation back to its course. 'So will you write to your mother for a reference do you think?'

'Most certainly not!' Etta beheld her as if she were mad. 'I said that merely to put the abominable woman in her place. I have absolutely no intention of lowering myself to ask my mother for a reference!' It was too shaming. 'Besides which it would be utterly pointless. The minute Father spots my handwriting on the envelope he'll tear it up.'

'You don't know that.' Red tried to project optimism but only succeeded in annoying Etta.

'I do!'

'Better humble pie than starvation,' cut in Uncle Mal as Red fell asleep.

'That's true,' admitted Etta with a sigh. 'I didn't receive as much for my locket as I'd expected, barely enough to buy food for another week – and even that depends on whether the rent collector manages to catch me. Oh heavens, the confounded fellow will be here again on Friday, what on earth am I to do?' She rubbed her face vigorously, then, over the tips of her fingers, threw a look of resignation at her mother-in-law. 'I have little choice, do I? I shall have to go now and write to Mother. I do hope she won't keep me waiting too long for an answer.'

Etta's wish was granted, a response coming within twenty-four hours of writing. It appeared that Red had been correct in saying that Pybus Ibbetson would not destroy his daughter's letter without reading it, for, tellingly, the reply was delivered to the correct address. However, once opened, its content was less heart-warming; not only did it bear Etta's original letter in eight pieces, but an instruction from a senior manservant, obviously dictated by Ibbetson himself, advising Etta that the occupants of Swanford Hall had no desire to correspond with her.

Hating herself for being persuaded into this humiliating surrender by her mother-in-law, Etta was terse when Aggie enquired if she had heard anything of benefit from her parents. 'That depends on one's viewpoint,' she said archly. 'I certainly consider it a benefit that I shan't have to grovel to that pig again.'

Though sympathising with the girl's hurt, Aggie rebuked her. ''Tis no way to speak of your father.'

'Would you prefer that I call him louse?' demanded Etta. 'You certainly don't expect me to compliment a man who ignores the plight of his destitute grandchildren?'

'You laid that out in your letter, then?'

'No, I didn't even mention it to Mother, but they must realise I have children! I've been married for seven years – at least I *was* married until that other pig deserted me. Now I'm totally at a loss as to how I should describe my marital state.' She saw Aggie's lips tighten and added vehemently, 'I'm sorry, I know he's your son, but the mess he's left us with . . . I could kill him!'

Aggie dealt a weary nod of acquiescence.

'By Friday we could be homeless!'

Her mother-in-law pondered this. With Maggie and Elizabeth in service now, only the two boys still at home, there was more room. 'I suppose you must move in with us then.'

If the tone of Aggie's offer had been reluctant then Etta's response was equally so. 'Oh, I think we'll keep that as a last resort.'

'There's thanks for you,' sniped Aggie to Uncle Mal

'Yes, it did sound most ungrateful, I do apologise,' said Etta. 'But you have little enough space as it is – and it would feel as if I were giving in. I don't see why I should lose my home through no fault of my own.'

Aggie denounced the idea. 'Seems crazy, you spending money to rent and heat a place that'll be empty most of the day. I mean, it'll be well past the nippers' bedtime by the time you're home from work, 'twould make more sense and kinder too if I put them to bed here.'

'I suppose it would, but then I should never see them at all.' Etta remained entrenched in her decision. 'No, I should prefer to maintain my own residence, and for that I must find a job.' This, of course, involved backing down a little. Swallowing her haughtiness she queried meekly, 'Would you mind taking care of Willie and collecting the others from school whilst I go and search?'

Aggie showed virtue. 'Mind? They're my grandchildren, for pity's sake.' And she took possession of the baby. 'Will I mash some brains for his dinner?'

Etta nodded thankfully and prepared to leave. However, her exit was preceded by a tap and a halloo.

Aggie groaned at the arrival of her sister-in-law, then adopted a tone of welcome. 'Come in, 'tis open!'

Joan's beady eyes gleamed when they fell on Etta. 'I hoped I might find you here! I've just come from your house – are you going there now? I'll walk with you.'

Etta explained that she was going into town.

'So you'll have to make do with the poor relations,' said Aggie.

'Oh that's all right, I'll accompany Etta!' said Joan hastily.

'I'm afraid I shan't be much company,' replied her victim, and briefly explained her reason for going to town.

Joan touched her breast in shock. 'How dreadful! I never thought Marty was one to do a thing like that – you shouldn't have to lower yourself by going out to work.'

'I have no alternative if I'm to keep a roof over our heads. Now I really must go and search for employment. I pray I'll be luckier than on the last occasion.'

Informed of Etta's failure at the department store, Joan again delayed the other's exit. 'But you should have come to me! I'd have asked my neighbour to put in a good word for you – here, let me write his name down for you then you can reapply for the post and mention that you know him. I believe he's very big in the underwear department.'

Etta threw an involuntary smirk at Aggie, then declined. 'That's good of you, Aunt Joan, but I've no wish to be insulted again. I'm sure I'll find something eventually. I shan't return until I do.' Thanking her mother-in-law for looking after the children, she left.

Spurning the employment agencies, for they would take a cut of any wage, Etta went about town, seeking posters in shop windows that might advertise for assistants. But the innate sense of optimism which initially led her to the better establishments gradually began to fade with each successive rebuttal, forcing her to lower her sights and then to despair as afternoon turned to evening and still she had to find anyone willing to interview, let alone employ, a married woman.

There was, of course, a way to solve this. But Etta steadfastly refused to deny her marital status to any of these petty dictators. She *was* married, her husband *would* be coming back . . . sometime.

It was past six o'clock, her abdomen was grumbling with hunger and her feet were dotted with blisters as she wandered the streets. The sunlight had weakened in its descent towards the irregular roofline of antiquated buildings, yet still the air remained stifling and, with the dust stirred up by traffic and no drink past her lips since morning, her throat felt like parchment. Coming across a poster advertising for an assistant at a shoe shop, she sighed, not welcoming the thought of all those sweaty feet, but told herself that beggars could not afford principles and did as she should have done hours ago: she took off her wedding ring. It felt such a huge act of self-betrayal and she clung to one thought on committing the deed: in her heart she was married. Bracing her shoulders, she entered with a smile for the first person she encountered.

The male assistant at first looked piqued at the arrival of a customer at closing time, but, swayed by her beauty and her genteel request, personally escorted her to a tiny office in a corner of the shop, the lower half timber, the upper of glass, wherein sat a portly and balding individual. Her guide was very pleasant, tapping on the glass pane to make the request for her. 'A young lady here to ask about the job, Mr Burdock.'

In his cashier's absence due to sickness, it was left to the manager to tally up the day's takings, and his expression upon looking up was frazzled. 'It's hardly conven—' But at the vision of young beauty, his pasty, perspiring face immediately brightened, and, jumping from his chair and tugging at his waistcoat, he invited her to join him in the booth.

Etta did not resort to false hope, for the same had occurred at other establishments until they had heard she was married, and Burdock's old-fashioned garb of frock-coat and winged collar announced that his views would be similarly inclined. However, this time was different in that she was prepared to lie. She beamed and squeezed her way into the cramped space. 'Thank you, Mr Burdock, I'm most grateful to you for seeing me when you must be so busy.'

'Not at all, Miss . . . ?'

'Lanegan.' Etta did not disabuse him of her virgin status.

270

'Please, be seated, Miss Lanegan.' Obviously dazzled, Burdock offered her the one and only chair.

'How kind, thank you.' She had always balked at using her femininity as a weapon, but now she employed it liberally, holding the chubby figure with her dark, sparkling eyes, responding with the utmost admiration and respect.

'I fear you might not think me so when you hear what I have to say.' Mr Burdock leaned his plump backside against a cupboard. 'Our policy is to take on only school-leavers. It's our experience, you see, that young women of your age will in all probability leave in a few months to get married.'

Feeling that she just could not win, Etta held the pasty face and said firmly, 'I assure you, Mr Burdock, that I have no intention of marrying.'

'Ah, that's what they all say, Miss Lanegan!' He donned an indulgent smile. 'The number of young women to whom I've given the benefit of my experience, trained them for weeks, and then off they sail with a husband. In fact I'm surprised that a pretty young thing such as yourself wasn't snapped up ages ago.'

Etta wanted to scream.

'However . . .' Mr Burdock studied her thoughtfully, '. . . the post has been advertised for some weeks and you are the only one to apply. So, Miss Lanegan,' he announced with a beam, 'I'm pleased to say I'm prepared to give you a chance.'

Etta bit her tongue at the condescending tone and replied graciously, 'Why, thank you!'

'You can start tomorrow at a quarter to nine,' added Burdock. 'The wage will be eleven shillings per week minus stoppages. Naturally you'll have to work a week in hand.'

Alarmed to hear both adjuncts – she had been accustomed to receiving thirty-five or even forty shillings from Marty – Etta told herself that at least it was a job, as she rose and was escorted from his office and thenceforth from the shop.

With a sigh of gratitude, she made her weary way home. But there was to be no welcome, an agitated Aggie bearing down on her the moment she entered. 'Where've you been all this time?'

Exhausted, Etta felt like strangling her. 'I've *been* –'

'Ssh! You'll wake the nippers, I've shoved them in bed with Jimmy-Joe. We've been waiting on you to come, I've found yese a nice wee house down the street, one like this with a back entrance too.' Some of those on the other side lacked this facility. 'Peter Bechetti's horse has been hitched up for ages, he's waiting to shift your furniture!'

'*Now?*' Etta gaped.

'Well, unless you want to fork out that nineteen and six back-rent,' riposted Aggie.

Etta covered her mouth, but did not think too long about the offer, especially when her mother-in-law added that she and Red had generously paid for the initial lease. Forgoing the longed-for cup of tea and the need to gaze upon her sleeping children, she hurried back into the night. By midnight, her furniture was once again ensconced in Hope Street.

Unprepared for the move, her pictures, ornaments and other belongings all willy-nilly where Mr Bechetti had dumped them after the clandestine flit, Etta had been overwhelmed by the task of putting everything into some semblance of order and had broken down in tears before finally staggering off to bed for the few hours that were left before she must rise again.

Mercifully, with the children already at Aggie's, she had only herself to dress and feed. Even so, not daring to be late she tore through a hasty slice of bread whilst also buttering one to take for lunch, managing only half a cup of hot tea before she was on her way.

All that rushing was needless. When she arrived, the interior of the shop was still in darkness. After peering through the glass door, she wandered out of the shadows to consult a church-tower clock. There were fifteen minutes to go. Rather than dither here and fall under the curious eye of street-sweepers, she decided to stroll up and down the parade of shops which, one by one, were opening.

Perhaps, though, she had underestimated the time this would take, for when she returned the doors to the shoe shop were ajar and the manager was sitting behind the glass partition of the cash office. Instead of a smile of greeting he took his watch from his waistcoat and consulted it disapprovingly as she entered.

Etta quickly explained. 'I was here earlier but there was no one around.'

Her affability was not returned. With a sound of intolerance he came out of the booth, grasped the revers of his frockcoat and told her, 'Your colleagues are already upstairs in the staff room – come, I'll introduce you.'

Meekly, she followed him up the dark staircase.

At the intrusion everyone turned – though she had to blink in order to see them through a choking haze of cigarette smoke. Apart from the man she had met yesterday, they didn't appear a very friendly lot, looking her up and down without a word of welcome, though Etta conceded this might have something to do with the earliness of the hour if they felt as bad as her.

'This is your new colleague Miss Lanegan,' Mr Burdock told them, then briskly pointed each of them out to Etta. 'Mr Tupman . . .'

Etta extended her hand to the middle-aged man with the wavy ginger hair and flashed a smile, which induced the same response, his grip warm and dry.

'Mr Vant . . .' A decrepit but immaculately suited old codger rose slightly, who, it appeared, was the one responsible for filling the room with smoke. Before shaking her hand he took a lengthy drag of his cigarette, as if desperate to get his money's worth.

'Mr Ficklepenny, our trainee manager – in my absence he will instruct you in your duties.'

One glance at the fuzzy cheeks told Etta that Mr Ficklepenny was a recent newcomer to long trousers and she felt loath to grace the lad with a title and even less so to take orders from him. Nevertheless, she swallowed her pride and offered her hand respectfully. 'How do you do, Mr Ficklepenny?'

This gained instant favour, the youth dealing her a schoolboyish grin and a brisk handshake.

'Miss Sullivan, Miss Jackley, Miss Wimp, Miss Binks . . .'

The first three merely nodded, but the latter, a dull-looking girl provided her Christian name. 'Mary-Ann.'

'But not on the shop floor,' Burdock warned sternly. 'And finally Miss Bunyon, our book-keeper and cashier.'

Etta couldn't resist a friendly titter. 'An apt name for a shoe-shop assistant!'

Miss Bunyon was lofty. 'It's B-u-n-y-o-n, not b-u-n-i-o-n. And I'm not an assistant.'

Etta murmured an apology and touched her chin self-consciously, noting with distaste that her hand reeked of stale tobacco courtesy of Mr Vant.

Having completed introductions the manager went downstairs, the cashier closely following. With lame expression, Etta glanced around at the collection of rickety chairs then perched on one.

'Take no notice of her,' advised Mary-Ann, who without smiling managed to convey amicability. 'She reckons she's a cut above. Now, let's see if we've got an old overall in the cupboard till you've time to go for a fitting.'

'I trust that will be soon.' Her eyes beginning to water as a result of Mr Vant's chain-smoking, Etta was dismayed by the article that was presented to her, which looked clean enough but billowed with staleness when she tried it on.

'Oh, not till Wednesday afternoon when we're closed,' replied Mary-Ann.

'That's a good fit,' observed Maude Wimp, a bespectacled, middle-aged spinster with translucent skin that was marbled with a network of blue veins. 'Miss Duncan was skinny like you. Doubt she'll be coming back for it now, you might be able to keep it.'

'What luck.' Etta hardly dared breathe.

Misinterpreting the sardonic comment, the dull-looking Mary-Ann nodded, 'Yes, then you'll only have to buy one.'

Etta looked shocked. 'No one mentioned that I'd be required to buy two overalls!'

Mary-Ann explained in simple terms, 'One for wearing while you wash the other.'

'I meant –' Etta broke off, looking testy at being interrupted by a racking cough from the elderly smoker. 'I meant, how am I to afford them?'

Mr Tupman, who had been admiring her from a distance, sought to ease the fraught expression. 'They knock it off your wages, threepence a week, so it's not as bad as it sounds.'

Etta responded indignantly, 'It is when every farthing counts!'

All turned to eye her curiously.

Flushing, she told them, 'I live in lodgings with no one else to support me and I've been without work for some time and fallen behind on the rent, so you might imagine my reluctance to part with hard-earned cash.'

There were murmurs of empathy from the women.

Then young Mr Ficklepenny consulted his watch and announced bumptiously, 'Come along now, ladies and gentlemen, time to go down!'

Etta finished buttoning her overall. Mr Vant wrapped his grey wrinkled mouth around his cigarette to take a final deep inhalation. Mesmerised, Etta pictured him sucking his socks up through his legs into his chest, so strenuously did he pull on it. Her last button fastened, she looked down at herself despondently, wondering if she would be able to bear the stench of the overall and hoping she could make do with just the one by washing it overnight.

The youth clapped his hands as one would to a child. 'You too, Miss Lanegan, let's start as we mean to go on!'

Hating being under such rule but having no choice, Etta went down to begin instruction.

However, later in the morning, after a ten-minute break for tea, when the manager went out into town for a cup of coffee, she was to discover that there remained enough of the schoolboy in Mr Ficklepenny to provide a humorous interval, his main party-piece being to tip methylated spirits onto a counter and set it alight.

'Ooh, he's a card,' sniggered Mary-Ann, hand over mouth as blue flames danced across the counter before the pyromaniac expertly smothered them with a flourish. 'He'll get copped one of these days.'

'Nay, I'm too wick,' bragged Cyril Ficklepenny, acting the showman. Withdrawing a bag from his pocket he thrust it at Etta. 'Here, have one.'

About to delve into it, she noted with surprise, 'It looks like India rubber.'

'It is. He cuts them into bits and scoffs them.' Mr Tupman wandered up to join the circle that had gathered, the atmosphere more relaxed in the manager's absence. 'He's flipping crackers.'

Etta watched in astonishment as a grinning Mr Ficklepenny partook of the contents of the bag, relishing the pieces of eraser as if they were sweets.

'Here, have a proper one.' Mary-Ann handed round a bag of toffee, Miss Sullivan and Miss Jackley from the children's department being first to delve in.

Etta rarely ate this confection but accepted a lump just to be sociable, looking from the corner of her eye at the cashier who remained aloof in her small glass booth. 'Miss Bunyon looks disapproving. Will she tell?'

'No, she hates Dandy as much as we do,' said Maude Wimp.

'Dandy?'

'Our esteemed manager,' provided Tupman, toffee in cheek. 'Short for Dandelion, you know, as in dandelion and burdock. Mindst, he's been called all sorts. We used to call him Buttercup at one time.'

Etta laughed at the apt description, and agreed that the shape of his face with its limpid brown eyes reminded her too of a cow's, especially as on either side of the bald pate was a little tuft of hair, the placing and arrangement of these making them appear like horns. The red-haired man grinned back at her, this and the smiles of others engendering a feeling of camaraderie. Perhaps things were not going to be so loathsome here after all.

'Oh damn,' issued Maude at the entry of a prospective customer. 'I knew somebody'd come in the minute I'd put this in my mouth.'

'As the actress said to the bishop,' leered Mr Ficklepenny.

'What do you mean?' enquired Tupman, straight-faced.

'You know!' the youth grinned lasciviously.

Tupman remained mildly puzzled. 'No, we don't, do we, Mr Vant? Tell us.'

'Well, it's just – it's just summat you say!'

'You don't know, sonny, do you?' admonished the older man. 'In that case it would be wiser not to voice such vulgarities in front of ladies.'

'Especially as you're meant to be in a position of authority,' added Mr Vant, wagging a shoehorn.

Ficklepenny blushed crimson, his amusement petering out at being so humiliated. Etta had no understanding of the comment, and neither, she suspected from their blank expressions, did the other women, but she was grateful to Mr Tupman and Mr Vant for their chivalry.

Unfortunately, her smile brought her under attack from the trainee manager. 'Don't just stand there, go with Miss Wimp and learn your job!'

Following Maude's example, she discreetly spat the lump of toffee into a twist of paper and rushed to attend the customer.

For the next seven hours, except for the one allocated for lunch and a short tea-break in the afternoon, Etta was inducted into the ways of the shoe trade. She attempted to retain all that she was taught, the rules and regulations, especially the one that decreed that the customer was always right even if he or she was blatantly offensive, this latter rule being the most difficult to uphold and the new assistant very nearly finding herself sacked on her first day when a woman took exception to being told that the shoes she had selected did not flatter her and walked out.

'But she requested my opinion!' a tired Etta objected, upon the manager's reprimand.

'She expected you to tell her they looked splendid,' scolded Mr Burdock, the fat on his double chin wobbling. 'And so do I. Your role, Miss Lanegan, is to sell the product.'

Towards the end of a very long day when it looked as if another awkward customer might cost her her job, Etta despaired as she scanned the wall of shoe boxes for a solution, her own footwear having rubbed blisters on the two swollen lumps of hot meat on the end of her aching legs, when she felt a sweaty presence at her side.

'Take her these.' Mr Burdock's pudgy hand tugged a box from the fixture. 'They match the colour of her hat.'

'They're not what she asked for; she won't like them.'

'Miss Lanegan, have you listened to nothing?' The fat, impatient face jutted towards hers. 'Make her like them. That is the art of a saleswoman.'

278

Moving slightly away, she beheld him in protest. A dark shadow of stubble had begun to sprout on the perspiring, lardish jaw. On top of his manner she found it immensely irritating. 'I can't force her to buy them.'

Burdock was firm. 'No, but with a little charm you might persuade her. And as an added incentive, this one carries a spiff.' He pointed to a ticket on the box. 'Every pair of old stock you move will earn you an extra sixpence in your wage packet at the end of the quarter.'

For someone on eleven shillings per week this was sufficient to make Etta put aside her principles. Perking up, she bore the outmoded shoes directly to the customer, telling her, 'I omitted to show you these, madam. They are just in and very modern – but perhaps too modern for madam's tastes.'

Watching her, Burdock groaned at the new assistant's idea of charm.

But there was a certain method to Etta's words as she added, 'All the young ladies are wearing them.'

'You're not.' With acid features, the mature-looking woman glanced down, then indicated Mary-Ann. 'And neither is she.'

'Only because I'm unable to afford them,' confessed Etta sadly. 'They are rather superior quality to the ones I buy – such a pretty colour too.' She affected to admire the garish hue. 'In fact, they're an exact match for the ribbon on your hat.'

The woman sought out a mirror and her suspicious frown departed. 'So they are.' And, though still dubious, she tried them on and paraded before the admiring assistant. 'Well, they were not what I came in for . . . but you're right in saying they match my hat. Do they suit me, do you think?'

'Admirably,' confirmed Etta.

'Mmm . . .' a moment's indecision. Then, 'I'll take them.'

A triumphant Etta was picking the spiff off the box

before wrapping it when she felt the manager's hot breath in her ear. 'Well done, Miss Lanegan – but wait, if you can persuade her to buy a handbag there'll be another little bonus in it for you.'

Her tactics this time proved not so successful. Even so, Etta was grateful to have earned herself a precious extra sixpence, and yet more grateful upon being told that it was time to take her receipt book to the office in preparation of closing.

At long last the working day ended and she said perfunctory goodbyes to the other assistants. Whilst not as bad as she had feared upon being introduced to them this morning, none of them were of the type with whom she could strike up a close friendship – but then she was not there to make friends but to keep a roof over her children's heads. How desperate she was to cuddle her brood after being apart from them since yesterday morning.

Alas, when she went to pick them up from their grand-mother's they were too drowsy to care, the youngest one being particularly crabby at this disruption to his life. Etta wanted to weep, and yet again cursed Martin for destroying her family.

And no sooner had she taken them home than it was morning and time to give them back. So exhausted was she that it hardly registered how oddly Aggie greeted her when she entered, and she did not notice or comment on all the scurrying and guilty looks.

Besides which, Aggie spoke first, her awkward expression being quickly replaced by a look of eagled-eyed concern as she demanded, 'Where's your wedding ring?'

It was Etta's turn to shrink with guilt then. She had expected someone to comment on this last night but, probably because it was dark, no one had noticed. Defensively, she retorted, 'I don't even know if I am still married. Your son hasn't granted me the courtesy of knowing whether he's alive.'

Uncle Mal shared an uncomfortable look with Red then shuffled out to the closet with a newspaper.

Aggie remained intent on Etta's denuded ring finger. 'Ye haven't pawned it?' she gasped.

Etta shook her head and spoke truthfully. 'I've been forced into taking it off because no one would employ a married woman.'

Aggie gave a murmur of sympathy as she watched Etta kiss each of her children prior to leaving for work. 'It must be terrible hard having to deny these little mites.'

Etta's quick nod foretold that it was heartbreaking. 'But I must keep up the lie or lose my job.' Then she cocked her head. 'You know, I've been thinking: why should you have to look after Martin's children?'

'I've said I don't mind,' Aggie told her.

'But you shouldn't be forced into it! And, for that matter, neither should I, when all I need do is apply to the Parish and they'd trace him for –'

'Oh, don't do that!' warned her mother-in-law hastily.

'But he should be made to attend his responsibil—'

'No, no, ye mustn't!' Aggie was adamant.

Red, too, looked alarmed. 'We're well as we are, deary. They'll send a constable, we can't be having any truck with the polis.'

'But I don't earn enough to contribute to the children's upkeep,' she reasoned.

'No need, darlin'!' Aggie remained emphatic. 'We've ample money now the girls are sending their wages home. Don't go making the situation worse by instructing them busybodies.'

'You're very generous,' concluded Etta with a look of gratitude. 'Well, then, I'd better go. I don't want to be late again.' She blew a last kiss to the children and left.

Aggie sagged in relief and opined to her husband, 'That

was a close call.' She turned to look at Red, then, noticing he had fallen asleep, she clicked her tongue and muttered, 'Talking to my bloody self again.' And, now that it was safe, she gave her grandchildren a drink of milk then pulled out the letter that upon her daughter-in-law's entry had been hastily stashed behind the clock, and continued reading it.

13

By the end of that first week, the sheer physical effort of having to be on her feet all day made Etta thoroughly jaded, and she remained dead to the world for most of Sunday morning, or at least until her children began to whine impatiently for breakfast. Eyes like slits, she indulged them by letting them snuggle into her bed for as long as they would remain still; then, after dinner at Aggie's, devoted the entire afternoon to their enjoyment, prescribing a nature walk before bedtime stories at the end of an all too short day of rest.

Still, it hurt that she saw so little of them for the rest of the week. The working day, purported to be eight hours long, often extended much longer than this if custom required it, and sometimes Etta could still be there at eight or even nine at night if there was stocktaking to be done, so the little ones were invariably asleep when she got home and, not long afterwards, so was she. Even when she did have them to herself there were things to intrude. Possessed of a solitary overall, she had only Sunday on which to launder it. This meant that by the middle of the week it was far from pristine, which earned the manager's disapproval, and so she was compelled to wash it on her Wednesday afternoon off as well – more disruption to her time with the children – and to rise half an hour earlier in order to iron the wretched thing. The only good thing she could say about the job, other than that it would eventually bring in money, was that it had brought male admirers who, thinking this beauty unwed, were falling over themselves to assist her. It was rather touching when one's husband obviously no longer cared.

Payday came at last, and whilst it was very welcome this buoyant feeling did not last long. Once the cash had been allocated it was back to lean pickings for another week. Always quick to damn her mother-in-law, Etta now gave praise for Aggie, without whose help her children would have starved. It was only at her in-laws' house that she herself tasted meat nowadays, at home existing mainly on bread and condensed milk. Fortunately it was summer and savings could be made on fuel, but there was nothing to spare for clothing, however desperately she might need it.

Struggling to survive on the eight shillings that was left after the rent had been deducted, Etta inwardly raged. *Surely* she could do better for herself? As she hurried back and forth to work through town, her eyes could not resist being drawn to the window of each artistic embroidery shop. Why, the examples of needlework displayed were no better than she herself produced for fun, or had done once. No longer able to afford the goods within, lucky even to scrape together fourpence for a ball of white mending cotton, she eyed the silks wistfully. She had in fact applied to all these establishments, but there had been no vacancies. However . . . An idea began to form. It was futile to dream of renting premises but she could acquire a sewing machine by hire purchase and thenceforth work from home. Sparked by enthusiasm, she decided to go out in her lunch break and make enquiries at the Singer Sewing Machine Company.

But to her crushing disappointment, quite apart from the deposit, the weekly instalments would be half a crown, far more than she was able to spare. Certainly, once she was established the rewards would more than cover this amount, but how could she afford the initial outlay? She could move in with her in-laws to save on rent – some might say it was ridiculous not to do so – but Etta was loath to relinquish what little independence she had. Besides which, life would still be a struggle. So, it appeared she was trapped in the shoe shop until the time came when she could afford to put a little money by.

Thoughts of money, or rather the lack of it, were to become all-consuming. Despite the fact that it made things worse, Etta could not resist counting the days up to the quarterly disbursement when she might reap the benefit of her sales technique.

With the latter continuing to improve, by the time the long, hot summer drew to a close she had learned every trick in the trade. These included all manner of lies to an unsuspecting patron, and where Etta might once have disdained to involve herself in such dupery she now rushed to participate if it meant affording bacon as opposed to offal. Besides, after hours of pandering to customers' whims and being subjected to their sweaty feet in varying degrees of decomposition, she had come to view them as the enemy and therefore fair game.

Mr Burdock himself had also come to be included in this category. Whilst quite an amicable man, and obviously as admiring of her looks as his male underlings, he had been very patronising in bestowing her with his great experience and she had no qualms about joining her colleagues in mocking him. These humorous intervals had been somewhat enhanced lately by the fact that the unfortunate fellow had developed an intimate complaint. The female assistants in particular found it most entertaining to spy upon him when, imagining himself unobserved, he groped beneath his frockcoat, performing contortions in trying to reach the excruciating itch between his chubby buttocks.

He was at it again today. Behind his back, spying round a pillar, Etta and Mary-Ann clutched each other in mirth, almost hysterical with silent laughter as he strained on tiptoe to alleviate the irritation. 'Ooh, he's like a ballerina!' giggled Mary-Ann, tears in her eyes.

Etta mopped her own streaming face with a handkerchief, blurting, 'Do you think I should fetch him the sink plunger?' Allowed to enjoy the mischief for a while longer until another customer required serving, she broke off and wiped her face with the declaration, 'Gosh, what fun – and payday too.' And a quarterly payday at that. It was certainly worth the wait. Etta found upon tearing open her brown packet in the staff room at lunchtime that there was almost an additional week's wages from all the extra pennies and shillings she had accrued.

Mary-Ann was pleased with hers too. 'Spiffing! I can finish paying off my hat.' Unable to afford the said item in one go she had been forking out weekly instalments. 'What will you buy with yours, Ett?'

'Oh, it'll just go on bills.'

'*Surely* you can afford a little treat?' Mary-Ann and everyone else remained ignorant of Etta's true circumstances. 'Come to the De Grey Rooms with me tonight!'

Etta smiled at the dull-looking face. 'Thank you for asking but it's out of the question. My funds are already allocated.'

Mary-Ann shrugged her hefty shoulders. 'What a dreary life for a young woman to have.'

'It won't be forever,' announced Etta. 'I intend putting what little I can save to good use. The moment I have a deposit I shall hire a sewing machine and be my own mistress.' She divulged her other ambition of setting up an artistic embroidery shop.

Some were impressed, others were not, the cashier forming a smirk of derision as she gathered her belongings and headed downstairs. 'Should be good at that with all the embroidering you've done so far. To hear the way you talk, you're obviously too good to work here.'

'Oh, I didn't mean to insinuate that at all!' Etta turned

apologetically to the others. 'It's just my little dream . . .'

Mary-Ann waited until the sound of the cashier's footsteps had faded before commenting, 'She can talk. There's no one more stuck up than she is. Take no notice of the jealous cat, Etta, we know you're not like that. Good luck to you, I hope you get your sewing machine. Wonder what *she'll* come back with today. Half of Marshall and Snelgrove's like last bonus day, no doubt.'

Etta frowned in confusion. 'But how does she get a bonus when she doesn't sell anything?'

'If Dandy sells any old stock he lets her have the spiffs,' confided her informant. 'Miss Wimp overheard them talking. She collected almost a pound last time, didn't she, Miss Wimp?'

Mr Tupman mocked them playfully. 'Tittle-tattle, tittle-tattle!'

Etta flashed him a brief smile but her tone showed resentment. 'It doesn't seem right that we have to work so hard for our little bit extra whilst she contributes nothing.'

Mary-Ann was pragmatic. 'Oh, it's not just her, it's a perk of the cashier's job – 'cause they don't have chance to earn it for themselves, you see. Matter of fact, I applied for the post when the last one left but I wasn't clever enough.'

Etta announced, 'I shall bear that in mind next time a vacancy arises. If I'm up to the task, of course,' she added quickly.

'If looks were the only requisite you would more than qualify, my dear,' complimented Mr Tupman, rising. 'Speaking for myself I hope it occurs. It'd be such a pleasant change not to suffer that haddock gob every time I visit the cash office.'

'You're terrible!' accused Etta, but chuckled with the others.

'I know, but you love me,' grinned Tupman, who, having taken an earlier lunch, now went down to relieve the other male assistants. 'Coming, ladies?'

'Just got to do my hair and change my shoes,' was Miss Wimp's reply as he left, accompanied by Miss Jackley.

At this point Etta spotted something lying beneath the chair upon which he had just been sitting. She bent to retrieve it and was about to call after him. 'Oh, you've dro –' Then her eyes suddenly noted the amount on the wage slip and her lips parted in amazement.

'Don't let Mr Burdock catch you looking at that,' warned Mary-Ann. 'We're not allowed to discuss how much we earn.'

'I'm not surprised!' Etta was indignant as she revealed Tupman's earnings. 'He receives over twice the amount I do!'

Mary-Ann spoke evenly. 'Don't forget it includes his spiff money.'

'I'm referring to his basic wage – twenty-seven shillings!' Etta's temper was rising.

The other women gaped at each other. Then Miss Wimp wrinkled her bespectacled nose and offered in fairness, 'Well, he's a married man, he has a family to support.'

Etta was furious. 'So do –' my God, she had almost given herself away, '– lots of women too! Widows, daughters with invalid parents – why should he get twenty-seven shillings for doing the same job as us just because he's a man? Do either of you think it fair?'

Alarmed at the outburst, Miss Wimp shoved her glasses back up her nose, leaving Mary-Ann to say thoughtfully, 'Well, I only have myself to clothe. Me mam and dad are kind, they don't take as much as they could. But you've got your mother depending on you, haven't you, Miss Wimp?' Her tone suggested that the other might care to object.

However, Maude paused only slightly as she combed her lank hair in the mirror. 'It would be nice to have a little more, I agree. But that's just the way of things.' She gave a feeble shrug.

'Who decreed this?' cried Etta, infuriated as much by their acceptance as the unfairness of it all. 'I'm beginning to revise my opinion of Mrs Pankhurst.'

'Ooh, you're not one of them suffragists, are you?' breathed Mary-Ann. 'Mr Burdock won't have that sort of thing.'

'I have no affiliation, but I do begin to recognise why we women are barred from politics.' It had been bad enough under her father's despotic rule, but not until she had been compelled to support herself financially had Etta really begun to see the need for suffrage. Robbed of any social standing, she certainly saw the wisdom behind it now. 'Do you not think that if women had the vote they could command a better living?'

When her audience prevaricated, she returned to her main topic. 'And what about Mr Ficklepenny?'

At this point the young man bounded in. 'Do I feel my lugs burning?' He made a hungry grab for his sandwich tin, flopped his buttocks onto a chair and his highly polished boots onto another.

Mary-Ann warned Etta but the latter ignored her and said stiffly, 'We were wondering how much you are paid.'

Stunned by her forthrightness, the youngster took a quick bite before replying through a mangle of bread and cheese, 'The going rate.'

'Which is?' persisted Etta.

He chewed quickly and swallowed. 'That's not a question to put to one's superior! If Mr Burdock heard –'

'I'd like to know how much *he* takes home!' cut in Etta.

'A lot more than any of us, I'll be bound,' opined Ficklepenny, incising another large crescent from his sandwich. 'What's started all this off anyway?'

'Mr Tupman's wage slip.' Etta brandished it.

'Eh, you shouldn't have that – give it to me!' He leapt up and snatched it with his free hand, though it was too late to matter, Etta being already fired up.

'Am I to assume you receive a similar amount?' she demanded.

Still he refused to tell, stuffing the wage slip into his pocket and sitting back to eat. 'I might do, it's nowt to do with you.'

'It most certainly is!' She turned to exhort the other women, 'Does no one else see the injustice in this?'

'What can we do?' asked Mary-Ann, a hopeless sag to her fleshy lips.

'We can petition Mr Burdock for a fairer wage!'

'Ooh, I daren't,' quailed Miss Wimp. 'I couldn't risk the sack.'

Neither could Etta, but, 'It wouldn't have to be so drastic if we band together with Miss Jackley and Miss Sullivan.'

'Not much of a union with only five people,' observed Ficklepenny, chomping contentedly whilst sprawled across two chairs.

'It's all very well for you!' scolded Etta. 'You've no family to support.'

'Neither have you,' he countered with a laugh.

Etta wanted to smack the brash little face, but instead squealed in frustration.

'Ladies, gentlemen, what on earth is all this squabbling?' The manager rushed in to censure them. 'You can be heard in the shop!'

Far from being subdued like the others, Etta came right out with her objection. 'Mr Burdock, it has come to our attention that certain members of staff earn disproportionate amounts to others.'

Burdock's attitude changed. He was at once suspicious, looking around at the rest, all of whom avoided his eye and pretended to busy themselves. 'You know the policy about discussing wages.'

'It was an accidental indiscretion,' said Etta, not wanting to land anyone in trouble.

Ficklepenny quickly swallowed his mouthful to say, 'She

290

found this, Mr Burdock.' In the manner of the class sneak, he handed over his colleague's wage slip.

Burdock became even sterner. 'I shall have words with Mr Tupman! Now, enough of –'

'My point is,' interrupted Etta with strained politeness, 'it seems grossly unfair that he's paid more than twice as much as we women for doing a similar job.'

The manager was succinct. 'Then find other employment, Miss Lanegan.'

Etta stalled and looked to the others for unity, but Miss Wimp seemed more intent on tying her shoes and Mary-Ann was immersed in rifling the contents of her handbag. Without backing, she had no recourse but to appear penitent. 'I didn't mean to imply –'

'Do you wish to remain here or not?' snapped Burdock.

'Yes of course, it's just that I –'

'Then enough of this nonsense!' he concluded briskly. 'Miss Wimp, weren't you on first lunch?'

'Yes, I'm just off, Mr Burdock!' She finished tying her laces and, with a hasty repositioning of her spectacles, jumped up.

Gripping the edges of his frockcoat, the stern-faced manager stood aside for her to scuttle past. Mary-Ann too grasped the opportunity to go out shopping. Bereft of support, Etta could only stand there and fume at the discrimination. But if Burdock thought he had subdued her he had another think coming. By fair means or foul she was determined to increase her pay.

After the dressing down for his laxity with the wage slip, Mr Tupman's attitude towards Etta underwent a cool change for the rest of that day, indeed for most of the week to come. She tried to explain that she had not intended to land him in trouble, had simply wanted fairness for herself, but he had taken the event to heart and ignored any of her attempts to charm him. As a formerly pleasant work colleague, his jokes helping to alleviate the daily grind, this was quite a loss, and it took a great deal of work from Etta to rekindle the bonhomie. Only by reason of him being a dreadful flirt and unable to resist a pretty face did he finally succumb, even able to joke about the episode on the next payday.

'Better make sure I've not left anything lying around today else milady'll have her little hands on it!' He made great play of folding his wage slip into his pocket as Etta came into the staff room, and nudged her suggestively as she came past.

Despite her failure to attain equal pay, Etta took it in good part, and, happy to have good feeling restored, even dealt him a playful push for his impishness.

To endorse that they were once again friends, his teasing continued into Saturday, and even though the shop was busy he managed to convey mischief, albeit in a silent fashion when Mr Burdock wasn't looking and more overtly when the manager went out for an afternoon cup of coffee.

With a brief lull in trade, only a solitary customer in the shop and Etta the one to serve her, others joined in the fun, their mood enhanced by the fact that this was the last day of the week. Taking it in turns, they tried to distract her behind the customer's back, Tupman being even worse than Ficklepenny in some respects; for a supposed adult his antics were very silly.

Etta tried not to laugh and forced herself to concentrate on her task. The customer had asked for a particular pair of shoes she had seen in the window. Knowing this style was limited in its size range, Etta had at first taken several others for the woman's inspection, but was unable to divert her from the original choice. Eventually she was forced to admit, 'I'm afraid we don't have a size four – however, if you'd care to try the three and a half I think you'll find them a generous fit.' She tried to avoid looking at Mr Tupman's clownish gesticulations.

Rather than be disappointed the woman agreed to try them, but her face was dubious as she strolled up and down the carpet. 'I had set my heart on them, and you were correct in saying they are large-fitting . . . though the left one nips a little.'

'Oh we can soon alter that!' Etta jumped up brightly. 'Slip it off and I'll just take it through to Mr Beasley in the back, he'll put it on the stretcher for you.'

'You can do that, can you?'

'Why, yes!' She fought to ignore Mr Tupman who mouthed theatrically, *what a liar*, and hoped her smirk did not show. 'They suit you so perfectly that it would be a shame not to resort to a little manipulation.' Given the shoe, she marched through a doorway and rammed it onto a broom handle, hauling and riving it into the toe for a minute or two, warming the leather in her hands and trying to make it more supple, before finally taking it back to the customer, who pronounced:

'Why, that's much better – how amazing!'

'Yes, he's a marvel with the stretcher, our Mr Beasley.' Etta tried to blinker herself to Mr Tupman, who stood across the floor tut-tutting and shaking his head at her lies.

'He certainly is – I'll take them!'

'Thank you, madam. Would madam care to peruse a selection of our hosiery whilst I wrap these?'

Only when the customer had departed with the ill-fitting shoes and a bagful of sundries did Etta take the opportunity to chastise her tormentor. 'You're determined to get me the sack, aren't you?' she laughingly accused.

'Never! I love you too much, my dear.' Mr Tupman grinned and, with the shop still divest of customers, came to help her pack the assortment of unwanted footwear back into boxes.

Mary-Ann, now dusting away at the fixtures in a spare moment, joked to her companion, 'Never helps us, does he, Miss Wimp? We're obviously not pretty enough for him.'

'Oh, go on then!' The ginger-haired man grabbed a feather duster and minced across the room, performing more silly antics to their laughter.

A smiling Etta shook her head, piled the boxes and returned them to their rightful place, parrying jokes along her way.

In the quiet of the stockroom, having replaced all the footwear, she bent to adjust her wrinkled hose prior to going back into the shop. Involved in smoothing the stocking around her thigh she did not notice that the door had opened and someone stood there admiring the view.

Upon looking up, she expressed startlement and hurriedly lowered her skirt before rebuking him laughingly, 'Mr Tupman, how unseemly!'

Arms crossed, he grinned unabashed.

Expecting him to move aside, she made to pass, but then he caught her arm and pressed his groin against her. The assault lasted only a second but it so shocked Etta that she dealt him an angry shove, which took him off-guard and sent him sprawling backwards into the shop.

Mr Ficklepenny had begun his virtuoso piece for the amusement of the rest of the staff and had just put a lighted match to the puddle of methylated spirits on the counter which burst into flame, but at the sight of Tupman's undignified ejection from the cupboard he forgot about this and exploded into guffaws, inviting others to join the spectacle.

All but Etta seemed highly amused, Mr Vant falling prey to a violent smoker's cough, hawking and wheezing fit to expire, until Mary-Ann hissed a sudden warning, 'Dandy's back!' and those that heard, scattered.

Tears running down his face, Mr Ficklepenny panicked. 'Ooh shit!' Immediately he tried to beat out the flames but in doing so managed to ignite his cuff and was still beating at it frantically as Mr Burdock came through the main door.

But he need not have worried for the manager's ire was focused on Mr Tupman, who was just picking himself up from the floor to much ridicule from the Saturday girls who had just come down from their tea-break.

'Disgraceful!' Horns bristling, nostrils flared like those of an enraged cow, the manager rushed forth to condemn his salesman. 'Tupman, on your feet at once! What the devil has been going on here – don't tell me! You can issue your explanation after closing time. Back to your posts, all of you!'

Mr Tupman was furious and glared at Etta, muttering as he stormed past her, 'Little bitch, if you get me sacked . . .'

She gasped in outrage but had no chance of redress for Burdock caught the interchange and announced damningly, 'I can see you are involved in this, Miss Lanegan. You shall stay behind too!'

With the manager keeping watch on the culprits for the rest of the day and trade resuming its normal Saturday briskness, there was little opportunity for discourse – besides which, Etta had no wish to speak to her molester. After an agonising wait, not only for closing time but for the takings to be cashed up too and everyone else to be allowed to leave, the miscreants eventually faced their destiny.

Mr Burdock saw them individually in the staff room, Tupman being addressed first and emerging with a face like thunder. Etta detected not just anger but a warning in his eye, though without knowing what he had said she was unsure how much to offer in her defence. However, she was quickly to learn, as Mr Burdock followed him out and addressed her in his presence.

'Mr Tupman has acquainted me with all the silliness that transpired this afternoon, and I have to say I am disgusted by such antics from the pair of you. Pushing each other about like children in the schoolyard – I will not suffer such tomfoolery in my shop!'

From this Etta deduced that Tupman had presented the episode as some innocent prank and not the sexual assault

295

it had been. Obviously he did not want to chance being dismissed and his wife finding out the reason. Not wanting to risk dismissal either, she went along with it for now.

'It's fortunate for you, Miss Lanegan, that you have been here so long! If I was of a mind to waste the time it's taken me to train you you'd be out on your ear and no mistake.'

She nodded, vastly relieved that she was not about to lose her job.

'How you could have the audacity even to suggest that you are worth the same pay as Mr Tupman . . .' He shook his head in disgust. 'Now, you will apologise to your senior colleague.'

Disbelief caused her to bristle. 'But I've done nothing wrong!'

'Are you denying that you pushed Mr Tupman to the floor?'

'Well, no, but with good rea—'

'No buts! There can be no excuse for such behaviour. My goodness, what if there had been customers present? Now, apologise to Mr Tupman or face dismissal.'

Seething with outrage, Etta had no option but to mutter an apology, though it tasted like vomit.

'Very well, consider yourselves reprimanded, and I trust that will be an end to it.' Burdock embraced both parties in his warning, then said, 'You may go, Mr Tupman. I'd like a further word with Miss Lanegan before she leaves.'

Once they were alone, he became friendlier towards her, though to just as insulting an effect. 'Now, I understand that a young lady possessed of such attributes as yourself might not understand what impact those charms have on a fellow, especially when accompanied by such flirtation as we have come to expect from our Miss Lanegan, flashing those sparkling black eyes . . .' He all but wagged a finger.

Etta was astounded. Flirting? She had simply been pleasant and friendly. But from what had just been said it appeared that Tupman *had* revealed the true extent of the situation – then why had Burdock not dismissed him?

'You must appreciate that Mr Tupman is a married man and it's quite wrong of you to tease hi—'

'I beg your pardon!' Etta cut in. 'If he chooses to misinterpret a friendly smile as an attempt to seduce him, surely the fault lies within his character?'

'Come, come, Miss Lanegan.' Though scolding her, Burdock was to maintain his avuncular manner. He even laid an arm across her back, cupping one of her shoulders in his pudgy little mitt. 'That is most improper speech, and, I might add, a most improper suggestion. Mr Tupman did not seek to lay fault at your door, and has had the decency to admit that he might have been led astray by the gaiety of the moment. You must accept some of the blame. If we cannot reach an understanding with your colleagues it will be impossible for you to continue working here, and that would be a shame, especially for those of us who appreciate the decorative effect you have on the place.'

Etta stiffened. Was this one about to molest her too?

But no, Burdock was far too proper, seemingly content just to have this beautiful creature in proximity, to look and perhaps to administer a little harmless if unwelcome touch.

'If I have misconstrued the situation, then I am very sorry,' replied Etta, fighting her inner revulsion, for she could not lose this precious job. 'I shall endeavour to be more thoughtful towards Mr Tupman.' And not to place myself in the stockroom at the same time as him, came the dark thought.

'Splendid!' Oblivious to how angry he had made her, Burdock dealt her a happy beam and a final unwanted squeeze, then took her completely by surprise. 'Now, don't worry your pretty little head any longer. Having accepted your oath of good behaviour I have a proposition . . .'

She gave an inward groan at her own naivety and braced herself for some lewd proposal.

'Miss Bunyon has today rather inconveniently given notice that she intends to marry in two weeks' time. It would save me a great deal of interviewing if you would take over the job of cashier.'

Etta could not prevent a gasp.

'I'm glad to see it was as big a surprise to you as it was to me,' nodded Burdock. 'It was very remiss of her to keep it under her hat until the last minute. I expected more from someone who's been here since she left school. Anyway, you seem quite an intelligent young woman and are familiar with the workings of the shop. It wouldn't take long for you to pick up the book-keeping system – thereby giving you the increase in pay that you so obviously covet – though I make it clear here and now there will be no shenanigans.' He broke off to laugh at his unintended pun. 'No shenanigans, Miss Lanegan! If you agree, I shall ask Miss Bunyon to show you the ropes before she leaves next Saturday.'

If that idiot can do it than I'm damned sure I can, thought a somewhat stunned Etta, but kept this retort to herself as she made quick acceptance of his offer. 'I should be delighted, Mr Burdock.' Delight was hardly the word – after such a terrible afternoon and the expectation that she was about to be sacked, she was ecstatic.

The manager seemed delighted too. 'Then we shall see you in the office on Monday.' He beamed and dealt her a series of affectionate little pats before ending with a joke. 'And let us hope that enclosing you in a glass booth goes some way to keeping you out of mischief – run along now!'

14

The new job might be welcome but that first week was incredibly testing, being patronised by Burdock and Bunyon alike, and receiving vexed glares from Tupman, who had obviously hoped to see her sacked in revenge for her rejection of him and instead found her promoted.

'I wonder how she managed to twist Dandy round her finger?' she overheard Mr Vant muse between fits of coughing.

And Tupman's wicked reply: 'More relevantly, I wonder what she's giving in return.'

What could she do to quash the rumours? Any attack on Tupman would bring instant dismissal, as would admitting that she was a married woman, but such gossip was offensive to her.

There was no option but to grin and bear it, and at least some of the bad feeling would come to an end when Miss Bunyon finally left on Saturday night. However, before then she was to give Etta much to endure. Loving every minute of having someone there to whom she could delegate the less attractive side of the job, the cashier made her polish every section of wood panelling in the office, plus every brass handle and each glass partition.

Knowing it was futile to object, Etta undertook every task, polishing until her arms felt as though they might drop off, but still it was not good enough for Bunyon.

'You'll have to make a better job of it than this.' The arrogant cashier pointed out a few smears left on the glass.

Pretending to be unaffected, Etta swiftly buffed these away, telling herself that in another few days her oppressor would be off.

Yet, even as she exited the staff room for the final time Miss Bunyon found the capacity for one last hurtful comment. When, along with the others, Etta gave her best wishes for the coming nuptials, there came a smug reply. 'That's very magnanimous of you. I'm sure you must be eager to see me go, it is rather crowded in the office. Now you and Mr Burdock will be able to have it to yourselves.'

That was all Etta could take. 'I'll say this once!' she boomed for all to hear. 'I would never so much as consider besmirching my honour with a married man and anyone who makes such a suggestion should be thoroughly ashamed.' She looked round at the shifty expressions. 'Yes, I *have* heard the gossip!'

Mr Tupman gave a careless shrug, threw his mackintosh over his arm and went home. Mr Vant studied the shabby linoleum and drew long on his cigarette, whilst Miss Bunyon merely offered an innocent smirk. 'I was merely commenting on the size of the office. What you make of that is all in your dirty mind.' And she left.

'We know you'd never do anything like that,' Mary-Ann murmured soothingly, passing Etta her coat from the cupboard. 'Don't we, Miss Wimp?'

Maude gave earnest reply, though Etta knew she was not without blame for the gossip. Nevertheless, she replied, 'Thank you. Well, at least that's one of my enemies out of the way – and good riddance to her!' she added with feeling.

But, left to do the job by herself, Etta found it somewhat daunting. Mr Burdock was eager to help in his puffed-up way, though the sight of their heads close together as they scrutinised the accounts did nothing to scotch the rumours.

It was all very annoying, but, attempting to cope alone this afternoon, Etta had more important matters to occupy her as she struggled to come to grips with the piles of receipts and invoices, the stocktaking and banking . . . and more. How the devil was one meant to work in such a confined space? Squashed against the desk by Burdock, who was involved in a telephone conversation with his superior, his weight on one leg and his fat backside taking up even more room than usual, she heaved a sigh, cleared her throat and threw him a look of annoyance over her shoulder, all of which he failed to heed. With a gasp, she turned away from the jutting backside and tried to concentrate on her ledger – but in seconds her head shot up again in response to a feminine squeal.

'Wasn't me!' Tupman held up his hands as a protestation of innocence when the manager glared immediately at him.

'A mouse!' Mary-Ann, who had been carrying a waste-paper basket with the intention of emptying it, now threw it in the air and danced about hysterically as the rodent sprang out and in a blur of movement shot across the floor with everyone after it, customers looking on in bafflement.

Etta interrupted her book-keeping to watch the excited pursuit that wound its way back and forth across the shop, covering her mouth and laughing in anticipation of what would happen next.

Behind her, still leaning against the panelled wall with the receiver pressed to his ear as his superior droned on, Mr Burdock itched to deal with the explosion of noise but, for now, the only outlet for his annoyance was a tapping of his foot and a disapproving frown, for he dared not break off the important dialogue. It transpired he did not have to. In an extraordinary sequence of events the mouse ran into the office – straight under Burdock's foot which instantly snapped down on it like a trap.

Its pursuers stopped dead with a unified exclamation for

the manager's skill, before Burdock shooed them away with a wordless command, leaving only Etta to stare in horror and to watch the life being squashed out of the tiny body. Under his foot, the mouse struggled briefly then was dead.

Still on the telephone, Burdock reassured his superior – 'Noise, sir? Oh, it's from outside!' – and maintained the conversation whilst gesticulating to his staff to get about their business and for Etta to remove the body from under his shoe.

Revolted, she scraped it up using two receipt books and carried it to the dustbin, her heart still thudding from the shock. Marty would never have done such a cruel thing. Gazing sadly upon the crushed mouse in the dustbin, the glaze of death upon its eyes, something inside her died too. He wasn't coming back, was he? She couldn't pretend any longer. He had truly gone. A wave of emotion threatened to swamp her. After working nine, ten, sometimes even eleven hours a day for months she had begun to appreciate how gallantly Marty had struggled to provide for them. Small wonder he had not the energy for anything else, small wonder he had been short-tempered with her. Why had she taken his efforts so much for granted? Well, she must no longer take it for granted that someone else would look after her. She was on her own.

Slamming the dustbin lid over the mouse with a noisy clang, she hurried indoors and tried to forget.

Which was impossible, for later it was discovered that before its demise the rodent had multiplied. In fact, the outside yard where they stacked the flattened cardboard boxes was suddenly alive with them.

'I've just seen another!' announced an excited Mary-Ann. 'A right big un – oh, look, it's there again!' From the window of the staff room she pointed down into the yard.

'That's no mouse, it's a bloody rat!' exclaimed Mr Vant in a fit of apoplectic coughing over his cigarette.

His colleagues agreed, but the tight-fisted Burdock

refused to believe it and, insisting it was only a few mice, instructed Etta to take some money from the petty-cash tin and go and buy a couple of traps.

Huffing at this sudden demotion to lackey, Etta nevertheless welcomed the opportunity to wander through town and to spend the penny change on three stale buns for her children, a treat her own wage would never allow. Above anything else – mice, rats, or condescending managers – it was this that gave her most cause for anger. For, having access to all the confidential records she was now acquainted with the amount each member of staff received in comparison to her own pittance. Whilst she was indeed now better off than the other female assistants, despite the supposed importance of her position the men still received higher wages – why, even the schoolboy earned more than she did just because he was male! Though infuriated by the injustice of this, Etta was to think twice before doing anything about it.

Not until she had accrued several more weeks' experience in the post and was therefore not so easy to replace did she confront her superior. Still, it was no easy fight.

'A rise?' stuttered Burdock's fat mouth in response to her tremulous enquiry. 'But you've already had one in being promoted to the cashier's job, Miss Lanegan.'

She toyed with a corner of her ledger that had been nibbled by rodents. 'I understand that and I'm very grateful to you, Mr Burdock. I wouldn't even consider asking unless my need was very great . . .'

He gave a curt laugh. 'So is mine, Miss Lanegan, but I doubt my superior would take kindly to my application for more. He would ask, "What makes you think you are worth it?" And I ask that of you.'

Knowing that any form of arrogance spelt financial death, Etta lowered her gaze and tried to look humble. 'I'm sure I'm most unworthy, Mr Burdock. Please forget I said anything.' Quickly dipping her pen into the inkwell she made as if to resume her book-keeping.

'No, no!' Burdock responded to her piteous stance. 'I'm not a man to dismiss such a request out of hand.'

She lifted her eyes from the ledger, allowing her winsome expression to plead on her behalf, feeling Burdock's gaze upon her and despising him.

'Well . . .' he said eventually, his brown eyes beginning to soften and to dart a look into the shop to see if others were in earshot. 'I'm bound to say you're doing a magnificent job, and I must say you've taken no time at all to pick it up. Most impressive.' He bent nearer to whisper. 'But if I did agree to recommend you to head office I shouldn't like any of the others to know; they'd surely see it as favouritism.'

Etta formed her lips to issue thanks, but her bright expectation was instantly quashed.

'I haven't made my mind up yet –' came his stern addition.

'Of course.' She hung her head again, playing the game that he demanded of her.

'– but I'll certainly consider putting in a good word for you.' Realising that Tupman was taking an interest the manager smoothed his tufts of hair, gave her a barely perceptible wink then raised his voice again. 'And let us hear no more about it, Miss Lanegan!'

In the staff room Tupman teased her as he had always been wont to do, but now there was a malevolent edge to it. 'Lover-boy fallen out with you, has he?'

'What are you talking about?' Etta sighed impatiently as her ink-stained fingers unwrapped the slice of bread-and-margarine that served as lunch.

'Heard you trying to wheedle a pay rise out of Dandy, but he didn't seem too receptive. You must be losing your grip.'

Knowing he was goading her into a response that might earn her the sack, Etta tried to keep her temper. 'Yes, well, some might consider it unfair to have all that responsibility and not be adequately compensated.'

Tupman scoffed. 'What, for sitting on your derriere all day pushing a pen? There's no responsibility in that.'

'And you'd be a firm proponent of responsibility,' retorted Etta.

Tupman brushed this aside with a cunning laugh. 'We all know the reason you got that job, and it isn't your brains.'

Stung, she revealed unwisely, 'Apparently Mr Burdock does not agree. He has said he will consider my request.'

Tupman frowned. 'If his fancy-piece is getting a rise I'll want one an' all.' The other listeners echoed this feeling.

'And do you intend to phrase your request like that?' enquired Etta lightly, hoping it would conceal her anger. 'I shouldn't think Mr Burdock would take kindly to it.' And with that she set upon her lunch.

'Got him nicely under control, haven't you?' sniped Tupman. 'I wonder how he'll respond when he hears you've been moonlighting.'

'What nonsense, you silly man.' Etta remained unmoved, until he sprang his trump card.

'Me and the missus saw you in Coney Street on Wednesday with a pram and three kids in tow. Doing a bit of nannying on the quiet, aren't you?' Though almost bursting with his discovery for the last couple of days, he had been biding his time in order to make the utmost impact and had obviously succeeded. Drained of colour, watched closely by her colleagues, his adversary fought for a reply.

'What difference does it make to you if she is?' Mary-Ann sprang to her aid. 'We'd all like a bit of extra cash.'

'Aye, but most of us have families to support. She hasn't, she's just raking it in so that she can buy that blasted sewing machine and open her shop and lord it over us.'

'Etta isn't like that,' sneered Mary-Ann. 'You're just maungy because she spurned your advances – and quite right she was too.'

Tupman flicked a dismissive hand at her. 'You don't know what you're on about.'

'I do.' Mary-Ann looked crafty. 'She told me you tried it on with her.'

Etta groaned inwardly for this betrayal of confidence.

He snorted. 'And you believe her? She's just got too high an opinion of herself. Stuck up madam, looking down on us, talking with a plum in her mouth.'

'Just because she talks nice doesn't make her stuck up. If I spoke like that I wouldn't want to work here neither.'

'Why are you fighting her corner? She's not bothered about you, just how much she can cram into her own pocket.'

'When you've quite finished!' Etta had finally had enough of being discussed as if she were not there. 'Mr Tupman, you were mistaken when you said I was moonlighting. In fact, those were my own children you saw me escorting.' Giving him only time to gasp, she went on, 'And before you spring to any more of your scurrilous conclusions, no, they are not illegitimate. I am married to their father, who abandoned me – *that* is the only reason for my enduring the last six months of lewd innuendo and physical assault upon my person, so that my children might keep a roof above their heads and not starve!'

No one spoke, their mouths slack with amazement.

'Now! May one eat one's lunch in peace?' Etta made brave play of biting into her sandwich.

Tupman stared at her for a moment, then without a word turned and left.

Etta felt the others staring at her and tried to appear unaffected, chewing quite casually.

Mary-Ann seemed amazed, not just by the revelation but by Etta's cool reaction. 'Don't you ever wonder where your husband is?' she asked eventually.

Etta swung to face her, her immediate reaction to shout, *Of course I do, you idiot, I think about him every bloody night!* But the enquiry was made with such genuine sympathy that she merely responded, 'Sometimes . . . but it's best not to. Mary-Ann, I'm sorry for lying to you, to all of you,' she looked around beseechingly, 'but no one would employ me and I was so desperate . . .'

Despite all efforts not to appear weak, tears bulged over her lower lids. Her audience beheld her awkwardly as she dashed them away, Mr Vant clearing his throat and, with the hand that was not holding a cigarette, offering her something from his pocket. 'Here, have a Minto, love.'

She shook her head vigorously at the tobacco-tainted offering but passed a damply grateful smile at him before sighing, 'I suppose he's gone straight to Dandy, hasn't he?'

The others pulled faces to show that they shared this view, and in fact all were correct. The moment she returned to her office after lunch Mr Burdock demanded she explain herself. 'I am informed you acquired your employment by false pretences, *Mrs* Lanegan.'

Etta sighed heavily. 'I don't need to ask who told you.'

'Don't try to blame anyone else!' Mr Burdock glanced to see whether the customers had heard, then lowered his voice to a stern hiss. 'It's you who are in the dock.'

Only as a last resort had she used her femininity to curry favour, but now in danger of losing precious income and knowing how susceptible the manager was, she unloosed a waterfall to drench him, affecting to weep – not having to try very hard – and telling Burdock of the manner of her husband's leaving. 'He deserted his family without a word! Please accept my apology for the deception, but with four children to feed I was in such dire need of work that I was compelled to say I was unwed, otherwise you wouldn't have employed me.'

Burdock still frowned, yet was sympathetic as he lifted a hand to smooth distractedly at his little horns of hair. 'Well, I agree that is understandable. No wonder you asked for a rise in pay. My, my . . .'

He ruminated for a while, leaving her to hang desperately on his every nuance. Only once did she tear her eyes away to accuse Tupman, who lurked on the far side of the shop, gloating at her misfortune.

Then the old-fashioned character said abruptly, 'Very well, I've reached my decision.'

She cocked her head expectantly. 'You mean about the rise?'

'You ungrateful litt – the very nerve!' Burdock's face almost bulged out of his starched, winged collar. 'You can put that right out of your head. I told you not to mention it to anyone but you had to go and let the cat out of the bag, didn't you? I *meant* my decision on whether to keep you on or not.' He viewed her sternly. 'I don't think you realise how seriously I regard being lied to, Miss Lan– Mrs – oh, just be quiet and let me finish!'

Dutifully, Etta waited to hear her fate. Across the shop Mr Tupman waited too, trying to gauge what was transpiring.

Composing himself, Burdock proceeded. 'Only the harshest critic would dismiss someone with Christmas almost upon us . . .'

Christmas? What difference does that make to a woman in my position, raged Etta, yet she clung optimistically to his sentence and waited for the rest of it.

'Therefore you may stay – but this is positively your last chance. Should you cause any more insurrection you shall be dismissed.'

She heaved with relief. 'Oh, Mr Burdock, thank you!'

'I trust you know how lucky you are, my girl?'

'Indeed, I do!' Etta managed to sound duly castigated, whilst keeping her true thoughts to herself: oh yes, so lucky to work in an office infested with rodents and be treated in such a condescending fashion by my superior.

Too crass to see past her teary ingratiating smile, Burdock nodded his satisfaction, then made way for her to be seated behind the desk. 'Very well, you may get back to your ledgers now.' Then he lowered his voice and spoke confidentially in her ear. 'Oh, and by the by, you shall continue to be referred to as Miss Lanegan. It wouldn't do if head office got to hear of my lenience.'

With an inward sigh, Etta nodded meek acceptance.

'And don't make too much of my merciful gesture to the others,' he advised, glancing at Mr Tupman who immediately busied himself in polishing stock. 'They might get the wrong idea.'

Naturally, there were those who did get the wrong idea. Whilst some congratulated Etta for managing to escape with a reprimand, and a few days later on Christmas Eve wished her all the best as the shop closed down for a two-day festival, Tupman remained waspish, acting as if they had never been friends.

Leaving the shop to trudge through dark, wet streets, teeth chattering as the damp chill pierced her threadbare coat, Etta told herself what did it matter? In receipt of a quarterly bonus and with two whole days' leisure ahead, why should she care about petty arguments? But, even at the thought of being with her children, there was little anticipation of Christmas jollity: the carol singers, the brass bands, the scent of pine, the bright shop windows with their festive displays, the merry last-minute shoppers staggering under mounds of parcels all leaving her uninspired. The only thing for which she was truly thankful was that someone else would be shouldering the work, for, traditionally, the entire Lanegan clan always gathered at Aggie's for Christmas dinner.

Stopping only to exchange a florin for four sixpenny books for the children and a few more necessary provisions, she had almost reached home when she caught sight of a neighbour she had not seen for some time rushing towards her with a look of self-importance on her face. Feeling too weary to submit herself to gossip, she was unable to avoid her.

'Hello, Mrs Lanegan! I've been hoping to catch you. Did

you hear our John had joined up the other week?'

Etta wanted to demand tiredly *What's so bloody important about that?* But she managed to be polite whilst still maintaining her approach to her own door. 'I didn't know that, no. I hope he's enjoying being a soldier?'

'Aye, thank you,' Mrs Reilly flicked a hand, 'but that's not what I want to tell you. I just had a letter from him and guess who he's seen? Your husband!'

Etta was stunned and fought to recover whilst the woman babbled on.

'They're in the same regiment – would you believe it? John saw him on the parade ground but hasn't had time to speak to him yet. Eh, what a small world!'

'Isn't it?' She smiled tightly, and, though her heart was beating furiously, managed to sound casual. 'Well, I'd better stir the fire into life before the children come clamouring for my attention.'

'I thought I'd best let you know!' said the other to her retreating back. 'I know how difficult it's been for you . . .'

'Thank you, Mrs Reilly, that's most kind.' Etta inserted her key, furious that it took a stranger to provide the whereabouts of her delinquent husband. Oh and wouldn't people round here have a field day when Mrs Reilly broadcast it to all and sundry.

'Will you pass the news on to your mother-in-law or shall I?'

'I'll tell her,' said Etta quickly. 'Thank you.' She fought bad-temperedly with the unresponsive key as she struggled to escape. *Turn*, damn you!

'I thought you might like to write to him, so here's the name of his battalion!' Mrs Reilly had followed her and held out a scrap of paper.

'I'm very grateful to you for taking the trouble.' Etta put it straight into her pocket and donated a last tight smile before closing the door on the neighbour's, 'Merry Christmas—!'

In truth she could have wept. After groping her way

through the dark, she grabbed the poker and rammed it into the almost dead fire, inducing a pathetic flame. In six months not a word – not a sign even!

Well she didn't need him, the turncoat. Retrieving the slip of paper from her pocket, she took quick, disdainful note of the words thereon, then crumpled it disparagingly and threw it on the coals.

She mentioned none of this to Aggie when she went to fetch the children. Didn't mention it for fear she might weep. Only upon going to bed did she finally give rein to her desolation, bundling a corner of the pillow into her face so that she might shed her bitter tears in silence. She did need Marty – oh, how she missed and needed him. But obviously he did not need her.

The Lanegan house was packed on Christmas Day, bursting at the seams with married couples: Aggie and Red, Lou and Dan, Bridget and Mick, Mary and Ed, Annie and Joe . . . their arrangement at the table making it patently obvious that Etta was the only woman lacking a husband. Being decent folk they tried to make up for this discrepancy, of course – as if holding themselves responsible for Marty's leaving her – but in doing so they merely appeared to overcompensate, rendering all the gaiety somewhat false and so making Etta feel ten times worse. In addition there was the guilt of keeping his whereabouts to herself, for she knew that if she told them they would demand to know why she did not rush there now and drag him back. It was awful. *Awful*.

Moreover, her children were the only ones without a father. How heartrending it was for her, watching them trying to find a substitute in various male relatives – not that they seemed particularly sad themselves. Nor were their appetites spoiled for all that was on the table, tucking into mounds of roast pork and showing even more delight upon coming across a silver threepence each in their bowl of

Christmas pudding – though this was rather marred when their grandmother stood at the door collecting the coins back off each child as they departed, saying she would put them to sensible use for the recipients – 'You'll only go frittering it on sweets.'

Etta, assuming this to be the cause of her offsprings' sullen mood as they trundled their way home through the dark, was unprepared for her eldest child's remark.

'I hate you for sending Father away,' denounced Celia out of the blue as she walked beside the pram, looking straight ahead but injecting her voice with venom.

Etta stopped dead, the cold night rushing in at her. Deeply shocked, she stared down at her six-year-old daughter, at all her children. Struggling for words, she answered lamely, 'I didn't mean to, Celie . . . I miss him as much as you do.'

'Then fetch him back,' begged Edward, the reflection of a gas-lamp flickering in his earnest green eyes.

'I can't, darling.' One hand rocking the grumbling babe inside the pram, she stooped to tend her son, trying not to cry. 'I don't know where he is.'

Under their pitiful, sullen stares, she damned herself as a liar, a hypocrite. What kind of mother would put her own pride before her children's happiness? And, as she studied them, she saw in their features both herself and Marty combined, the love that had conceived them, and the deep desire for him came flooding back.

'We'll help you to look,' offered Celia, Edward and Alex, nodding enthusiastically.

Etta smiled sadly, then, one hand holding Edward's, the other steering the pram, she shepherded her children onwards, still fighting her emotions. 'I wouldn't know where to start.'

Yes, you do, liar, she accused herself. And it would be such a simple task. How can you rob them of a father's love, knowing what it is to be so deprived yourself?

But what if Marty rejects me? Her spirit recoiled. I

couldn't bear it, I couldn't. Tears came just at the very thought.

Then, after a painful hiatus came momentous decision. She squeezed the little hand that held hers and promised, 'But I'll try.'

The infants were immediately transformed, beaming as they set off at a hop, skip and jump between the puddles of light on the dark, wet pavement towards home. Using two hands now to steer the pram, their mother smiled after them, fond yet still sad. How easy it had been to make their lives happier.

She could only hope it would be so easy to broach the subject with Aggie. God in heaven, what an ordeal the holiday had been, it would almost be a relief to have it over.

Aggie seemed to think so too, giving a less than enthusiastic welcome when Etta appeared the following day with the children.

'Don't worry, we shan't stop.' Etta summoned a weak smile.

'Thank God,' said her mother-in-law, only half-joking as she fell back into her chair to display near exhaustion. 'Boxing Day already and I've not so much as sucked a tangerine.'

Etta thanked her once again for putting on such a wonderful spread. 'We're off for a walk to Heslington to blow away the cobwebs and just wondered if any of you would care to join us.'

'Oh, I haven't the energy, darlin'.' Aggie echoed the others' thoughts.

'But you must come, Granny,' urged little Alex. 'We're going to look for Father.'

Finding herself under sharp surveillance from Aggie, Red and Mal, Etta gave a sad chuckle to make a joke of it and said to them, 'Actually, we're going to look for squirrels, but I can see that you need your rest so we'll leave you in peace until tomorrow.' And she dragged the children from the house before any more secrets could be divulged.

In fact, she had come here with the full intention of admitting that she knew where Marty was, and to inform her in-laws that she had decided to take him back. But after all she had said about their son, every curse, every insult – not to mention that she had injured him with a teapot – it would be a most disagreeable task, and so fearful was she of being embarrassed over her climb-down that it had only taken some childish prattle to dissuade her.

'You said we were going to look for Father.' From within the huge pleated brim of her winter bonnet, Celia's face accused her.

'And we are! But not today.'

'When?' demanded Alex, ringlets bouncing as she skipped alongside.

As soon as I can pluck up the courage to admit to his mother that I was at fault for his leaving, thought Etta. Heaven only knows when that will be. But to her children, she said, 'Soon, I promise. But you mustn't say anything about it to Granny.'

'Why?' asked Alex.

'Because I want it to be a lovely surprise when we do find him,' said Etta, knowing that this was the only way to make them keep quiet. 'For now it's to be our secret.'

Naturally one could not expect a four-year-old to know what a secret was, let alone to preserve it, but Etta was able to explain away Alexandra's words to Aggie as a childish fantasy.

For a time, too, she was able to pacify her children with the reply that, yes, she had begun the search for their father, was trying desperately hard to find him, and that she would meet with success very, very soon, she could vouch for that.

In truth, the search for her errant husband was proving

314

to be more difficult than she had anticipated. Her written enquiry to the regiment in which she believed him to be had as yet received no answer. Frustrated over the fact that she had sent it weeks ago, unable to do anything more practical through having to earn a living, Etta was thus compelled to sit there day after day in her cramped booth, flicking mouse droppings from her ledger, adding up columns, counting out currency, having to endure fat little Dandy whose hot breath continually abused her ear telling her how fortunate she was to be there, and Tupman, who habitually tormented her with cruel innuendo, whilst her emotions varied erratically between desperately wanting Marty back and damning him to hell for being responsible for her plight.

Three months passed with no answer. Three months of trying to pacify her elder children with the lame excuse that she was doing all she could. Then, one evening she arrived home to find an official-looking envelope on the doormat. Without hesitation she tore it open.

'*Madam*,' she read quickly, '*with reference to your husband Martin Lanegan, we regret to inform you that there is no person of that name serving with this battalion* . . .'

Etta's heart plummeted. Through a blur of disappointment, her eyes took in the remainder of the letter. It offered no solace. Allowing her hand to fall to her side and the letter to drop to the floor, she asked herself dully what was she to do now? Could she have made an error, misread the neighbour's scrawl before throwing the scrap of paper on the fire? No, it was branded on her mind. Perhaps Mrs Reilly was the one to make the mistake. She would go and ask.

But just a moment, she had overlooked something: had her neighbour mentioned this to Aggie? She had known Etta wanted to relay the news but that might not have stopped her nor anyone else from also divulging it in passing.

No, Aggie was sure to have confronted Etta if she had been told.

After mopping away all trace of tears she went along the street to collect her brood. But the moment she laid eyes on her children the thought of their disappointment pricked her eyes again.

Aggie caught the gleam. 'Hard day, was it, love?'

Etta fought the urge to cry and instead blamed the paper-thin soles of her footwear, saying bad-temperedly, 'My feet are crippling me.'

From his chair by the hearth, surrounded by a heap of scrap metal through which he had been prospecting for gold or silver, Red craned his neck. 'You'd think that working in a shoe shop would have its benefits. Take them off and I'll put them on the last.'

'And have yourself a cup of tea while you're waiting,' offered Mal, though he made no move to get it.

Etta threw both a smile of appreciation and passed over her shoes, and whilst Red worked on cutting pieces of leather from an old pair of boots to patch the soles of these, she drowned her upset in a cup of hot tea. 'A pity you can't fix Edward's so easily.' Her son had outgrown his and was now sporting his elder sister's cast-offs. 'His toes are to the end of those already.'

'Here.' Without quibble, Aggie dipped into a tin and proffered a handful of silver. 'Bring him some home tomorrow.'

Etta stared at her. However generous of spirit in feeding and tending her grandchildren, the other rarely parted with hard cash, but this was the third time in recent weeks that Aggie had made such a gesture. However, she wasn't about to refuse. 'Why thank you! I shall.'

Aggie gave a curt nod, but then changed the subject completely. 'Tell your mother what you've learned at school today, Eddie.'

Ready for bed, his green eyes heavy with sleep, the five-year-old came away from watching his grandfather tap-tap-tap at the shoe on the last and leaned against his mother's knee. 'We learned how to put a splint on an arm.'

His mother cheered up, smiling along with the other adults. 'Really? How informative.'

'Isn't it indeed?' said Aggie.

'I volunteered to fall down and break mine on purpose,' joked Uncle Mal, 'just so's he could practise his skills, but Aggie wouldn't let me, thought it was taking things too far.'

His niece gave a dismissive smirk. 'Wouldn't let ye? I'd gladly break your neck.'

Etta chuckled, feeling somewhat better. Then she glanced down at her little son, who, with his eyelids drooping in tiredness, appeared more like his father than ever, and she felt the disappointment rushing back. As soon as Red finished hammering tacks into the repaired soles, she slipped her shoes on, gathered her children and left.

'Mind on other things,' Red responded to his wife's objection that Etta had gone without reaffirming her thanks for the donation.

In fact, Etta was to forget about almost everything other than her vanished husband and how to find him, only just remembering to purchase the shoes for her son before going home the next night. The thoughts that resounded within began to drive her to distraction. Whilst absent-mindedness had always been a trait, her own desires preceding any household chore, now this was compounded by having so many more important issues over which to mull, to the detriment of her book-keeping.

Unable to balance the daily sheet with the contents of the till one evening, her reckoning out by five pounds, Etta racked her brain as to where a mistake could have been made. To see a ten-pound note was extremely rare, and there had been none tendered that day, so it was impossible that she could have given the wrong change. She was therefore compelled to go through her entries again and again, sighing heavily and trying to spot the inconsistency, but to no avail.

In the end, when almost everyone else had gone and the hour was close to eight, Mr Burdock said testily, 'Leave it now, Miss Lanegan, and try again in the morning when you're a little more alert.'

But the morning brought no solution. Time after time, Etta went through every receipt, completely removed the drawer that served as a till and peered into the cavity in case a note had somehow become jammed behind, lifted every ledger from the shelf and riffled its pages, moved every obstacle beneath which a note could have slipped, but the evidence was clear: five pounds had vanished.

Where could it be? If she had no idea the manager certainly did.

'This is very difficult for me to say, Miss Lanegan.' He hooked his thumbs into the lapels of his frockcoat. 'But as you have made it plain that you are in desperate need of cash . . .'

Etta gaped at the bovine face, her skin pricked by shock. 'Are you –' She broke off and lowered her voice as others were watching. 'Are you accusing me of taking it?'

'I can reach no other conclusion. No one else is permitted in the office except you and I. Needless to say, it is not my habit to borrow the takings, but if that is the situation, if you merely sought to borrow –'

'I most certainly did not!' Her chest ballooned with outrage, though it did her no good.

He fixed her with a baleful eye. 'It has been brought to my notice that you harbour a desire for a sewing machine . . .'

'How would I afford one on my wage?' snapped Etta, wondering who had told him.

'My thoughts exactly. The rearing of offspring robs us of many a personal desire.' He tapped his lips thoughtfully.

318

'I recollect that you recently purchased some shoes for your son . . .'

'With cash I was given!' Her cheeks were pink at being confronted like this in the presence of her peers.

'Given, by whom?'

'My –' Etta bit her tongue and looked aloof. It really was none of his business, nor any of the others, who pretended to go about their affairs but were obviously listening. 'The five-pound note has just gone missing, I bought the shoes days ago, how could –'

'It is interesting that you refer to the missing cash as a five-pound note.' Burdock's eyes immediately lit up.

'It doesn't take Sherlock Holmes to deduce that!' rallied Etta. 'It would hardly have walked off in separate denominations!'

'I'll thank you not to adopt that tone with me!' snapped the manager.

Exasperated, Etta tugged at the pockets of her overall, turning them inside out to show they were empty. 'See – and you may search my coat if you wish!'

'There'd be little point in that, the thief would hardly be still in possession.' He laced his plump fingers across his abdomen, a hint of finality to his tone. 'Now, remember I told you before Christmas that I was giving you one last chance –'

'But I've done nothing!' cried Etta, so that all eavesdroppers were suitably informed of this vile slander.

Burdock was not to be shifted from the belief that she had taken it. 'In extenuating circumstances I could be persuaded to stretch that chance; if you were in dire need I am sure you could be forgiven, but I must have the truth here and now.'

'I did *not* take it!' insisted Etta.

For a moment, Burdock viewed her emphatic stance with obvious disbelief, then sighed regretfully. 'You understand that if you are dismissed in such circumstances it would take effect immediately and you would be granted no reference?'

'I've been handling hundreds of pounds for months! If I were dishonest do you think I'd be satisfied with a paltry fiver?' Then she frowned. 'Wait a minute! I could have sworn I left five pounds amongst the float after cashing up on the previous night – yes, that's right! A customer tendered it just before closing so it should still have been in the till, but when I came in yesterday morning there were only coins. I remember thinking it odd . . .' Her thoughts raced. Someone could have sneaked in before she arrived – it could be Tupman! He was obviously intent on causing trouble since her rebuttal of his advances, he could have orchestrated this. 'Am I the only person to be interrogated?' she demanded now, causing those in the background to exchange looks of concern.

But the turned-down mouth indicated that Burdock considered this futile. 'As I said before, only you and I have access to this office.'

'Bu—'

'Further argument is useless, Miss Lanegan. I take a very dim view of having my generosity thrown back in my face – all the little extras I gave you, yet still you greed for more. Now, I will not search your coat but I should like you to put it on and leave the premises.' When she did not immediately respond but stood there raging helplessly, he added, 'Consider yourself fortunate that I choose not to involve the police.'

Etta glared ineffectively for a few more seconds, then turned abruptly, rushed upstairs to grab her coat and, with all eyes upon her, finally left the shop.

Only when she reached home did she break down in tears.

She remained there for most of the day, fuming and clenching her fists at the injustice, wondering what on earth to do now. Well, with no reference and little chance of getting another job there was nothing else she could do but go and reclaim her husband. But where to find him? *Where?* Rubbing her palms briskly over her cheeks, leaving them clamped there for a while as her reddened eyes stared into space, she asked herself did she truly desire to have Marty back, or was it simply that she had been forced into this corner? She did not have to think long before reaching her conclusion: life was not worth living without him.

First, though, there was the disagreeable task of informing her mother-in-law of her intentions, and, even worse, she would have to admit that she had been keeping from Aggie the information that her son was in the army. She glanced at the clock. The children would have left school by now, they'd possibly be having tea. She would be forced to make her admittance in front of them. No . . . she just could not have them witness the terrible rumpus that would arise, not on top of today's upset. The shame of being labelled a thief! How would she possibly convey this to others?

No, she had made up her mind. She would go and collect the children at the normal hour, then she would put tomorrow's enforced day of idleness to good use and make a few enquiries at the barracks as to how one went about finding a soldier that did not want to be found. Maybe then she would have some constructive news for Aggie, who hopefully would forgive her for this digression.

Forty-eight hours later Etta was to ask herself, what had been the use of prolonging the agony? She might as well have asked the man in the moon how to find her husband as those at the barracks. Whilst the officer had been sympathetic, suggesting that she visit the Infantry Record Office, he had given her not the slightest cause for optimism. No wiser than two days ago, she would be defenceless against Aggie's wrath.

She carried her confession and a heavy heart to the house

at the far end of the street, steeled herself and went in. Those around the table showed surprise at her premature appearance. Having finished their meal, the children sought immediate permission to get down, then tumbled to greet their mother who hugged them fondly and shared a brief conversation, before explaining her early arrival to Aggie, Red and Uncle Mal.

'I've lost my job.'

The adults groaned. 'Ah, dear . . . for what reason?' asked Aggie, pouring Etta a cup of tea. Reluctant to voice the truth in front of her children, Etta delved in her purse and handed three halfpennies to Celia. 'Did you eat all your tea? Then take your brother and sister to buy some lollipops.'

This was unheard of since their father had been away! Before a disapproving Granny could veto this, Celia grabbed the coins and scampered from the house, the others chasing her, only baby William left behind to protest.

Etta smiled and bent to pet the dark-haired infant, though her eyes were sad.

'Ah well, can't be too bad if you're throwing your money about,' Uncle Mal tendered lightly.

'Oh, it is.' Etta's tone remained dull. 'My dismissal was two days ago. I couldn't bring myself to say anything to you before . . .' It hurt even now to say it. 'Five pounds went missing from the takings, they think it was I who took it.'

Aggie sat up, objecting, 'We know you better than that!'

'Thank you.' She threw her mother-in-law a half-smile of gratitude, took a few sips from the cup of tea that had been poured for her, then replaced it on the table and went to flop into a chair, staring blankly at the fire.

Red gave an ominous yawn.

'You must be sure of another job if you're wasting money on goodies though,' quizzed Aggie.

Etta shook her head. 'I'm sure it's highly irresponsible

322

of me, but I just wanted them to have a little treat.' She was building up to her confession. 'They haven't had the best time of it lately. They're missing their father dreadfully.'

'Ach, I know,' murmured Aggie, noting that her daughter-in-law seemed reluctant to meet her eye. Feeling sorry for Etta, who had grown so very thin, she watched her playing with the material of her dress that had been purchased in the sales. A dull green, it had been the only colour available at so cheap a price and sucked the life from her skin, making it corpselike. Not the vivacious creature of whom Marty had been so proud.

Then, suddenly, Etta buried her face in her hands, saying with such utter despair that it greatly alarmed the onlookers, 'This can't go on.'

Aggie employed euphemism. 'You're not thinking to do anything silly?'

Scornful eyes shot up to meet her. 'I'm not about to end my life if that's what you infer! No, I meant I have to go and find that blessed husband of mine.'

Aggie breathed a sigh of relief. 'Well, it makes a change to hear you've accepted ownership at last – he's usually "that son of mine".'

Etta could not raise a smile. 'Have the children said anything to you about him?'

'Not much.' Aggie threw a shifty glance at Red who looked equally ill-at-ease and occupied himself in filling his pipe with tobacco. 'Just Alex getting mixed up and saying you're going to find him.'

'Yes, well, I know I said that, but in fact she's not mixed up.' Etta took a deep breath and plunged in. 'I do intend to look for Martin. I decided at Christmas.'

'Oh . . .' Aggie looked at her husband and Uncle Mal, her attitude brightening. 'Well, that's good . . . that's good.'

'The trouble is, I have no idea where to start.' Coming to the worst bit, Etta dealt her mother-in-law a sincere look of apology. 'Mrs Reilly informed me that her son had come across Martin in the army –' at the expressions of shock on their faces she added immediately '– I know I should have told you and I'm so sorry! I just didn't even want to think about it at the time, let alone talk about it, it was too painful.' She sighed again, her eyes desolate as she rushed on. 'Then on Christmas Day it was so hideous . . .' She could not even begin to voice the pain she felt at Celia's declaration of hatred. 'Anyhow, the point is that I decided to write to the regiment and ask about Martin. It took months even to receive a reply, and when it came they had no record of him at all.' Her face crumpled at the memory of that disappointment and she bent her head again.

The listeners were silent for some twenty seconds, Uncle Mal clearing his throat and forming a noiseless whistle, Aggie looking indecisively at her husband, who in a matter of seconds fell asleep, woke, then fell asleep again, before she said in measured tone, 'They've no record of a Martin Lanegan, but they should have a Martin Lonergan. If they were looking for the name alphabetically it would appear much lower down the list and they might have given up before reaching it.'

'Oh, yes, I suppose people do often spell it incorrectly.' Having expected fireworks, a somewhat relieved Etta pondered on this inspired guess from her mother-in-law.

'Well, apparently that was what happened and your man didn't bother to put them right. But if you have his army number you should have no more trouble in contacting him.'

For a moment Etta was oblivious to what was being revealed in that statement. Then, she blinked tearfully and frowned at her mother-in-law, who had left her seat to rummage in a drawer.

'I know I promised him, but I can't allow this to go on,' said Aggie, her tone softly apologetic as she scribbled on a piece of paper.

Etta continued to stare as the note was calmly handed

to her. Only when her eyes saw the truth writ large did she finally come to grips with the reality. '*You knew?*' She rose to her feet and erupted, 'He's been writing to you, and for nine months you've watched me struggle, be humiliated –'

'Marty didn't think you wanted him any more!' Aggie defended herself, the onlookers most uncomfortable. 'I thought otherwise but it wasn't up to me, so I kept my nose out of it until you decided for yourself that you did want him back.'

'Don't you realise how callous, how . . .' Etta was too furious to say more but jerked her arms in the air with a stifled shriek.

'I said you should've told her,' scolded Red, puffing anxiously on his pipe. 'About the money at lea—' He fell instantly asleep again.

Etta gasped and became so red in the face it appeared she might burst. 'He's been sending money?'

'Well how else d'ye think I've been managing to feed and clothe your children all this time?' retorted Aggie, ignoring the knock that came at the front door, hurrying instead to prevent the fallen pipe from burning another hole in her husband's clothing.

'I could have looked after them myself if you'd had the courtesy to let me know!' a furious Etta yelled back at her.

'Aggie just told you,' Uncle Mal leaned forward to plead on his niece's behalf, 'Marty didn't want ye to know.'

Etta turned to rage at the old man, shocking him back into his chair. 'But everyone else in the world could be privy to his whereabouts – I'm his wife, I had a right to know!'

'It's no fault of ours if he can't stand being married to you!' snapped Aggie, finally charging to the door in response to the persistent knocking.

Etta used the hiatus to try and compose herself, but it was difficult with her heart thudding in anger. The children streamed in then, opening their bags to display the sweets they had bought.

Etta gave a terse smile and said, 'Lovely! You sit and eat them quietly now.' And at once they obeyed, leaving her to cross her trembling arms over her breast and shake her head in exasperation at Uncle Mal; then when Aggie came back to growl at her 'It's for you!' she heaved a frustrated sigh and went to investigate with a scowling demand.

'What?'

'Sorry for botherin' you!' Taken aback by the rude greeting, Mary-Ann Binks wrung her hands.

'Oh, Mary-Ann . . .' Etta tried but failed to calm her palpitating heart, then frowned. 'How did you find me here?'

'Mr Burdock told me!'

Etta nodded impatiently. Ah yes, she had originally given this address as her lodgings.

'I thought to let you know as soon as possible, he says you can have your job back!' Hands clasped, Mary-Ann waited with an expectant smile for Etta to digest the news.

Unmoved, her mind on other things, Etta demanded suspiciously, 'And to what do I owe this change of heart?'

Mary-Ann built up to her announcement as if rolling a snowball down a hill. 'You know that rodent problem we had? Well, just after you went the other day Mr Tupman sat on a mouse! Oh, real comical it was, least it was for them as aren't squeamish –'

'Mary-Ann, it's very fascinating but –'

'Yes, well, anyway, Miss Wimp was sick in front of a customer and old Dandelion got real angry and said he must get the problem sorted out, so he called in a rat-catcher and guess what they found when they pulled away the wainscoting?'

'Let me see – a rat perhaps?' Etta's jaw ached from clenching her teeth.

'A whole nest of them, and they'd used a chewed-up

fiver as bedding! So you see, it wasn't you what took it!'

'Really?' Etta's lips had a sardonic twist. 'Well, thank you for taking the trouble to relay this news. However, I was already aware that I was not the one to steal it.'

'Oh, I knew that really! And so does Mr Burdock. He says the only explanation is that the rat somehow managed to get into the drawer that held the overnight float and pinch the fiver – he says you can have your job back!'

'How very magnanimous,' came Etta's taut reply.

'So you'll come back to work tomorrow, then? I promise it's safe, the rats have been exterminated.'

'Oh, I rather think there are more to be dealt with yet,' snorted Etta, referring to the one who had sacked her out of hand, not to mention the one who had molested her, but this was wasted on Mary-Ann who merely gawped in puzzlement. 'Regrettably, tell Mr Burdock I shall have to decline his most generous offer as I have to deal with a rat of my own – the one who deserted me!' Etta began to close the door, then was further inspired. 'Better still, do you remember where Mr Burdock had his terrible itch?'

Mary-Ann tittered.

'Well, tell him to shove his job there!' concluded Etta.

15

Etta's fury over Marty's connivance with his mother took days to expire, and during this phase her yen to have him back underwent a complete reversal. She was his wife, for heaven's sake, yet to whom did he send his earnings? As if she herself were too useless to apportion them! Nine months, *nine months* she had slaved, been humiliated . . .

But no more. Now she knew he had been sending money she would have no need to trail about looking for him, nor to lose her house, nor even to go out to work. She would demand that Aggie hand over the next payment at once. How dare the pair of them insinuate that she was too stupid to look after her own children? Well, she *had* been looking after them quite competently enough since the discovery of the treacherous pact and would continue to do so. Oh yes, that was the last Aggie would see of her grandchildren.

At last, though, she calmed down enough to see that this state of affairs could not proceed, for not only did she require money, but she wanted answers too. After taking her children to school that morning, she braced herself for confrontation.

Aggie looked initially shocked upon answering the door to find her daughter-in-law, but soon recovered to say, 'You don't have to knock . . .'

'I rather think I do.' Etta was brusque. 'I hate to impose upon the close relationship you have with your son, but –'

'Ah stop being so bloody self-righteous!' rasped Aggie, throwing open the door. 'Get yourself inside and I'll tell you everything.'

'Rather late in the day for that,' muttered Etta, but nevertheless she left the sleeping baby in his pram and slipped haughtily into the living room.

At her imperious entry, both Red and Mal started to rise. She gestured them back into their seats and took one herself, then instructed her mother-in-law to, 'Begin.'

'Are the nippers at school?' Aggie came to sit down too.

'Yes. So we may say what we must.' Etta remained cool.

'We've missed not having them here, have we not, Red?' Seeing that Etta was not about to countenance small-talk, Aggie rubbed her aproned knees, then launched in. 'Right, well, Marty wrote to you a few weeks after he left, enclosing a money order, but he sent it to your old address, and –'

'Of course I was no longer there, having had to do a moonlight flit thanks to him!'

'Are ye going to keep jumping in like a flea or will I be allowed to finish?' Aggie fixed her with a glacial eye.

'I beg your pardon.' Suitably rebuked, Etta inclined her head stiffly. 'Please go on.'

'Thank you.' Aggie was just as curt. 'Anyhow, somebody opened the letter –' She broke off with a warning glower as it looked like Etta might butt in again, then proceeded, '– don't ask me who, I don't know and I don't care, I just know it got sent back to him and he thought you'd read it and taken the money and returned the letter out of spite or whatever, and he thought you didn't want him back – I know!' Eyes closed in exasperation, she held up her palm to stave off another outburst from Etta. 'It was stupid of him, I told him all that had happened, and about that man only giving you a lift in his car when the pram broke, but he was adamant, said if you didn't want him back then he didn't want you either.'

With Etta looking as if she had been slapped in the face,

329

Aggie went on, 'But one thing I'll say about Marty, maddening though he can be, he wouldn't see his children go without, and when I told him they were living with his father and me most of the ti—'

'Only because I was forced to go out and earn a living!' cut in Etta, highly offended.

'For *whatever* reason.' Aggie's patience was wearing thin, as her tone conveyed. 'When he heard, he started sending the money to me. I've spent every penny on them, haven't taken so much as a farthing for meself.'

I'll bet you haven't, Etta wanted to fling at her, but resisted.

'I wanted to tell you about it much earlier than this,' went on Aggie, 'but he asked me not to.'

'Why?' came the clipped response.

Her mother-in-law began to fidget with her apron. 'Well, like I said, he didn't think ye wanted him . . .'

Etta sensed there was more. 'Have you kept the letters? May I be permitted to read them for myself?'

Behind his daughter-in-law's back, Red advised his wife not to do this by means of a brisk shake of his head, though Aggie was already of the same opinion. 'You won't like them.'

Etta tossed her head. 'I'm sure I shan't, but at least I'll know what my husband really thinks of me.'

Reluctantly, Aggie went to fetch them. 'There aren't that many. Marty's not much of a letter-writer, some of them are only a few scribbled words to accompany the postal order.'

'Nevertheless . . .' Firm of face, Etta held out her palm for them.

As she began to read, the other occupants made themselves as unobtrusive as possible, Aggie reaching for a flat iron, Red shambling off to hawk various items he had scavenged, old Mal using a magnifying glass to study the newspaper for runners.

Immediately, Etta saw that Marty's address differed from the one given by Mrs Reilly. She read on. Most of what Aggie said was true. Marty had forbidden his mother to tell her where he was. But that was not all he had to say. Etta's face darkened as she read the next line: '*It's the best thing for her, teach her to stand on her own two feet, fend for herself for a while, then she might see how hard it is . . .*'

An irritating noise forced her to look up. Aggie was scraping the layer of soot from the bottom of her flat iron with a piece of emery paper. When her prickly look had no effect, Etta pursed her lips, tried to inure herself to the rasping and continued to read.

There was no explanation for joining the army in the first place, other than drunken stupidity. Well, thank goodness he had not mentioned the teapot business. She was still ashamed about that. Apart from the few derogatory sentences about herself, most of his words were for his children, asking how they were, and the remainder devoted to telling his parents about life in the army. Then, right at the end she saw written: '*I'd dearly like to say give my love to Etta and the kids, but of course that would let the cat out of the bag. Even so, I think about them all the time. Maybe one day I'll write to her. I still love her you know . . .*'

Etta felt her eyes pricked by tears. That was the stupidest thing about all this, she still loved him too . . .

She sat there for a while staring into space, the letter resting on her lap. Then, feeling herself under inspection, she mustered her wits and said to her mother-in-law in the same detached tone she had used before, 'I suppose one of us ought to deal with this sensibly. I promised the children they would have their father back. So, I had better go and fetch him.'

Having made the decision, she was to act upon it immediately, backing down enough from her intransigence towards

331

her mother-in-law in order to procure a minder for the children whilst she was away.

'Sure, you'll be after writing to him first,' Aggie had prompted. 'A stamp is a lot cheaper than a train ticket.'

But Etta had shaken her head. Like Marty, she had never been very good at putting her thoughts onto paper and she wanted no chance of a misunderstanding now. 'I'd rather speak to him in person,' she had said, before taking herself off first to the pawn shop with an assortment of goods to raise the train fare, then to the railway station.

In the hours it had taken her to journey the hundred miles or so to Lichfield she had rehearsed what to say, first to the commanding officer, then to Marty. For all her unforgiving rants, she found herself looking forward to seeing him again. Would they be allowed a private meeting straightaway? She hoped so, for she had no money for lodgings and there was much to convey before her return to York. She pictured their meeting after almost a year apart: both of them hesitant at first, Marty looking down at her with that droopy-lidded gaze of his that had always managed to turn her inside out even when she was angry with him. She pictured him standing there in his uniform, the pair of them making up for lost time . . . but of course there would be none of that at first. None of anything if she didn't pluck up enough courage to go through those blessed garrison gates instead of dallying here staring at them.

Bracing her shoulders, she approached the sentry and asked to see the commanding officer.

Some minutes later she found herself being presented to a charming adjutant who first directed this shabby but extremely genteel and attractive young woman to a chair, then apologised for the colonel's unavailability before asking what he could do to help.

Outlining her story, Etta told him that she had made a written enquiry before and produced the letter she had received in reply, 'But then I was not in possession of my husband's regimental number nor the correct battalion, so it was understandable that there was some mix-up with the spelling of his name . . .'

The adjutant frowned over the letter, then looked up at her. 'Even so, I must apologise for the great inconvenience it must have caused you. Anyway, now that we are no longer relating at cross-purposes I might be of more assistance. On second thoughts,' he rose and went to summon a man in the outer office, 'let us have Private Lonergan's company commander in, perhaps he will be able to shed light on your predicament.'

Etta thanked him with her sweetest smile.

The adjutant told her not to mention it and seemed most happy to chat to the alluring young woman until another entered. 'Ah, here is Captain Palm now!'

For the benefit of the newcomer, the adjutant gave a précis of Etta's dilemma, Etta herself finishing with the polite enquiry, 'I wonder if I might be permitted to see my husband today? I understand that it would be inconvenient, but as I have not spoken to him for several months . . .'

But Captain Palm was at a loss. 'Madam, I'm afraid you have me at a disadvantage. I was under the distinct impression that Private Lonergan visited you regularly. He has been issued with a pass to that effect.'

'I can assure you, Captain Palm, that I have not seen him since May of last year. That is why I'm –' Etta's smile froze as the truth hit her.

It hit Captain Palm at exactly the same moment. He looked slightly vexed, then dipped his head as a gesture of apology. 'Forgive me, madam, this could be a case of mistaken identity . . .'

The adjutant smiled in slight confusion at his captain. 'No, I think we've established we have the right man.'

'Indeed you have,' murmured a stupefied Etta, under

assault from her feelings, the most forceful of these being wrath. *The swine! The dog!* How she managed to keep her tone on an even keel was a miracle. 'It is just that I was previously unaware as to the extent of his misdeeds. I had thought him merely to have deserted us.' She gave a mirthless little bark of a laugh and shook her head. 'I say *merely*, when I do not mean that at . . . at all . . .' Her voice caught, but her eyes retained the brightness of fury as they searched the room for a way out.

The adjutant was, by now, frowning from one to another in complete bafflement. 'You must think me incredibly dim, Mrs Lonergan, but let us state this clearly so there is no danger of us misunderstanding one another. Your reason for being here is to make an official complaint of desertion against Private Lonergan?'

'It most certainly is!'

He nodded slowly, a hint of pity in his blue eyes. 'Then first I must regrettably inform you that as more than six months have passed since attestation, I cannot apply for your husband to be discharged. However, I can –'

'I don't wish him to be discharged!' railed Etta, shifting in her chair. 'You're welcome to keep him!'

The adjutant patiently finished his statement. 'Be that as it may, I shall apply to the brigade commander to withhold his pay so that you may have financial support.'

Regaining her manners, Etta fought to moderate her angry approach. 'Thank you, Major, that's most considerate of you, but he's already sending money. My reason for coming here was to see him, to tell –' Anguish forbade her to say any more on the subject and she rose abruptly. 'Thank you, gentlemen, for your information. I should very much like to leave now.'

'But you must have an explanation from Private Lonergan!' objected the adjutant, jumping to his feet. 'Captain Palm will –'

'That won't be necessary, thank you!' Etta rushed for

the door, which the captain hurriedly opened for her. The cheating, miserable wretch! No wonder he hadn't needed to come home to her.

'Then allow me to – Sergeant-major!' The adjutant interrupted himself to call to the man in the outer room. 'Please show Mrs Lonergan to the gate.' But Etta's shoes were already performing an angry tip-tap along the corridor in desperation to be out of there, the sergeant-major racing to catch up.

'We shall have Lonergan in at any rate,' said an extremely brusque adjutant to his captain. 'And find out what's damn-well going on!'

'I can tell you that,' muttered Captain Palm. 'It seems our chappie has two wives on the go.'

Marty was enjoying a moment of relaxation in the dry canteen, as usual making others laugh, this time with an impersonation of their company sergeant, contorting his mouth so acutely that the words seemed to emerge from just beneath his ear. Ah, but it was good to be able to get this response once more. There had been times when he thought he'd never laugh again.

'Lonergan!'

At the summons, he shot a frightened look over his shoulder, causing his friends to poke fun as this popular member of their group breathed a sigh of relief. 'Christ, I thought it was him for a minute.'

'Your presence is required by the Captain!'

With not the vaguest inkling what it might concern, he rose and quipped to his companions, 'Oh, it'll be that medal he's been promising me.'

His friends mocked, though in fact there was a grain of realism in the joke. Popular with men and officers alike, everyone knew that Marty was ambitious, and despite being a clown in his spare time had been soldiering hard to gain promotion. He was quite buoyant as he left them.

But this light-heartedness was to dwindle upon being escorted into the company commander's office and seeing his face.

'Ah, Private Lonergan!' Captain Palm's tone was brightly caustic. 'I have just had the pleasure of speaking to your wife.'

Marty wrinkled his brow.

'Well you may frown! Are you not curious as to which wife I refer?'

For a second he failed to comprehend – then the walls came rushing in at him. Etta had come here! A sweat of panic sprang up all over his body, prickling the hair beneath his armpits.

Captain Palm sat back in his chair, his patrician face hard and knowing. 'I can see just by your expression that you are fully aware of whom I speak.'

'I can expl—'

'*Explain!*' The officer showed derision. 'Please do not insult me with that well-worn phrase, Private Lonergan, it is the refuge of every wrongdoer in history, the bolthole of a scoundrel . . .' He glared at the soldier before him. 'First, what have you to say to Mrs Lonergan's charge of desertion?'

Desertion? His old wounds suddenly ripped wide open again, Marty was transported rudely back in time, to relive the months of anguish. He had thought them over, but here he was dragged back to the beginning . . .

Joining the army had taken an instant weight off his shoulders. Yes, life was hard, but then it always had been and here he didn't have to think for himself. He was fed at regular intervals and though the discipline was stringent it had helped him forget about Etta . . . for a while. But then the question of families had arisen and he had had to face it. He missed his children so acutely that the thought of never seeing them again was like acid pouring into his soul. And, remembering the good times, he was compelled to admit that he missed Etta too, and along with these thoughts guilt had begun to gnaw. He couldn't leave her without money for the children. So he had written to her, told her where he was, and if not exactly saying he was sorry had enclosed a postal order as a token of his desire to reconcile.

But then the letter had come back, minus postal order, as effective and painful as a blow from a teapot, reminding him how desperate things had become between them, and he had asked himself, did he really want to start it all up again? No – yes – no, because she didn't want him or she would have come looking for him. So . . . that was that.

Except that it wasn't that, because he still loved her. Even though he had found the warm and generous Amelia, who asked nought of him, who, upon his visits, dropped anything she might be doing to treat him like a king, to feed him and love him . . . even with all this he still thought about Etta, yearned and cried out with his entire being for her, especially when his mother had written to tell him it had all been a big mistake, that man had only been giving her a lift in his car, and that Etta was out of her mind with worry over him. Yes, that had caused a pang of conscience, had made him regret his betrayal of her with another woman, regret even more stringing poor Amelia along, when all the time his body used her his heart belonged to Etta . . . And now she had been here, accusing him of desertion . . .

He cleared his thoughts and admitted to the captain, 'I suppose technically I am guilty as charged, sir, though I have been sending money home every week for the upkeep of my children.'

This did little to affect the officer's mood. 'Yes, Mrs Lonergan did tell me that. However, she was most put-out to say the least when I unwittingly informed her that her husband had been going home to his wife every weekend.'

Marty cringed. 'I thought she didn't want me back, sir!'

'So you went and found yourself another! Private Lonergan, perhaps you fail to grasp the rudiments of a Christian society: your entitlement is to one wife, not two, or three, or half a dozen for all I might know.'

'Sir, I just –'

'Enough! You'll have an opportunity to speak when you appear before the Colonel.' Captain Palm glowered at him for long seconds, before ending peevishly, 'However, I should like to have all the details at hand when I am called upon to say why I allotted your pass. I'm very disappointed in your lying to me, Lonergan. I took you for a better man.'

'Sorry, sir.' Marty projected suitable shame.

'As well you may be! And what is all this ridiculous business with the misspelling of your name? You caused all manner of inconvenience for those trying to find you. Why sign the attestation form if it was so obviously wrong?'

'Well, I did try to correct the recruiting sergeant, sir,' Marty felt a dart of disapproval from the sergeant who stood beside him, 'but he told me the army doesn't like troublemakers.'

'You would have done well to heed him,' replied the captain gravely, indicating further charges.

Marty felt sick. Even so, he chanced more rebuke to ask with a modicum of hope, 'My wife, sir, is she still –?'

'Gone home!' The captain's reply squashed any optimism. 'At least I must presume so from the state she was in.'

Etta had indeed gone directly to the railway station, for what would have been the point of tarrying? Even so, she was subjected to an excruciating wait of an hour until her train arrived, during which she could barely keep still, her feet striding up and down the platform as she asked herself furiously over and over how she could have been so stupid not to see it, picturing him with that . . . that thing! What else could one call a woman who stole another's husband?

338

Nothing else concerned her, not the fact that she had pawned all manner of belongings in order to be there, nor what others on the platform might think of her frantic prowling – she could only see Marty in the arms of another, tormented herself with the vision of him kissing, touching, loving . . . it made her squirm like a maggot impaled on a hook.

By the time the train arrived she was almost ready to vomit, and the moment a man opened the door of a carriage for her, she leapt on board and flung herself into the darkest recess of a compartment, crossing her arms over her breast to signify that she had no wish to socialise, urging the engine to get a move on, and remaining sick with fury all the way to York.

Dreading the moment when she would have to tell the children, she did not go immediately to collect them but returned to her own empty house, and, seated there in the fireless kitchen, burst into tears at the thought of how they would react. She should never have told them that she was going to see their father. *How could he do this to her?*

What a fool! She had always considered him loyal, for he had repeatedly defended her against his parents, but now she realised that his support had merely been partisan; now he had found someone of more use to him he had ruthlessly abandoned her. Spurred by rage, she jumped up and began to seek any personal item of his. She found the mug he used for shaving and hurled it at the wall, gaining no satisfaction when it shattered and having great difficulty in restraining herself from smashing more valuable objects. Rushing upstairs, she wrenched open a drawer and withdrew the few items of clothing he had left – everything worthwhile had been pawned long ago – grasped the patched woollen combinations by the legs and tried to rip them apart, and, failing this, stood on them and heaved with all her might until they eventually gave at the seams, whereupon she inserted her fingers into the rent and clawed it viciously apart, tossing the two halves of the ruined article aside and reaching for another, going through the rest of his drawer in similar violent fashion, wanting to do to him what he had done to her. How *dare* he cast her aside like some old boot? And all the while she sweated and squealed and cursed and ripped, she was telling herself how stupid she had been to meekly accept what she had been told, to come home with her tail between her legs, when instead she should have demanded to know the address of the woman who had replaced her in his affections. Well, he might think he had got away with it, but just let him see what he had unleashed! She would go back there tomorrow and confront them! Hurling the last rag aside she dashed back downstairs and began to pick things up and put them down, searching for items to pawn so as to acquire the train fare, a jug here, a picture there, a cushion, a pan, all being noisily stacked in a pile on the table. Her wild eyes sought the room for more booty – she would even pawn the clothes in which she stood and drag him back if need be!

But to what end? The rude thought served to interrupt her fevered searching, and Etta stood there panting to undergo more measured argument. The children might have their father back, but what about her? Oh, she would have gladly carried out her plan, would have fought tooth and nail if it meant winning back Marty's love. But what was the point in fighting when he did not want her?

After further sporadic eruptions of tears, she eventually sank into a trough of despair, just sat there twisting the wedding ring on her finger, the one she had only just put back. She was to remain in this same pose for most of the evening, barely stirring even when the gas ran out and plunged the room into darkness, for she could feel no darker in spirit than she already did.

Even the next morning she continued her avoidance of the children, waiting until after school began before slipping from the house to go and collect William. A neighbour, Mrs Carter, was on her hands and knees scrubbing the pavement in front of her own house. Etta stepped into the road so as not to disturb her.

'Thanks, love,' said Mrs Carter, pausing her scrubbing to smile. 'But I think I might be wasting my time by the look of that sky.'

'Perhaps we all are,' muttered Etta, lifting her bloodshot eyes to appraise the thick grey blanket of cloud and in doing so catching sight of the name plate on the wall across the road. Hope Street? Oh yes, hope in abundance, came her anguished, bitter thought.

The instant Aggie saw her daughter-in-law's blotchy face her heart sank. 'Ye didn't make it up then, the pair o' yese?'

'I didn't even see him.' Etta reached out for her youngest, wrapped her arms around his warm little body and pressed her head against his, trying to draw solace. 'And I'd no wish to after what I was told. He's found himself another woman.'

'*What?*' Aggie shot a glance at her uncle, who looked just as shocked. 'How long's this been going on?'

Etta hid her face in the child's delicate neck. 'Quite some time apparently. His officer was under the impression that he'd been coming home to his wife every weekend.'

'That stupid little –' Aggie was furious.

'I couldn't bring myself to speak to him.'

'And rightly so!' Aggie's heart went out to Etta, who looked most forlorn. Groping for something of comfort, she tendered quietly, 'Will you be having some toast with your cup of tea, love?'

Etta shook her head. She had been unable to stomach anything, and felt sick even though there was nought to come up.

341

Loath to upset her further, Aggie chose not to press for more information, waiting for it to be volunteered whilst she brewed the pot of tea. Eventually the injured party was to tell her all that had occurred, at which she pronounced with feeling, 'God, that boy! Wait till his father hears about this, 'twill kill him.'

Uncle Mal, who had been quiet till now, chipped in with a doom-laden prophesy, 'Marty could be in serious trouble over this.' When both women glared at him he added quickly, 'With the army, I mean. Sure, I know what they're like, he could be in for a rough time.'

'Not as rough as the one I'm in for!' Etta hurled back at the old man. 'I'm the one who has to tell the children their father isn't coming back. How on earth am I to –' Her voice cracked with emotion.

Aggie reached out awkwardly to administer a comforting stroke. 'Don't go upsetting them over it yet. Once Marty knows you've been to see him he'll buck his ideas up. He'll be back, you'll see –'

'I don't want him back!' raged Etta as if to a fool. 'Not ever! How could he do this to us?'

Aggie withdrew her hand and crossed her arms, looking embarrassed. 'I don't know, darlin',' she said quietly. 'But sure, he'll be paying for it now.'

'Good!' spat Etta. 'Financially, too, I hope. And whilst we're on the subject –'

'Oh yes, I'll pass on any money that comes,' Aggie assured her, but deep down her concerns were more for her son's welfare. Marty could be facing a court-martial over this.

Receiving no news on the matter from the culprit himself, Aggie was to remain anxious that her son could be in serious trouble, and, with another week passing without word, her misgivings were bound to increase, this leading to more than one medicinal glass of sherry.

When an envelope finally did arrive there was to be little relief, for it did not bear Marty's handwriting and was addressed to the younger Mrs Lanegan. Even so, Aggie was not about to adhere to protocol and without qualm ripped it open.

But still, she was not to be briefed on her son's fate, for inside was only the usual money order. Whilst retaining her worry, she took this round to her daughter-in-law's house straightaway.

She was to find Etta in the yard, attacking one of her dining chairs with an axe.

'For the fire?' shrieked Aggie upon being informed. 'Glory be, you could've got two bob for that – half a week's rent!' Her daughter-in-law had again fallen behind with the latter. 'Ah well, what's done is done.' Sighing, she helped Etta to gather the splintered wood and took some of it indoors, where she also handed over the letter. 'Here, this might cheer you up.'

But the money did nothing to lift Etta's melancholy. 'Seven shillings,' she uttered in dismay.

'Sure, that's what he always sends, but there's usually a note with it,' said Aggie, eyeing the other impatiently. 'Have you had any news yourself?'

Still despondent, Etta shook her head, sat down and dragged a whining toddler onto her lap.

Aggie sat back with a worried expression. What on earth had happened to Marty that he could not send word? But she knew better than to voice this to Etta. She took to studying the other's face, guessing the thoughts that must be going through her head. 'The offer's still open if you want to move in with us.'

Despite the weight of debt, still Etta showed reluctance to give in. 'I suppose I could take in a lodger.' Appearing distracted, she came across a dying flea on Willie's clothes, and in a matter-of-fact way, nipped it off him and threw it into the fire where it sizzled for a millisecond.

343

'Lodger indeed,' scoffed Aggie. 'Why, you can't even look after yourself! Look at the cut of you, all skin and bone.'

The fight gone out of her, Etta merely stared, before giving a weary nod. Whether she wanted to or not, there was nowhere else to go.

So, lock, stock and barrel, the younger Mrs Lanegan and her brood set up home in her mother-in-law's front parlour. Knowing she must find paid work, Etta worried that none would take her on without a reference from her previous employer; however, within hours and with further assistance from Aggie, she was to be taken on as a part-time assistant with a local provision dealer, the proximity to home and the shorter hours meaning she would not be away from her children so long as before. Thank God, for, cast adrift by her feckless husband, they were the only emotional anchor she possessed. On an economic front, so long as the money orders kept arriving, she could just about survive on her wage – but whether this would extend to her spiritual wellbeing was another matter.

Aggie, too, was apprehensive about this. How could the girl bear to sit there doing nothing for hours? To prevent this she told her new lodger that she must not feel as if she had to stay in the designated living space but was free to come and join her in the back sitting-room. This had been intended to make Etta see that there was work to be shared, but all the girl did was to exchange her chair in the front parlour for one in the back, sitting opposite Uncle Mal, staring dolefully at the embers. It made the old man awkward too. Finding her there again in the middle of the day whilst she herself laboured, Aggie bit her tongue for a while and went into the scullery to change her bucket of water and also to sneak a glass of stout which, in the absence of sherry, had to suffice, listening as Uncle Mal tried yet again to start a conversation.

He cleared his throat. 'A ferocious amount of rain we've been having.'

Etta looked up, gave a wan smile at the aged figure and nodded, then went back to her fire-gazing.

Unable to bear any more, Aggie put aside her glass, stepped forth and announced briskly, 'Hold out your hand', then planted something on the upturned palm. 'There! Don't go saying I never give you anything.'

Etta looked upon the lump of stone bemusedly. 'What is it?'

Aggie showed exasperation. 'Donkey – now shift yourself from that chair and go clean the front step and sills! If I want a pair of Toby jugs I'll buy them.'

Apologising, Etta slunk away, promising truthfully to give more help around the house, which satisfied Aggie to some extent, though she was to retain her concerns over her son's collapsed marriage and today's glass of stout was to be far from her last.

Red had his worries too, and, like his wife, decided to act upon them, though he resorted to different tactics. Commiserating sincerely with Etta that his son had got her into this mess by dragging her away from her life and estranging her from her own family, he sighed and announced as he reached casually for his pipe one evening, 'But sure that's Marty all over, always wants what he can't have, then as soon as he gets it he doesn't want it any more.'

Etta was furious to be portrayed as some cast-off garment. 'Others may tolerate such capriciousness – I shall not! He has responsibilities and I shall hold him to them!'

'Will it work, d' you think?' quizzed Aggie when her daughter-in-law had stormed from the room.

Red feigned innocence. 'Sure, I don't know what you're talking about, do you, Mal?'

The old man gave a shrug. 'I do not.'

'He's thinking to provoke the lass into going after Marty

345

and having things out!' Aggie explained to the old man. 'Let's hope it doesn't backfire and she takes her temper out on us instead.'

'Ah, 'tis a great, great shame,' lamented Mal. 'I do pray to God your plot works, Red. It breaks my heart to see Marty's little family so ruined.'

'I'll grant it breaks Etta's heart too,' murmured Aggie, and, sharing a worried look with Red, added, 'Let's hope 'tis not too badly-broken for your mischief to take effect.'

Whatever Etta was feeling inside, her parents-in-law could take credit that their words had had some impact, for she did appear to buck up enough to do her share of house-work without having to be commandeered all the time. Still, Aggie detected an air of wistfulness as Etta went about her laundering and polishing, or, on this particular afternoon, her ironing, and not for the first time she felt a little guilty for having kept Marty's whereabouts a secret from her – for it was obviously himself who was on her mind.

As a matter of fact, Etta's reverie was of a different nature, much further in the past than her failed marriage. As her hand steered the iron into folds and pleats, the vivid pictures in her mind were of herself as an eight-year-old, with her dear old nanny, her mother and her brother John – what a nice boy he had been then, careering through a garden hand-in-hand with her, picking her up when she tumbled and getting out his handkerchief to rub the graze from her palm. The scene included other children, and beau-tifully dressed ladies with whom she had shared a picnic by a lake at a big house – whose house she did not know or care, the pertinent thing being the mood of intense happi-ness she had felt then, remembered so clearly now, perhaps because her childhood had come to an abrupt end not long afterwards when Nanny had been dismissed, and she had never really felt that way again until her wedding . . .

'Get kettle on, then!' Her trance was interrupted by the shouted demand from across the neighbouring wall to Aggie, who was out in the yard folding up her washing line, and within seconds the house was invaded by Mrs Thrush, whose loud presence put paid to any mind-wanderings.

'I can't stop long!' The beefy posterior in its grey dress was lowered onto a wooden chair, its owner proceeding to survey Etta's endeavours with the iron. It was common knowledge that Aggie's daughter-in-law was none too adept at domesticity, but now there seemed a definite improvement. Leaning forward to tweak a section of white linen, Mrs Thrush remarked to Aggie, 'She's not doing bad for somebody who couldn't even tell the difference between a box o' starch and a bag o' flour not so very long ago.'

Despite being slightly offended that her shortcomings had obviously been discussed in public, Etta took the observance in good part. 'Yes, I made some terribly stiff pastry until someone rectified my blunders.'

Adding her own compliment to Mrs Thrush's backhanded one, Aggie mashed a pot of tea and poured four cups, giving one to Uncle Mal who sat quietly in his corner, then, for once, she was compelled to tell Etta, 'Leave that ironing and rest your legs for a while.'

Glad of the break, Etta stretched her aching muscles then sat down and joined the conversation, though this was only to last for as long as it took to drain the cups, Mrs Thrush finally announcing, 'Well, it's no good me sat sitting here, I've a pile of mending to do. I'd rather dig holes in t'road. And if me needle comes unthreaded I'm done for – I can't see, you know, specially if I'm working on owt dark-coloured.'

Aggie agreed that the advancing years brought many drawbacks, grunting and wincing as she too rose from her chair to clear away the crockery. 'It's rotten growing old.'

'Old?' Uncle Mal piped up in amusement. 'A mere slip of a girl.'

'Tell that to my joints.' Aggie rubbed her fingers. 'I think I'm getting arthritis.'

'You're not the only one!' Mrs Thrush rose with a grimace of empathy. 'Right, off to that blessed mending then.'

Moving to take up her iron again, Etta said, 'I'll do it for you, Mrs Thrush, if you're in no hurry that is.'

The neighbour exchanged a surprised glance with Aggie, before saying, 'There's quite a bit to do . . .'

'It won't trouble me – rather mending than laundry any day!'

To counter any misgivings on Etta's skill, Aggie told her neighbour, 'She does all ours. A dab hand at needlework, she is.'

Mrs Thrush accepted the kind offer. 'Well, thank you, lass – and you with all your troubles thinking of me. I'll fetch it round. Eh, she's a good un, bless her!' Then, an afterthought, 'Would sixpence be adequate?'

Etta hungered for the cash but knew the widow couldn't afford it. 'I couldn't possibly accept. Besides, it won't take me long.'

'Right! In that case,' said a grateful Mrs Thrush, 'whenever you want a hand with your mangling just give us a shout over t'wall – I've arms like a navvy. I mean it now.'

And she went to fetch the stack of mending, which was indeed undertaken in no time, whilst in turn, the following week Mrs Thrush's brawny arms were to wade through Etta's pile of washing.

When word got round of Etta's nimbleness with a needle, others sought to barter too – a threadbare sheet trimmed and stitched down the middle, hems expertly raised or lowered – in exchange for a pile of the hated ironing. And so it was that on the afternoons when she was not working at the shop, Etta found herself doing the thing she did best

– the only pity being that it would never grow into a proper business, for, at two and sixpence per week to hire, a sewing machine was definitely out of reach.

Glad at her deeper involvement in the community, Aggie and Red were nevertheless to remain worried over the military matters regarding their son, about whom there had still been no word. A good many weeks were to pass until, along with one of the postal orders, there came a letter from the man himself. Etta's first instinct was to throw this on the fire, but luckily his anxious mother was there to grab it.

'Praise be to God!' Upon reading the first few lines Aggie let out a breath of relief. ''Tis all over and done with.' She read the letter aloud, the gist of which was that, after thorough investigation, Marty had been deemed to have committed no major offence. There had been no false attestation, no attempt to profit financially by applying to go on the married roll. His only subterfuge had been one of omission rather than downright falsehood. Therefore, the commanding officer had leniently reduced his punishment to seven days' detention. Marty did not reveal all the humiliation that had gone with this, but wrote merely that he considered himself lucky.

Indeed, this was Etta's scornful opinion as her mother-in-law conveyed the news. '*Seven days* – for deserting his wife and children?'

'It wasn't exactly for that,' corrected Aggie, attempting to take in the rest of the letter until she saw it was too personal. 'Oh . . . you'd better be reading this for yourself.' When Etta declined to take the missive she flourished it at her rattily. 'Look, I know he doesn't deserve it, but at least pay the lad that courtesy before ye go throwing away your marriage.'

Etta's face showed condescension as she grabbed the letter and read it, and remained unforgiving as she handed it back. 'There, I've done as you asked. Now will you permit me similar courtesy?' At Aggie's nod she voiced her cool request. 'When you write to him, I should like you to say that other than any financial contribution I have no wish to receive any communication from him ever again.'

Upon receiving this crushing blow via his mother's pen, Marty took this to mean he had been barred from his children too, and his whole reason for being came tumbling down to flatten the life out of him. If Etta was seeking to punish him then she could have done it no better way. As the weeks went by, obsessed with such dreadful loss, he began to see his little ones in everything he did: as he cleaned his rifle he thought of Edward, as he shaved his face he saw Celia's reflection, as he dug a ditch he thought of Alex and her mud pies, as he polished his buttons he thought of Willie's baby fingers playing with them – the agony was indescribable. And there could be no comfort, no tender female arms in which to take solace, for Amelia, too, was now out of bounds.

Well, it wasn't right, he would stand for it no longer, and he wrote and told his mother so.

The go-between was to relay his demand to his wife. 'Marty wants to see his children.'

At the unexpected sound of his name over the remnants of dinner, Etta flinched as the rawness returned to seep through all-too-fragile scars. 'Oh, *does* he?'

Aggie's ice-blue eyes glanced up from the letter, she and Etta the only ones left in the room. 'I know he's done wrong, but he's hardly some sort of Casanova. I mean, he'd need clean underpants for that.'

Etta simply fumed.

'He made one mistake, and he's paying for it,' defended his mother. 'It's bad enough he can't see his wife, don't prevent him seeing his children too, it's not fair on them.'

Etta objected. 'I've never said he can't see them!'

'Well that's what he was led to believe, and so was I

350

come to that – I mean, you got me to do the dirty work, instructed me to write and tell him you wanted no further truck with him, what else was he to think?'

Etta closed her eyes in exasperation, thinking she should have done the job herself. 'I merely wished to convey that I have no desire to correspond, I never even mentioned the children.'

Aggie brightened. 'So he can see them?'

Etta granted a somewhat reluctant concession. 'I suppose so – but if he expects them to meet his floozy –'

'No! Give him some credit,' said Aggie, back to perusing the letter, 'he's been granted a week's leave, says he'll be coming up here on Saturday.'

Etta tried not to display the panic she felt at his imminent reappearance. 'Then I shall have to prepare them . . .' And herself too. Oh damnation, why was he coming here to stir it all up again?

'You have no objection to his coming to visit them, then?'

'I have every objection!' Still inflamed from his betrayal, she pushed away the half-finished cup of tea and rose to get ready for work. 'But I can hardly prevent it considering that they live with you, unless I drag them out to pound the streets all week.' She began to brush vigorously at her long hair, raking the harsh bristles across her scalp.

Aggie indicated the letter. 'So will I tell him he can come?'

Etta nodded as she wound the hair into a chignon and stabbed it with half a dozen pins, but her face made it plain she had no wish to be there when he arrived and she added tightly as she made to leave the house, 'I myself will have to find other lodgings.'

'Ach, there's no need for you to go forking out money.' Aggie felt that as Etta had compromised she herself must reciprocate. 'Marty can stop at Lou's.'

Pausing at the door, Etta projected gratitude. 'But he'll still want to come here and see his parents. Could you let me know in advance of his arrival so that I may endeavour to stay out of his way?'

'If that's the way you do be wanting it,' said Aggie, though she herself was looking forward to meeting her son again after almost a year's absence.

'I do,' said Etta, then left.

Informed by his mother's letter that his wife had no desire to see him and that he must lodge with his sister Marty experienced deep hurt but did not press the issue. He was sufficiently relieved at being permitted access to the children.

Directly upon depositing his kitbag at Lou's he went round to visit them. In compliance with Etta's demand he had previously written to inform his mother what hour he would be there. Accordingly, his wife was clear of the house by the time he entered.

It was all rather odd at first. Though there was much kissing and handshaking and joking from his parents and his siblings and Uncle Mal, who had shrunk to a bird-like figure in his absence, his own small band seemed to regard him as a stranger, keeping their distance until urged to come forth and greet their father, and even after doing this retreating once more to the margins from where they watched the goings-on with shy curiosity.

'Same old Marty,' he heard Uncle Mal comment as he left some two hours later, but he wasn't the same and neither was anyone else. He wondered, as he wended his doleful way back to his sister's house, if things would ever be the same again.

However, events were much brighter the next afternoon when he went to revisit his children and found communication between them start to ease. One by one, as he gently cajoled, the barriers were gradually dismantled, his youngsters ceasing to regard him in awe and beginning to edge in closer, and before he left they were jostling for attention. It was such a relief. As the days progressed so did their relationship, and by the end of the week Celia, Edward and Alex were standing on the step awaiting his arrival, and upon spotting him came streaming up the street to meet him and to squabble over which two would hold his hands.

How utterly devastating that he must leave them again so soon.

'Your final day, Marty,' said his great-uncle during a lull in the conversation towards the end of his Friday afternoon visit.

'Thanks for stating the obvious, Uncle Mal.' Marty chuckled but his heart was weighed down, for apart from having to face this wrench, there was more terrible news to divulge. 'And this is the last you're going to see of me for quite a while, I'm afraid.' Wearing a smile of apology, he looked at his mother and father, then at his children. 'The reason they were so generous with the leave is they're sending us to the emerald isle.'

The mood of the room plunged dramatically, his father falling instantly asleep. Whilst little William was too young to understand, the elder ones felt the impending loss keenly, Celia mouthing their objection.

'But you've only just come back to us!'

'I know.' He sighed, though tried to sound cheerful as he wound his arm around her. 'I hate it too, but I have to go where I'm sent. I'll be back as soon as I can, though.' Glancing vaguely towards the corner where his father slept, he was the only one who noticed a surreptitious hand grope around from behind the chair, grab the pipe that had fallen onto his chest and spirit it away out of sight, a few rapid puffs of smoke arising before the pipe was returned to the slumberer's chest. He smiled to himself, remembering a time when he had played this trick, and did not give Jimmy-Joe away.

Red awoke with a startled harrumph and picked up his pipe as if nothing had occurred.

'What would happen if you didn't do as you were told?' ventured Edward.

'I'd be locked up, no question.'

Alex joined the coercion. 'You could always wear a disguise.'

'I could.' Marty squatted to address her, taking a handful of her long dark hair and arranging it round his chin. 'What do I look like with a beard?' Succeeding in making his children laugh, he patted Alex and rose. 'Ah no, 'tis away I must go and no argument.'

A hoarse old voice invaded the moment of poignancy. 'Why, you'd think he was being sent to the North Pole the way you're carrying on.' Uncle Mal might be shrunken to a bundle of twigs, but his boastful nature was not. 'Compared to the places I've been 'tis a stone's throw. Jamaica, New Zealand –'

'My God, don't get him started,' Aggie begged the children, then to her son, 'Ah, sure we'll be sad not to see ye, darlin', specially the way things are for you.' To cover her own upset she sprang up to flit about the room. 'But sure, I might as well make use of your trip by giving you a few things to take with yese. Now let me see . . .' She began to gather various items, instructing her son on their purpose. 'This here is for your Uncle Mick, and that's for Patty Doran who lives in Tullamore, he lent me it years ago and I never –'

'Ma!' Marty laughed, 'I'm not going on holiday! I'll be stationed in Belfast, I can't go leppin about all over Ireland.'

Aggie nodded and put a curb on her enthusiastic gathering. 'Indeed – but now ye must go and see all the ould folk when ye get the chance.'

'I will,' he promised, then turned his attention back to Celia and the others to try and make the most of the time he had left.

But as the moment drew nearer for him to depart he became increasingly less chatty, unable to concentrate on anything other than the coming separation from his children. Feeling wretched, he rose and went out to the lavatory. When he came back his mother was in the scullery, waiting to pose the question she had been itching all week to ask.

'Tell me, son, are ye still seeing the other one?'

Knowing she meant Amelia and fearing a tongue-lashing, he shook his head. 'That was put paid to straightaway.'

'Ah that's a great relief,' was all she said as she quietly patted his arm.

'Is it?' he tendered dully. 'I don't know that it'll do me any good.'

Aggie cocked her wizened face and gave shrewd reply. 'You never know. I shall tell Etta anyway, that it's all over and done with.'

'And so is my leave, I'm afraid.' He heaved a great sigh and bent to kiss her cheek, then went back into the living room to say goodbye to everyone there, shaking hands with his father and Uncle Mal and his brothers.

'Won't you stay with us, Father?' Edward made a last-ditch entreaty.

'I can't, son, I've told you I'd be in big trouble.'

Edward started to cry. Immediately twelve-year-old Tom stepped in. 'Away now, come and tell the fairies about that loose tooth of yours.' He lifted the little boy up to the mantel clock wherein lived the fairies.

Fighting emotion, trying to jolly everyone, Marty reached out and ruffled Edward's hair. 'I promise I'll come to see you all again as soon as I get back from Ireland.' So saying, he kissed each one, sweeping the youngest up into the crook of his arm.

'May we walk with you to the end of the street?' asked Celia.

Though it would make the parting a thousand times harder he said they could, and, lowering baby William back to the carpet, he took hold of his daughter's hand. There was an immediate fight as to who would hold the other, Alex refusing to give sway. In the end, Edward was placated by being allowed to wear the soldier's cap. Then it was finally time to go.

They had sworn to be good and go straight back down the street when it was time for their father to part, but once arrived at the junction they tried to cajole him. 'Come to the shop with us and see Mother.'

'Ah no,' he said softly, 'I've still to pick up my bag from Aunty Lou's, if I go anywhere else I'll miss my train – give us a kiss now and run home to Granny.'

They complied with the first part, but Celia had a last question. 'Will you ever live with us and Mother again?'

Stabbed through the heart, he could only reply, 'I don't know, honey. I'd love to, but your mammy . . . Look, I really have to go! Off you run home now.' And after an authoritative gesture which set them on the correct route, he turned and strode away.

Hard at work in the provisions shop on Walmgate, Etta was weighing out bags of sugar when she caught sight of her husband passing the window and her heart leapt to the skies. Nothing had changed, nothing and everything, for in spite of his betrayal the overwhelming desire she held for Marty was as strong as ever. As if by some sixth sense he felt her watching him and turned towards the window. Panicking, she immediately wheeled away to busy herself. When she looked out again he had gone.

Her heart had still not reverted to its normal rhythm when Aggie came into the shop some half an hour later to say in confidential whisper, 'I thought to let ye know the lad's gone, so you're safe to come home whenever ye like.'

Etta nodded and continued scooping sugar onto the scales, then into pound bags, not mentioning that she had seen him.

Aggie turned to go, then thought to inform her daughter-in-law, 'He told me he isn't seeing that other one any more, hasn't been for a long time.'

Etta shrugged as if she did not care, at which point her mother-in-law left the shop. Only then did Etta allow her façade to drop, and she stared out into the street, envisioning Marty walking straight past her again and again.

16

Notwithstanding the money orders, Etta was to hear nothing more from her husband until Christmas, when, out of the blue, a very elaborate card arrived from Ireland, along with a one-page letter and some small gifts for the children. She was far from elated. Just when it felt that her heart had begun to heal, that she could face the day without the yawning bleakness he had left in his wake, he had to go and stir it all up again.

She did not reply.

This seemed not to deter Marty, for he sent another letter at Easter, again to no acknowledgement from Etta, and another in summer. This latest one, however, demanded a response.

Dear Etta, she read with pursed lips, *I won't bore you with all the things that are going on over here as I don't suppose you are that bothered. This is just to tell you once again that I truly regret all the hurt I have caused you. There is nothing I would like more than for us to be man and wife again, and if I thought there was a chance I would keep on trying, but as I have heard nothing from you I don't know where I stand. Can you please let me know whether I am wasting my time and I will stop pestering you. If I don't hear I will take it to mean that our marriage is finally over and I will not write again . . .*

There was no room for complacency now. She had finally

been made to face the question: Did she want him back or not? If anything, Etta felt even angrier with him for forcing her into this decision. She did reply, but her nib was tipped with vitriol, asking how dare he put her in this position? *I have done nothing wrong, you're the one who deserted me and found someone else. You're deliberately putting me on the spot so you can say to the children that their mother was the one who wrecked this marriage, that you tried your best to reconcile but Mother wouldn't have it – well, I won't be browbeaten . . .*

And a furious husband dashed back a reply in similar vein: *How can you say you've done nothing wrong? I've a scar on my head to prove it.*

Well, I'm certainly not going to get a reply to that, thought Marty. But if this was the end then he might as well purge himself of all other resentments, and this he proceeded to do, scribbling down as many as he could recount before ramming them into an envelope that was much thicker than usual and sealing the flap with an angry bash from the edge of his fist.

For a couple of desolate weeks it appeared that his candid epistle had indeed set the final seal on a dying marriage, and, with nothing else to live for save the hope that he might one day see his children again, Marty devoted himself to the rigorous regime of the army. Then, one morning, a response arrived. Less than excited, for it would be nothing good for sure, he opened it with trepid fingers, wondering how stingingly inventive she had been this time with her attempt to have the last word. But, to his great surprise, the tone of the letter was conciliatory, sheepish even. Yes, Etta accepted much of what he said: she was a deficient housewife, perhaps she could have done more – she had failed to appreciate how hard he had worked to provide food and shelter . . . yes, of course he must keep in touch for the children's sake . . . she would try to be more civil to him in future . . . No words of love, but at last a shred

359

of hope. Marty's grim expression was transformed into one of astonished pleasure.

'On a promise, are we?'

He glanced up from the letter to find himself under amused observation from fellow soldiers.

'He's looking very pleased with himself.' Private Burns's eye held a knowing gleam as it winked at his comrades. 'In my experience there's only one thing produces a grin like that.'

'Ah no, I wouldn't go so far as to say it's a promise.' Fingering the letter, Marty stared into the distance for a while before turning to his wife's words again. 'But we live in hope, my friend, we live in hope.'

Throughout the rest of 1913 the correspondence between Marty and Etta was to become more civilised – warm even, which was perhaps understandable when the topics under discussion were their children, whom both adored. Not once, though, apart from being a fraction less hostile, did Etta give Marty any cause to believe that she had forgiven him or might some day take him back; nor dared he risk their current fragile rapport by posing the question outright. He must for the present be satisfied with the concession she was prepared to make.

However, this was considerable when measured against the state of affairs between them a year ago, and when Marty received a card from her on his second Christmas in Ireland and an invitation to commune with his entire family upon his return, one would have thought she had given him the world. Being forced to wait three more months before this came to fruition was absolute torture.

Eventually, though, the order was received for he and his pals to embark for home, whereupon they were granted passes to visit family and friends whom they had not seen for over eighteen months. Marty was first out of barracks, nervous as a child on its first day at school as he boarded the morning train to York.

Perhaps he should have written first. The look on Etta's face when she heard someone enter and turned to see the identity of the visitor could have sent lesser men dashing for cover.

'Sorry if I made you jump!' he said quickly, hoping to convey with his apologetic smile and his shining eyes just how glad he was to see her again.

'Yes, you did!' Face bright red as she turned from the mirror, she didn't seem at all pleased to see him.

'It's just that you said for me to visit when I came home . . .'

'It might have been an idea to send prior warning!' Shocked that his impromptu appearance should have such a heart-tugging effect on her, angry that he seemed to think just because she had been civil in her letters he could waltz in here unannounced with that smile of his – and just as angry with herself for being moved by it – she donned her white overall and, along with it, her composure, adding aloofly, 'Everyone's out, I'm afraid – and I'm just about to leave too. I'm due at work in five minutes.' She grabbed two black patent-leather armlets, used to protect the sleeves of her overall, and shoved one over each wrist.

Though his heart sank, Marty accepted the rebuke without question and turned to leave. 'Right, I'll go round to Lou's then and call again when it's more convenient.'

Already regretting her cool welcome, Etta called hastily, 'The children will be in around four!' When he turned back she added in what she hoped was a reasonable tone, 'Everyone else has gone to a funeral.'

Marty frowned. 'Who –?'

'Oh, it's only Mrs Doyle.' Swiftly she placated the look of concern. 'The old girl at twenty-four.'

That was a relief at least. He gave a quick nod. 'Right, I'll be back this afternoon then.' And without another word he left, feeling vastly disappointed both with the reception and the lack of invitation to dinner, his stomach feeling as raw as his emotions.

Etta sagged. If only he could see into her heart, seen how it had leapt for joy at the sight of those shining green-grey eyes in the tanned face, how much she wanted to rush to him, hold him, press her cheek against his own, once so beloved . . . but after all the hurtful exchanges she was too afraid of rejection. Besides, had he not betrayed her?

Heart still pounding, limbs weak from shock, she scribbled a brief note to let Aggie and Red know of their son's whereabouts then left for work.

Arriving home from the funeral, Aggie was instantly uplifted to hear of her son's homecoming and set off across town to her eldest daughter's abode, therein spending much of the afternoon catching up with Marty's news.

Around three thirty, though, she was forced to rise. 'Well, I'd better be getting back for the kiddiwinkles or Uncle Mal will be teaching them bad habits. You'll be coming with me, son?'

'Ah, no.' His face reluctant, he brushed vaguely at his trousers. 'I fully intended to, but the reception I got this morning from me wife, well, I think I'd best give her time to calm down.'

His mother was dismissive, Louisa chipping in with strenuous agreement. 'Pay no heed to that one! You've a right to see your children.'

'All the same, Ma, I'll leave it till tomorrow – it being Saturday like, I can enjoy a whole day with them – and you and Da,' he added hastily.

With an understanding nod, Aggie went to the door. 'You've seen plenty enough of me for the moment, and your father will wait. We'll go pay your Aunty Carmel a visit. I'll make sure we're all out by half past nine so you can have a few hours in peace with your family before dinner.'

'Sure, I don't know about peace,' said Marty, but his smile was appreciative.

Uncle Mal was none too appreciative at being told he must be out of the house so early, and in a starched collar and suit too. ''Tis only Marty who's coming, not the Queen of Sheba. Why must my routine be buggered up?'

'God in heaven, one would think ye had the country to run!' scolded Aggie. 'You can sit in Carmel's closet all morning, if ye so choose.'

Still his wrinkled old face protested. 'I can't go in a strange lavatory.'

'Sure, isn't one blessed lavatory the same as any other!'

'Tell that to my haemorrhoids,' grumbled Mal. 'Once my routine's mucked up they'll be swinging like a bunch of grapes for wee—'

'*Thank* you!' Palm upraised, eyes disdainful, Aggie spoke over him. 'Haven't we been educated enough on your habits for one morning. Now get your coat on – are you three ready yet?' This to Red and the boys.

'There's really no need for you all to be put out like this,' said Etta, watching the exodus.

'How can the pair of you sort things out with this old relict so keen to regale us with his plumbing?' Aggie jabbed a thumb over her shoulder at the old man.

'There'll be little discussed with the children here,' pointed out Etta.

'That's true enough.' Aggie was thoughtful as she buttoned her brown coat. 'Well, maybe I could take them out for a while this afternoon, give you and Marty time to patch up your differences.'

'It will take a lot longer than an afternoon.' Etta felt as if she were being corralled into a reconciliation. 'Besides, I'll be at work.'

Aggie tutted. 'Ach, I forgot – well, how about tomorrow then?' She put on a brown felt hat.

'I'm not even sure what I want,' argued Etta.

'Nevertheless,' Aggie persisted as she handed out caps to the males, 'the longer the pair of you are left to your own devices the more space you'll have to consider it. Now, 'tis a cold dinner so there's nothing for you to see to.'

'Thank you,' replied Etta sincerely.

'We'll be back at noon.' Aggie turned to follow her menfolk from the house but found Red still there. 'God help us, the wretch has dropped off again, and him keeping me awake the entire night!' She jabbed him.

'Wha –, who –?' Red awoke, completely disorientated.

'We're going to Carmel's!' Aggie reminded him, her voice betraying impatience as she attempted to haul him to his feet.

The boys were called back to help their father on his way. Etta looked on, sharing some of her mother-in-law's irritation over this strange ailment that disrupted the entire household. It was not even consistent. Sometimes, Red would wake and continue his sentences, yet at other times it was as if his memory had been wiped clean.

With her menfolk finally evacuated, Aggie delayed her own exit to throw a few disgruntled words at Etta, ''Tis all right for him, he can catch up with his sleep any time he likes – if I'd known what I'd have to put up with before I married him . . . !'

It had been meant as a quip, but, now that there were only the two of them there, Etta, with her own troubled marriage in mind, enquired out of interest, 'Was his affliction not always evident?'

Taken by surprise at this intimate query, Aggie was hesitant in her reply. 'Why, no, we'd been together three years before it showed.'

'But, if you had known what was to come,' Etta pressed gently, anxiously, 'would it have made a difference? Would you still have married him?' She seemed to remember her manners then and added quickly, 'I'm sorry, it's most rude of me to pry . . .'

'No, no . . .' Aggie gave the question but a moment's thought, repositioning her hat before announcing with genuine assurance, 'Yes, I would, because Red is the sweetest creature I ever met. I loved him the minute I laid eyes on him.' She looked suddenly embarrassed over this declaration, adding flippantly, 'And me with a heart like a slab of stone.'

'I know that's untrue,' smiled Etta.

'Hah! Well don't go asking himself the same question, I'm not sure the answer you'd get!' Her mother-in-law started to back out before any more probing questions could be asked. 'Whatever the case, with nine children between us and no one else likely to put up with our faults, we're stuck with each other – right, I'm off!' And hoping she had left Etta with food for thought, she hurriedly withdrew.

Etta heaved a nervous sigh and contemplated Marty's arrival.

Informed that their father was coming, the children had been waiting for him on the pavement, and as Marty turned into Hope Street he saw them hovering excitedly at the sight of him. But they did not immediately abandon their bunch of playmates, and after so long an absence their apprehensive expressions showed they would have to get used to him all over again.

'Who's that?' he heard a snotty-nosed boy ask as he gave them a wave in approaching.

'It's our father,' answered Celia.

'Didn't know you had a dad. Why doesn't he live with you?'

None of Marty's children replied, their attention glued to their father, who eventually reached them. He smiled a greeting and ushered them indoors.

Etta was waiting to meet him, and all the old feelings came rushing back for them both.

But for Etta there was still much in the way. Her hands clasped protectively in front of her, she noted the scar on his forehead that disappeared into his hairline, before offering an awkward apology. 'I'm sorry about yester—'

'No harm done!' He tried to sound carefree. 'I should have written to warn you.'

Unsure whether or not she would accept his kiss, Marty took a faltering step towards her then thought better of it and handed over the flowers he had bought on the way there. 'I don't know what they are. Narcissus, I think the woman said, and flit—, thrit— God, I can't even get me tongue round it!'

'Fritillaries,' supplied Etta, then added an appreciative murmur and held them to her nose. 'They're lovely, thank you. Would you like a cup of tea?'

He nodded and rubbed his hands self-consciously. 'That'll be grand.'

Whilst Etta turned away to brew the tea and then to put the flowers in water, Marty turned to his children, who were still beholding him with shy smiles. 'No school today?'

'It's Saturday!' Celia laughed.

'So it is, what an eejit.' Marty feigned stupidity and pulled a face, causing the youngsters to laugh too and inch closer.

'Well now . . . haven't you all shot up?' The last time he had been there William had been a baby. Now he was three. Pretending not to see him peeping from behind a chair, Marty frowned and looked about him. 'But are there only the three o' yese? I thought there was another . . .'

Chortling, the others pointed.

'Sure, is that our Willie? Why, I'd never have recognised him he's grown so big – and look at the cut of Eddie, why he's almost a man!' Gradually their inhibitions began to wane and they gathered round to drape themselves over his limbs. 'And what have you all been learning at school while I've been away?'

Alex jumped in first, her warm little hands pressed to his thigh. 'Mr Brown taught us about mountain climbing.'

'Is that so? There's a lot of call for that in York.' Marty chanced a grin at Etta who smiled benignly as she placed the vase of flowers on the table.

Then Marty gave an exclamation. 'I think it's somebody's birthday coming up soon, is it not?'

Both Celia and Edward bellowed into his face, 'Mine!'

Their father pretended to be deafened, then reached into his pocket. 'Here you are then.' He presented the eight-year-old with an embroidered handkerchief. 'Look, it's got a C for Celia on it – come all the way from Ireland with the shamrocks on it an' all. And this is for you.' He handed over a tin whistle to Eddie.

'Oh, thank you most kindly,' Etta offered insincerely at the discordant shrieks that followed, 'I'll enjoy listening to that.' But a wry smile overthrew the look of disapproval.

Marty smiled back, aching to take her in his arms. Then, turning again to his children he saw that Alex and Willie were looking extremely disappointed and he quickly appeased them. 'I know it isn't your birthdays for a while, but I thought I'd bring the pair of you an early gift.' And out came some emerald-green ribbon for his daughter and a bubble pipe for the youngest.

'Grandad!' Willie stuck the pipe in his mouth, crouched over and puffed on it in an imitation of his grandfather, making the adults laugh.

Etta patted the little boy fondly. 'I shall make you some bubbles for it later if you sit quietly and allow Father and I to talk.'

'And to make it easier, here, take these.' Their father handed over four sticks of barley sugar, which were eagerly grabbed.

Then, whilst the children's mouths were occupied, Marty sat back in a wicker chair and, over a cup of tea, looked warmly at his wife who was now seated opposite. 'Well, now . . . here we are.'

Her only response was a faint smile and a sip from her cup. She looked far from relaxed.

Faced with such lack of communication, Marty saw that the first move must be his. He set his cup and saucer aside. 'You can't know how much I've longed for this, Ett.'

Briefly her eyes caressed him yet remained guarded, this wariness displayed in her change of topic. 'How many years have you to serve?'

'Another three, I'm afraid.' He looked gloomy. 'I won't be out till 1917.'

'Still, you're looking very healthy on it.' Despite inner reservations, Etta found herself issuing this compliment, then, hoping to disguise just how wonderfully attractive she found him, raised her cup to her lips.

He grinned. 'All that fresh air and exercise – and might I say you're looking very well yourself.'

With a diffident tilt to her head she took another quick sip of her tea, concentrating more on this than on him.

There was a lengthy silence, then Marty asked outright, 'D'you think you'll ever forgive me, Ett?'

'Right, children!' She put aside her cup and jumped up with artificial gaiety. 'Time to make those bubbles!'

Interpreting this act of cowardice, Marty set his jaw and dealt his children a sad smile as all abandoned him in their exodus for the yard.

But when Etta left them playing and returned to her seat and to sip from her half-finished teacup, she was to face the same daunting question.

'So, now they're out of the way, you can speak frankly. Will you ever forgive me?'

Even with the children gone she felt reluctant to embark on intimate discussion, forcing herself to look up into his face, studying him deeply, then, after another long interval, said simply, 'I don't know, Martin.'

His tone and expression disputed this. 'You must have some idea how you feel.'

Immediately she bristled. 'How can you expect me just to forget about your other so-called wife?'

'I don't expect that!' He put aside his cup, the wicker chair creaking as he leaned forward earnestly. 'I wasn't being pushy, I just want you to know that I never felt for her what I feel for you.' He shifted onto the very edge of his chair, wanting desperately to stroke her, to make her see. 'I mean, Amelia was a lovely person but –'

'Don't!' She held up a hand to silence him, her cup and saucer rattling in protest.

'I'm just trying to –'

'I don't want to know!' Her dark eyes teemed with suppressed horror, even the woman's name causing affront.

Marty gave a nod of surrender, and, sitting back in his chair and retrieving his cup of tea, was to utter naught of substance for the remainder of the morning. He just waffled on about what he had been doing in Ireland, the people he had met, the weather, anything to disguise the long silences and the creaking of the wicker chair.

Hence, when Aggie and the rest of the family returned there had been nothing more intimate than a few exchanged smiles. Weighed down by defeat, now that others were here and wanting to share news, Marty did not let it show but chatted amiably, projecting marvel when Uncle Mal boasted, 'I'm eighty-eight, now ye know, Marty,' though throughout he constantly watched Etta from the corner of his eye.

After dinner, with his wife at work that afternoon there was no hope of any attempt at conciliation, and so he was to pass the time by taking his children for a walk, aided by his younger brothers, and afterwards helping his father sort through a pile of scrap metal.

Seeing him still there when she got back in the evening, Etta was alarmed that Aggie might be trying to engineer them into spending the night in the same bed, at which she would have strenuously protested, but, half an hour after the children had gone upstairs Marty patted his knees and rose, saying it was time he too was making a move.

'Will you be coming for dinner tomorrow?' asked his father.

He glanced humbly at Etta. 'If I'm welcome.'

Upon her brief nod, he said he would look forward to it, then left.

'Sure, your man's looking as handsome as a mackerel,' opined Uncle Mal after the door had closed on Marty, to which there were nods and murmurs of agreement, except from Etta, who sat quietly contemplating her husband's return.

On Sunday afternoon, after much serious thought overnight, Etta deigned to accompany Marty on his walk with the children around Heslington, although other than this the day was spent much the same as the day before, with nothing of significance being uttered between them.

On Monday the children went back to school, but not without posing the anxious query: would Father still be there when they came home?

Much to their relief, Father *was* there and continued to be so for much of the week, during which the atmosphere between the parents improved so well that by Wednesday Marty was almost back to his old jaunty self, in his children's eyes at least. For some reason this appeared to make Etta peeved, for she snapped at him out of the blue that he needn't think that fatherly duties were confined to having fun and games – Alexandra had a toothache, he could take her to have the offending molar removed by the cobbler's pincers. However, that he did this without quibble seemed to win her over and they were soon once again on an even keel.

Though privately frantic that nothing had been settled between himself and his wife, Marty wanted to make this, his last evening, an event that his children would remember, and was in the throes of organising a shadowgraph theatre for them, his deeper intention being to have that vital conversation with Etta once the show was over and they had gone to bed. Considerately, his parents and Uncle Mal were off visiting another relative. There were still his younger brothers to be taken care of but that would be relatively easy to fix, and he did so now.

'This is going to be too tame for a man of your years, Tom, so here y'are!' He handed over a sixpence. 'Take yourself and Jimmy-Joe off for some chips or fags or whatever takes your fancy.'

Issuing effusive thanks, his brothers grabbed their coats and dashed off.

'Right!' Marty clapped his hands and, with a sheet strung across the room, he addressed his young audience who sat cross-legged on the floor. 'Do I have everyone's attention?'

Alex bemoaned to her brother, 'Jesus, Mary 'n' Joseph, will you ever stop tooting that bloody whistle!'

Stunned, and only now realising that her children were developing an Irish accent, Etta gaped at Marty, the spark of amusement kindling in both their eyes, before she responded firmly, 'That's quite enough of that, thank you! Father is speaking.'

Marty put aside his mirth and took on the role of compere. 'Thank you, Mother – if you'd be so kind as to pass me that lamp and draw the curtains, I should like to introduce you to The Great – the *Magnificent* – Lanegano!'

Etta chuckled as she took her seat and her husband gave a bow. 'Lanegano?'

'Oh, ye must have an Italian name if you're a showman,' he instructed her and the children with a most serious expression, 'it's compulsory. Now, using only my bare hands, I shall begin!' With a last flourish he dived behind the curtain where, with the aid of a strategically placed lamp, he was to project onto the sheet a series of impres-

371

sions. 'First – a rabbit!' Encouraged by the round of polite applause instigated by his wife, he went on, 'Next – a horse!'

Etta chuckled again. 'It looks the same as the rabbit.'

Marty's head popped from behind the curtain. 'You're splitting hairs – hares, get it?' At the laughing groans he grinned and ducked back behind the curtain, there to perform for the next fifteen minutes or so a menagerie of silhouettes with his hands, often having to repeat the same ones several times, his repertoire being limited. But the children seemed greatly impressed, as did Etta, who instigated the round of applause which followed and also led calls of, 'Encore!'

Afterwards there was tea and bread for supper, then finally it was time for Marty to give his children one last kiss, a time he had been dreading, for until now they had no idea that he would not be there tomorrow when they came in from school.

Naturally they could not hide their disappointment and anxiety, Alex wanting to know, 'Will you be coming back?'

Before he could respond, Etta cut in, 'Of course he will!'

Heartened by this, Marty used similar endorsement. 'Of course I will – as soon as the army'll let me. They're a bit stingy with the leave so it might not be till summer, but be assured I'll be back. Be good for your mammy now.' He gave each one a tight hug, inhaling each individual scent before waving brightly as Etta took them off to bed.

But the moment they had gone he sank onto the sofa and rubbed his hands over a face that was drawn and worried. He was left to contemplate this state of despair for a good five minutes, Etta having to supervise prayers, to tuck each child in and to pay them the appropriate amount of affection before coming down, finally, to sit beside her husband.

'Well, they seemed to enjoy your little theatre.' She smiled at him.

'Does that mean you didn't? I'm hurt.' He pretended to look wounded, though in fact he was heartened by her proximity.

'No, no,' she chuckled, 'I thoroughly enjoyed it too.'

'Even if the horses looked the same as rabbits?' he joked.

'Oh, I was only teasing.' She did not look at him directly, for the lazy droop of those eyelids and the sensuous bow of those lips had such magnetic appeal that she feared she might spontaneously weaken, but her voice was kind. 'They were really very good.'

'Ah, well.' He stretched his limbs for no particular reason. 'I've had a lot of time to practise – army life can be very boring.'

Etta nodded thoughtfully, then maintained the topic. 'Have you anything else in your repertoire?'

He shook his head. Then a wicked glint appeared in his eye. 'Oh, hang on, you might like this, though.' Reaching for a packet, he removed the one cigarette that was in it and put it on the table then began to fold and tear little sections from the flattened card, eventually handing her the result.

'Oh, it's a little man,' smiled Etta.

'Pull on his feet,' advised Marty.

Intrigued, she did as instructed and was rewarded by the appearance of an extra piece of male anatomy and immediately gasped over this risqué performance and dealt him a scolding. 'That's completely outrageous!' But it was delivered with a laugh and he laughed too and leaned towards her in intimate fashion, his eyes twinkling. 'Not really the thing to do for a man desperate to be forgiven, is it?'

'It most certainly is not!' For a brief moment her eyes sparkled back at him. 'Naughty boy, now behave, or I shall put you in the corner and make you recite fritillaries a hundred times.'

He continued to smile at her warmly, his eyes holding a certain plea. 'And after that might I hope for absolution?'

When she did not immediately reply, though her gaze remained warm, he added, 'Seriously, Ett, we need to discuss what's going to happen to us: am I just to keep visiting like this or can I expect something more permanent?'

Her face altered then and she looked away, quickly objecting, 'It's too much of a rush.'

'I have to rush.' He seized her hand imploringly. 'I'm leaving tomorrow. I don't know when we might get the chance to talk again. We've been getting along well this week, haven't we?'

'Well enough.' Her heart had begun to race and she extricated her fingers from his grip. To Etta the act of holding hands was one of the deepest intimacies a couple could enjoy, and she would not reinstate it lightly. 'But you can't expect an instant transformation, Martin.'

'I don't expect one, especially after what's happened, what I did . . .' He looked at his rejected fingers for a while, picking at his nails, trying to summon the words, then he looked up at her again. 'But even in the middle of it all I never stopped loving you, Ett. I always will.'

Frowning, she turned again to study him, her heart and mind at war. Much as her body leapt with desire for that lovely face, to be held in those arms, to press her mouth to those beautiful lips, another instinct warned that this would be letting herself down. It had been bad enough him running away, though in the circumstances it had been understandable and she could have eventually forgiven that digression, but his infidelity had wounded her too deeply . . . How could she be sure that if she allowed him back into her life he would not do it again? How could she even be sure that she herself would ever be able to allow him to touch her without the loathsome image of that other woman in between them?

She took a deep breath. 'We've only been together a matter of days, and in someone else's house. How can we possibly know how things would be?'

He thought he caught a glimmer of surrender in her eyes and quickly took advantage. 'I've been thinking about that. Maybe you could move down to Lichfi—'

'I'm not dragging the children down there, away from everyone!'

'Hear me out!' he urged earnestly. 'You wouldn't be living in barracks, we could rent a nice house and I could apply for a pass so's I could get to see you more regularly.' His transgression with the bogus 'wife' had long been forgotten by his commanding officer if not by Etta, 'It'd give us more chance to be like a family again – see, as things stand I'll only be able to get up here every once in a while, and with three more years to serve –'

'No!' she intervened loudly. Unnerved by the closeness of him, she shuffled along the sofa to insert a space. 'Stop trying to bully me, Martin.'

'I'm not!' he cried instantly.

'You are!' This was getting dangerously close to an argument. Etta toned down her response. 'You might not mean to – but you seem to think everything must revolve around your needs, and there are five other people involved. Now, let's maintain the status quo for a while and see what happens.'

'But I might not get up again for months!'

'Then it will give each of us time to consider what went wrong before so that it doesn't happen again – take things slowly.'

Disappointed, he was forced to nod compliance. If she wanted him to court her then he would. In the pensive interval that followed, he pondered on how ironic this was: there had never been the need to woo her before their marriage, her impulsive streak had matched his own and she had needed no persuasion to run away with him.

She felt him watching her, wondered over the thoughts that might be going through his mind, then said, 'I don't think you'll ever really understand how much you hurt me.'

At her words his face crumpled, and he tried unsuccessfully to put a hand to her cheek. 'I'm so sorry, oh God, I've been such a bloody fool. If I could turn back the clock, get back what we had –'

'You can't,' she said bluntly.

He looked devastated. 'But you led me to believe –'

'That I'll try,' she corrected him firmly. 'But even if we do get back together, things can never be as they were.'

How much more of this scourging could he take? A hint of irrevocability burdened his tone as he realised that even if he did take this as slowly as she demanded, there was no hope of a total healing. 'Then I don't know if I'll be able to stand it,' he told her, 'being near you but having you hate me.'

Etta sat back slightly and furrowed her brow. 'You're the father of my children, how could I hate you? I don't ever recall saying I did.'

'But you've stopped loving me.'

'I don't recall saying that either.'

His eyes flickered with renewed hope as he said cautiously, 'So, you do still feel something?'

'I feel all manner of things – betrayal, grief, wretchedness . . .' Those feelings came rushing back to choke her now, to override any physical desire, causing her eyes to burn and glisten, '. . . but I never stopped loving you.'

He heaved with relief and made a lunge for her, but she pressed a hand to his chest to fend him off. 'I meant what I said about taking things slowly.'

Forced to sit back, Marty nodded and studied her, looking deep into her eyes before folding his arms gently around her and holding her to him until the sound of the back gate broke the spell.

When Aggie and the men came in, Marty and Etta were seated as distantly from each other as ever. But something in her son's demeanour told Aggie that things had changed for the better, and when he finally made to leave she dared to suggest that he might like to spend his last night there.

'You could sleep on the sofa in here,' she said hurriedly lest Etta thought she was trying to arrange some kind of rapprochement. 'No call wasting your leave if you're not due back till nightfall, and 'twould be nice to give the nippers a few more hours with their daddy before ye have to catch your train – they could come and wave you off at the railway station.'

'Oh, Christ, no,' said Marty with feeling, shutting his eyes against the very thought. It would be difficult enough leaving as it was. He donned his coat, then formed a goodbye to his wife, a sad smile on his lips.

Experiencing similar emotions, Etta sought to offer compassion. 'Well, I'm sure you'll be back to see us in no time.'

17

Unable to communicate with his wife in any other way than by letter, and unskilled in the art of poetry, during the next couple of months Marty struggled to court her with only the aid of pencil and paper. But how? It never even occurred to him to begin *my dearest darling wife*, which was the thought that was in his heart – much too embarrassing for a working man – yet *Dear Etta* sounded as if he were addressing a mere acquaintance. Even *My dearest wife* was not right at all – it could lead her to believe he was drawing comparisons between her and Amelia. Well, that might be true in a way, he did think of Amelia occasionally, how could he not when she had been there for him in a time of crisis, providing for his needs? But not for a second had he considered her his one true love; that crown belonged to Etta . . . though how to make her believe this was a daunting task. Back to where he had started, he heaved a sigh, licked the tip of his pencil and began in the time-honoured fashion, hoping that the simple terms he used to convey his longing might one day lead her to share the sentiment.

Etta did share it – at least in the struggle to communi-cate her feelings. Unable to afford either the time or the money to visit him, a letter was a poor substitute and, with absence lending her the time to reflect on how she had felt at their last meeting, she found herself yearning to commune with him again in the flesh.

Looking back, as their weekly missives piled up, neither of them could pinpoint a date when the realisation dawned that there was going to be a war in Europe. For Etta the threat was nebulous, gleaned through outpourings of doom from Uncle Mal and, ignored as senile rambling, relegated to the back of her mind by the more immediate concern of civil unrest nearer to home. 'I do hope this trouble in Ireland dies down soon,' she expressed her concerns to Aggie, who responded with a fatalistic sigh:

'There'll always be trouble in Ireland. 'Tis the nature of the place.'

'Yes, but they're talking about a civil war . . .' Etta's gaze was distant and anxious. 'I couldn't stand it if Marty were dragged back there to put his life at risk, before we've had a chance to be together again, properly I mean . . .'

And with her mind focused thus, she had no inkling that they might be parted through another violent source.

For Marty, though, the grave conclusion was reached much earlier. There had been rumours flying around for weeks that a European war could be imminent, though neither he nor his fellow soldiers had taken it seriously at first – the German Kaiser had always been a gasbag and the supposed threat a couple of years back had come to nothing – but now, to growing unease, clues had begun to appear that they were indeed being prepared for active service. Training had become more rigorous; battalion orders gave a list of requirements that must be carried in their pack at parade; each man must conserve his own ration as on the battlefield. He could not bring himself to reveal these fears in his letters, allowing Etta to assume that the only reason he had not yet been up to visit her was that leave was doled out sparingly, when in actual fact all passes had been cancelled. Now, however, the Germans had invaded Belgium and only a fool could not see what lay ahead. For some this manifested itself in panic buying, provision stores being inundated with requests for bacon

379

and flour, keeping Etta so busy that by the close of one humid August afternoon there was not an ounce left for her to take home for tea. But for her there was much greater concern than lining one's belly, and for Marty too.

When the announcement finally came a great cheer went up throughout the barracks along with a fervent desire to be at the murderous Hun, a will that resounded across the breadth of England. Were Marty and Etta the only ones whose blood ran cold? It mattered not that it was to be a short war – over by Christmas, everyone opined – but Marty's fatalistic streak told him that a man could be killed on his first day out, and sure as hell that man would be himself. More desperate than ever to reconcile with his wife, he rushed to apply for leave to visit her, his normally unsympathetic sergeant championing his application to the company commander.

Captain Palm appraised the situation compassionately. The battalion could go nowhere until it was up to full strength and they were still waiting for some reservists to arrive. Most of the other married men had their wives and children, if not living in barracks, then in the near vicinity. Aware that Lanegan – or Lonergan as he called him still despite the records being amended – had been attempting to repair his marriage, he asked, 'Can you manage to be there and back and do what you have to between now and tattoo?'

'Yes, sir!' barked Marty without consulting a clock, though knowing it was going to be a terrible rush for it was now mid-morning.

'Then I shall grant your request – but on the strict understanding that you'll be packed up and ready to march the instant you return.' Captain Palm briskly stamped the pass and handed it over.

Portraying gratitude, Marty rushed to store his personal chattels in his ditty-box, folding his dress tunic and white belt into tissue paper in order to keep them clean, for it might be weeks before he needed them again. Then, with everything done, he hurried to the station.

With the schools being closed for the summer holiday there were children everywhere, many of them chattering excitedly about the war to him and any other soldier on the platform. He tried to be pleasant, whilst inside his stomach churned at the thought that such conversation with his own sons and daughters would be limited: by the time he reached York it would be almost time to come back. But it was thoughts of Etta that concerned him most. If only he could have telegraphed ahead to let her know he was coming . . .

Finally arriving in York, he was first off the train and almost elbowing people aside in his haste to reach the cab rank. Luckily there was no queue, but the traffic was dreadful, most of it being caused by the military, and to his agitation it took twice as long as normal to get to Hope Street. Once at his mother's house he grabbed the door knob but one twist told him it was locked and that could only mean that everyone would be out for the day. Damn! He rubbed an agitated hand over his jaw, his grey-green eyes searching for an answer. There was no problem getting in, all he had to do was stick his hand through the letter box and retrieve the key on its piece of string, but what would be the point when there was no one home? On his way here in the cab he had craned his neck to peer into the shop where his wife worked and had not seen her, but now, thinking he could have been mistaken, he ran back to check. Informed by another assistant that it was Etta's afternoon off he began an immediate search for her, starting with his eldest sister's abode.

In the middle of ironing, Lou was at first shocked when he burst into her kitchen, then her face lit up in welcome. 'Hello, stranger!'

Breathing heavily, for he had run all the way through town, he asked, 'Is Ma here? . . . Sorry, Lou, that was no greeting, how are ye?' He grabbed her to dab an appeasing kiss to her cheek, adding quickly, 'But I've only a few hours –'

'Oh, Marty, they've all gone to Scarborough!' Louisa abandoned her ironing to concentrate on him, her eyes oozing sympathy.

'What, Etta too?' At her piteous nod he clasped his head as if in agony. 'Oh, shite!'

Guessing his reason for being there, Lou hurried to stroke him. 'Is it going away to war you are?'

He nodded despairingly. 'I couldn't leave without seeing Etta and the kids . . . but it looks like I might have to.'

The mother of five tried to comfort her younger brother as she had done for him as a child when he had hurt himself, directing him to an armchair and pressing him into it. 'Maybe not, they'll be home about six, they won't want to be out late 'cause of the little ones' bedtime – what time do you have to be back by?'

'Ten at the latest.' Slumped in the chair, he cast a pointless look at the green imitation marble clock, working out if he had time to get to Scarborough and look for them. It was futile, of course.

'Well then!' Lou tried to sound cheerful. 'You should catch an hour or so with them. I know it's not much but . . .' Her kind blue eyes offered encouragement and she went to make a pot of tea. 'Can I do you something to eat? Bread and jam all right?'

He nodded without enthusiasm. 'And they've all gone, ye say?'

'All except Dad,' she continued to speak whilst sawing at a loaf, 'he's managed to find himself some labouring.'

Marty frowned. 'How on earth did they afford the train tickets?'

'Oh, they didn't go on the train!' Casting a smile at him, she plastered the bread with butter then scraped most of it off again. 'One of the customers who comes into Etta's shop for his bacon, well, he's a chauffeur for some big nob and he gets to use the car when the boss is away up in Scotland. Etta sweet-talked him into taking them to the seaside – mindst, I think he assumed he was just taking her, not the entire Lanegan family! I wouldn't fancy Uncle Mal in the back o' my posh car if I had one – don't look like that, there's nothing funny going on, Etta was just giving the kids a treat – anyhow, she decided it would be too busy on the Bank Holiday so she arranged it for her afternoon off. Just her luck that the Huns decided to go on their picnic at the same time. If she'd known you were coming . . . anyway, now, you sit and eat that while I tell you all that's been going on. Did ye hear Jimmy-Joe got himself a job as an errand boy after school? No? Oh well, you'll get a laugh out o' this, sure, he only walked in on Mrs O'Hara when she was . . .' And she proceeded to burble on maddeningly whilst a doleful Marty ate his sandwich.

With nowhere else to go, he was to spend an anxious afternoon with his sister, waiting until her children came in from their day's adventures and sparing a few jocular moments with them before making his way back to see if his father was home.

Red was delighted at the arrival of his eldest son. 'Marty, how great to see you – now I can have a cup o' tea instead of bloody water!'

The reply was sour. 'Oh, thanks, I'm glad I have my uses.'

'Ach, ye know what I mean!' Red cuffed him lightly and directed his son to put the kettle on the fire, which he himself was not permitted to do in case of accident, nor even to smoke his pipe if unaccompanied. 'Here, share this with me.' Generously he offered the cold meal left by Aggie in case she was late.

'Thanks, Da, but make sure you give yourself plenty though,' warned Marty, having attended to the kettle, watching his father divide the platter, saving his news for later. 'You look as if you need it – have you been falling over again?'

Red touched the bloody graze on his head and winced. 'Aye, fell off a cart as I was up there loading and bashed me head on the iron wheel-rim – nearly did for me, so it did – here now, wrap your gob around this.' Both set to eating.

But Red's delight at seeing Marty turned to shock upon learning that he might be off to war in the next day or so, this causing him periodically to fall asleep throughout his son's brief visit.

Six o'clock came and there was no sign of Etta. There was a spark of hope when someone poked their head in but it was only Mrs Gledhill.

'Marty, hello!' She entered, smiling, just as Red woke up. 'I didn't know you were coming! I were just saying to Mrs Thrush, I'll have to look in on Mr Lanegan in case he's had any little accidents . . .'

'Ye make it sound like I've messed my breeches!' objected Red.

'Clot, I meant with the fire!'

'Got you checking up on me, has she?' he growled.

A Yorkshire woman through and through, Mrs Gledhill suffered no back-chat, jocular or not, and wagged a finger at him. 'Now you know Aggie's only looking out for you.'

Red's face was stern but his eyes twinkled at Marty. 'Oh yes? I'd have had to put up with bread and water if it wasn't for this boy here – going off gallivanting to the seaside while the man o' the house starves.'

Out of politeness, though his heart was not really in it, Marty shared the banter, then asked the neighbour, 'How's your Albert these days, Mrs Gledhill? I'm told he's at the glassworks now.'

'Don't you mention that name to me!' Pretending outrage, she bent towards Marty and bellowed, 'He's only gone and joined up! His father's *absolutely* livid – says he must be mad to risk chucking up a good job like that – if

384

it's a scrap he wants there's plenty round here would give him one without trailing all the way to France! And it'll all be over before he's got off the bally boat.'

'Let's hope so,' nodded Marty.

'Oh, you're off an' all, are you? Well, it's different for you, you have to go where you're sent, but that daft bugger of mine . . .' Calmer now, Mrs Gledhill smoothed her plump, aproned breast and wrinkled her nose to project forbearance. 'Well, I suppose I am proud of him really . . . he always was quick to jump in when he saw any bullying. His heart's in the right place even if his brain isn't.' She grinned and made to go. 'Right, I'll leave you lads to it, nice to see you again, Marty.'

'Aye, and you, Mrs Gledhill. Give my regards to Albert.' It was hardly believable that the small boy who had once hero-worshipped him was now off to fight a war. 'I still think of him as nine, you know.' He went with her to the door, his main reason being to cast a frantic eye up and down the street, though to little benefit.

Coming back inside, he said dully to his father, 'They're not coming, are they?'

Red sighed and shook his bushy head. 'I'm sorry, son.'

It grieved Marty to say it, but, 'I can't wait any longer.'

Red offered a scrap of encouragement. 'You might pass them on your way.'

His son nodded despondently, then with a last flicker of optimism said, 'But if she should happen to come in five minutes after I leave would you ask her if it's humanly possible for her to come to the station and see me off?'

'That I will.' Pressing a supportive hand to the other's shoulder, Red accompanied his son to the street, where they were instantly accosted by another of Aggie's 'spies'. With polite excuse to the neighbour, and another futile look up and down the street, Marty shook his father's hand and hurried away.

*

When Etta and the others returned at a quarter past six, Red was asleep. Aggie rolled her eyes at the latest abrasion on his forehead, then, whilst Uncle Mal shuffled out to the lavatory, she picked up the kettle. 'I'll make the tea, Ett, you share the chips out – you children come wash your hands.'

Etta began to unwrap the bundles of newspaper. 'What about Red?'

'Throw a bucket o' water over him.'

She laughed at her mother-in-law. 'I meant what about his meal, shall I put it on a plate or . . . ?'

'Ach, stick some in the oven for him.' Lifting the teapot and finding it lukewarm, Aggie raised the lid and clicked her tongue in irritation. 'He'd better not have touched that kettle himself or I'll flay him!' She went to dispose of the dregs.

The meal was well underway when Red finally woke. A smiling, sunburned Etta rose and removed his portion from the black-leaded range and placed it on the table.

'Thank ye, deary.' Her father-in-law's delicate countenance smiled back at her and he pushed himself from the chair and went to join the diners. He had taken a mouthful before remembering his family had been out all day, and addressed the congregation. 'Oh, sure, I don't need to ask if ye had a good trip – you all look like a bouquet of roses.'

Etta dissuaded her son from peeling the skin from his nose. 'Yes, we've had a lovely time paddling in the sea and building sandcastles, haven't we?'

'And rides on a donkey!' the youngest piped up.

'Did you indeed?' His grandfather beamed at him.

'Couldn't get him off,' said Aggie, her wizened face glowing with health. 'Screamed the blessed place down, had everyone looking.'

'Sure, I think we'll have a donkey ourselves one day.' With his usual stock phrase Red tranquillized the little boy. 'What else did you see – oh, and what was it like to ride in the motor car?'

They took turns in telling him all about the wonderful time they had had, chattering away until told to attend to their chips, which were growing cold.

Drifting and snoring his way through the rest of his meal, Red finally nodded off completely and woke with a start, his face in his dinner. Whilst he picked bits of batter from his cheeks, the plate was snatched by his long-suffering wife. 'Go light your pipe and I'll fetch you a cup of tea – and don't think I'm blind to the fact that you've had one already! Who did ye drag off the street to make it for ye?'

Back in his armchair, about to share his tobacco pouch with Uncle Mal, a flash of panic crossed his face and he eyed the clock. 'Oh, bloody hell to buggery!'

'What is it now?' sighed an exasperated Aggie, having learned from painful experience that this facial expression meant he had just remembered some vital snippet of information that had been temporarily erased by his narcolepsy.

'Marty!'

Etta's ears were instantly pricked as her father-in-law rose from his chair and reached out to her, contrition in his watery eyes.

'I'm so sorry, deary, I was meant to tell yese – he was here all afternoon, waiting!'

Etta cried out, which was echoed by a gasp of disgust from Aggie.

Red's face had become distraught as he looked from one to the other. 'He couldn't hang on any longer or he'd miss his train!'

'For the love of Christ!' Aggie berated him. 'How long ago was this?'

His expression remained tortured. 'Too long for, you to catch him, I think – and him so keen to see Etta before he goes off to France that he'd got special lea—'

'He's going then?' The thing Etta had most dreaded, the reason she had arranged today's light-hearted trip in order to take her mind off it, was come to pass more swiftly than she had envisaged. She clutched at her breast where anger joined the fear. 'When?'

'Er, I'm not sure.' Concentrating hard to stay awake, Red pressed a hand to his brow, struggling to remember. 'I think it could be any day, he asked if ye got home in time would you follow him to the station.' His face appealed to her for pardon. 'Ach, I'm really sorry I forgot to give ye the message – 'twas awful bad luck ye didn't pass him on your way home.'

'We came by the fish shop!' His wife was testy.

But his daughter-in-law was even harsher. Devastated that Marty had gone off to war and could be killed without ever knowing that she wanted him back, she hurled at Red, 'You useless, *idiotic* man, you've jeopardised my marriage – he'll think I don't care!'

Whilst Red did nothing to defend himself, just stood there hanging his head whilst she harangued him and everyone else looked on in shock, Aggie stepped in with a pointed finger. 'Don't you dare –'

But ignoring any rebuke and abandoning her children, Etta flew from the house, leaving the door swinging violently on its hinges, and set off at a run along Hope Street.

Uncle Mal was disgusted. 'She's a nasty gob on her and no mistake.' And, rising, he extended bony tendrils of comfort to the devastated man's shoulder. 'Pay no heed, Red, 'tis herself who destroyed that marriage . . .'

Oblivious to aught else, Etta pelted across the junction with George Street, hurtled down the slope of Lead Mill Lane and under Fishergate Postern in the direction of the station. A tram was humming alongside her, but without a coin she was forced to let it pass, racing onwards over Castle Mills and Skeldergate bridges, dodging traffic to continue along Nunnery Lane, slowing only to relieve her tortured lungs, then on again, hair coming loose from its pins, worn-out shoes slopping on and off and threatening to trip her, muscles screaming as she pounded laboriously up and over the railway bridge and down the other side, finally staggering into the station some fifteen minutes after leaving the house, only to find that Marty's train was long gone.

Close to tears, excluded from the platform by the ticket barrier she clung to its iron bars, chest heaving as she fought to regain her breath, straining for a glimpse of those who congregated beyond, in the hope that she might yet see him, wondering what must have been going through his head after coming all this way for naught. Then, realising the futility of standing there torturing herself, she turned and made her stricken way home.

There was trouble waiting. As much as Aggie might grumble and grouse over Red's affliction she was fiercely protective of all her menfolk and descended on Etta the moment she entered. 'Right, milady!' Her eyes were glaciers, her finger a lance. 'Don't you *ever* speak to my husband again in that manner! All these years Red's looked after you and your –'

'I know!' Etta's face projected genuine contrition. 'It was unforgiv—'

'If anyone's to blame for your marriage breaking down 'tis not himself!' snapped Aggie, turning away abruptly to stalk up and down and gather the children's discarded clothing, they themselves having been put to bed. 'You're so full of your own importance! Did you never once stop to imagine what utter agony it must be to fall asleep at the blink of an eye, no matter what vital task you're in the middle of, whether it be carrying the best china or carrying your baby; to be mocked as a figure of amusement when you're trying to get from one side of the road to the other without being flattened; not even to be trusted to strike a match in case you burn your house down and your family with it; to have folk spit on you in the gutter and call you a drunkard and a waster – to miss out on half a bloody lifetime?'

Bruised and dejected, Etta turned tear-filled eyes to Red, her apology profuse. 'I'm so terribly sorry, my behaviour was appalling. I do appreciate how you must suffer . . .'

Not entirely appeased, Red spread his arms in an attitude of despair and managed to emit between a series of five-second naps, 'The Lord knows . . . I feel dreadful enough . . . about forgetting, without being told . . . what an eejit I am, but I can't help it, ye se—'

'The fault is entirely mine.' Etta raised a firm hand to prevent him saying more. 'Please don't feel in any way responsible, I was just taking out my frustration on you. I was angry at myself, I should have been here – I only arranged the trip to take our minds off this dreadful business in Europe. It's not an excuse, there can be no excuse for the way I spoke to you and I'm truly sorry.' She clasped her brow and heaved a sigh. 'One blessed day at the seaside, the first time I've been anywhere of note for over a decade, and what happens? Marty trails all that way to see his wife before going off to fight for his country and she's out enjoying herself!'

'Ah well, you weren't to know he was coming.' Red shrugged forgiveness and reached for his pipe. 'Nobody's to blame, 'tis just the war pulling us this way and that.'

Etta nodded woefully. 'You're very understanding. I only pray that Marty understands why I wasn't here. I can't bear the thought of him going off to war thinking I don't care about him.'

'You could drop him a line.' Seeing how badly this had affected her daughter-in-law, Aggie was not so censorious now.

'I intend to.' Taking herself in order, Etta wasted no more time and went to seek out an envelope and paper upon which she was to scribble a hasty explanation, an apology, and a wish for her husband's speedy return. Then she dashed out to post it in the hope that when he marched off to war it was in the knowledge that she loved him.

*

Following the initial commotion, apart from dramatic head-lines in the press and an increase in traffic from the barracks – indeed from all corners of the city as flag-waving children waved their fathers off to war – life at home soon reverted to normal. Similarly at the provision dealer's, where, after those few days of panic, it was business as usual. Well, not quite as usual, noted Etta, for once new deliveries arrived her enterprising boss put up the price of bacon by tuppence a pound, and flour by ten pence a stone. But she herself was to continue in mundane fashion, weighing out her bags of sugar and tea whilst anxiously awaiting a reply to her letter. After a burst of patriotism the rush to enlist had slowed down too. Still, with hundreds of reservists called from their jobs there was more scope for those seeking gainful employment, and Etta was quick to spot this, applying for the post of clerical officer at an engineering works. It would mean working more hours, she told Aggie, but at least it would give her the whole weekend off in which to help around the house.

Maddeningly, there was the need to compete with other young women from more privileged backgrounds who volunteered their services through a loyal desire to help – and also from those who had fallen redundant due to the war – but with several such vacancies on offer Etta was eventually to find herself successful, and within a few weeks had exchanged her grocer's overall for a neat black skirt and cardigan. It might only be temporary whilst Mr Smith went off to do his duty, and she held the suspicion that she was paid much less than the usual holder of the position, but in the meantime it would boost her own income, allowing her to save towards a rental property of her own in which to welcome Marty home. To date there had been no reply to her letter, but then he would be so very busy preparing for battle, perhaps already in France and her letter yet to catch up with him, and with this thought she proceeded to comfort herself – if comfort one could term it.

Then, about six weeks after the outbreak of war, one morning the postman finally brought relief.

'He's in Aldershot! Oh, thank God he's still safe – I could go down and see him!' Etta buried her head in the letter whilst the others waited eagerly for news, occasionally throwing them snippets, whilst keeping the more personal items to herself. Disappointingly, these were brief, but Marty explained that the battalion had been kept so busy training and travelling from camp to camp that he had simply not had the time to reply in depth, but at least he acknowledged receipt of her letter and excused her for not being there when he had come to York, and really all that mattered was that he knew she loved him.

But then a bombshell: upon re-reading it Etta noted the date. 'Why, this was written weeks ago!' She looked up at the listeners, her expression one of outrage. 'How come it's only just reached me?'

Whilst others looked blank, Uncle Mal thought he knew. 'The army wallahs like to play their cards close to their chest. They wouldn't want to risk the Germans getting to hear anything about where or when we plan to land in France before it happens.'

Etta's heart suffered a jolt. 'Are you saying that Marty must already be there?'

'Not necessarily, I wouldn't want to worry yese.' Uncle Mal's rheumy eyes glanced at Aggie, who was similarly affected by his disclosure.

'Stands to reason, though, if we've only just got Marty's letter . . .' Red, too, looked concerned between napping and waking.

Etta tried to appear more cheerful as she addressed the children, whose eagerness to hear from their father had now turned to apprehension. 'But we can't be sure, and at least he was safe and well when he wrote this, so we mustn't be too worried.'

Naturally, though, she herself was to remain worried,

and before going off to work each day she hovered in wait for the postman. But not until the following Saturday, when they were all having breakfast, did he actually bring confirmation that Marty was indeed in France, Aggie bustling in with the missive and delivering it to Etta's eager hands.

'Oh . . .' Etta's excitement paled into disappointment as she saw that it was only a postcard bearing pre-printed messages, all of which had been deleted except the one that said Marty was safe and well.

Aggie read her face, saying kindly as she re-seated herself at the table, 'Well, I suppose he's busy, what with one thing and another. He just wanted to let you know as quickly as possible that he was all right.'

Etta nodded wanly. 'And that's the main thing. Poor dear, I must write to him later and cheer him up.'

'Fair play to ye.' Red downed his cup of tea, saying to Tom and Jimmy-Joe, 'Away now, boys, we've a day's work to do,' and off they went to pick fruit, leaving the rest to finish at their leisure. Whilst Etta fingered the card worriedly, her thoughts far away, Aggie refilled their teacups.

'Please may I have that, Mother?'

Etta looked blankly at her elder daughter. 'What? Oh . . . I suppose you may.' She handed over the postcard, which immediately set the others at loggerheads. With a sigh she scolded them and dragged the loudest complainant, William, onto her lap and pacified him with a slice of toast. Once the fuss had died down, she and Aggie discussed their plans for the day, though there was little peace to be had for long.

'William, please do be still!' Crossly, Etta interrupted her conversation to shove him from her lap, rubbing at her shin.

'I'm sorry, Mother, my shoes are biting me.'

She conceded with a sigh that they did need replacing. She and Aggie then conspired to involve themselves in some juggling, Celia's shoes being passed to Edward, the latter's to his younger sister, who gave hers to William. But it was still painfully evident that their mother would have to buy at least one pair and she sighed again – more of her precious funds gone astray. 'Well, Celia, it seems you are to be the lucky recipient.'

Alexandra was unimpressed. 'But she had the postcard! I need new ones too.'

'You'd *like* new ones, but those still have plenty of room in them,' reproved her mother.

'It's not fair! Celia always gets –'

'No!' Turning to her eldest daughter, Etta said briskly, 'Come along then, we shall go to town before it gets too busy.'

In the hope of some small treat the others begged for inclusion. Their grandmother invited Etta to leave them with her.

'I see little enough of them as it is,' replied Etta. 'They can carry the shopping and make themselves useful.' First, she made herself useful by taking the breakfast pots to wash, though Aggie knew from experience that these would have to be re-done to remove all the stuck-on crumbs that Etta, in her careless fashion, left on them. Everything about Etta was surface deep; everything except her love for Marty. Bearing witness to the girl's suffering all these months, Aggie had come to recognise that now.

'Can you fetch me a length of braid to fancy-up that dress stuff I bought?'

'Yes, it is a bit cottony, isn't it,' denounced Etta.

Aggie darted a sharp look at her daughter-in-law, saw that she was teasing over a recent remark by Joan, and elbowed her laughingly as she leapt up to fetch payment. 'To hell with your cheek!'

Etta laughed back, indulging the fondness that had sprung up between the pair of them of late. 'Oh, don't bother about cash, it'll only be a few pence.'

'That's my reason for wanting it, so's to get rid of this blasted ten bob note thing that the ould fella drew in his pension and fetch me some proper money.' Aggie used forefinger and thumb to brandish the new red banknote with a look of distaste.

Sharing another chuckle with her mother-in-law, Etta took the note and went off into town with her children, feeling much happier now that Marty had replied, however brief his words. The town centre was reached in five minutes. There they set about comparing the price and style of children's shoes in each window, a sluggish sun finally emerging through a blanket of cloud and drawing forth the scent of horse dung and motor oil from the busy granite setts. Uplifted to know that Father was well, they chattered all the while, Etta occasionally laughing at some childish joke, between muttering at the expense of such small shoes and moving on to the next window.

William sought to help. 'You can have some of my money if you like, Mother.'

His siblings brayed with laughter, but his mother bestowed a fond smile. 'Why, you are a generous boy.'

'I must have quite a sum in my moneybox now.'

Etta raised an eyebrow at this news. 'You have a moneybox?'

'Yes, I keep it at Granny's under the stairs where no robbers can find it. It's very clever, you drop your coin through a slot then twist a knob and it falls in.' Then he frowned. 'I'm not sure how you get the money out again, Granny only showed me how to put it in.'

'Yes, I'll bet she did,' muttered Etta, half-annoyed, half-amused as she realised he meant the gas meter.

She was still shaking her head and sighing over Aggie's deception when she rounded a corner and came face to face with her mother.

There was no diplomatic means of escape for Isabella, who looked in turns anguished and aloof as she remained stock-still before her daughter. Etta, too, was unnerved, trying to decipher the expression in her mother's eyes as the latter struggled to decide whether to stop or to go. It had been ten years since either had set eyes on the other. What did one say?

Though obviously stunned, Isabella was first to recover her voice, offering a polite, 'Good morning. What a coincidence, I'm only in York overnight . . .' With those few stilted words a decision seemed to have been made, Isabella gesturing with a gloved hand to the female servant who carried her parcels and ordering civilly, 'Run along, Susan, and I shall meet you at the hotel.' Not until the maid had safely gone did she continue the awkward conversation with her daughter. 'I almost didn't recognise you, Henrietta.'

'Hardly surprising.'

Isabella flinched. 'You look . . . well.'

'As well as anyone, with this terrible business.' Though Etta's eyes were levelled dispassionately at the other, her heart thumped as she was plunged back to childhood.

Isabella smiled in woeful agreement, and left the next words to her daughter.

'I expect John . . . ?'

'Yes,' said Isabella quickly, 'your brother is already in France. A captain in the East Yorkshire Regiment. We're very proud . . .' Realising the implication of these words she allowed her voice to trail away.

Etta nodded, watching her mother struggle to maintain the dialogue, unable and unwilling to help her, the pair of them standing there blocking the pavement whilst irritated shoppers milled around them. The once dark hair at Mrs Ibbetson's temples was now streaked with grey, and, though still a handsome woman, she looked frailer than her daughter remembered.

Without Marty given so much as a mention, the two women briefly discussed the war, though only in terms of the latest newspaper reports and how long it would last.

396

The children soon grew bored, Celia twanging the elastic of her little sister's hat, snapping it against her chin and making her cry, at which point Etta looked down testily and shushed them.

'Where are your manners? Mother's speaking.' Since living with Aggie they had become quite harum-scarum.

Isabella too looked down at her daughter's companions, apparently noticing them for the first time, though in fact she had been darting unconscious little glances at them throughout the conversation. 'And these are your children?'

'Yes, your grandchildren.' There was a defiant edge to Etta's reply as she mopped Alexandra's eyes. Taking little enjoyment from the look of guilt she had inflicted on Isabella's face, she named them individually, then instructed, 'Say how do you do to your grandmamma, children.'

First came confusion. 'But Granny's at home,' pointed out the youngest.

'You have two grandmothers,' Etta patiently told William. 'Everyone has two sets of grandparents.'

Still confused, they offered a greeting to the smiling, elegant lady in the grey silk dress and large hat.

Isabella inclined her head graciously, conveying interest. 'Are you come to town for a treat?'

'No, new shoes,' replied Alex, whose tears had quickly dried.

Isabella misunderstood, thinking that all were to be shod. 'But surely that is a treat? My, aren't you lucky children?'

At this Etta said scathingly, 'Oh no, just Celia, I'm afraid. The others must wait.'

After a piteous glance at the shoddy footwear, the little girls' grandmother smiled down at them and said, 'Still, you have very pretty dresses.'

'Made from one of their mother's cast-offs.' Etta could not resist this gibe. 'It was difficult enough to afford things before the war, but now . . .' She shook her head in disgust.

Somewhat appalled, Isabella immediately reached into

her purse and offered money. Etta did not reach for it but merely held the giver's eye. 'To appease your conscience, Mother?'

Dismayed, Isabella blurted, 'Many a time I wanted to write to you, but your father forbade it.'

When Etta simply gazed back at her coolly, making no move to take the coin, Isabella replaced it in her purse. Then, as an afterthought, she took out one of smaller denomination and sought Etta's permission before handing it to one of the children, similarly rewarding the others.

'Thank you, Grandmamma!' They grinned up at her delightedly.

'What charming little dears,' murmured Isabella, hardly daring to look her daughter in the eye. 'Very beautiful. I regret that it's taken so long for me to meet them.'

Still hurting from reopened wounds, Etta said, 'It was of your own choosing, Mother.'

Isabella glanced away to the unfamiliar faces that eddied round them. 'If only the matter was as simple as you make out.'

'It was perfectly simple to me.'

Isabella's focus returned. 'But then you were always so much braver than I.' Unable to cope with the condemnation in her daughter's eyes, she tried to mask her own emotions by saying with a tentative smile, 'I should like to get to know them now, if it's not too late. I was just about to take morning tea. Would you care to come?'

Made suddenly aware by the grunts of passers-by that she and her children were blocking the footpath, Etta made as if to be on her way. 'We've still to find some shoes. Besides, I hardly think Father would approve.'

'He won't know, he's away shooting. Come to my hotel – we could purchase the shoes beforehand – I'd be delighted to buy them all a pair.'

In no uncertain terms, Etta drew the line at this.

Her mother acquiesced, but persisted with her invitation

for them to dine with her. 'Please, I should like it very much.' There was a genuine plea in Isabella's eyes.

Etta studied her mother, then looked down at her children, so loved and cherished by their parents. Part of her wanted to lash out at her mother for robbing her of similar experience, but a growing maturity advised that she should not inflict her own bitter opinions on her offspring, should not deny them this opportunity to learn of their heritage, even if they never saw Grandmamma Ibbetson again. 'Well, if you're certain it will cause no difficulty for you . . .'

Isabella shook her head vigorously. 'Come, my dear!' Smiling, she held out gloved fingers to one of the little ones.

And Etta, seeing how naturally Edward accepted his grandmother's hand, nodded to convey permission to the girls and watched them skip happily to the shoe shop.

The shoes, plus the feast of biscuits, cakes and ice-cream that followed, were to provide a topic of conversation between the children all the way home. Regarding the meeting with her mother as a never-to-be-repeated fluke, even though Isabella had promised to keep in touch, Etta tried to discourage any talk of when they might see their other grandmother again, saying they should be content with the one they had. 'And better not to mention it when we get home, Granny Lanegan will be most upset if you keep prattling on about it.'

'She can go with us too!' declared Edward.

'It's not for you to make the invitation,' scolded his mother.

'I'm sure our other grandmamma wouldn't mind. She's very –'

'Desist!' warned Etta sternly. 'I shall hear no more about it. Give me the pennies Grandmamma Ibbetson gave you and I'll keep them in a safe place.' She held out her hand.

Hoping she would have to issue no further warning, Etta was slightly concerned over what they might say when they got home. But as it turned out, Aggie was in no mood to take notice of any childish prattle, and neither was Etta when the news was conveyed. Mrs Gledhill had received a telegram that announced her son Albert's death. He was the first soldier in the street to die.

18

He had thought himself afraid of Etta's father; he had thought himself afraid of the drill-sergeant; but he had never known the true meaning of fear until he had come to this place. It was a landscape of rolling hills, steep river valleys and woods; it could have been England, but for the fact that across that wide and gently flowing river were thousands of men who wanted to kill him.

It was halfway through September. Only two weeks after landing in France they had been plunged into vicious fighting, which continued to-date. Marty considered himself an experienced soldier, fit and ready to take on any comer, but his reactions here were not so slick as in rehearsal. The years of instruction obliterated by terror, he could only point his rifle and keep pulling the trigger until his finger was numb, in the hope that he would hit the enemy. His comrades spoke benignly of the Germans, just shrugged and said they're just like us, but Marty felt no such kinship. He loathed them with all his might for what they were putting him through; rejoiced to see them blown to bloody fragments by his gunners. Yet still they came . . .

Orders were to grab the crossing places from the German rear guard, then move against the steep escarpment on the northern bank eventually to seize the road at the top, but this did not compare with taking an exercise field defended by one's fellow soldiers. No matter how much screaming

401

and baring of teeth and stabbing of bayonets into straw-filled sacks, it could not have prepared them for the blood that spilled from real men, nor for the hazardous bombardment of hostile artillery and shrapnel that filled the air with banshees; nor for the machine-gun bullets that sprayed the river meadows on both banks; nor for the revulsion of being daily spattered with the flesh and fat, brains, splinters of bone, the excreta of bowels and undigested stomach contents of one's comrades as their number was savagely whittled from a thousand to two hundred.

Nor, when the river had at last been breached to even more grievous loss, did their minds and bodies gain relief, for, pinned down by the relentless onslaught, they could only attempt to secure a footing, the Germans launching counter-attacks at every hour of day and night so that one could barely catch a wink of sleep amidst the incessant alarms and the flares that lit up the sky. They could only wait for the barrage of hate to subside.

Even the weather conspired to hamper their frantic attempts to scoop out places of cover. Cold and miserable, it had begun to rain hard three days ago. The ground was now churned to a quagmire as Marty and those around him, drenched to the skin, struggled to carve their entrenchments under hostile fire, the parapets toppling as soon as they were built, desperate hands slapping and plastering and shoring up the walls with sandbags. Within a matter of days the corridors were flooded with six inches of mud and eighteen inches of water. Any relief that the rats had eschewed these waterlogged conditions and departed to higher ground was short-lived, for the absent lodgers were replaced by frogs and beetles and even more repulsive slugs that slithered about the walls, occasionally tumbling to land on Marty's face, making him feel as if he were buried alive. And in this stagnant cesspit, beneath a pall of cordite and the stench of rotting carcasses that no amount of chloride could disguise, under a never-ending torrent of rain, Marty

402

was forced to eat and sleep as best he could, his feet almost crippled from the wet and cold, the one consoling thought being that even if all valiant attempts to gain ground had, so far, been unrewarding, then the Germans too had been repulsed in their aims.

Another grey dawn arose, the tension of the night relieved by the usual staccato burst of machine guns and rifle fire. Exhausted from lack of sleep, stiff from being huddled on a ledge to avoid the cold water, Marty could barely keep his eyes open. He did not actually recall cleaning his rifle, though he must have done for it had passed inspection and he was now eating breakfast flavoured by the tang of gunpowder. At least one could expect a brief peace whilst the Germans ate theirs, if not for long. Whilst he was assigned to the repair of the parapet, which had yet again capsized, others employed pumping equipment, though this was of little use for the water would soon seep back to its own level. Covered in slime from head to foot, the wind cutting through his wet shirt, he grimaced and applied his weight to the wall of sandbags, hoping they would stay where he had fashioned them into the mud. Achieving temporary success, he tottered and skidded his way back along the trench to attend to more personal tasks. He had received another despatch from Etta, incurring a pang of guilt that he had not even had the time to think about her, let alone write, his only thoughts being to keep himself and his comrades alive. He devoted his mind to her now, but it was pointless trying to write back in this downpour, the paper would turn to mush in no time. However, he could read her words over in his mind. Wiping the cold rain from his face, he was contemplating this when he heard a plaintive Yorkshire voice.

'Can somebody help me? I'm stuck.'

It came from the far side of the parapet. He trained narrow eyes on the lance corporal with whom he was sharing a cigarette, Ged Burns, one of the few old pals who had survived, who was teetering on a plank nearby, his face and clothes like those of everyone else, caked with mud and gaunt from the horrors of war. 'Did you hear that? Stick your head up and have a look, Ged.'

'Er, I don't think you've quite got the hang of this regulation lark, Private Lanegan. It's me what gives the bloody orders.' Ged cast a sarcastic eye at others who crouched nearby, and, repossessing his cigarette, took a leisurely drag.

Marty gasped at his companions. 'He's a proper little Napoleon Bonaparte since he got that bloody stripe.' And directly to Ged, 'You only got the promotion 'cause there's no bugger left.'

There returned a denigrating laugh. 'And what does that say about you?'

Marty conceded this was true. Some of his jocular efforts to make life bearable had been misinterpreted by his officers; they obviously did not regard him as serious enough to take command. But, for once, his ambitions to further himself could not have mattered less; his only objective being to stay alive.

The disembodied voice came again. 'Please, *please* help.'

Marty was about to scramble to his feet, but the lance corporal handed back the cigarette, bidding, 'Oh, stay there you idle sod, I'm nearest.'

The periscope giving no clearer view, Ged clambered onto the fire step to risk a cautious look over the top. His observation was curtailed by the crack of rifle fire. He fell back with a splash, a hole in his forehead from which emerged thin runnels of red that crazed the mud-daubed cheeks for an instant then stopped. A group clustered round his supine form, revolted by the horrible gurgling that continued to emerge even though Burns was stone dead. Despite all the carnage he had witnessed, Marty found that he could still be shocked, and he stared down with racing heart into the sightless eyes of his friend, watched the heavy rain sluice the blood from his face, experienced an inner conflict of guilt and relief that it was not himself lying there, before being overcome by a wave of futility. Whilst others stretchered Ged away, he took a long drag of the cigarette, used his toe to flick mud over the fragments of skull, then turned to attend the disembodied voice, and asked in flat tone:

'Are you still there?'

'Not from choice,' came the quivering reply.

'What're you doing?'

'Went out to mend the wire t'other night, got separated and couldn't find me way till it got light – but me feet have gone down this 'ole and they're wedged tight in t'mud, I can't pull 'em out.' There came the sound of frantic squelching. Then, 'Oh Christ, I'm up to me knees now!'

He sounded terrified, but those on the other side of the wall were unable to help him.

The voice was unfamiliar to Marty, but then the majority of those around him were strangers now since his own regiment had been decimated, his CO and most of the company commanders dead, along with three-quarters of the men, he and the survivors from other battalions being rounded up to form this new unit. 'What's your name, chum?'

'Salmon.'

'I thought there was something fishy about him.' To try and staunch the horror he was still experiencing over the death of his friend, Marty could not resist a bad joke to his companions. If one did not laugh, one was done for.

'Ha bloody ha,' came the unamused voice.

'Well, sorry, Fishy old chum,' said another, 'you'll just have to keep your head down till after dark.'

'I can't stay here for ten bloody hours!' The victim must have tried to free himself again for there came another rifle crack.

'Salmon? *Salmon?*'

'I'm still here,' whimpered the voice to the group's relief.

'Just keep still, he'll think he's done for ye,' urged Marty.

'We'll get to you as soon as we can.' And he went back to his cigarette.

Hours passed, he and the others offering the occasional word of encouragement as they squelched about their business, reassuring the trapped man after each bombardment. Hot rations were brought up but there was little that could be shared with poor Salmon, who by midday sounded thoroughly demented for he shrieked at every burst of fire.

Marty rammed a lump of bread onto the end of his bayonet and called, 'Prepare to receive rations, Fishy!' Taking his rifle by the butt he slid it up and over the parapet and, straining against the wall of sandbags, tried to lower its bayonet as best he could in the supposed direction of Salmon. 'Got it?'

There was no reply.

'Salmon!' Marty had seen horses drown in these conditions; he feared the worst.

'Hang on, nearly – got it!'

'Jeez, I thought you'd swum away for a minute.' Issuing a note of relief, Marty quickly withdrew his bayonet to see that the bread had been taken.

Salmon gave tremulous thanks, and despite being half-paralysed with terror managed a quip as he kept his head down and gnawed at the bread. 'Is there trifle for afters?'

'Better – a lump of fruitcake.' This was Marty's own, sent to him by his mother, but sharing it was the least he could do for a comrade. Transferring it in the same manner was difficult, and it slipped from bayonet to mud before reaching Salmon. However, there was a more positive addition. 'Your sniper friend seems to have gone, least he hasn't taken advantage of me handing this over, so we might be able to get you out earlier than planned.'

But the sniper had only been having games with them, allowing Salmon to relax a little before landing a bullet half an inch from his elbow that had him squealing for assistance and trying to camouflage himself by wriggling into the mud like a crab. From then until nightfall they were forced to take it in turns to feed and to reassure him, passing him titbits on the ends of their bayonets whilst his demeanour became gradually more uncontrolled. Only when darkness fell could Marty and another slither over the parapet with their shovels and dig him out. His trembling body was eased through the morass and carried to safety, this at least lending those involved some satisfaction in this hellish place.

In due course they were on the move, though making slow progress, their route impeded by roads clogged with mud, shells dropping all around them, strafed by the Germans from their seemingly impregnable position in a line of trenches along the edge of the woods that crowned the slope. The greater part of the week was passed in bombardment and foiling counter-attacks, again to heavy loss. Eventually they reached the comparative safety of higher ground and, once ensconced in a wooded area, they took cover and awaited fresh orders. A shower of hail, a shower of shrapnel: each made similar noise as it came rushing through the trees. Relieved to have escaped the deadly effect of the leaden variety, Marty uncurled and looked about him, studying the ravaged branches, and saw what appeared to be a shrivelled monkey's ear, attached to a piece of fur by which it dangled from a twig. Knowing it for human, he stared at it in fascination as the raindrops hit it, causing it to rotate and jiggle.

And then it was onwards again, he and his fellows despatched in small groups up the wooded slope, the fighting chaotic as they ran from tree to tree, friend shooting friend in the panic-fuelled bid to stay alive. A village intervened. Breaking from the woods, Marty and his group set off at a crouching run along streets littered with corpses from both sides, dashing from ruined cottage to blood-spattered shell-hole, firing at those who fired upon him.

407

Then, suddenly, Germans were looming up before them, lunging with bayonets. Too close to shoot the one that came at him, Marty whacked the blade aside with his own rifle, struggling briefly, brutally, before stabbing the enemy and moving on to another, and another, and another . . .

Amidst brave deeds and ugly combat, their trial was victorious, the village was taken and on Sunday a break in the clouds permitted them to attend their sodden clothes, though the sun was too feeble to be of much use. It was just as well, for the rotting corpses smelt bad enough as it was. Haunted by the loss of his own humanity, his hands yet sticky with blood, Marty sought out a patch of sunlight and re-read his wife's last letter before making an attempt to reply, the first real opportunity he had had. But what to say apart from that he missed her? He couldn't tell her of the awful things he had seen, nor of the constant nightmares, nor the expectation that any minute he would die. He longed to have closer contact with her – not just in body but in spirit, longed with all his being, was consumed by the funny little things she used to say and do, cursed the stupid immaturity that had led him to run away and so be in this position now, and prayed it was not too late to put things right.

Not long afterwards, the Hun, too, seized advantage of the more clement weather, launching a counter-attack, and again at dusk. The night filled with the roar of express trains. And so it went on . . .

Mrs Gledhill's son was to be the first of many. Less than two months after the declaration of war, long lists of casualties began to appear in the newspaper, amongst them many from Marty's regiment. Now, every time Etta saw a telegram boy in the street she held her breath until he had pedalled by her door. But even though he might be past, the fear and danger were not, for talk had it that instead of being over by Christmas the war might go on for much longer.

What was most distressing of all was the lack of correspondence from her husband. Sick of trying to control her palpitations every time there came a knock at the door, after one such incident too many, Etta finally announced, 'I can abide this no longer, doing nothing whilst Martin's under such threat, feeling useless . . .'

'You're doing your bit, as am I,' pointed out Aggie. The pair of them, indeed all the female members of the clan, had taken to doing voluntary work in what little spare time they had.

'Yes, but I need to undertake something more useful,' argued her daughter-in-law.

'The munitions factory needs people,' ventured Red, scraping up the last of his dinner.

'I'll be damned if I'll make bombs to prolong their blessed war!' retorted Etta. 'My intention is to go out there and find him.'

Aggie was astounded. 'You can't do that!' she said, grabbing her husband before he fell off his chair. ''Tis too dangerous.'

'Hundreds are out there already with the VAD,' pointed out Etta.

'And is it that you're intending to join them?' asked Aggie, thinking that her daughter-in-law would not be one's most natural choice for a nurse.

'No,' Etta was firm. 'I'm sure it's all very noble and of course I'll assist wherever possible, but my main concern is Marty.'

'War's no place for a woman,' opined Uncle Mal, picking meat from his teeth.

'It's no place for a man either,' she snapped back.

'And what do you intend to do when, *if*, you find him?' asked Aggie, a fistful of Red's shirt in one hand whilst using the other to try and stack the dinner plates.

'I don't know.' Vexed, Etta clasped her temples. 'Just be with him to offer support, I suppose. I've thought about it a lot, I'll use my savings —'

'Ye said you were putting that by for when Marty comes home.' With her husband awake again, Aggie relaxed her support of him. 'What happens if you go swanning off wasting your money in France and the war's all over next week? Just bide a while, then we'll help if we can. He knows you're thinking about him. Sure, we all are.' Alerted by the delivery of the afternoon post, she went to fetch it and returned triumphant. 'There! Didn't I tell you he'd write when he could?'

At once a relieved Etta ripped the envelope open.

'What does he say?' The rest of the family hovered eagerly.

A pause whilst the reader's eyes flicked back and forth. 'Very little . . . he asks that we send something to make him smell nice.'

'Wasn't he always the vain one,' mocked Red to a similarly amused Uncle Mal.

Etta sprang to her husband's defence. 'Apparently the conditions are atrocious, there's nowhere for him to get a proper wash . . . He says the food's all right, though he'd appreciate some Bovril and some razor blades . . .'

'Shall I send Father that bottle of violet scent which Aunt Joan gave me for my birthday?' asked seven-year-old Alex. 'It's got orange blobs in it but it still smells nice.'

Etta smiled at her. 'I'm sure he'd love it, dear.' The next section she read aloud: *Please apologise to Ma for my not writing –*'

'Sure, I'm not bothered about that,' cut in Aggie. 'So long as he's safe.' She played nervously with the skin of her throat. 'Ye read such awful things . . .'

'Has he shot many Germans?' Tom and his twelve-year-old brother were desperate to know.

Etta looked up to issue a frowning rebuke, which was all it took for them to apologise and hang their heads for they adored their sister-in-law. She forgave them, looking down again to read and saying kindly, 'He doesn't say –

he has some foreign souvenirs for you, though.'

'And for me?' Edward felt left out.

Etta said she was sure that he had, but sought to alert her children that, 'Father has much more important things to think about.' For the benefit of all, she went on, 'He says not to worry if we don't hear from him very often, but they've been very busy pressing forward and their battle led to great success – that must be the one we read about in the paper.' Whilst the others underwent a bout of murmuring, Etta kept the last few lines to herself, her lips forming a sad, secret smile, her eyes portraying empathy as she read how much he missed her and longed for the day when they would be together again.

'Hadn't you better be off to work?'

Aggie's voice alerting her to the time, Etta nodded and, returning to the mundane, she folded the letter away. 'I intended to leave earlier than this. I want to call in on Mrs Gledhill on the way, the poor soul looked completely lost yesterday.'

'That's a nice thought.' But Aggie was not surprised by this. Living at close quarters, she had long ago reversed her opinion of Etta being selfish. Indeed, she was very warm-hearted and, besides mucking in with all the neighbourly sharing that had to be done in these times of food shortages, had involved herself in visiting every bereaved wife and mother in the area.

'It's only what she'd do for me,' said Etta as she kissed her children and went off to work.

'And let's hope that's an end to her crazy ideas,' murmured Red to his wife.

The rain began to drain away, October opening fine and warm, though the nights grew increasingly colder. Since the battle they had became static, which was somehow worse than ever for the long periods of boredom gave Marty time to dwell on the terrifying notion that he could die at any moment – he had seen so many killed, how rudely death came – and this could be only briefly alleviated by the arrival of letters and parcels from home. There was always something for him. Sometimes several items arrived from his mother, sisters, aunts, but something always came from Etta. Never had she let him down, never did she scold for his own lack of correspondence, letting him know gently that it would be nice to hear from him whenever he had the time.

In a dormant moment now, at rest camp well away from the front lines, he pulled out her latest missive and pored over it again. She wanted to know specifically where he was. Even had it been permitted he couldn't have told her. Shunted from pillar to post, bombarded, strafed, exhausted, Marty didn't know where he was himself half the time. Nor did he care, all he wanted was to be home with his beloved and his dear children, his ma and his da and his brothers and sisters and Uncle Mal's bowels. He longed to be back in dirty old York, with its soot-coated factories and dog-shit pavements, its boisterous pubs, its blunt-speaking residents . . . but to dwell too long on thoughts such as these had driven others to insanity. Wondering how long he himself would be able to resist mental collapse, he tucked his letter away and answered the call to parade.

Here they were given news: they were shortly to move again up to Flanders. In addition to this, ten men were singled out for detail, Marty amongst them. Worried that this could mean some dangerous mission, he debated this with the others, and was to be even more unnerved when rumour reached them that their detail was to form a firing squad.

'The cherrynobs brought in a deserter,' revealed the goggle-eyed harbinger.

Marty was shaken to the core. It was not so much that the man was being shot, for he, like many others, had a low opinion of those who ran away. He had felt like running away himself, but that would have meant leaving his friends to face the danger, something he would never countenance. No, it was the fact of being told to shoot a fellow Briton that upset him most.

'Who is it?' he asked quietly.

Huddled in a bunch, consulting each other uneasily, no one knew.

'It's not right,' objected Marty, feeling sick. 'We're here to shoot Germans, not our own. What harm has he ever done me?'

'I'll tell you what he's done.' At the sound of their sergeant's voice their faces whipped round to portray guilt, though their eyes retained a look of repugnance for what they were being commanded to do.

'He's let you down,' said the sergeant. 'You, his comrades.'

'Begging your pardon, sarnt,' chanced Marty, his grey eyes troubled, 'but that's my point. We're his comrades, why should we have to –'

'You *were* his comrades,' emphasised the sergeant darkly. 'As from the time Salmon decided to run away, abandon his duty and leave us in the lurch, he was no friend of mine, nor yours neither.'

'*Salmon*? Oh, Christ, I know that man!' Marty begged in earnest, 'Oh, please, sarnt, don't make a murderer out o' me. I'll do anything else you ask, but please don't make me do that!'

The sergeant remained grim as others joined their wheedling voices to Marty's. 'I don't like it any more than you do, but somebody's got to carry out the order, and if it isn't you it'll be somebody else – don't bother to argue, Lanegan!' Seeing Marty's lips part yet again he nipped any further insurrection in the bud. At the bleak nods of concurence he finished on a sympathetic note. 'I'll see if I can wangle you some rum . . .'

This he did, but even alcohol could not remove from their minds what lay ahead. Marty could not sleep at the

413

best of times, but tonight was even worse as he smoked one cigarette after another, fretted and drank and prayed and wondered what must be going through the condemned fellow's mind. When dawn rose over the crenellated outline of ruined buildings he was awake to meet it, sullenly assembling with the others to have his rifle checked by the attending officer. In the centre of the ground selected as Tyburn was an empty chair: a dazed and inebriated Private Salmon was half-carried, half-dragged out of an abandoned, bomb-damaged house and tied to it. Marty experienced a jolt of shock at how young he looked, the eyes bewildered. It was awful to watch him struggling to free himself – how naturally, how fiercely would he himself struggle were the positions reversed. A white disc was pinned over his heart by the medical officer and a blindfold applied to his gyrating head. Wanting to vomit, to rebel against this cruelty, Marty crossed himself, then, with trembling limbs, shouldered his rifle, wondering what the others intended to do, for he himself knew exactly: when the order was given to fire he would obey but would aim above Salmon's head; he was damned if they would make a murderer out of him.

At the order to fire, a volley crackled through the cold grey morn. Peppered with bullets, none of which was fatal, the condemned man groaned and tried blindly to stand, but only succeeded in toppling the chair. The officer's face suffused with fury. Immediately he rushed to where Salmon lay, aimed his revolver and shot him through the head. Shot him in cold blood. As horror-stricken as his comrades, some of whom were vomiting, Marty looked on as death was certified, then the young officer turned angrily on them.

'Damn you ignorant fools!' His eyes were red and threatened tears. 'You simply prolonged his agony! Get out of my sight before I have you all on a charge!'

And with this terrible image seared into his breast, Marty slunk away.

*

Limbs torn off trees, limbs torn off men. First snow, then ice. Now his pleas to Etta were for warm socks and gloves, as many as she could muster lest he should succumb, like others, to frostbite. Everyone had expected the war to be over by Christmas, but Christmas had passed and now the ground was frozen; as was his soul. He wondered if he would ever be rid of that look of bewilderment on Salmon's youthful face. Petrified by the overwhelming odds that he might never see his wife and children again, he hurt so much he felt it might kill him even before the Germans did. From a rock-hard lair, a feral beast, he stared out at the wintry landscape, eyes fixed dolefully on the frozen footprints of men who had long since died. Only now, as the threat of death became ever more realistic, was he able to elaborate his feelings for her, on filth-streaked paper, with blunted lead and trembling chilblained fingers scrawling the words *darling* and *beloved* to such poetic effect that he could barely believe it came from his own hand.

Neither could Etta, who was stunned by the new eloquence of her husband's writings. She should have been delighted; instead she was afraid. To add to her consternation, the lists of casualties grew ever longer, complete with smiling photographs of the valiant dead which seemed to make the loss even more poignant somehow. Ironically, due to the war, she was no longer the only one without a husband at the Christmas table, for most of her brothers-in-law had joined up too, but this brought not the slightest comfort to Etta. Nor did the pay rise in spring, which at one time might have been enough to make her smile but now merely provoked the utterance that she would give every penny she had in return for her husband's safe return. Besides which, the increase was soon gobbled up by the rising cost of food.

As the year went on the outlook was to become even more depressing, for the newspapers told of terrible gas attacks by the dastardly Germans, and a shortage of munitions placed the beleaguered troops at even higher risk. Etta felt useless in going about her own affairs, and wished she could do more for Marty than supply a few home comforts. There had been no letter from him for some weeks. As August brought the first anniversary of the war, along with the anniversary of her eleven years of marriage, she began seriously to resurrect her plan to go and find him.

Searing summer days. Between the flowers of the field sprawled black and bloated corpses rank with flies, their tumbled entrails dried to rope, their stench omnipresent, permeating the very weave of Marty's garb until he was aware of little else, save his own filth, no longer a man, just a breeding ground for lice.

Prolonged by extra hours of sun, the mood of the day veered twixt sheer terror and abject boredom, the constant pummelling by enemy guns forbidding aught other than to lie low. Only under cover of darkness did those imprisoned gain respite in activity, the labyrinth of trenches resembling city streets on a Saturday afternoon, men rushing this way and that, trying to make repairs, fetching up supplies, venturing into No Man's Land to renew barbed wire or to launch raids or to bury dead, before dawn brought fresh mayhem.

And what was the object of such violent contention? A hole. A colossal crater to be exact, possession of which seemed to have become every man's reason for being. Along with a ruined château it had been held by the British until just over a week ago, when the enemy had taken it back. Having thought to have seen the ultimate horror, Marty had been unprepared for the diabolical barbarity of that attack, thanked God he was only a witness and not one of those brave souls who had perished. Yet never would the memory be put to rest: the eerie quiet that preceded it, the hiss of the dragon before its breath lit up the dawn, turning it a raging crimson with jets of flame, great spurts of burning fuel that arced over No Man's Land to roast all those in its path . . .

Since then the nightmares had intensified. Even awake he had lived in fear of being burnt alive, had quaked at the order to counter-attack but had done so nonetheless, with naught to protect him but a new tin hat and the colonel's 'God bless you', had ventured stoically against bomb and bullet into that bloody hole where he had fought the Germans hand-to-hand until all were vanquished and the hole was once again a British hole.

Now, thank God, his battered battalion had been relieved, and an exhausted Marty was on his way to rest.

But there were many miles to travel through a network of trenches, and the pom-pom-pom of the heavy guns dogged him all the way, shaking the earth so violently that its reverberations extended to the fillings in his teeth. Even as the sun rose it saw them still a good distance from their billets. One minute plodding, the next waking to find himself on the ground, a confused Marty realised he had fallen asleep whilst marching. Unable to drag his feet another step, he gasped wearily to the man who hauled him to his feet, 'It's no use, Tommo, I'll have to nip into that barn for a kip. Will ye cover for me? I know where you're headed, I'll catch you up.' And with the fellow's nod he stole a quick look around for officers, then ducked into the barn and immediately dragged himself up a ladder into a loft, where he threw off his military paraphernalia and collapsed on a bed of straw. Before the sound of tramping boots had died away he was claimed by oblivion.

It was still daylight when he awoke, though the quality of that light told him that more than a few hours had passed. Had he slumbered all afternoon and all night too? From the way he felt this was probably correct. Robbed of proper sleep for days – nay months – due to nightmares over that firing squad, he was now sufficiently equipped to tackle the rest of the march. He lay there for a moment, wondering, thinking, yearning, rubbing pensively at the stubble on his shorn scalp, picking at the blood-encrusted scabs inflicted by his own razor in an attempt to avoid playing host to nits. Then, he stretched his limbs wide, farted, and raked his head with black fingernails, before finally coming round and sitting up. It was abnormally quiet this morning. True, the big guns were still hammering away in the distance, but there was not the usual sound of barked orders, men's conversations, the jingle of harness, or anything much at all except the trill of a lark. It was only when he risked a glance over the edge of the hayloft that he remembered he was alone. Any improvement he had felt was quickly dispersed by the knowledge that he would be in serious trouble if he did not find his unit quickly, and snatching up his pack and rifle, he slung them on, scrambled down the ladder and bounded outside. Knowing where the billets were located he felt no undue panic and, after emptying his bladder and bowels, embarked on his own way there, looking forward to a meal, for he was famished.

But when he arrived at the bomb-damaged village, though there were troops amassed, his own unit was nowhere in evidence, and in the confusion no one could tell him where they resided. Panic did flare then. It was anyone's guess which way they had gone. The footsteps in the trampled verges were directed at every point on the compass. Flashing a dirty, nervous face to right then left, he scanned the pockmarked countryside in between, then made a very rash decision. He set out to find them.

He jogged for as long as he could, accompanied only by the clinks and clanks of his equipment and the short sharp bursts of his own breath until he could run no more, when he slowed to a walk, alternating in this manner for most of the morning until he stopped to partake of his iron rations. He ate only a third of the tin of bully beef and one of the biscuits – best to eke them out just in case his search took more than twenty-four hours. He ran and walked and ran again for much of the afternoon too, hauled his heavy pack and his exhausted carcass down this lane and that, traversed the countryside in search of his battalion until nightfall, when his pace abated to a tortured limp and finally he could walk no more. At which point, with no barn and no hedgerows, he slept where he fell. Another morning dawned to the ominous cawing of rooks. Having slept hardly at all, his belly raw from hunger, he devoured the rest of his bully beef and another of the biscuits. Not wishing to draw attention to himself by lighting a fire on which to boil a can, the ration of tea and sugar and the Oxo cubes had to be left in their wrapping and the paltry meal washed down with water. After relieving himself in the open field he set off again, accompanied by no small amount of concern.

By midday, absolutely ravenous, he threw caution to the wind and lit a fire in order to boil some water for one of his Oxo cubes, in which was steeped the last two biscuits, for his teeth and gums were sore from gnawing at the hard tack.

Evening put paid to the remainder of his rations, though he hung on to the old tea leaves, which would provide another brew in the morning. There was no shortage of water, for the area was traversed by countless little streams and ditches into which, in his weakened state, he occasionally stumbled. Wondering how long one could last without food, he lay down and closed his eyes.

More filthy, more frightened by the day, existing on fruit and one battered tin of meat discarded by some soldier in a hedge bottom, his weighty pack and equipment long abandoned but grimly hanging on to his rifle, for to cast it away was a crime, he was to wander around for almost a week.

*

With no office work to attend that Saturday afternoon, the children out at play and the men out too, Etta pondered telling Aggie of her decision as the pair of them collected bits and pieces to be included in a parcel to the Front – a batch of newspapers, socks, underwear, cigarettes, soap and chocolate – but then the postman came, and, hoping he might bring news of Marty, she beat her mother-in-law to the door.

She was to return looking disappointed yet thoughtful, as she recognised the writing on the envelope.

'Not from Marty then.' Aggie's voice was dull.

'No, my mother.' Etta studied the letter pensively for a moment, then opened it. 'She's staying the night in York and invites the children and myself to dine with her this afternoon.'

'You could sound happier.' Aggie picked bits of lint off some socks that were destined for the parcel.

Etta looked dubious. 'I'd feel as if I were betraying Marty somehow.'

'Why on earth would you think that? She's your mother.'

'Yes, but would she invite my husband if he were here? I doubt it. He's having such a beastly time of it over there . . .'

'Doesn't mean you have to have one as well.' Aggie was charitable. 'And when he comes home you can stick up for him then, but you've been given this opportunity to make things up with your family, 'twould be a shame to throw it away.'

Etta looked guilty. 'Well, actually, it's not the first time I've seen Mother . . .'

'Sure, I know that.' Aggie hardly batted an eyelid as she went on with her task. 'Didn't those children of yours tell me the minute you were out the door.'

Etta looked embarrassed. 'I'm sorry, I instructed them not to upset you by gabbling on about her over-indulgences.'

'As if to make me jealous? Nonsense, their grandmother's just trying to make up for all the years she's lost. Be off with you and get the children ready.'

Etta passed her a smiling nod of gratitude, wiped the beads of perspiration from her forehead and looked through the window at the sky. 'I wonder whether I'll need an umbrella. We could do with a shower, it's so close.'

'Ye never can predict lately.' Aggie mopped her own brow. 'It's all them blessed bombs going off that's messed the weather up.'

Etta nodded and prepared to go out, but then Joan arrived and for this reason she tarried to lend Aggie support.

'Oh, these must be for our brave Marty.' Joan smiled over the array of items that lay on the brown paper ready to be wrapped. 'I sent him one of those but mine was a good one.'

Aggie flared her nostrils and turned away. 'Cup of tea, Joan?'

The dainty little creature demurred, wafting her glowing face. 'No, I'll just have a glass of water if it's no trouble. My goodness, it's a bit, er, a bit –' she groped for a word to describe the climate.

'Cottony?' suggested Etta helpfully.

Joan looked at her sharply, heard the snigger that came from Aggie, and pursed her lips looking most put-out. But before she could respond Etta went to answer a knock at the door.

On her return she held a telegram, her face deathly pale. 'He's missing.'

Joan immediately exchanged her look of reproach for one of pity, reaching out a sympathetic hand.

But strangely, Aggie did not, as might be expected, create instant hullabaloo, her ice-blue eyes totally calm and her voice steady as she told Etta, 'He's not dead. I'd know if one of my children was dead.'

For the moment Etta could not respond, her limbs turned to jelly, her mind and stomach churned.

'He's not dead I tell ye,' said Aggie in as airy a tone as she could muster.

'You're right of course.' From somewhere beneath the layer of bile, Etta found the power of speech, though her response was far from confident.

'Anyway, weren't you going out?' Aggie reminded her.

'I can't go now!' protested Etta.

'And what good will that do Marty, you sitting and worrying about him all afternoon?' Aggie snatched the telegram from her. 'Now off with you and see your mother.'

Joan's sad demeanour changed to one of alertness. 'You're going to see your mother?' Swiftly she gathered her belongings. 'Perhaps I should accompany you if you don't feel up to going alo—'

'Sit down!' commanded Aggie. 'You can save your grovelling introductions for another day.' And Joan meekly complied.

Though Etta hardly felt like going anywhere, was too consumed by worry to contemplate the small feast that her mother would undoubtedly lay on, and feared she might burst into tears at any minute, she decided to put on a brave face for the children, and, composing herself into some sort of order, duly took them out to meet Grandmamma Ibbetson at the hotel.

Their meeting was almost as awkward as the last time, both withholding comment whilst a young waiter delivered a trolley to Isabella's suite, and set out items on a starched linen tablecloth. When asked if there was anything else the ladies required before he left, Isabella thought she detected a foreign accent and frowned suspiciously. 'You're not German, are you?'

'No, madam, I'm from Northumberland.'

She dealt a satisfied nod and signalled briskly for him to proceed, before leaning to murmur to Etta, 'One never quite knows if one is doing the right thing in being civil to them. Well now, sit down, children, and let us have tea!'

Even if the somewhat aloof barrier was to remain

422

between mother and daughter, Isabella made great effort to pierce it by asking as she extended a plate of sandwiches, 'What is the latest of Martin, I do trust he's not having too hard a time out there?'

Greatly surprised to hear the forbidden name from her mother's lips and feeling a rush of gratitude, Etta felt tears burn her eyes, but fought them and soon recovered her voice to say, 'Yes, thank you, as far as we know he's safe . . . This is an excellent spread Grandmamma has put on for us,' she said briskly to the children, 'I think we should all say thank you.' And nothing much more was said as everyone tucked in.

Even later, when the youngsters had taken their fill and had been granted permission to leave the table and go across to the window that overlooked the city, Etta declined to admit her true worries to her mother.

'You've hardly eaten a thing, Henrietta,' ventured her hostess, polite but kind. 'Can I not tempt you with some of this delicious cake?'

Etta simply shook her head.

Isabella thought she knew the cause, issuing thoughtfully, 'It's a strain not knowing if they're safe, isn't it? I worry terribly about John. At least he doesn't have a wife to fret about him. Life must be even more difficult for you without a husband. The children must be missing their father too.'

Across the table, Etta nodded quietly, fighting tears.

Then her mother amazed her even more by referring to the cause of their previous estrangement. 'Eleven years,' breathed Isabella, as if disbelieving the passage of time, 'and there was I foolish enough to imagine it was only a girlish romance, that you'd come back to us when you realised your mistake . . . I should never have doubted your fortitude.'

Etta looked slightly pained. 'You make it sound like an ordeal. My years with Martin have been wonderful.' She

423

chose not to mention the rift, did not even want to think of it. But she had come partly to understand the reason her mother had chosen to stand by her own husband and not her child, and could only hope that she herself would not one day have to make that same decision.

'I'm glad,' said her mother. 'Really I am. I'd much rather my daughter be happy than have had all those years gone to ruin.'

Etta took a deep breath. 'So, you're prepared to admit that my life hasn't been wasted as you feared?'

'Most certainly,' confirmed Isabella. 'How could one dismiss it so when it has produced such a charming brood.' She turned her elegant head to smile at her grandchildren who stood looking out of the window at the street scene below. 'Good as gold.'

'I didn't like to say in front of them,' blurted Etta, 'but I am rather worried.' And she divulged to a shocked Isabella about the telegram.

'Etta, how dreadful,' breathed her mother, 'were the children not present when it arrived?'

Etta shook her head and said they had been out at play. 'Martin's mother thinks it must be a mistake, says she'd feel it if anything had happened to him, and I tend to concur . . .'

Isabella nodded. 'I agree, absolutely.'

'But one can't help wondering.' Etta's distracted eyes went to the children, who were too involved in giggling over some joke to overhear.

'Naturally,' said Isabella with feeling. 'My dear, I'm so desperately sorry . . .' Lost for words, she grasped the silver teapot and refilled her daughter's cup.

'I'm going to look for him.'

'To France?' Her mother was stunned, dribbling tea into the saucer before setting the pot down. 'Oh, Henrietta, it's so dangerous! You were always so impulsive.' But recognising the depth of feeling Etta had for her husband, she

424

voiced her desire to assist. 'I wish that there was more I could do, but all I can offer is money and I'm afraid to insult you again.'

Etta shook her head. 'I shouldn't have behaved so rudely to you on our last meeting.'

'Then please take this!' Isabella reached for her bag, pulled out a fistful of cash and thrust it at her.

'But your hotel bill . . .'

'I can write a cheque! Please, take it.'

Despite her anxiety, Etta was compelled to chuckle. 'And you label me impulsive.' But, to her mother's gratification, she took the money all the same.

Isabella smiled, and played with the fastener on her handbag. 'So, how shall you get to France? Do you have a passport?'

'I shall have to look into it. I'm afraid I know little of such things.'

'We must make enquiries this afternoon!'

'I'm sure your presence would be of great assistance,' Etta told her mother warmly.

'Then we shall go and have your photograph taken!' Isabella began to look quite excited at being involved. 'And you must be inoculated against enteric. Shall you join some organisation? I believe it's pretty difficult to obtain a permit otherwise – but please, not the VAD, I wouldn't wish that for you. Elizabeth Netherwood has joined and some of the things she has to deal with are quite disgusting, I believe. Her parents are so mortified they prefer us to believe she's serving tea and coffee – oh, what a brainwave! I may be able to help you in that field. Lady Fenton has opened a canteen for soldiers in . . . now, what is the blessed name of that place, I can't remember – oh, some wretched little town in France!' She gave an irritable flick of her wrist and went on, 'It has the full approval of the Red Cross so it's quite near to the front. I could persuade your father to make a donation so that you may go and work there

425

too. You wouldn't have to stay, of course, but it would gain you the permit you need to travel about. Naturally, I won't divulge that it would benefit yo—' She broke off to issue a sadly apologetic smile. 'I'm sorry, dear, I didn't mean to hurt you, but your father won't have your name mentioned.'

Etta waved this away. 'It would be such a great help.'

'Then I shall attend to it immediately I'm home. You shall have all the permission you need within the shortest time possible.'

The children came back at this point and the subject was hurriedly closed. Apropos the passport, however, there followed a trip to a studio where Etta had her photograph taken. After this it was back to unconstrained fun for the children, Etta and their grandmother taking them for a walk around the Bar Walls, then for another round of cakes at the hotel before it was time to go home, a most heart-warming afternoon being spent by all.

'Do let me know how you fare,' begged Isabella upon parting.

'I will – and thank you.' Etta dealt her mother a respectful peck on the cheek, then went home.

True to Isabella's word, the required paperwork was to arrive within three days, along with a letter advising the beneficiary to use Lady Fenton's name wherever she needed to smooth her passage. Yet, even financially equipped for an expedition to France, Etta held reservations as to the wisdom of her trip. Much as she feared for Marty, much as she ached to be with him, if she left her children in order to search for him who knew how long she would be away? Or even if she would return at all. It would be as if she were abandoning them as her parents had once abandoned her.

But Marty's mother declared this was nonsense. 'Abandoning them? Doesn't their Granny Lanegan love them as much as anyone? They'll be happy enough here till their parents come home, as surely both will.'

Still unsure, Etta picked up the newspaper then, to be met by the announcement of her brother's death. At such tragic event any doubt was banished.

19

Steeped in grief over her brother's death, Etta was to delay her intended voyage for twenty-four hours, during which she wondered whether there would be any funeral or if John would be buried in France. She debated how to convey her sadness to her mother without raking up a storm from her father, and remembered the good times she and John had enjoyed as children, rather than the bad.

But there was no doubt in her mind now that she would go to find her husband. She would never forgive herself if something happened without Marty hearing directly from her lips how much she loved and cherished him.

'Have you a plan?' enquired Red when, that evening, she confirmed her decision to go.

'Other than to find him, no.' Whenever Marty had written 'we are at a place called', the name of that place had been censored. There had been crude maps in the newspaper, indicating the progress of the war and the various battles that had occurred, and Etta had been studying these for a hint of where to start, though she was little wiser. 'Perhaps I'll begin by going to the canteen as Mother arranged for me.' She had at least managed to locate that place via an atlas in the library. 'With the amount of soldiers that pass through there, surely one of them must be able to point me in the right direction.'

'Sure, I don't like this at all, you going so near to the

battlefront.' Red shook his head. 'Marty left you in my care, I ought to forbid it.' Seeing Etta's dangerous expression, he sighed and declared, 'Well, if your mind is made up there'll be things you need,' and he went upstairs, from where they were to hear a lot of banging of floorboards.

'Is he taking the house apart?' tutted Aggie, before he came back down to say:

'If you won't take my advice then take this.'

Expecting a suitcase, Etta could not have been more surprised at what was passed into her hand. It was a pistol.

'Where the divil –' began Aggie, then spun accusingly on her elderly uncle.

'Don't be looking at me!' objected old Mal.

His cheeks sprouting fluff and his voice like a man, Jimmy-Joe made as if to pounce, asking reproachfully, 'Aw, Da! How long have you had that?'

He received a cuff from his father and an order to, 'Leave off! 'Tis not a toy.'

'Then what are you doing flashing it about with children still here?' demanded Aggie, jerking her head at the row of grandchildren sitting quietly in awe. 'And that's an officer's pistol if I'm not mistaken.'

Fingering the leather holster and strap, Red agreed that it was, then explained to all, 'I came by it in the ould country. 'Twas in a sack of rags I paid tuppence for – quite a bargain, don't ye think? I knew 'twould come in handy one o' these days.'

'Handy?' cried Aggie. 'You crafty rascal, how long have you been hiding it away from me?'

'About the same amount of time you've been hiding your bottles of liquor from me.' He nodded curtly as she blushed and bridled.

'It's not the same thing! Ye could bring the polis on us – ye'll have Etta arrested, encouraging her to carry that thing!'

Her husband remained calm. 'It might be news to you,

Ag, but there are a lot of people with guns in France.'

'She's got to get there yet!' His wife's voice betrayed a scathing pessimism.

'Unfortunately there's no bullets to go with it,' Red told his daughter-in-law, 'but still, it might ward off unwanted attention.' He sat down abruptly and fell asleep.

'Pass it over,' croaked Uncle Mal. 'I'll get you some ammo.'

'Oh, that'd go down a treat,' scoffed Aggie, 'an Irishman going round the shops asking for ammunition.'

'Is it stupid you're calling me? I was thinking to ask Billy Watson, he's sure to have some in that shed o' his.'

Etta was unsure about carrying a loaded gun, but thought the firearm itself a good idea, for, 'One might bump into Germans.' The pistol was therefore designated for travel.

'Well, we'd better gather the rest of your kit then,' sighed a defeated Aggie. 'What'll you be wearing to travel in?'

'One of those cotton dresses I bought.' Etta hoped to make herself less conspicuous by furnishing herself in attire befitting a nurse; there were so many volunteers wearing such unofficial uniform that she should blend in nicely. 'But that'll be no good if it rains so I'm going to buy a water-proof cape on my way. This is the most unpredictable August I've ever known; one never knows what to put on, the mornings start so cold then by midday it's absolutely boiling.'

The ancient uncle shook with laughter. 'There's folk bashing the tripe out of each other and the pair of you are concerned with the weather!'

Aggie's eyes ordered the old fool to remember the children, who appeared apprehensive about their mother's involvement. 'But of course, Etta won't be going anywhere near the trouble.'

He took note and said confidently. 'Why, to be sure she will not.'

Red, who had woken as quickly as he had fallen asleep, grabbed the newspaper and sought to deflect his grandchildren's worry. 'Here now, there's a circus come to town – would you look at this splendid creature!' He showed them the picture of the elephant leading the procession.

'Will we have one of those one day, Grandad?' enquired Willie, thereby spurring light-hearted laughter amongst the adults.

'No, but you shall have some sweeties.' Etta smiled indulgently and, grabbing her purse, asked, 'Does anyone else want anything from the shop?'

'Not for me,' said Aggie, but by means of covert hand signals made a request for a bottle of stout, pretending to scratch her head when Red looked sharply in her direction.

Etta paid a brief visit to the shop, encountering Aggie's closest neighbours on her way. Breaking off her conversation, Mrs Thrush was keen to verify the rumour. 'Eh, Ett, is it right you're off to the war to find your lad?' There was a note of admiration in her voice.

Etta nodded and turned to smile sadly at the other person present. Mrs Gledhill, dressed from head to foot in black, the grief over Albert's death still haunting her face, reached out to press a hand to her arm, saying warmly, 'Good luck, love. God keep you safe.' And both women gave murmuring agreement as they watched the younger woman go on her way that she had improved out of all recognition to the girl Marty had married.

Etta returned with bags of sweets for the children, some tobacco for the men and Aggie's bottle of stout, and tried not to smile as the recipient affected great surprise.

'Oh, you naughty girl, you shouldn't have!' Aggie responded innocently to her husband's disapproval by saying, ''Twould be rude of me to ask her to take it back now, wouldn't it?' And with a crafty wink at Etta she went to pour it into a glass.

In between gulps, in return for the favour, the matriarch spent a good deal of time sorting out the necessary provisions and items that might come in handy for Etta's expedition, plus some small gifts for Marty when he was found – cigarettes, soap, and muslin bags of lavender that the children had sewed – packing all of these in a small brown suitcase, which was finally handed to her daughter-in-law. 'There, I think that's just about everything . . .'

Etta beheld her warmly. 'Thanks, Ma. Thank you for all you've done.' And on impulse she put her arms around the other in a much more open show of fondness than she had been able to share with her own mother.

Surprised and touched, Aggie indulged this embarrassing behaviour for a moment, then patted her and escaped the embrace, looking self-conscious as she shrugged off her daughter-in-law's thanks. 'Sure, 'tis only a small little thing, for heaven's sake.' Though Etta's gesture had delighted her no end.

Uncle Mal was also apportioned Etta's affection, along with Tom and Jimmy-Joe, and finally Red, who gripped her paternally by the shoulders.

'I've the greatest admiration for you, Etta,' Marty's father told her.

Aggie was to endorse this. 'We've every faith you'll find your man and bring him home safe to us.'

'Not such a dilatory biddy now, then?' teased Etta, a sparkle in her eye.

Momentarily taken aback that her past insults had been overheard, Aggie could laugh at herself. 'Indeed you are not. There are others who might bake a better pie, but they've not half your adventurous spirit.'

Despite the latter, fully aware of how dangerous her mission, Etta was to spend a long time with her children that night, reading them story after story without complaint, explaining to them where she was going and how long it might take, assuring them she would be in no danger, kissing and holding them in preparation for the parting.

When they awoke the next day she had gone.

*

After closing the door behind her Etta seemed to be constantly on the move. First by train to London where she changed her money to francs, then a ferry to Boulogne. Thankfully the sea was quite calm, though the zigzag course of the boat and the knowledge that it was doing this to avoid enemy submarines did produce a thrill, and there was no need to take up the knitting she had brought along in order to stave off boredom. Advantageously, she was not alone in her quest, for, apart from French and Belgian travellers and the official groups of VADs and Red Cross workers – from whom she tried to steer clear in case she was commandeered – there were a few solitary females, anxious and hollow-eyed, wrapped in their thoughts. Naturally drawn towards them, Etta was to discover that they too had come to find their soldier husbands. An immediate rapport was struck up. Alas, the difference was that their men had been grievously wounded and were at a hospital in Rouen, meaning that, unlike her, they knew exactly where to go, and Etta's hope of procuring a travelling companion was rudely thwarted. Upon reaching foreign shores she was still alone.

A short period of tension whilst her papers were inspected, then she was onto French soil. Thenceforth she was plunged into another world. Already tired and grubby from her travels, she felt her head begin to spin as she was engulfed by a malodorous sea of khaki, troops of all nationalities, jabbering swathes of foreigners, women of dubious character and competent-looking nurses, all of whom appeared to know exactly where they were going. Affecting to appear similarly knowledgeable, yet without any real sense of direction, she pulled her crumpled summer dress to order and, with her cape over one arm and her suitcase in the other, tagged onto the crowd and struck out smartly towards what she assumed to be the railway station.

Here, confused even more by trying to read all the foreign names on the notice board, she experienced a moment of panic and rushed for the nearest retreat, a canteen, but upon entry she saw that the inhabitants were nearly all soldiers, and the hubbub was only marginally less than outside. Unsure whether this place catered for the general public, she deposited her cape on a stand and her luggage at its base, then hovered for a moment, imbibing her surroundings, the clink of teaspoons in cups producing an involuntary thirst, unaware that eyes turned to look at her for she had long been accustomed to male admiration. Then, feeling rather foolish, she told herself how ridiculous and disorganised she was being and decided she had better start asking for directions. After tucking a strand of loose hair back under the white cotton triangle that enfolded her head, her hand moved involuntarily to the bulge in her nurse-like uniform as she wondered, not for the first time, if anyone would guess she had a pistol strapped beneath.

'Two teas, please, dear, when you're ready!'

She glanced down at the soldiers seated on a bench nearby, about to explain politely that she was not a wait-ress, but then veneration for their heroism got the better of her and, with a nod and a smile, she made her way between the throng and approached a woman in charge of an urn, wondering how she would make herself understood if the other were foreign.

However, it transpired that all the staff were English volunteers. Upon discovering this she introduced herself.

'Oh, good-oh, are you come to join us?' asked the jolly looking matron who wore similar attire to herself, her voice raised above the clatter of crockery and the buzz of male conversation.

'I'm afraid not!' Etta raised her voice too. 'I'm here to look for my husband.' It seemed safe enough to drop the pretence now that she had the necessary permit to travel about France. However, her conscience pricked, she added hastily, 'But I'll help for a while if I can. The chaps over there have asked for two teas . . .'

'Two teas coming up!' Her bosom thrust proudly, the other duly filled the mugs and presented them along with a small bundle of cigarettes.

Keeping her elbows pressed to her sides for fear of causing spillage, Etta made her way through the throng of tired-looking soldiers and handed the mugs to those waiting; then, being accosted for service on her way, was to attend to numerous others, some very charming French ones, going back and forth for a good while before finally being able to make her own request to the woman on the urn.

'Do you cater only for soldiers? I've had nothing for hours and I'm absolutely gasping.' She brandished her purse. 'I'll pay of course.'

'Gosh, no, you deserve a cup for mucking in – you only came in here to look for your husband, you said?'

'Oh, I didn't mean he's in here,' Etta hurried to explain. 'At least I don't think so, that would be luck indeed. No, he's somewhere out there, amongst the fighting.'

'All the more reason you deserve a cup of tea then,' said the jolly woman. 'Here, have a bun too.'

'Thanks.' Etta was deeply grateful, then realised aloud, 'I've had nothing since breakfast.'

'I say! Then you should be having more than that.' She told Etta where a reasonably priced meal could be had, and, upon learning that she was a complete stranger to France, gave her all manner of useful information.

Racked by guilt in the face of such friendly treatment, Etta decided that she would after all go to Lady Fenton's canteen as promised, and confessed to her new acquaintance, 'I feel so wretched. I'm here under false pretences. I'm supposed to begin canteen work myself but I used it as an excuse to come and search for my husband.'

The other merely shrugged. 'It's natural one should pay greater importance to one's own.' She cast wistful eyes around the roomful of soldiers.

'Yes, but there's nothing to prevent me helping others

435

whilst I'm looking,' said Etta firmly, and, unsure how to pronounce the name of her destination, she exhibited the piece of paper with her mother's writing on it. 'So can you advise me how to get there?'

The other could, but, 'You are aware how close to the front it is?'

Ignorant as to what this entailed, Etta nodded and said she would catch the first available train.

'You'll have a long wait,' the other busied herself whilst giving her reply, gathering dirty mugs for washing, 'there's not another due till this evening – if only you'd asked someone earlier you would have made the last one.'

Etta sighed and said it was her own silly fault. Reluctantly, she agreed it was better not to arrive at a strange venue in the dark. 'Do you know anywhere cheap I might stay?'

'There's a relatives' hostel.' The woman scribbled on a piece of paper. 'Or if they can't fit you in there, there's another place that's quite reasonable.'

Etta nodded and said she would delay her journey till morning. However, after consuming the bun and the mug of tea, she decided there was nothing to prevent her making a start on her investigations into the whereabouts of Marty's unit. 'I didn't like to pester your customers before . . . Do you think they'd regard it as a monstrous cheek if I ask them to which regiment they belong?'

'No, so long as you don't go empty-handed.' The other grinned slyly and extended more mugs of tea towards her.

And for the rest of the afternoon, Etta found herself thus involved. But, apart from being made to feel of some small use to those who had been fighting on her behalf and seemed to take great pleasure in conversing with her, she found little to be gained from the exercise. When she bedded down for the night in the cheap hotel she still had no definite course of action. Still, tomorrow she would head in the general direction of Lady Fenton's canteen and see what fate provided.

Another train, another cramped, soot-speckled journey with many miles to travel, sometimes at a crawl and often shunted into sidings to make way for a troop train to pass, finally to alight several hours later at Amiens. Lady Fenton's canteen was many miles to the south of here, but Etta had decided she could go no further today and would find a place to spend the night, meanwhile using the rest of the afternoon to make further enquiries about her husband.

It was somewhat peculiar, being in quite civilised surroundings but able to hear the big guns growling in the distance, and frightening to know she would soon be heading towards them, but exhilarating too. However, with no jolly accomplice to provide her with an address of somewhere to stay, her lodgings might prove more difficult, for the city was crammed with soldiers of every nationality, and so she made a start without delay. Second nature led her to forgo any grand hotel and opt for more modest accommodation, though her prospective hostess seemed not keen to take a female guest, saying her rooms were reserved for the brave *soldats* who had been fighting, and only when Etta made a concerted charm offensive and explained her desperate reason for coming there was Madame persuaded.

Immediately after slaking her hunger, Etta set about her enquiries, asking anyone who might listen if they knew of the exact whereabouts of her husband's unit. She wandered from every café to every restaurant and every bar, meandered within the Gothic cathedral, here not to admire but to scrutinise each male face, praying that one of them might be his. She gazed through the windows of barbers' shops at lathered jaws, attempting to define the features behind the foam, wondering if those green eyes swathed within the hot towel could be Marty's, but no . . .

Back to treading the streets, the thin soles of her shoes

affording no redress and her feet on fire, she paused tiredly to inspect a column of French soldiers on the march, noting the weary faces and unpleasant odour that emanated from their ranks; more powerful than mere sweat. This was, she guessed, the stench of war.

By early evening, having come almost full circle, the constant squinting against the sun giving her a headache, she stood in a patch of shade for a moment by a high-class hotel to observe the stream of red-hatted staff officers going in and out. How silly that she had not thought of this first: if anyone should know how to locate an army unit, they would. Without a second thought, she accosted one of them politely as he passed, explaining briefly that she was here to search for her husband.

After flicking his eyes up and down her form, he responded to her question as if she had no right to ask it. 'My good woman, if you suppose that I have nothing other to occupy me than the personal dealings of one private soldier, you know little about the organisation of war.'

Etta was instantly furious, losing her dignity into the bargain. 'You know little about courtesy either!' she flung at his retreating back. Still, this did not deter her from asking another.

This one was barely less discourteous, though he was more knowledgeable, priding himself on statistics. 'Let me see, that would make his battalion with the eighteenth brigade, which is with the Sixth Division . . .'

Etta was instantly excited. 'And can you tell me precisely where I might find them?'

'Certainly not.' He strode on.

Etta refused to be cowed and persisted in her approach to others, but, constantly frustrated, she was about to admit defeat and return to her pension when someone appeared at her elbow.

'Pardon me, ma'am, might I be of assistance?' She turned to see a man of perhaps forty, quite tall and thickset, clearly not one of the staff officers for he was infinitely more polite, and, though his hazel eyes had a shrewd vulpine gleam about them and his wide, heavily pocked face had lost any shred of innocence it might once have had, it wore the most engaging smile. He also had a North American accent. 'I couldn't help but overhear you say you're looking for your husband.'

She threw herself on his mercy. 'Yes! All they'll tell me is that his unit is with the Sixth Division, but they won't say precisely where.'

'That's probably because they have no idea themselves.' He smiled.

She looked dubiously at his garb. 'Are you involved with the military?'

'I'm a journalist.' The man doffed his Panama hat and introduced himself. 'Robert Williams.'

'How do you do, my name is Lanegan.' Etta extended her hand. 'Thank you so much for your intervention. I do hope you'll be able to help.'

'I shall endeavour to, Mrs Lanegan.' Not content with covering accounts of valour, Williams had spotted a smaller but no less interesting tale of a beautiful young woman come to the battleground in search of her missing husband. 'Though I must warn you that I'm as persona non grata to the British Army as yourself when it comes to information.' He indicated the hotel foyer. 'Would you care to tell me all about your intrepid venture over dinner?'

'Intrepid?' She laughed this away. 'Merely desperate, I'm afraid.' Aware that she could be being duped, Etta nevertheless decided this could be her only chance, and hence, after apologising for her dusty attire, accompanied him into the hotel. Here, over an exquisitely laid table, she was not only to spend the best part of two hours regaling him with her dilemma, but rather unwisely opening her heart, for somehow without even seeming to, Mr Williams extracted from her much of her life history, including the identity of her tyrannical father.

Despite this, her faith in him was repaid. In exchange for her story, Robert Williams was to donate the valuable information that the 6th Division was in the vicinity of Ypres in Flanders.

At first, dismay. 'So I've been travelling in completely the wrong direction!'

But then salvation, for on top of putting her on the right track her host offered to escort her as far as was possible in his motor car. 'Unlike our Fleet Street brethren we neutrals have the advantage of being allowed to go pretty much where we like.'

She disallowed herself to become too excited. 'This is inordinately generous, Mr Williams.'

'Not at all.' He dealt his mouth a final pat of the table napkin. 'I was thinking of heading there myself anyway.' Ascertaining the whereabouts of her lodgings, he said he would meet her there early in the morning.

Astounded by this change of fortune and by the speed of it, Etta could not really believe as she left the hotel and returned to her modest pension that she would see Mr Williams again, let alone that he would lead her to Marty, and she determined to make alternative plans for the morning. These feelings were added to by the elderly Madame, who, upon being made privy to Etta's progress later that evening over black coffee in her cosy parlour, cautioned against going so deep into the battleground, saying in impeccable English, 'I do not want to alarm you, but could it be that your husband has been wounded and is in one of the hospitals?'

'That has crossed my mind,' replied Etta gravely, pausing in her knitting and allowing it to rest on her lap, her eyes travelling over the religious artefacts and lace doilies that made this parlour very like Aggie's except for its more ornate furniture. 'But the telegram made no mention of it and I really need a starting point. the most sensible thing would be to find his unit and start from there rather than visit every hospital in France.'

'There are so many casualties that it must be hard to keep track of them,' said Madame in her charming lilt, she too working on an item of comfort for a soldier. 'They bring many here. Perhaps, before you go all that way, would it not be wise to check?' Tugging a fresh supply from her ball of wool, she pulled her shawl more closely around her and continued knitting, going on to inform Etta that there was a casualty clearing station near to Amiens in an old asylum. 'Maybe your journalist friend can take you to look there?'

Etta nodded and thanked Madame for her help, though as she finally put away her needles and went off to bed she was still not expecting Mr Williams to turn up.

But, to her extreme gratitude, the black motor car which arrived outside the pension early next morning did contain the journalist in its rear passenger seat. Trying not to express her surprise that he had been true to his word, Etta relinquished her luggage to the driver who installed it in the boot next to Williams's typewriter, then told her new friend of Madame's suggestion and asked if he would take her to the asylum before anything else.

He gave a shrewd smile, this extending to a glint in his hazel eyes as he held the car door open for her. 'I've already included it on the itinerary. Thought about it last night.'

Etta smiled back warmly as she slid along the leather seat and pulled down her skirt, which had ridden up to display her black-stockinged calves. 'I'm gratified to hear you've paid so much consideration to my welfare.'

'My motive's not entirely selfless,' admitted Williams as he climbed in beside her and instructed the driver to move off. 'I'm hoping that your good fortune might also shed a little on me.' He told her how, regarding information, the British Army put every obstacle in his way, which was why he could so readily sympathise with her plight.

441

However, there was an extra reason for his kindness, which he chose to keep from her. Inured to many features of this war, even the most horrific, there was something about this young woman that moved him, despite her friendly, confident nature, an air of vulnerability in those brown eyes that managed to pierce the hide of this hard-bitten old hack and made him want to look after her. He feared he had fallen in love. It worried him.

They drove to the asylum where, earlier, a stream of ambulances had deposited hundreds more cases, most of them being too badly wounded to be interviewed. Observing these as they lay in the yard, waiting to be categorised, Etta was so shocked that for the moment she could do nothing but stare. It was one thing to read of wounded men in a newspaper, a completely different matter to have them presented in the flesh, with their grossly disfigured faces, seeping bandages and suppurating wounds. Involuntarily, she covered her mouth. She had considered the previous bodily smells bad enough, but this cloying stench made her want to retch. Yet others went about their task quite calmly, making sense out of chaos, talking to the wretched creatures on those stretchers as if they were human beings. Which is what they are, Etta told herself sternly, and tried to pull herself together and to remember the purpose of her quest. The white collar and cuffs of her dress marked her as a nurse, but now she felt completely ashamed and useless. She was, however, able to wander amongst those with less critical injuries who were still lying unattended in the open, to hand out cigarettes and light them whilst gently pumping the men for news of Marty, until her lack of medical attention revealed her as an impostor, at which point she was told to stop bothering them by a very possessive genuine nurse.

Williams, who had been quietly watching Etta, now lifted his hat and sought to plead on her behalf. 'I beg your pardon, Sister, this young woman is attempting to find her husband.'

Flattered by the title, yet remaining intolerant, the over-worked nurse directed Etta to someone else who might be able to search a list of names to see if her husband's was on it. 'In there!' Even as she flicked an impatient finger she was already turning away to attend to someone more needy.

Issuing profuse thanks to the nurse's back, Etta went with Robert Williams in the direction she had indicated. Somewhere along the way they managed to take a wrong turn and went into an outbuilding containing a pile of arms and legs. They hurried out again, finally to come upon the one who held the relevant list. Marty's name was not on it.

In spite of an ability to charm with his sudden smile, it came to light that Etta's travelling companion was by and large a taciturn man, of which she was quite glad, for she had no inclination for idle chat. Unaware of the troubling thoughts that consumed Williams, that a part of him hoped for her husband's death so that she might turn to him for comfort, she was content to look out of the window as the motor car carried them north.

Along the dusty, bumpy miles her glazed eyes were to encounter a procession of bullock carts piled high with mattresses and household goods, dispatch riders on motor-bikes, motor-lorries, horse-drawn ambulances, peasants going about their everyday business as best they could, and, of course, the ever-present tramping soldiers. There were refugees too. As the car was steered carefully around them, Etta's heart went out to a young barefooted girl pushing a wheelbarrow in which was a toddler and a baby. That made her think of her own dear children and she thanked God they were safe in England.

An hour after midday, she and her travelling companion stopped to buy food at a small town, where, by coinci-dence, a string of VAD ambulances were bringing wounded to the railway sidings. Forgoing the opportunity to eat and leaving Williams to type his notes, an anxious Etta went immediately to inspect the men on stretchers as each was laboriously transferred to the train. She walked amongst those still lying and sitting on the platform, clasped the hands of those strong enough to reach out to her in cheery greeting, lighted cigarettes for them, asked if there was anything else she could do.

One issued cheek despite his blood-stained bandages. 'Yes, you can give us a kiss.'

'Gladly,' she said, without hesitation pressing her lips to his brow, to much stoical jocularity from others and pleas for her to do the same for them. 'I'm sure my husband wouldn't mind.'

There were groans. 'Might've known a corker like you would be married!'

Which gave her the opening to ask if any of them knew Marty, or at least knew of his unit. But alas, no one did.

So, after a quick bite to eat it was back on the road again, stirring up the dust for another thirty miles or so, when, stiff and uncomfortable from the tortuously slow pace of travel due to all the obstacles and the poor state of the roads, they stopped again and knocked at the door of a cottage to ask if the owner could provide food and drink. This impromptu course of action was to be repeated as, veering northeastwards, they drove throughout the late afternoon across the border into Belgium, the villagers happy to oblige with what refreshment they had, sometimes charging exorbitant rates, sometimes nothing at all. Neither language nor dialect formed a barrier, the rather weary-looking inhabitants seeming to understand what was required, which was as well, for just when Etta had begun to grasp a few Gallic phrases the local tongue became predominantly Flemish. Every outbuilding, every barn now seemed to house those who had been dispossessed and driven out by the enemy, forced from the place that she herself was travelling towards; every other field an army

444

encampment. Since having their passports stamped, the driver had become increasingly nervous that they were getting very close to the war zone and now announced himself not keen to go further, until Williams offered a hefty bribe, then on they went, showing their passes at village after village, towards the sound of the guns.

Yet even as they drew nearer the theatre of war there were pockets of tranquillity to be found. Considering it was now early evening they decided to put-up for the night, but unable to find a hostelry that was not crammed with military, they drove onwards for a little while along the narrow back-roads and eventually came across an inn, which, being on higher ground, had a splendid view of the surrounding area. Here, after allowing herself to be treated to egg and chips, Etta voiced a desire to take an evening stroll in the sunshine, and with her journalist companion was to wander unmolested amongst flowers, birds and butterflies, to gaze upon a vista of windmills and hop gardens, the countless church spires of this deeply religious country adding paradox – when no more than five or six miles away across that green plain could quite clearly be seen the white tents of an advanced dressing station, and, only a little further, the puffs of white smoke as the artillery of friend and foe harangued each other in fine voice.

The sun began to set, the gunfire to diminish. A soldier appeared on the scene, reminding them that civilians must be in by dark, and so they made their way back to the inn, here to capture what was left of the balmy evening, sipping drinks by an open window. On the breeze, from the direction of the camp hospital, came the faint strains of a bugle. Overwhelmed by thoughts and fears for Marty, Etta suddenly bent her head and wept. Gently, Williams took the glass from her hand, replacing it with a handkerchief. Etta buried her grateful face within and surrendered to the tears, barely noticing the large supportive hand on her shoulder until its warmth lingered just a fraction too long, and at this she moved away as politely as she could to extricate herself and retreat to her room, wishing not to offend but to be alone.

Dawn broke to a horrible din, its effects causing a slight tremor of the breakfast cups and saucers. From then on life became exceedingly more tense, papers being demanded at every turn of the way, the only other presence on the road now being army personnel. Long convoys of motor-wagons carrying ammunition and rations from the railheads, stirring up clouds of dust. Behind them and restricted to a crawl, the car bumped its way over the worn pave, taking three hours to cover three miles. Long before this there had been signs of the violence, homes tumbledown and abandoned. Now, though, came gruesome indication of how close they actually were: dead farm animals, some horribly mutilated, others whole but inflated by gas, their rigid limbs directed at the sky.

'We must be in shell range.'

Even without Robert Williams's grave assertion, Etta guessed for herself that their vehicle would inevitably be stopped, and when they came upon a traffic post with its massing troops and a provost barred their way she was not altogether surprised.

'I'm afraid I can't let you go any further,' the redcap told the driver first, becoming doubly adamant upon seeing that one of the occupants was a woman.

Williams leaned forward from the back seat and introduced himself. 'I'm trying to help this young lady who's searching for her missing husband. We have permits.'

Until now Etta's innate confidence had helped her to bluff a way through any hurdle. With this same air she produced her authority to be in Belgium, interjecting the loud whizzes and explosions and the crackle of rifle fire to say, 'I'm a volunteer with Lady Fenton.'

But the provost was unimpressed, glowering coldly from

beneath the slashed peak of his cap. 'I don't care who or what you are, that's not the right permit and you're not going any further without one.'

'I must protest most vigorously!'

'Protest all you like!' With this ungallant retort the redcap ordered the driver of the car to steer into a farm gateway and turn it around.

'Well,' sighed Etta's companion as they headed back at snail's pace along the congested road for the village they had just left, 'I don't know what to suggest you do now, Mrs Lanegan.'

'Thank you for all your help anyway, Mr Williams,' replied Etta sincerely. 'If you'd be so good as to ask the driver to stop once we're out of sight of that military policeman I'll get out and attempt to find my way via another route.' When he looked at her questioningly, she added, 'I've no intention of giving up after I've come so far.'

'And I've no intention of deserting you so close to the war zone,' he told her sternly.

'I shall be perfectly all right,' came her airy response. 'I have a gun.'

He blurted an amazed laugh. 'Then I'm most definitely not leaving you to your own devices!'

'Please don't address me as if I'm a simpleton!'

'That's exactly what you are! Don't you know you could be shot as a spy? You're staying with me till we decide what to do.'

And with that Etta had little option but to return with him to the place they had just left.

Unable to persuade her to hand over the firearm but accepting her promise that she would not try to use it, Williams spent the rest of that day talking matters over with her, and tried to find a mayor or someone in authority who could give them the correct paperwork. When this failed, he drew up various plans, none of which were to

447

Etta's approval, though she kept quiet for now. Her companion made great effort to cheer her spirits throughout that long day, concluding with as nice a supper and bottle of wine as could be bought in this small village, seemingly as keen as herself to bring the story to a happy conclusion. Yet something alerted her to the fact that this was not the case; some word, some look in those veteran eyes over the wine glass that made her realise his intentions towards her were not quite all they seemed. And though he never made a wrong move, and promised that he would continue to act as her escort and if need be accompany her on foot in the morning, her nod of gratitude veiled a deeper intention.

With the household still asleep, she crept away in the night.

Knowing she was at risk of being shot for breaking the curfew, camouflaged by her dark cape, Etta distanced herself from the road and took a furtive route across country, first groping her way through the field she had inspected last evening in order to ensure that it would pose few obstacles, aided by the occasional flare that burst in spidery fashion upon the night sky, and, once well away, resting in a small copse to await sunrise.

Then, on she went, shivering through the morning mist that was laced with the smell of heavy explosives, damp from the overnight dew; sweltering in the midday sun, through fields of poppies and gardens of hops, with singing larks and thunderous guns, occasionally stumbling upon areas of churned-up earth and barbed wire and splintered trees and dead farm animals, shocked even more by a small graveyard of wooden crosses. She provided an incongruous sight, with her little suitcase in hand as if on a trip to the seaside. Upon being fortunate enough to find an occupied dwelling where the farmer's wife gave her bread and water, she paused only to consume this, before marching ever onwards in her single-minded pursuit. It was quite amazing to find civilians still living and working so close to the line – gratifying too, for a woman like herself, grubby and unkempt as she had become, might blend in as a peasant all the better. There was no doubt that she was heading in the right direction, for the constant boom of artillery was much louder now; moreover, the landscape was almost as flat as a bowling green, and on the distant horizon could be seen the skeleton of a large town where a cloud of smoke signified some violent disturbance, its acrid, billowing fumes thick enough to taste.

But her perspective of the landscape was ill-formed, her goal much further than the sound and smell of the guns would indicate. Exhausted and hungry, with places of shelter few and far between, she paused for a while at a bombed-out cottage to relieve herself behind a wall, then to gorge on the pears and soft fruit that grew in the garden, to relax for a time as best she could with the intermittent thrash of warfare pounding in her head. Finally she splashed herself with water from a pump to remove the dust kicked up from the parched fields, though there was little to be done about the grubbiness of her attire. She examined the rent hem of her dress and tried to rub the brick-dust from it, before heaving a sigh and setting off again.

That day seemed never-ending. God knew how many hours must have passed before she was forced to stop again. Remaining vigilant for local policemen, she spread her cape, sat down, took off her shoes and rubbed at the pink skin of her feet through the honeycomb of holes in her black stockings. Trying to gain further relief for her throbbing toes by rubbing them through the cool grass, she ate one after another of the pears that she had tucked into her case, meanwhile casting her despairing eyes upwards to watch, between the fleecy clouds, two aeroplanes engage in combat, held fascinated till one of them suddenly exploded into flames and plummeted to earth, its pilot and gunner with it. Unable to stomach any more fruit, Etta put her shoes back on and rose, hefted her suitcase, draped her cape over her arm and staggered on.

With her garments drenched in perspiration, her fingers in agony from being curled around the handle of the case even after alternating it from one hand to the other, every ligament throbbing, she wanted to burst into tears but would not allow it, forcing herself to concentrate on the man she loved and the quest to find him.

And then her prayers were answered. There, just a hundred yards beyond, was a field amassed with soldiers at rest. Panting and perspiring, limbs racked with pain, from Etta's parched lips a gasp of hopeful laughter emerged. She gazed for a second, taking in the scene: lines of picketed horses, men shaving, washing their clothes and spreading them out to dry along the hop scaffolds, others playing football, writing letters. Keeping her eyes alert for military policemen who might prevent her mission, she hurried towards the makeshift camp – and then another miracle! From a cluster of red-roofed farm buildings a group of young peasant women appeared with baskets of fruit, and they too proceeded towards the soldiers, thus providing Etta with a shield! At once, she took advantage and rushed to join them, just as the jubilant soldiers made a similar beeline.

Immediately encircled by young men desperate for female company, the local girls attempted to display their fruit. But Etta was not here to hawk wares. Grasping one man's arm and drawing him aside, she said, 'Excuse me, I'm sorry to bother you, but can you direct me?'

Remarking on the incongruity of her request and its delivery in a refined English accent, this soldier and others now flocked around her, wanting to know where the dust-coated maid had sprung from. 'How did you get so close to the lines, Sister? Did nobody try to prevent you?'

She felt exhilarated. 'Yes, but the only way they would

have succeeded in that would have been to hold hands and form a chain across the entire continent – I came across the fields!'

They laughed and admitted that there were still great gaps where no troops were to be found. 'Let's hope Fritz doesn't do the same!'

'Don't suppose you've got any soap in there, have you?' One pointed to her luggage.

'Oh, certainly!' She stooped quickly and threw open the case. 'At least for one of you – are these lavender bags any use?' These were eagerly snatched, the soldiers badgering her for whatever else she might be able to spare and quickly cleaning her out of the small gifts she had brought.

'What happened to your face, Sister?'

She touched her cheek, which had been inflicted with several grazes in her stumbling passage over the detritus of war, imagining that she must look a mess; but, unwilling to be diverted from her true ambition, said simply, 'I fell.' Then she told them she was not actually a nurse as they assumed, but had come here to seek her husband, at which they further marvelled.

'Blimey,' joked one, 'I'm glad my missus isn't like you, I see enough of her at home.'

Patiently listening to their quips, Etta finally explained which regiment she was seeking and was greatly surprised when another of them replied, 'You've found it, blossom.'

But to her vast, heart-shattering disappointment she learned that this was only one of the many territorial battalions in the regiment. Her husband had been with the regular army. Despite this, she gave his name.

They shook their heads sadly. 'Sorry, don't know him.'

She sagged. 'You must think my question ridiculous – that you could possibly know him out of thousands . . .'

'It's not daft at all, Mrs Lanegan,' said one, others agreeing. 'My cousin lives in London, I've only seen him a couple of times in my life but I saw him here last week!

So, buck up, you're sure to come across somebody who knows him.'

Then, one of them broke off peeling the orange he had just bought and said, 'Hang on, the name sounds familiar. I think Cyril was with that mob till he got sent to us.' And he cupped his mouth and called to a man some twenty yards away who was gathered with others at a water cart refilling his bottle. 'Have you heard of a bloke called Lanegan?'

'Ham and egg?' Deafened by the months of perpetual bombing and the current background noise of guns, the other misheard and came hurrying over.

'Eh, he's always thinking of his belly.' His friend laughed and called again, 'Lanegan!'

Cyril finally arrived to be told the reason behind the enquiry. Frowning at Etta, he said in a Yorkshire accent, 'I know a Marty Lanegan.'

She cried out in joy and seized his arm. 'Yes! Do you know where he is?'

'I haven't seen him for ages.'

From his odd reaction, she sensed that he was holding back and begged him with earnest brown eyes, 'But do you know where I might find him? Please, you must tell me, I'm his wife!'

He looked awkward then and she had to prise the information out of him. 'Well, it's only rumour . . .'

One of his pals gave a murmur of recognition then, 'Oh it's that bloke what –'

'What, man, what?' Greatly irritated, Etta pressed him.

'I'm sorry, missus, I heard he's been arrested.'

She sucked in her breath. 'Arrested – for what?'

Again he seemed reticent.

'For pity's sake, man!'

'Desertion,' he said sheepishly, then, at her speechlessness, he looked around to include his comrades, more of whom had begun to gather around this shapely woman as

452

he gave his opinion, 'but it can't be right, he's a good bloke is Marty.'

Etta's sunburned cheeks had turned white. 'Tell me all you know,' she directed unhesitatingly. 'Where shall I find him?'

'I don't want to send you on a wild goose chase, but well, what I heard was the redcaps took him back down the line a few days ago.'

'To be tried?' At his sympathetic nod she almost collapsed, envisaging Marty in prison.

Before anything much else could be uttered a sergeant appeared on the scene and the soldiers were called away, issuing hasty farewells to Etta.

She remained there for a moment as the troops milled around her, too distraught to move, tears blurring her vision. Eyeing her on their return from their errand, the peasant girls noted her troubled mien, one of them pausing and, with no English but a sympathetic gesture, handing Etta the last orange in her basket before moving on.

What in God's name to do now? She stared bleakly at the fruit in her hand, then made as if to trail after the girls – but in a bout of quick thinking instead she ran after the soldiers who had informed her, calling out to them, asking where she could find the nearest headquarters where she might learn more.

Fortune had it that Divisional HQ was not so far away, and so, tucking the orange into her skirt pocket, and retrieving her belongings, Etta went rambling yet again through hordes of military traffic, choked by clouds of dust thrown up by lorries, in search of the deserted estaminet that was HQ.

Assumed to be a local peasant, she was for a while allowed to roam at will. Yet before too long came the inevitable picket to bar her way.

'Bong jour, mamselle!' The greeting was stern; a rifle emphasised the point. 'Vous marchez the wrong way.' The soldier made a twirling motion with his hand, indicating for her to turn around.

For a few seconds, Etta continued to stare at him obstinately, wondering whether it would aid or hinder her to address him in English. No, it was probably best to have the army think she was local; it might at least allow her to remain in the vicinity. Reluctantly, despondent, she turned around and wandered back along the road, wondering over her next move.

After several steps, thoroughly worn-out from her travels and also from despair, she flopped down on the dusty verge. Immediately, flies began to buzz about her. She gave a half-hearted swipe at them, then, taking the orange from her pocket, she began distractedly to remove its peel, her mind on other things, her eyes still searching the faces of passing troops in the forlorn hope that the information she had just been given might be wrong, that she might yet see Marty walking past; that, like before, there had been some mix-up with the surname.

But what would happen if it truly was he who had been apprehended? She bit into a skein of orange, grateful for the juice upon her parched tongue. When would he be tried? Would she be allowed to be there to lend support? Swallowing the portion of skein, she inserted the other half, chewing thoughtfully as she tried to think what to do, demolishing the orange bit by bit. Remembering the awful staff officers in Amiens she dreaded coming up against similar treatment, especially now that she had come so far, so ironically far, only to be told that Marty was no longer here.

Abstractedly, she inserted the remaining half-skein. Instantly she balked at the sharp pain at the back of her tongue and in a highly unladylike manner tried to rid her mouth of the half-chewed orange, spitting it out along with the wasp that had been sitting on it.

Within seconds she was feeling unwell. Within minutes

she was struggling to breathe. Aware that her tortured choking sounds had brought men running, she reached out to them, eyes bulging, overwhelmed by terror that she would never see Marty and her children again. She was going to die.

20

When her eyes opened again, wide in fear, her immediate
impulse was to put a hand to her throat. No longer suffo-
cating, she nevertheless had the sense of some foreign body
in her windpipe and tried to remove it. But to her horror
her hands were bound. Got to get to Marty, she wanted to
say, but no words emerged.

'You're all right!' The loud voice attempted to calm her.
'You're able to breathe now, it'll just take a few minutes
to get used to the tube. Just try and relax, don't try to
speak, that's it, stay calm.'

Struggling to come round, assailed by the smell of ether,
Etta saw that she was in a tent, the faces around her all
male. Still trying to grope her way back to consciousness,
she felt herself being hefted onto a stretcher, trundled away,
and someone calling in a harassed voice, 'Nelson, you speak
the language, come and calm this trachie down. She keeps
trying to pull out her tube.'

And, still being jolted on the stretcher, Etta's blurred eyes
saw a face loom into hers and heard words she could not
grasp. Then it occurred to her that they too assumed her
to be local, and she tried to speak but still could not. She
must have passed out at that point.

When she regained her faculties it was to find herself in
some sort of outbuilding along with other casualties, her
bodice spattered with dried blood, and, from the mere fact

that she still could not speak, she deduced that it must be her own. When in panic she tried to rise, someone pressed her shoulders down.

'Why didn't I learn this blinkin' lingo before I came here,' sighed the one who held her captive, then mouthed loudly to Etta, 'Keep still, I need to check your tube! Do you understand English?'

Her eyes opening wide to project fear, Etta gave a quick nod.

'Oh, right . . .' Having considered her exotic with her dark hair and eyes, the old orderly was momentarily disconcerted, then spoke again, still exaggerating the formation of his words. 'You can't speak because they had to cut your windpipe, you were choking. Your hands are only tied down so you didn't try to pull out your tube when you woke up. If you promise not to do it now I'll untie them.' At the signal that she had understood he released her. 'I know it takes some getting used to but you won't need it in for very long.' Impatient and frustrated, her throat feeling raw, Etta performed a scribbling movement with her hand. Understanding this gesture, the orderly reached into his pocket for a stub of pencil and a notebook, upon which the patient scrawled frantically, *'I'm English. Need to find my husband.'*

The man expressed surprise on reading the first part. 'Oh? You don't look it.' Then he scolded her over the second, 'Just you worry about yourself.'

But Etta wrote feverishly, *'Urgent! How long was I unconscious?'*

'Not long.' He took the notebook away. 'I don't know how on earth you managed it, not even nurses are allowed this close to the line. Now, I'll be back to check your tube again in a while, I've others to see to you know.'

And, too shaken and feeble to object, Etta was left to lie there, fuming and worrying amidst the mayhem.

The orderly did come back seemingly ages later to clean

her tube, and also to say that she was to be moved to a safer place, which did not meet with her approval.

I can't go! Etta raged wordlessly, trying to drag at the other's sleeve. Don't you understand? I have to get to Marty! She gestured for his notebook but was ignored. Then, despite all grimacing protest, she was lifted up and loaded into an ambulance and, along with a groaning selection of bloodied soldiers, packed into its dark interior and driven away.

Hot tears of helpless rage welled in her eyes, spilled onto her cheeks and trickled down her neck into her hair as she was packed off like a parcel. Marty, oh Marty!

Stacked like sardines, Etta and her fellow patients were taken far behind the lines, back to where she'd been, from where she had fought so hard to come. Separated from the rest now and also from her suitcase, which had been lost, though her rolled-up cape travelled with her, she was handed over to a company of nuns who, using their own stretcher, toted her towards a waiting cart. Made giddy by the countless faces that flashed past her horizontal form, Etta thought at first she was mistaken, thought in her delirious state that he was some mirage. But it *was* him – and the stretcher was carrying her away.

She groped for the nearest arm, tugged and tried to gain their attention, and when they would not heed she attempted to raise herself precariously, jabbing and pointing frantically so that the stretcher was in danger of being tipped up, until those who transported her guessed that she wanted them to stop. Still gesturing, she directed her hand in his direction, whence they called to the one in civilian clothes who turned at their summons and was now frowning at their patient.

'Monsieur, do you know this lady?' one of them asked the portly gentleman with the greying beard.

And, still frowning, Pybus Ibbetson strolled up to her stretcher, looked down at his daughter and said without emotion, 'Yes, I know her.'

458

Their eyes locked. In the intensity of his gaze she read the thought that was going through his brain: why wasn't it you who died, and not my son?

'The lady cannot speak, monsieur,' said one of the nuns, and quickly explained what had happened and where they were taking her. 'Do you wish to accompany her?'

Totally at his mercy, for he might be the only one who could find out what was happening to Marty, Etta's dark eyes begged with all their might for him not to abandon her as he had done before.

After a tense moment, he said curtly that he would follow in his own transport.

It was not a large town but the slowness of the journey was agonising. Upon being put to bed in a cell-like room at the convent, Etta's first action was to indicate frantically that she needed a pencil and paper in order to communicate. However, this had already been thought of, and as her father was shown in they were handed to her. Immediately she scribbled the rumour of Marty's arrest and asked if her father would find anything out for her.

'Don't you even want to know what I'm doing in Flanders?' he demanded in a low, incredulous tone.

Trying to convey with tear-filled eyes that she already knew, she wrote one word: *'John.'* Ibbetson tried to appear stalwart, though his own eyes gave him away and his voice, when he managed to respond, was hollow with grief. 'I came to see the place where he died.'

There was a short silence whilst both composed themselves. Then Ibbetson changed the subject. 'So what is this about that ne'er do well husband of yours? He's been arrested, you say? I'm hardly surprised.'

Trying to contain her feeling of outrage at this slur, Etta scribbled anxiously: *'Only rumour. Not heard from him in weeks. Can you find out? Please.'* And under this she pencilled Marty's regimental number before presenting it for his gaze.

Ibbetson looked without compassion at her scrawlings, stared for so long and so detachedly that Etta feared he was going to refuse. She reached out to clasp his arm but he was not near enough, nor did he move any closer to oblige. But at least he said eventually, 'I'll see what I can do,' before abruptly he left.

Unable to call out and ask when he would be back, left to wait and to wonder in these austere surroundings, a frantic Etta could scarcely believe it when he returned that same afternoon with news of Marty's whereabouts.

'It's not good,' he told her unblinkingly. 'You were correct in being told that he has been arrested. In fact he's already been tried and found guilty of desertion.'

Devastated, Etta seized her pad and scribbled: *Is he in prison?*

'It's worse than that,' said her father. 'He's been sentenced to death.'

When the hysteria had died, when the silent scream no longer distorted her face, she had solicited the concerned nun at her bedside to go and search for her father and fetch him back, for she had omitted to ask where he was staying and feared he would be gone before she could enlist his help, which was now vital. But the sister had smiled benignly and said he was only waiting outside.

Why he was still there, Etta did not know, but she was grateful for the fact that he continued to visit her during the days it took for her to learn how to speak again, even though neither of them were to issue apology for past deeds, and interacted as strangers. In this time she was to discover that a man under sentence of execution was not immediately put to death but was entitled to have the proceedings reviewed at each higher level, and that pleas could be entered at any stage all the way up the chain of command, before the Commander in Chief gave final authorisation for the penalty to be carried out. She begged and pleaded with her father to help her save Marty, desperately wishing that she could shout her point of view instead of this pathetic, croaking whisper. 'What can be done?' he asked uninterestedly, having found out the details of the trial and relayed these to her. 'The facts cannot be argued with, your husband deserted.'

'No, I don't believe it, there must be some compelling reason!' Seated on a chair now, her tube removed but her wound still tender, Etta pressed her hand to her bandaged throat in order to hiss a painful defence, having to make up for the weakness of her vocal cords by injecting forcefulness with her eyes. 'And even if he did, then should the rest of his family be punished for his misdeed? Please, please, can you not use your influence to save him?'

'Had I the power of life and death would I not have used it to save my own son?' he demanded gruffly. 'He who died so valiantly defending his country and his comrades, whilst that . . . feckless oaf you married ran away?'

'For the love of God!' Her distorted voice beseeched him. 'How can you remain so cold and unloving in the face of your child's anguish?'

'And where are your own children?' he accused with a theatrical look around the bare white cell.

'It's only out of love for their father that I left them!' hissed Etta. 'And they're not alone, they're with affectionate grandparents.' Then, still clutching her throat, her breast rising and falling with the effort, she frowned at him. 'How did you know –'

'That you have children? I made it a point to find out. Do you not think I know what goes on in my own house?'

From this she guessed, 'So you are aware of our meetings with Mother? And of her assistance in my coming here? I'm surprised you allowed it.'

His aloof shrug indicated that this was of no account.

Her cavernous eyes observed him with disdain. 'You never did set very much store by females, did you, Father?

461

I doubt you'd still be here now if you hadn't lost your son and heir and see that I'm the only one left.'

At last she had managed to provoke some sort of feeling from him. His eyes blazed at her. 'Oh, how right I was about you! How bitter and spiteful you are.'

'Spiteful?' Her throat chafed as she hissed back at him, 'No, I speak only the truth! You're the one displaying the ultimate spite – refusing to save my husband from death! Because now you've got what you always wanted!'

He poured scorn on this. 'You imagine I've made it my life's ambition to wreak vengeance? I gave him not a second's thought since that day, nor you neither.'

'Then if it no longer matters to you one way or another, I beg you to err on the side of compassion! You know so many powerful men. You might not care for me, but do it for Celia and Edward and Alexandra and William.' Naming them deliberately, she fixed her dark eyes to his, trying to solicit mercy. 'You knew about Mother meeting her grand-children, yet you never saw fit to make yourself known to them. Perhaps you will now that they're the only ones you'll ever have, much as you'd prefer them to be those of your beloved son.'

He was so furious she thought he was going to hit her, but she did not care – cared only that she might goad him into helping Marty.

'Why are you so hurtful to them? To little children, your flesh and blood.' Her fingers were aching from the act of clutching her throat in order to provide a voice, but her heart suffered more. She shook her head to convey utter disbelief. 'Why must you allow their father to be killed?'

'Because I have no say!' came his virulent response. 'Because he's useless to them, useless as a man. My greatest service to them is to restore their rightful heritage.'

Etta's expression changed. She formed a bitter laugh with her eyes. 'Oh, how stupid, I see it all now! It isn't me who'll take John's place as your heir, but my son.'

'You could never take his place.' He beheld her as if she were raving. 'And neither could your brats ... but they must suffice and I shall not let them down.'

She was expert at concealing her hurt, demanding in a tone as cold as her father's, 'Aren't you forgetting something? My children's name is not Ibbetson but Lanegan.'

'And imagine the shame they'll suffer to learn that the name which they hold has become synonymous with cowardice! Never could there be a greater burden.' He almost shuddered with disgust. 'Yet it does not have to be so. I can have them become Ibbetsons in the stroke of a pen.'

Etta could hardly believe he had reached such callous depths. 'And what of their mother? Shall she revert to being called Miss Ibbetson too? Be spurned for having borne illegitimate children, for that's what you conspire to make them by robbing them of their father's name.'

'I want you to come home too.' Despite the hint of pardon in his eyes, it was a command.

'And if I demur shall I be whipped into submission?' Her own much darker eyes seethed with loathing for him. 'You cannot treat me in such a manner any more, Father. Women have attained certain rights.'

'Then you will not need my help,' said Ibbetson bluntly, and without further ado, he left for good.

In the old days she would have screamed and wept and stamped her foot in order for him to take notice, but now, even if she could have managed it, there was no time for childish histrionics. In the deathly silence that followed his exit, knowing from reality that he would not repent, and that Marty could have only a few weeks or even days left, she was faced with the stark truth that she was alone in her fight to save him. And thus, even though she felt like sobbing, Etta reserved her emotional outpouring for a greater purpose. Instead she quickly sought practical assistance from the nuns, asked for pen and ink and stationery, the only weapons at her disposal. And thereto, she used the information her father had provided, wrote to Marty's battalion commander, pleaded for her husband's life, told of the four children who waited at home, of his parents who would die of shame if this sentence were carried out, of his great-uncle who had given his best years to the British Army, begged for a reprieve so that her husband might redeem himself. She used every grovelling tactic at her disposal, even resorted to falsehood and said that she herself was helping the war effort through her work with Lady Fenton, the scratching of pen on paper the only sound in this quiet place, finally coming to a halt with the request for him to forward this emotive plea to the Commander in Chief.

Satisfied to have done her best, she took up a fresh piece of paper, dipped her pen in the inkwell and wrote to her beloved husband, telling him to have strength for she was here, would not let him down, would fight to her last breath . . .

After this there remained only enough energy to scratch out a few words to her mother, to inform her what had occurred, and to tell her that Etta would never forgive her father for this ultimate cruelty.

Then, after making sure all three envelopes were immediately delivered, emotionally drained, she sat back to prepare herself for the worst, staring at the crucifix on an otherwise bare wall. And only then, in that quiet contemplation, did she perhaps begin to understand the true extent of her love for Marty: that she could never be whole without him; that his death was her death.

Sometimes, as a child, after he had come to understand by means of his grandmother's demise that he himself was mortal, Marty had wondered what it would be like to die. He had envisaged himself going under a train, or in a blazing house, or tumbling off a cliff, or cascading down a water-fall to rocks below. In his boyhood fantasies he had even imagined what it would be like to be shot – had imagined it so much more clearly during his twelve months at war – but not once had it occurred to him that he would know the exact date and time of his expiry. Oh, he had not officially been appraised of this yet nor even of the verdict of his court martial, but he might as well have been, for, if acquitted, he would have been released there and then; hence without a word being uttered he knew himself to be damned, that he was most probably to be executed by his own compatriots for a crime he had not committed. This latter aspect was the worst thing of all – except, of course, death itself – the injustice of it, the way no one would listen, the way it had all been decided in twenty minutes, the way his emotively written defence, which had taken him ages to compose, had been ignored, the way all his brave deeds of the past year had been disregarded, the way he was referred to as the prisoner, sneered upon by his captors, reviled. When all he had done was snatch a few illicit hours' sleep. Faced with eternal rest, to sleep was the hardest thing of all now, would have been impossible had he not been detailed for hard physical labour. Never sloth, he embraced wholeheartedly every exertion now, desperate for any chance to be outside, under sun or rain, would have braved snow and ice if it meant escape from these dreaded four walls that so concentrated the mind. Thus confined again following another day of transient liberty, his energy might be spent but his senses were in no way dulled. With light beginning to fade, every sound became heightened. He flinched at every clink of key or exclamation, both feared and valued each approaching footstep, wondering, was it someone come to kill him or to save him.

But who would be his saviour? His friends' attempts had been cack-handed. When he had failed to respond to his name at roll they had apparently told the officer that on the route march 'someone' had seen Lanegan gashed by shrapnel and that he had taken himself off to hospital, all in the hope that this would lend their pal time to catch up. Exposed as liars by the investigation, they too had been punished – Marty had felt guilty about that, learning of it from a sympathiser's whispered divulgence through the bars – though their punishment was not half so severe as his. Despite all the trouble he had caused his battalion commander, the major had spoken up for him at the court martial, given evidence of Lanegan's previous good character, recognised that he had still been in possession of his rifle when arrested, added that he did not feel this man should be made an example of simply to act as a deterrent to others, and had recommended mercy. But his adjudicators had preferred to unearth the disciplinary notes in Marty's conduct sheet; the ones that told of the seven days' imprisonment for his misdemeanour long before the war. They had pointed out that when found he had been many miles from where he should have been, which quite clearly indicated his intention to desert the battlefront. If the major could not save him, who would?

Through the bars in an outer wall of the civic centre his bleak eyes gazed through the dying light upon the market square of this small hop town, now a bustling garrison, and he gave thanks that his cell did not overlook the inner courtyard where the killing-post stood. But for all he tried to put this from his mind, it remained crammed with such thoughts. He thought of the poor sod whose execution he had bungled. He thought of his children, and, overcome by deep sadness, wept.

There was no sign of tears when the guard came to check on him. He even made a weak attempt at humour as he asked for permission to correspond with his wife. 'I'd better let her know about that money I hid under the floorboards, seeing as I won't be going home.'

But when he did sit down to write, it was not to appraise

her of his impending slaughter – he could not bear the shame, and nor would she – but to take this chance, perhaps his final chance, to express his adoration. These carefully chosen words of love were sent home, their author little knowing that Etta was barely ten miles away.

One of her letters met with swift response. The major was extremely moved by her distress – he knew that Private Lanegan was a fool but no coward and would assist in any way possible, but feared that this would be of little substance as his recommendations for mercy had so far carried no weight. Nevertheless, he had instructed that her letter be forwarded to Brigade Headquarters, whence it would be attached to the file of proceedings which would then be passed on to Divisional HQ and along the chain of command, eventually to reach the Adjutant General's department at GHQ where the Judge Advocate would instruct on the legality of the case. It was he who decreed whether or not the conviction should be quashed.

With this her only shred of hope, not knowing how long the outcome would take or even if they would let her know at all when they were going to kill her husband, Etta was to extend her stay in the convent for another week. At first, swaddled in a deathly silence broken only by the occasion clanking of a bucket and the swish of a nun's habit, upon recuperation and in need of more useful existence, she took to sitting with the sick and elderly who occupied a larger dormitory, to try and meet their physical needs without speaking their language, to stroke their hands in a universal gesture of support, and at other times to scrub floors and to hoe the vegetables in the high-walled garden, all the while yearning to receive personal news from Marty and racking her brain over what else could be done, other than to bombard the army with letters, which she continued to do.

'A lawyer!' she announced suddenly to the one who had come to check on her wound and had just given pronouncement that it was nicely healed. 'I must have a lawyer – this can't possibly be right. Do you know where I might find one, Sister?'

There was a faint whiff of carbolic as Sister Cecile withdrew, looked dubious and said, 'There used to be one in the town, but he was killed when his house was bombed.'

Etta simmered with frustration. 'I shouldn't think I could afford the fees anyway.' It was little comfort to know that what money she did have was still tucked safely behind the pistol in the leather holster, the latter having come through all the various traumas undetected until she herself had removed it in order to bathe. The nuns had expressed mild alarm until she had shown it wasn't loaded and was merely a cosmetic means of protection. However, she had thought it advisable to keep the weapon hidden on her person in case someone from the army came to see her and confiscated it. It might yet be needed.

Many more precious hours were fretted away, nothing being delivered to her room save a waft of boiled cabbage. Then, at last a letter arrived from Marty. It had reverted to its old disjointed style, in fact was much, much worse as he groped for words to describe the horror of his situation. He apologised for rambling, it was simply the shock of knowing that she was aware of his dilemma – but not totally appraised of the facts, he hastened to add, for he must state here and now that he had *not* deserted, had merely been unable to find his way back to his unit who, unknown to him, had been ordered elsewhere to stem a breach in the line whilst he had been asleep. That had been his only crime, he could not emphasise this strongly enough. He hated to have her think him a coward, begged her not to tell his parents or his children, but to say that he had died bravely, as he hoped he would when his time came . . .

Dashing away the mist of tears, Etta read on, coming

to understand now why she had received the telegram to say he was missing; how his unit had been shelled whilst on the march and how his friends had lied about seeing him wounded, how he had stumbled around for almost a week in his search for them, until finally he had been picked up by the provost and accused of that most heinous offence.

In closing lines he told her how good his commanding officer had been in making sure this letter would reach her as quickly as possible, and expressed again his astonishment that his dear, dear wife was so much nearer than he could ever have imagined. He praised her attempts to free him, said how much it gave him strength, even though the Major had warned him to prepare for the worst. They must both be prepared. If that happened, if he never got to see her again, he hoped that she would find it in her heart to forgive all the hurt he had caused her. He concluded with his undying love.

Dealing her eyes and nose an angry swipe of a handkerchief, she took up her pen and scratched out a fevered response immediately, ordering him to keep faith, for there was higher authority than his battalion commander and she was yet to hear from that quarter. Meanwhile, she would organise the correct paperwork that would enable her to visit him. He must not allow himself even to entertain the idea that all was lost, for she intended to save him, at whatever price. She was certain the news would be good, for no one could take a man's life for so trivial an offence.

But as another two days crept by, Etta became increasingly perturbed that she had had no response from anyone other than the major. This could only spell the worst. Yet, however fearful, whatever the amount of dread that weighed upon her heart, she had not truly believed it would happen until the reality finally dawned in the shape of a terse letter with an official stamp, which informed her that having reviewed all the evidence, the Judge Advocate ruled that all statutory requirements had been met. There was therefore no reason why sentence should not be carried out.

They really did intend to kill Marty.

Whilst Etta attempted to battle her way through the stultifying shock that followed, the nuns administered infinite succour, telling her of their prayers for Marty's soul, to which she finally managed to retort bitterly that he was not dead yet, the warrant had still to be signed by the Commander in Chief and whilst Marty remained alive there was hope. And it was in this last desperate spirit of hope that she seized up her pen and wrote to the battalion commander again, demanding to be allowed to visit her husband in his hour of crisis, hoping that once face to face with her, the major would be unable to resist her plea for compassion.

But the only compassion he showed was to have his reply delivered swiftly by despatch rider, telling her that in his humble opinion it would not be advisable for her to visit her husband, but to remember him as he had been in happier times. And this was to be endorsed by the sisters, who sought to prise her from the grip of spiritual despair, telling her that she was not alone, that their prayers for Marty would continue, and urging her to join them on their knees before the blue-mantled Virgin.

But Etta had not the time to waste on plaster saints; she could just as easily pray whilst on the move. 'I don't care what they say – they won't keep me from him!'

'But it is in the war zone!' protested Sister Bernadette, acquainted with the location of Marty's prison. 'You cannot go without a permit. You may be shot.'

Undaunted, Etta demanded, 'Then where do I apply?'

Sister Cecile spoke dubiously of all the form-filling that would be required before the civil authorities would grant it. 'I have known it take ten days . . .'

'Then I'll go without one!' declared Etta, before seeing

how futile this would be and, grasping the nun's arm, beseeched her, 'Please, please help me – they know you! If you intervene they might expedite matters . . .'

Looking at each other, the sisters agreed, saying it might also help if they were to write her a letter of introduction to the nuns at the local convent, and whilst Sister Cecile went off to seek leave from the Mother Superior, Etta pressed Sister Bernadette for as much information as she had on the town where Marty was being held.

Whilst Sister Cecile's pessimistic view was not upheld, it took Etta another whole precious day to cut through all the rigmarole and for the permit to be granted. Issuing effusive thanks to the sisters for their help with this and for their care, she appealed for one last favour: that they allow her to buy one of their large white pinafores that might keep her newly laundered dress a little cleaner.

Equipped with this and the precious documentation she departed next morning, stepping warily from the cloistered world of the convent into the military bustle of the old grey town. Her figure caped against the chilly but bright late-summer morn, she had no time to wait for a train. With only a brief diversion to obtain some necessary items, she struck out along the main road, bound for Marty's prison.

In his stark little cell, with its cool floor of bricks, its barred windows and planks for a bed, its only piece of furniture a bucket, Marty had read Etta's most recent letter many times in the last few days. He knew most of it off by heart. He had told her that knowing of her attempt to save him lent him strength, but it didn't, for he had come to understand that all raised hopes of an appeal were academic. His fate had been decided from the start. Deep down he had always known that.

Now, perhaps only hours of life remained. He should

have been preparing to meet his Maker. Instead, he was plotting his escape.

By means of a generous tip to an ambulance driver, Etta was now within reach of the town that served both as a rest camp and a centre for casualties. On the outskirts, small shacks came into view, built of biscuit tins and packing cases, straw, and anything that might house a refugee. Her nerves on edge, she paid them little heed; nor would she have remarked upon the large black dog harnessed to a cart had it not been blocking the way ahead, but she shared the driver's irritation until the dog's owner led it aside allowing the ambulance to sweep past.

Finally set down some streets away from her goal, she held her breath as she mingled with the crowd of army personnel, waiting for someone to demand her permit. The sun was out now and she held her cape rolled into a bundle. She had toyed briefly with the idea of pinning a cross of red material to the breast of her pinafore to make herself appear more official, but then this might leave her open to the attentions of some bossy matron, so she had decided to leave things as they were, relying on the introductory letter to the local nuns as reason enough for her to be here. The ambulance driver hadn't been concerned enough to interrogate her, just happy for her company and her money. Clutching the bundle under her arm, she followed his directions to the market square, praying that she was taking the right path. A young girl walked briskly ahead of her, the clickety-clack of her wooden clogs coinciding with the rapid beat of Etta's pulse. The noise in her own head was so deafening that she was barely aware of the distant explosions in the background. She had been told that Poperinghe was relatively safe from bombardment, and indeed it appeared to be so with its civilian population intact and its shops still doing business, though this made no difference to her state of apprehension. She needed desperately to visit the lavatory but tried to ignore the spasms in her gut by concentrating on her mission. One of the nuns knew this town well and had been good enough to tell her where the military prison, formerly the town hall, was situated, totally innocent that Etta was not merely going there to share a last kiss with her husband but to rescue him. Limbs like jelly, she tried to prevent her hand from constantly checking that the pistol was still beneath her skirt. Fully recognising that the consequence of wielding an unloaded weapon against an experienced soldier might be her own death, she just as soon dismissed it. She would never forgive herself if she did not try everything in her power to save her husband.

Her heart leapt; she could see the prison now; or at least she could the neo-Gothic spires of the town hall that the sister had described. She headed along the narrow cobbled street, not too slowly, not too quickly, every nerve on edge, every hair on end. Soldiers nodded to the attractive nurse as she passed, some respectful, others with an impudence born of living in constant threat of death. She responded to all with as steady a smile as she could muster, hoping they would not see the nervous twitch about her lips, moving ever nearer to her goal.

Another soldier sauntered towards her. She glanced at him, smiled and glanced away, when suddenly he grasped her free arm and turned her about.

'Don't say a word!'

At first, shock at the painful nip of her flesh, then a cry of recognition. 'Mar—'

'Ssh!' he told her, and, still gripping her arm he tucked it under his and steered her back the way she had come, 'Just try to look as if you're enjoying yourself.'

Overwhelmed by the joy of having Marty at her side, Etta's eyes held a lustre that had long been absent. She yearned to embrace him, but did as he ordered and said not another word as they walked as nonchalantly as they could through the human traffic.

'Where shall we go?' Heart racing, Etta told herself to be calm, and threw smiling glances at passers-by.

'Station,' came the succinct response, Marty grinning as if he were merely enjoying an excursion in the sunshine with a pretty nurse.

'Is it far?' She could scarcely breathe for excitement.

'I don't know.' He held on tightly to her arm. 'I just hope it's this way.'

After what seemed hundreds and hundreds of yards, the railway station finally came into view. But, 'Oh my God,' breathed Etta, 'look at all those people!' A fleet of ambulances had just arrived from the direction of Ypres and a squad of stretcher-bearers were busily transferring patients to a waiting train, whilst black-clad peasants stood patiently by, waiting to be allowed entry to the platform.

Some of the not too badly wounded were staggering unattended into the station. Stating that this might just help their cause, Marty pressed her onwards, and, as they drew nearer he affected to lean against her and to hobble, she supporting him as they made their way through the wicket and onto the platform. A steaming train awaited. It was useless to try and gain access to one of the carriages, for these were all fitted with white hospital beds. Instead, Marty and Etta hobbled their way to the end of the platform, to the station yard, where another train stood. Though its engine was dormant and it seemed to be going nowhere, in the hope that it eventually would they looked sharply about them before leaping into one of its carriages.

Here, at last, they were able to fling their arms round each other, pressing their bodies tightly together. They kissed and cried for joy – and in pity too, Etta unable to believe how Marty had changed, his poor, dear face stripped of youth.

Briefly tearing himself away to examine her, an elated Marty immediately noticed the scar. 'What's that on your throat?' His eyes flashed from green to grey in concern.

'I was stung by a wasp – they had to cut my windpipe.' Continually, between words, she pressed her lips to his face, hugged him and cuddled him to her breast.

'God! I thought you sounded husky.' He returned her fervent embrace, both of them crooning how wonderful it was, squeezing so tightly they could hardly breathe.

He pulled away to marvel again, breathing into her joyous visage, 'Well . . . fancy seeing you here! I almost didn't recognise ye.'

Etta laughed aloud, her eyes shining with the brightness of delirium. 'I know, I look a mess, don't I?'

'I don't give a monkey's what ye look like – you're here!'

'I was just coming to free you!' she told him. 'How did you manage to escape?'

'Just walked out!' Marty sounded equally amazed. 'The guards got used to chatting with me, knew I could be trusted to behave meself.' He laughed. 'When one of them left my door open while he went to fetch something I took me chance. There's usually a sentry, I don't know where the hell he'd gone, but God bless the bugger. Christ, I still can't believe you're here!' He hugged her again, rocked her to and fro, this way and that, both ecstatic.

'Thank *goodness* we met!' Warm face pressed to warm neck, her voice was feverishly shrill on his ear. 'I would have looked very foolish holding up the guard with my pistol for a man who'd already escaped!'

'You've got a gun?' Incredulous, he pushed her away again.

'It isn't loaded, more's the pity!' Proudly, she revealed the weapon through a slit in her skirt.

'I wondered what that hard thing was!' He hauled her back to him.

'Your father gave it to me,' she told him, laughing like a maniac.

'The ould bugger,' breathed Marty into her neck. 'God bless him.'

'Oh God, Marty, what are we to do now?' Even during the breathless conversation they refused to let each other go. 'Where were you bound for when we met?'

'To see you, or at least try.' Suddenly plunged back to awful reality, his arms grappled to hold her ever closer. 'I hadn't planned any further than that.'

'I have.' Etta lifted her face from his shoulder, but only to rub her cheek against his as she outlined her strategy. 'Those civilian clothes are for you.' She referred to the bundle that was now on the floor. It had been the very devil to obtain them, her inability to speak the language causing a great deal of frustration, until the universal language of paying double what they were worth had solved her problem.

'Oh God, Etta, do you realise how much trouble you'll be in by providing them?'

'I don't care! You'd better change into them now. Then the main thing is to reach the coast as swiftly as possible. Once there we stow away on a ship – not to England, we'd probably be apprehended on landing, but if we could reach Ireland that would make it harder for them. Then we could get word to your parents and have them bring the children across, and we could all go to America.'

'And have us live as fugitives?' His voice held dismay. 'To be forever on the move?'

'I don't know what else to do! I can't lose you, I can't!' Her tears were not of joy but of desperation now.

'I'm not so keen on dying meself,' came Marty's grave response as he rested his chin on her head and gazed into a bleak future. 'I just keep asking meself if there's any point in running. Should I be a man, go back and face what's coming?'

'No! It's nothing to do with being a man, it's just not right that you should die for something you haven't done! How could they reach such a conclusion?'

Mystified, he shook his head. 'There's no rhyme or reason, darlin'. I knew a man who deliberately went AWOL and they only gave him twenty-eight days.'

This only served to increase her anger and desperation. She clung to him. 'Please, please come with me!'

'They'll get me in the end.' He looked down into her crazed eyes, then administered tender kisses. 'They always do.' He had heard of men on the run for a year only to be captured and shot.

'Is that any reason not to try?' Etta shook him violently. 'Don't leave me, Marty! I won't let you!'

'All right.' He gave a quick decisive nod, dashed a last kiss to her face and began ripping off his army clothes. 'But, one thing: if we don't make it, will ye let Ma and Da know I'm not a coward?'

'Yes! But we will make it!' Shaking out the civilian jacket she grasped his arm and helped to direct it into a sleeve, urging him to hurry.

The carriage door was suddenly wrenched open, causing both to exclaim and to behold the provost in dismay. For one split second Marty was poised to leap out of the other door and onto the track, but when a revolver was levelled at him his arms immediately shot upwards in surrender. His face robbed of all hope, he turned again to his wife, his dear beloved wife, looked deeply, longingly into her face, then gave in to the inevitable.

But Etta fought on as the redcap and another hauled Marty off the train, yelled her protest and grabbed at the arm of one of them, trying to drag him off. And when this failed she pulled out her pistol and in the moment of uncertainty that followed screamed at him, 'Run, Marty, run!'

But to her anguish all he did was to stand there in horror.

477

'Ett, don't be – she doesn't mean it!' he cried swiftly, urging his captors not to shoot. 'It's not loaded!'

At which she was roughly disarmed and placed under arrest too.

Then they were parted, Marty to his prison cell to await certain death; Etta keening her eternal love for him as she was taken from the town under guard to be shipped back to Blighty.

Come finally to accept his fate, Marty knew he should be preparing to face his Creator, should more closely attend the comforting words of the padre who, along with many a slug of rum, would see him through the ordeal; but for now, in these few last rays of sunlight, he could concentrate on naught except Etta and his children. And it was in writing to each of them, and to his mother and father, that he spent his time until darkness reigned.

Trying to think of words to say, he meditated on the path that had led him to this state. Had he been satisfied with his lot, accepted Etta as the brave and warm and wonderful if scatterbrained woman she was, instead of stupidly quibbling over her laziness around the house and trying to mould her into something she was not, then he would never have run away and joined the army. Maybe, yes maybe, he would still be in a similar position – there were plans to conscript those reluctant to fight – but left to chance, as a married man he might just have escaped the net. As it was, by his own vanity and discontent, he was the master of his own fate.

Filling his chest with air, he listened to the crump and rumble of artillery. This town was reasonably safe but, whilst he had been here it had received the occasional shell from long range to much devastation. Regarding it as merely disconcerting before, now he prayed that such a shell might come and flatten him and rescue him from a more ignoble death.

How much more acute his senses now, so acute that at the merest thought of what lay ahead he felt the pencil in his hand start to tremble, the tremors creeping up his arm into every limb and the panic start to prickle his scalp and to rise in a hot tide to engulf his entire being, and though he gripped his fists and raged and swore at himself to prevent it spilling over, it boiled and surged within his skull, making his feet tap uncontrollably, urging him to run . . .

A jangle of keys, a steadying voice, a cup of rum pressed into quaking hands.

His letter-writing postponed, Marty gulped great mouthfuls, felt the heat invade his gullet then his gut, drained the whole cup and held it out for more, swallowed some of this too, until the panic was eventually tamed. Then, resuming his epistle, he rushed to add a few final words, so that the recipient might be sure they were his and not the befuddled rantings of a drunkard. And after this, the crutch of alcohol forever by, he sat and prayed for God to lend him strength. He was to need every ounce of this when the key turned in his cell door and the guard admitted two staff officers.

Dawn. The mundane sounds of breakfast being prepared, the clank of dixies, the rumble of gunfire, the clip-clop of hoofs, the crunching of gears as a procession of ambulances arrived with more wounded from the battlefield, the shuffle and tramp of thousands of boots . . .

In the camp on the outskirts of town, the battalion to which Marty had once belonged was assembled to hear his sentence promulgated. Many of them wept, for they held him dear.

Seated on the edge of his bed of planks, waiting for breakfast, Marty heard a cheer go up and wondered if it was for him. Even now, hours after he himself had heard the incredible news, he was still reeling, unable to fathom how it had happened, nor who had gained his reprieve. It might still be only a fleeting reprieve, for instead of killing him today, the Commander in Chief had decreed that Private Lanegan's sentence be suspended and that he rejoin the lines for the duration of the war. Who knew how long that would be, nor if he might be hit tomorrow by a German bullet. But for today, thank God, he was alive. He was alive.

Epilogue

Neither woman felt in the mood for a party. It was impossible to concentrate on the trivia of bunting and buns for the Peace Celebrations after four, almost five gruelling years of shortages, the agonising worry over one's husband, one's son, yet Etta and Aggie had decided they should make some sort of effort for the children's sake. Dressed in black, each was silent, going over the business of sandwich-making automatically, scraping knives across bread, their thoughts otherwise engaged by memories. The room was silent, its only other occupant fast asleep in his fireside chair, pipe on chest, his nose and cheeks burnt bright red after an accidental nap under a blazing sun.

'Marty used to like these when he was a boy,' murmured Aggie, even in her best attire looking haggard as she stacked another round of condensed milk sandwiches on the plate with its paper-lace doily. 'Of course, that was before he developed expensive tastes. Nothing was ever good enough for him after that.'

Etta gave an absent smile, deep in her own thoughts as she sawed and sliced, contributing to the pyramid of sandwiches. It seemed like a lifetime ago that, after being let out of prison with all charges dropped, she had staggered back into this kitchen, thrown herself into Aggie's arms and sobbed out her misery, to be just as dramatically assuaged by a letter which told of the petition to the Commander in

Chief, organised by her mother, her meek little mother who had never uttered a defiant word in her life but had rallied her influential friends to save her daughter's husband. Whether this had swayed Sir John French's decision one could not say, but, with a telegram to confirm the reprieve, it had not mattered. For whatever reason, Marty had been spared execution. Had Etta but known it then, that even in such wondrous moment of relief there would be three more years to suffer . . .

'God!' An agitated Aggie paused abruptly in her task to rest her hands on the table and to shake her head, her face grim. 'I know I said I wasn't going to mention it and spoil the children's party, but I don't think I'll ever get over the shame. That boy . . .'

Etta paused too, looked at her sympathetically and parted her lips to speak, but her mother-in-law announced, 'No, don't say a word! I don't even want to think about it, not today.' And she got on with her frivolous chore.

'Any more plates, Granny Lanny?' fourteen-year-old Celia tripped in to ask.

'I'll give you Granny Lanny!'

The young woman laughed coquettishly, and, carrying the plates that were thrust at her, returned to the tables that had been set up in the street, from where others' happy laughter could be heard.

'I suppose we'd better join the party then,' sighed Aggie, smoothing her grey hair and casting a harassed glance at Red still asleep in his fireside chair, then at the empty one opposite. 'Much as I don't feel like it. Seems disrespectful to be kicking up our heels just after a wake.'

Etta sanctioned the need for them both to have fun. 'I don't think anyone would begrudge us after the hardship we've been through.'

Red woke up then with a grunt, cast his glowing face about him in mild surprise, before picking his pipe off his chest and puffing it back to life.

'I should buy you a lace waistcoat,' his wife chided him sourly. ''Twould save you the trouble of burning the holes in it.'

Red gave a philosophical brush at his chest. 'Have I missed the party?'

'No, we're still waiting on himself,' replied his wife, looking somewhat aggrieved.

All looked round as the back door opened.

'Oh, here you are at last,' chided Aggie. 'I thought I'd have to come and dig you out.'

'I can't help it, it's what you do go feeding me!' A grumbling Uncle Mal shuffled in at the speed of a tortoise, his twig-like hand upon a stick, having to summon help from Etta in negotiating the shallow step up from the scullery.

'My feelings exactly!' A younger male head poked itself round a different door and a voice chipped in, 'Is there nothing more interesting to scoff? Christ, I was stuck on condensed milk and bully beef for four years – this is meant to be a celebration, ye know, Ma.'

A grossly indignant Aggie put her hands on her hips and beheld Etta. 'Didn't I tell you he always wants what he can't damn-well have?' Feigning violence, a sparkle in her eye, she advanced on her grinning son.

'Call her off, Da!' begged Marty, but at the first sign of laughter Red fell instantly asleep, awaking every few seconds to issue a brief spurt of amusement before falling asleep again and again and again. 'I was only asking, Ma!' Marty yelped.

'And I'm only telling!' She smote and jabbed him. 'I haven't the money to waste on you after emptying my purse on the wake!'

'Nobody said you had to,' objected her son, laughingly trying to fend her off, bending this way and that to avoid her flailing hands.

Aggie pressed forth the mock attack, poked and prodded him till he shrieked for mercy in a boyish falsetto, whilst

483

her blue eyes sparkled with delight at having him home. 'I'm damned if I'm having your Aunt Joan, God rest her, sitting up there in her heavenly abode complaining to Uncle John that I didn't give them the very best send-off!'

'So we have to make do with a crummy shindig!' taunted Marty, green eyes twinkling as, having left off, his mother now came back to re-launch the assault. 'Ah, don't just stand there, Ett, save me, save me!' And for the benefit of his amused audience that now included little William, who had just come in and joined the game by helping Granny smack Father, he danced this way and that to avoid her blows.

'I shan't lift a finger,' announced Etta loftily, maintaining a steadying hold of Uncle Mal's arm. 'I thoroughly agree with your mother.'

'Oh, fine wife you turned out to be!' accused Marty, finally allowed to escape from Aggie's clutches, but his eyes were warm as they locked with Etta's dark brown ones. And for a moment they were to remain like this, each sharing the same thought, silently wondering what it had all been for, those years of suffering, when here they were in this little house as if he had never been away? Was Marty returned to a better world? A world fit for heroes? Different, certainly, but better? With all his heart he prayed so, not from any selfish desire for, unlike many, he had walked straight into a job that enabled him to rent a modest house, and so he didn't have to rely on his parents, and could feel like a man. No, his prayer, his fervent hope, was that his less fortunate comrades had not been trodden and pounded into the French earth simply to add to its fertility . . . for a second the nightmarish memories that he had managed to suppress for today's celebrations now came rushing back, the thunderous bang and whistle of artillery, the smell of burnt flesh, the pitiful cries of the dying that would ever reverberate . . .

But he fought them, for he was not dead, he was here,

alive, with his dear, brave wife and his beloved children and his parents and siblings and his brothers-in-law, all of whom had survived – few families could boast that – and here he would be, forever. Just in time – for Etta had gauged his flicker of despair causing her smile to falter – the warmth of contentment flooded back into his gaze, he and she composing their smiles as a more serious outpouring came from his mother, who undid her apron and tidied her hair for the party.

'As if I haven't enough expense with that blessed brother of yours rushing a wedding upon us – Holy Mother, I'll never get over the shame, never!' Aggie stopped in her tracks to press her cheeks in horror at the thought of Jimmy-Joe's impending fatherhood. Then her eyes were all of a sudden directing fake malevolence at Marty again. 'And I swore I wasn't going to let it worry me today, and now you've gone and reminded me of it, thank you very much!' And in an unstoppable attack she began to drive him towards the front door. 'Out, out with ye now, and not another word of complaint – go and have a party in your own street if this one isn't good enough for ye!'

'It's good enough!' cried Marty, covering his head and backing away, trying not to trip over a giggling William. 'Please don't hit me, Ma, I'm begging ye!'

'My God, he'll have the –' Red crashed into a few seconds of unconsciousness before finishing his sentence – 'polis on us with his daft goings-on.'

'Are we off then before all the food's gone?' croaked Uncle Mal.

A happy Etta shook her head laughingly, then slowly and patiently began to guide the frail nonagenarian towards the front door.

Managing to control his affliction, Red arose to shuffle after them, an expression of disbelief upon his burnt face. ''Tis a fine thing if you've only your belly to worry about, and you nudging your century!' And to Etta, 'If I'd known he was going to live so long I'd never have taken the ould bugger in. I can't believe he's still walking round with this flu knocking people off right, left and centre, like poor Johnny and Joan.'

'Neither can I,' marvelled Etta, and to her charge, 'Tell us your secret, Uncle Mal.'

With painful slowness, the old man cupped his ear with a bony, liver-spotted claw.

'What's your secret for a long life?' she repeated in louder tone.

'Keep breathing,' said the ancient, with a mischievous grin.

And to fond laughter, the Lanegans moved out into the sunshine, to join in the Hope Street celebrations.

A Complicated Woman

Sheelagh Kelly

Set in York and Australia between the World Wars, *A Complicated Woman* follows the fortunes of Oriel Maguire, whose parents' enthralling story was told in Shoddy Prince.

After twenty-two years' estrangement, Bright Maguire and Nat Prince have been joyously reunited and plan to start a new life in Melbourne, Australia. Only after much agonizing thought can their daughter Oriel put aside her opposition to the father who deserted her and decide to go too.

The horrors of the Great War have retreated, leaving a thirst for excitement and frivolity, and Oriel is one of the many gay young things eager to cast aside the restrictions of the bygone era. But unresolved tensions from her past have left her ill-equipped for life in the wider world and her air of loneliness and eagerness to be loved make her an easy victim for those who would take advantage. Committing one folly after another, she stumbles from a disastrous liaison into an unwise marriage, and a train of events is set in motion that results in scandal and ruin, propelling her ultimately to the brink of tragedy. Only then does she come face to face with the truth about herself, become reconciled to her family and claim the man she has dared to love.

0 00 649650 4

A Sense of Duty

Sheelagh Kelly

Flamboyant and fun-loving Kit Kilmaster rebels against the constraints of Victorian society and pursues her dreams. But, as Kit is to learn, there is a high price to pay for happiness . . .

While her brothers and sisters resign themselves to a life of drudgery, the voluptuous Katherine Kilmaster years for better things. Though her kin try to instil in her a sense of duty, Kit's cravings for the good things in life are too strong. And when her generous heart tempts her into dangerous situations with young men above her station, the family are scandalized by Kit's brazen attitude – although that doesn't prevent them accepting a share in the material rewards. For a time Kit revels in the life of a courtesan, launching herself upon London Society, until an unexpected consequence of her free-and-easy lifestyle stops her in her tracks.

Thrust back into claustrophobic village life, Kit falls prey to malicious gossip, and then to tragedy. Overwhelmed by events, she finally heeds the advice of her family, and is almost destroyed in the process. But then a chance encounter promises to deliver her the husband and children she has always wanted – provided her shameful secret is not revealed . . .

ISBN 0 00 651143 0